Pr

"Historical romance devotees wi__ Michels's adoring use of some of the classic tropes of the genre—the spare heir, the wrong brother as hero, the heroine in men's clothing—but what makes the book so enjoyable is the way Michels makes the familiar fresh. The book is at once a well-crafted mystery and a simmering romance."

—**Sarah MacLean**, *The Washington Post*
for *The Infamous Heir*

"Michels's latest is the complete package: a captivating romance with gripping suspense wrapped up in a novel to be savored."

—*Publishers Weekly* STARRED Review
for *The Infamous Heir*

"Readers are treated to Michels's strongest story yet. The engaging characters, intricate plotline, and powerful love story hold readers from beginning to end as they watch the changing relationship between headstrong lovers as they unravel a mystery. Savor this tale."

—*RT Book Reviews*, 4.5 Stars, TOP PICK!
for *The Infamous Heir*

"Playing with the themes of deception and authenticity, this romance delightfully emulates a Jane Austen-ish comedy of manners."

—*Kirkus Reviews* for *The Rebel Heir*

"Michels expertly delivers a heart-wrenching romance that will leave the reader eagerly anticipating future installments."

—*Publishers Weekly* STARRED Review
for *The Rebel Heir*

Also by Elizabeth Michels

Spare Heirs
The Infamous Heir
The Rebel Heir

Tricks of the Ton
Must Love Dukes
Desperately Seeking Suzanna
How to Lose a Lord in 10 Days or Less

The
WICKED HEIR

ELIZABETH
MICHELS

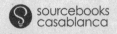

sourcebooks
casablanca

Published by Sourcebooks Casablanca, an imprint of Sourcebooks, Inc.
P.O. Box 4410, Naperville, Illinois 60567-4410
(630) 961-3900
Fax: (630) 961-2168
www.sourcebooks.com

Printed and bound in Canada.
MBP 10 9 8 7 6 5 4 3 2 1

For Lori Waters, my dear friend who always reminds me to dream big. May all of your dreams be large enough to be considered delusions of grandeur, and may every one of them come true.

One

SILHOUETTES OF FLOWERS AND SWIRLS OF INK FASHIONED into vines danced around the paper to form an ornate garden of shapes, framing the words written in the center. The artwork had been designed with care, crafted from precise black lines and finished with pale watercolor dots.

Large swooping letters at the top of the first page proclaimed this to be the diary of Lady Isabelle Fairlyn. All of her most personal thoughts would be detailed herein—details that were of vital importance if this mission were to be successful. *Knowledge leads to accomplishment*, wasn't that what St. James always said?

"It seems I listened," he whispered.

It was past time for the tide to shift against the man who'd wronged him so long ago. He aimed a smile at the closed door that led to the hall of the Fairlyn family's London home. Soon he would be the only one smiling.

Returning to his task, he ran his thumb over the

colorful first entry in the small leather-bound book, tracing the line of a leaf in the corner before he turned the page to find the information he had come for. An icy wind whipped through the open window, and the light from the candle beside him waved and flickered. He pulled his coat tighter around his shoulders and leaned in toward the light, scanning the words, committing them to memory.

Isabelle Fairlyn's Diary
January 1817

All gentlemen should strive to be more like Mr. Kelton Brice. He is fashionable, amiable, and a fine dancer—everything I require in a husband. I've never danced with him, mind you, but sometimes a lady simply knows these things, even from across a crowded ballroom. From the moment he entered our drive in his sharp red phaeton three years ago, I knew we would one day be married.

It was a chaotic time in the house the day he arrived. Father had recently acquired his title most unexpectedly from Uncle George, and our new home was a whirl of activity. Mother was calling orders to the footmen, having paintings hauled from this wall, and that while the sound of hammers echoed through the house. She and Father had been in another battle since dawn that day. I'd escaped to the garden for the morning, but one can only remain among the roses so long without a bite of food. I'd planned to slip in the side door and take one of the biscuits Father always left behind on the tea tray in the library. Only, when

I entered the room, I was caught between my parents as they raged over Father's inattention to the family, or perhaps it was mother's vanity with her new station—perhaps both.

Their anger surrounded me, holding me frozen, unable to escape. Then Mr. Brice was there. He was shown into the room, and a calm descended on the scene. He made a jest about the chaos of life with a title, and suddenly everyone was laughing, put to ease in an instant. He gave me a small wink as I finally took the biscuit from the tray and began to back away. Time stopped when he looked at me. And that was the day I fell in love. Some people may say love doesn't take hold in a single moment, but they are wrong and I am right. By some people, of course, I mean Victoria. Why must sisters be so irritating?

When she learned of my fondness for Mr. Brice, she pointed out quite cheerfully that he had been at our home only a few minutes to deliver a letter by hand to Father and we'd never truly spoken to each other. Even so, I'm certain we will share the kind of love that inspires poetry. Victoria didn't witness his kindness that day or feel the way he brings a bright joy wherever he goes. She doesn't know his true nature, but I do. I fairly melted into my half boots right there on the library floor, and if we were wed, no one in my household could ever be cross again. That is love.

I saw him again a few times over the course of my coming-out season last year. He didn't notice me then, but the upcoming season will be different. I'm certain of it. With my family's arrival in London, my plans can begin.

In spite of the cold weather, I convinced one of the maids to walk with me to the museum a few days a week instead of taking Father's carriage. I told her the street where he lives is the safest route for two women to take to Montague House and the British Museum, and she believed me. Thank goodness! Only yesterday I caught a glimpse of him through a window. He was wearing a green coat and leaning against the windowsill while he spoke with someone in his home. Perhaps tomorrow he'll turn around.

Soon I will finally gain Mr. Brice's attention, and he will fall desperately in love with me. We'll be married by special license and spend the rest of our days looking at one another in admiration, surrounded by the flowers he picked for me from a field on our estate. Just like something from a story. My dreams are about to come true. I can feel it in every sunbeam that shines down from the sky.

—*the future Mrs. Brice, Isabelle*

❧⸲⸲⸲❧

Spring 1817

Dreams were fickle little bastards.

Fallon St. James once had a dream—to attain enough wealth and power to spend his time as he wished. Reality, however, had a harsh bite. He had the wealth bit, and with an army of gentlemen at his command, now he certainly had the power. But if he were truly free to act as he wished, he would not be at this damned ball tonight. Yet here he was, searching the crowd for the one man who could destroy everything he'd built.

Fallon clung to the shadows of the ballroom as he moved toward the small parlor, Brice at his side. The only redeeming part of this evening was his current company. Even after years of operations with the man, Mr. Kelton Brice never ceased to amuse him. It was a wonder that everyone in attendance tonight didn't yet know of their search, since Brice felt the need to fill every gap in conversation with his booming voice. Fallon only smirked. He'd given up any attempt to hush the man years ago, understanding that some things couldn't be changed. He didn't wish to silence him even if he could have. Somehow Brice's loud demeanor and bright clothing only served to disguise the true nature of his work from those around him.

And it allowed Fallon time to think. He was always thinking—he had to be if he was to hold the Spare Heirs Society together and keep it profitable.

Two gentlemen nodded a silent greeting as he passed. He'd made trouble of sorts disappear for both men in the past year, and each of them now owed him a debt, something he acknowledged with a slight tilt of his chin. Their time to return his kindness would come, but not tonight. Tonight was dedicated to Mr. Reginald Grapling and stopping whatever plans he had now that he was roaming the streets and, if Brice could be believed, the ballrooms of London.

"I'm certain of what—or in this case who—I saw, St. James," Brice said as they entered the side parlor off the ballroom. The parlor contained tables laden with food and a few of the hungrier members of society. "At the ball last night and again a few minutes ago. He was moving in this direction."

"I believe you." Fallon scanned the room for Grapling as they circled behind the far table to get a better view. He needed to lay eyes on the man for himself, even if he did have Brice's word. "I only remarked that it was odd. Last we saw of him—"

"He was being led away in chains?" Brice cut in. "Prisoners do get released on occasion."

"Not that one. I gave specific instructions."

"You have men watching the prison? Guards on the payroll?" Brice asked as he plucked a grape from a tray on the table and popped it in his mouth. "It's not that I doubt you. It's only…mistakes happen. Prisoners can be released after a time. Do you trust those men?"

He didn't reply. He didn't need to.

"Of course you don't." Brice smirked and shook his head. "But you *can* trust me. Grapling has escaped. I know what I saw. I only wish I knew what he was after. I doubt he's been longing to try a waltz for the past four years. Can you imagine him, sitting in his cell at night wishing for a glass of the watery lemonade served at society events? Or better yet…"

Movement caught Fallon's eye, but he didn't turn toward it. If Grapling was watching, it was best to allow him to think they weren't aware of his presence until the time was right. It helped that Brice was still rambling at his side, creating a cover for Fallon's investigation. Much of the Spare Heirs Society's activity involved diversion and the nuance of timing. Hunting down this particular adversary was no different. Fallon glanced around under the guise of perusing the trays of sweets stacked high on the nearest end of the table. "We'll need to have every auxiliary parlor checked," he stated. Then he saw one heavily lashed, round blue eye peer around the tower of sweets.

A heartbeat later, the owner of the blue eye made a quick retreat behind the sweet trays, blond ringlets dancing in midair.

Someone was indeed watching them, but it wasn't Mr. Reginald Grapling.

"You take the card room while I stroll through the garden," Fallon said to Brice, collecting his thoughts. "If Grapling's still here, we'll find him and question him."

"A stroll through the garden? You're getting soft, St. James."

"On my way to my carriage," Fallon clarified, checking his pocket watch. As much as he would like to place eyes on Grapling and assess the threat he posed, Fallon had to be across town in an hour. "I have quite a few meetings planned for this evening. Only a handful of minutes are left for the untimely return of a former Spare Heir."

Fallon glanced once more to the tower of cakes and biscuits. The watchful eyes were back, this time in a gap where he was certain two slices of cake had been only a moment ago. He followed the line of sight back to his longtime friend, Brice.

Kelton Brice, who was a known bachelor and had no plans to change that fact? What lady in her right mind would glance in his direction if she were looking

for anything more than an evening's entertainment?
Or perhaps an evening's diversion was exactly what
this woman sought.

Fallon stepped closer to the table in an attempt to
see around the display. If someone was stalking one of
his men—even if it was only a light-skirted lady—he
needed to know of it. After all, he knew everything.

"I'll see to the card room and instruct the other
Spares to keep a wary eye," Brice said, pulling Fallon's
thoughts back to their present situation. "Will you
need anything further from me tonight? There's this
barmaid down at the—"

Fallon hit him in the arm before he could say more.
"You can tell me of it tomorrow."

"Go on about your stroll in the gardens, then. I'll
be on my way," Brice replied, eyeing Fallon and rubbing his arm in mock pain. "You didn't have to injure
me. You could simply say you're in a rush."

"You'll survive," Fallon assured him.

Brice smiled as he took a backward step toward the
door. He spread his arms wide in embrace of the night,
almost knocking a vase from a pedestal in the process.
"Survival—that *is* the excitement of it all, is it not? A
game of survival."

Brice might see it as a game, but for Fallon, protecting the Spares, his men, was much more than that—it
meant everything in his life. He was still watching
Brice leave when he heard a small feminine sigh from
behind the tower of sweets.

The lady who had been watching his friend
bumped into the table as she attempted to skirt it and
follow after Brice. The table shifted, knocking loose

a tiny pillar holding up one of the great, head-high platters of sweets.

The next moment slowed to a series of heartbeats.

Fallon watched as the display of fruit tarts and sugar-covered cakes wobbled ominously. Without thought, he reached out and caught the third tier from the top in an attempt to stabilize the display before the entire contraption could fall to pieces. His quick grab shifted the series of platters and stands in the opposite direction.

He sucked in a breath of vanilla-and-strawberry-scented air as the display began to slip toward the floor. Then a small gloved hand caught the other side, and he found himself face-to-face with the ever-watchful lady with eyes only for his friend.

When he imagined wood nymphs from mythology, this was how they appeared—with rosy cheeks, doe eyes, and blond curls cascading around a face lit with innocent, ethereal beauty.

Only this lady didn't belong in the woods with the other nymphs. Not dressed as she was. Fallon wasn't one to admire fashion, but her gown seemed to be made of stars, as thousands of beads caught the candle-light and skimmed over perfect curves. Who was this lady, and why was she lurking after the likes of Brice?

"Fancy a cake?" she asked, as her eyes cut over to the tower between them.

"Or fifty of them for that matter?" he returned, his gaze trapped, not leaving her.

She bit her lower lip and shifted her hold on the display. "I must admit, I'm rather surprised at the weight of this platter. I can see now why Mother gained a stone when she hired that new cook. Cakes always look so fluffy and light."

"Until you're balancing several score of them with the palm of your hand."

"Precisely," she said with a small laugh. "Why did you send Mr. Brice to the card room?"

Was this lady not at all concerned that if either of them moved the wrong way, the whole display could come tumbling down? She should be. He certainly was. "Wouldn't a better question be how are we going to remove ourselves from this predicament?"

"I suppose that depends on one's priorities," she murmured, her voice straining as she balanced the platter in her hand.

"And your priority is Mr. Brice." He eyed her. She wasn't old enough to be a widow, and the innocent sparkle in her eyes showed a decided lack of any clandestine ideas. That left only one explanation. "You must know he's a confirmed bachelor."

"That means he's available."

"How do you reason that?"

"He isn't married," she said, as if explaining something to a child. "That fact is confirmed. Therefore, he is available for the prospect of marriage. That's what *confirmed bachelor* means."

"Do you think so? Because I know Brice quite well and—"

"He showed me a kindness once, winked at me," she cut in.

"He winked at you?"

Her eyes lit up with clear delight over further discussion of the undoubtedly notable event. "He did. It was magical. He was visiting my father. He swooped in quite gallantly, and he winked. At me. There was a good-natured smile as well."

"Oh. All is explained then."

"Wonderful! I'm pleased it's settled. You can see now why I wouldn't want him to leave."

"Remind me to keep my grins to myself when in your company," he murmured.

"You think me that impetuous, that I go about hanging upon every smile of every gentleman?"

"No, I…" He didn't know what his thoughts were regarding this woman besides the obvious: perplexed.

"Go ahead then." She raised her chin in challenge. "If you dare. Smile. Do your best."

"Now?" He glanced around, noticing the room was empty—where were the blasted footmen? He had a job to do, somewhere to be, and it wasn't here holding cakes and smiling.

"Here is mine." She smiled, and dawn seemed to break in the candlelit room.

Her smile crept into every cold crevice of his mind and warmed it with its light. It wasn't until a moment later, when the edge of the platter began to cut off blood flow to his fingers, that he realized he was staring at her. "What's your name?"

"When you haven't even offered me a kind smile?"

"I've saved you from—" He broke off, knowing he'd yet to save her from anything at all. He sighed. "Very well." He exercised the muscles in his cheeks and exposed his teeth in a smile.

She sighed and gave him a pitying shake of her head. "You're safe from a leg shackle with that. I'm

Isabelle Fairlyn. You don't smile often, do you? I can see why. You really should work on it a bit more."

Fairlyn… Knottsby's daughter? Her name alone should have made him see the lady back to her chaperone and leave at once, but he was too busy being offended. "What's wrong with my smile?" His teeth were straight and white. No woman had ever complained of his looks before. And he'd never found fault in the mirror.

"Your smile lacks meaning." She adjusted her grip on the display. "Smiles should come from the heart."

"I'm holding up a tower of cakes and biscuits at the moment. My *heart* is elsewhere."

"If you say so."

"St. James," he supplied, wondering if she would recognize the name.

"Ah. You have a terrible lack of a heartfelt smile but a nice name, Mr. St. James."

"Thank you?" He found he was relieved that she didn't know of him yet oddly saddened at the same time.

How much business was really discussed while young ladies were present, though? He shouldn't have expected she would know him, nor did he want her to, though her family name was quite familiar to him. This was by far the strangest encounter he'd ever had with a lady, even without the cakes threatening to tumble to the ground around them.

"You're welcome," she practically sang in return. "Now, how are we to get ourselves out of this mess?"

"Carefully. Move your left hand to the right. Your right, not my right. That's your left."

"I moved to the right."

"There!" he commanded with a bit too much force

in an effort to still her movements. He glanced up and saw the top layer of the contraption wobble before stabilizing again. "Now, if we lift the top off, we can set it down on the table." He nodded toward his intended destination.

"On the fruit platter? We'll squash the berries!"

"I don't see another option, other than letting this thing crash to the floor and cover us both with icing. Or would you rather stay here forever? I could entertain you with my unnaturally affection-free smile."

To Fallon's disappointment, the reminder of his smile seemed to sway her thinking. "What about on the cold meats?"

"Berries have feelings about such things but ham doesn't? Think of the pigs when you say such a thing." Why was he arguing about this with her? He should set the damned platter down and leave for his meeting. He would be late as it was. Instead he was discussing pigs and berries? It was a good thing Brice had left when he did, or Fallon would never have heard the end of it.

"I didn't mean to insult the pigs," she explained, leaning in. "If you only knew my affinity for animals of all kinds—nature in general, really—you wouldn't suggest such a thing."

"Meanwhile this platter isn't getting any lighter. Let's move to that side table just there and set this contraption down where no foods will be harmed."

"All right," she agreed with another bright smile. "How should we do this? Count to three?"

Three... Yes, counting would keep him from staring at her again. "One, two, three... What are you doing? I said three."

"Was it to be on three or after three?" she asked.

"Three! Three! Just move!" He shouldn't order a lady, but she didn't appear to be capable of following his direction anyway.

"We're going to the table across the room?" She moved with him down the long table as if they were involved in some intricate new dance to which neither knew the steps.

"All to save the berries and swine," he murmured as he rounded the end of the table and walked backward across the open floor.

"It's quite far," she complained. Then with a gasp, she exclaimed, "My grip is…"

The tiered platter crashed to the floor between them, sending bits of cake flying into the air. They both jumped back just in time to avoid being completely covered in icing.

"Slipping," she finished with a grimace.

"It may be a bit too late to ask you this, Lady Isabelle, but do you have issue with *cake* being harmed?"

They both glanced down at the bits of cake littering the floor between them. The platter had landed in a large heap and splattered sugary confection across the tops of his boots and the hem of her gown. He could use a thorough cleaning now, but the sprinkling of icing on her gown would likely go unnoticed.

Looking up, her large blue eyes met his once more, this time rimmed with laughter. "As it happens, I believe I am quite fine with cake being harmed."

"Good. That's…good." He took her arm and pulled her toward the door until she was running to keep up.

"Where are we going?"

He glanced behind them and then back at her as they rounded the corner into the hall and kept moving. "If there's one thing I know, it's that you shouldn't ever be caught at the scene of a crime."

"That's the one thing you know? I know how to weave flowers together to make a wreath for my hair. And now I know how to bring terrible harm to a platter of cakes."

He began to laugh. His chest shook with it as if his body were knocking the cobwebs off of a seldom-used piece of furniture. He paused to look at her after they'd rounded another corner into a narrower hall.

"There," she said, staring up at him in amazement. For a long second, his chest contracted as he waited for her to explain her comment. Why was this wood nymph in a ball gown looking at him with such awe in her eyes? Her thoughts shouldn't matter to him. He was Fallon St. James. Men across the country feared and respected him for his work—that's what was truly important.

"You *are* capable of a heartfelt smile. You may need to worry about a leg shackle yet," she said, still looking up at him before blinking and taking a step away. "Not from me, of course. I have my sights set elsewhere. Nevertheless, you will do quite well this season."

He watched her as she took slow steps away from him. Some irrational voice inside didn't want her to leave. "I don't want to do well this season."

"That's silly. Everyone wants to do well in their endeavors."

"I'm not endeavoring," he said, forcing himself to remain still. "I never endeavor—not in what you speak of anyway."

"Is this more *confirmed bachelor* talk?" she asked, her eyes narrowed and fixed on him.

"I have obligations, business to see to—"

"With no time for dancing?" She gasped as she searched his face for some secret held there. "You don't dance, do you?"

Fallon let out a chuckle. When was the last time he'd laughed twice in an evening? "I really should..." he began and glanced away down the hall toward a door that led outside.

"You're planning to leave now, when it's still early in the evening," she replied with a tone of disapproval.

It wasn't often that anyone dared to disapprove of his actions. Aside from Brice's ribbing over almost everything he did, Lady Isabelle's own father had been quite opinionated over Fallon's actions, but that had been a long time ago. Perhaps disapproval ran though her veins...but laughter and smiles seemed this lady's usual inclination.

Lady Isabelle Fairlyn was more unexpected than the danger that had him searching the ball tonight. He turned back to her, not wanting to leave, not just yet anyway.

"I am thankful for your aid in my escape tonight, Mr. St. James." She glanced over her shoulder toward the ballroom and the waltz playing there.

"Of course. Is there somewhere I could escort you? To your family perhaps."

"I've already taken up enough of your time." She

took a few steps away before turning back to him once more. "Practice that smile in my absence."

He caught himself before promising to do just that. What was wrong with him? Others answered to *him*. He didn't answer to ladies—or even to wood nymphs disguised in ball gowns.

"Stay away from falling cakes," he called after her. *And gentlemen like Brice*, he finished to himself.

"I can't make any promises," she said with a laugh, and she disappeared around the corner.

Fallon stood looking at the empty hall for a moment to gain his bearings, feeling as if he'd been thrown into sudden darkness as Lady Isabelle waltzed away. But a second later he was moving toward the rear of the house. As late as he was already, he would make one more lap through the ground floor in search of Grapling and then be on his way.

His secret club that provided for younger sons of the nobility required all of his attention. He had nothing remaining for other *endeavors,* as Lady Isabelle had put it. Some gentlemen might have spare time for smiles, dancing, and staring after perplexing ladies, but he had the Spare Heirs Society to see to. And that was exactly how he preferred his life to be.

⁓

Isabelle dusted the crumbs from her gloves and slipped back into the ballroom as if the cake incident had never occurred. That *was* what St. James had advised, wasn't it? Escape the scene of the crime. It was all very clandestine and exciting until one was caught standing in a pile of spilled cakes.

What did St. James know of escaping danger, though?

Perhaps he was secretly a pirate. Her eyes grew wide with the possibilities. With his tall frame, dark hair pushed back from his face and worn a bit too long, and those piercing, deep-brown eyes, she could certainly envision him in command of a ship of lawless men. He traveled the high seas in search of adventure and was only here at this ball to sell off a stolen treasure. And pirates weren't likely to smile often—it all fit!

Either it was true and he was a pirate, or he was simply a gentleman who had spilled a great many desserts in his day and knew how to escape blame.

She giggled as she headed to the column where she'd left her sister. Whoever Mr. St. James was, she was glad he'd come to her aid for two reasons. One, she would have made an even larger mess of things without him. And two, because in spite of the situation, she'd had a rather enjoyable time in his company.

They should be friends. Ladies were allowed to be friendly with gentlemen as long as nothing untoward happened between them, weren't they? And it wasn't as if St. James was dangerous. He was friendly with Mr. Brice, after all. No one wicked could be friends with such a boisterous gentleman as Mr. Brice. "We shall be great friends," she murmured to herself as she joined Victoria to the side of the ballroom floor.

"You have cake icing on your gown," her sister said as she drained the last of the champagne in her glass and looked around for a footman with another.

"I'm not surprised." Isabelle smiled to herself. If Victoria only knew what had happened…

Dropping every sweet at the ball on the floor hadn't been her plan, but at least she'd gotten to see Mr. Brice for a few moments. And St. James had been quite sporting about the entire escapade. He was a pleasant fellow, even if he wasn't charming in the usual way. His choice of evening wear was far too dark, and his mannerisms were too businesslike. Yet there was a warmth held within the rich color of his eyes that inspired one to trust him, much like chocolate could be counted upon to be delicious. Trustworthiness was important in friendship.

Isabelle looked out across the swirls of brightly colored gowns as ladies danced in time to the music. Some lady here would tame St. James, force him to be fashionable and offer a heartfelt smile when called upon to do so. And his wife and Isabelle would someday laugh over how her friendship with the man had begun.

"You have that amused look on your face that you get when you talk of love, paintings, and flowers," Victoria said as she grabbed another glass of champagne from a passing footman.

"My talk of love and flowers *is* delightful," Isabelle returned, nudging her sister in the arm and causing her champagne to slosh about.

Victoria scoffed as she drank half the glass to prevent a spill. "Where have you been? You disappeared from our conversation midsentence a half hour ago. Have you been stalking Mr. Brice again?"

"Of course not." Isabelle wouldn't call it stalking; it was really more research, if anything.

She bit her lip as she considered her sister. Isabelle and Victoria were identical twins, true, yet when

Isabelle looked at her sister, she didn't see the similarities between them in the same way other people seemed to. She only saw Victoria. And her sister was quite Isabelle's opposite in every way possible. Isabelle noticed Victoria's too-pink cheeks from the drinks she was downing, the look of boredom in her eyes, and the hint of rouge she'd put on her lips, even though Victoria would deny it if asked.

"Yellow," Isabelle announced. "I do enjoy the cheerful nature of yellow. Or pink. Pink is a happy color too. Did you notice the color of Roselyn's gown earlier? It suits her, and it's a perfect representation of the color at its best. But yellow is ideal for adding a bit of sunshine to the evening."

"What?" Victoria turned from watching the quadrille to look at her in complete bewilderment. "I know we're supposed to have some type of bond as twin sisters, but I have no idea what you're talking about."

"You were disappointed that I didn't finish my thoughts earlier about the fashionable colors for gowns this season. I thought I would continue. Yellow..." She trailed off in confusion.

"Never mind that. I'm only glad you returned. Roselyn has wandered away somewhere, and Evangeline is nowhere to be found. That Lord Winfield of Evangeline's asked me to dance. It was dreadful. Do you know he doesn't enjoy visits to Tattersall's? What sort of gentleman doesn't enjoy speculating over the next great race horse? I don't know how Evie can abide a moment in that man's company."

"I don't believe Evie has any great love for Lord Winfield. Or race horses, for that matter."

"Great love or not, I can't make conversation with a gentleman who thinks rides in the park can be daring. Rides in the park! She's our cousin. We have to save her from such a dull marriage."

"Are they to be married now?" Isabelle drew back in shock. She'd been sure Evangeline's head had been turned by some mystery gentleman at the Dillsworths' ball only recently.

"Isn't marriage the very blasted reason all of us are here? All of you, anyway," Victoria corrected. "Since I have no plan to marry."

"Victoria, how many glasses of champagne have you had tonight?" Isabelle asked, though she could guess at the answer, and it was many.

"How many servings of cake did you eat to soil your gown to that degree?" Victoria countered.

"Two, but they were necessary," she offered with a smile. "I needed eye holes."

"I should ask, but since I'm certain it involves spying on a man you hardly know, I won't."

"I know him," Isabelle muttered, now searching for the footman with the champagne for her own consumption.

"Isabelle," Victoria said with a sigh, "when playing cards, no matter how you wish to have all the kings in the deck, you must play the ones in your own hand."

"I don't need *all the kings*," she countered, turning back to face her sister. "You make me sound like such the social climber. I don't care about ranking in society. Brice isn't even titled. I only want love."

"Then find a gentleman who is actually present this evening and wishes to dance with you," Victoria pleaded with a sympathetic smile before turning to survey the room. "What about that one over there?"

"With the faded cravat and receding hairline?"

"Heavens no. Do you think I hate you?"

"Sometimes I wonder," Isabelle muttered.

"Don't. I only want your happiness, and that gentleman there looks to be well suited for you." Her sister tipped her chin in the direction of a man to the left of the first.

"Victoria, is he even old enough to be allowed here? *That* is the sort of gentleman you think I'm suited for?" Isabelle hit her sister in the arm with her fan.

The gentleman in question could barely be of age. If Victoria had ever read the page of Isabelle's old diary about gentlemen's bums, she wouldn't think such a spindly youth would do for her at all. Isabelle unfurled her fan to hide her blush.

"That man over there seems to be staring in this direction a great deal," Victoria mused, her eyes flashing toward the shadowed corner of the room.

"Who?" Isabelle searched the room but saw no one looking their way.

"Just there, beneath the balcony. Although he looks rather—"

"Intent?" Isabelle returned, finally spotting the man to whom Victoria was referring.

He clung to the shadows of the room, but his gaze bore into her even at this distance. His eyes weren't bright and charming like Mr. Brice's, nor were they warm and endearing like Mr. St. James's. They were cold. His icy glare pierced through her, sending a shiver down her spine. Who was he? Perhaps they'd met last season and he was still at odds over not getting a place on her dance card. But wouldn't she recall an introduction to such a tall, dark-haired, and rather ominous-looking fellow? His sharp features alone...

She couldn't imagine forgetting him.

"If *intent* is the way you want to put it," Victoria replied. "I was going to advise we move to a different part of the ballroom and hope he doesn't follow us."

"I don't know," Isabelle murmured, searching for some explanation for his stare. "Perhaps it's only the rarity of seeing twin ladies. We do get looks of curiosity on occasion." Yet this man's wasn't that sort of expression. It was a stare that fairly screamed danger. Why was he staring so intently in their direction?

"Isabelle, I don't think he has any interest in the rarity of twin ladies," her sister warned. "We should move."

"Perhaps he's some distant relation we don't recall." Isabelle shifted to look at Victoria. "Or he could be an old friend of Father's. Father did have a rather different set of acquaintances before he inherited the title."

"I suppose that could be true."

Isabelle glanced back toward the main door to the ballroom but caught sight of only the back of the man's dark head as he disappeared into the crowd. She'd stood staring after him for just a moment when she saw St. James dart after him, both of them disappearing into the night.

"A piratical battle in the moonlight," she gasped.

"What?" Victoria asked.

"It could be an exchange of jewels with pistols drawn, or the retrieval of a stolen treasure map!"

"Or the thankful departure of a man looking at you with lecherous thoughts on his mind," her sister countered.

"We should follow after them. Pirates fighting in the street, Victoria! Can you imagine it?"

"Them? To whom are you referring?" Victoria asked, ignoring the notion of pirates as she did most of Isabelle's ideas.

"The intent man from the shadows and Mr. St. James," Isabelle supplied.

Her sister's eyes narrowed on her. "How do you know St. James?"

"How do *you* know him?" Isabelle countered.

"Everyone knows St. James…everyone with an interest in the good card games in town and wagers on race horses anyway."

"You told me you stopped wagering with gentlemen. If Father learns—" Isabelle broke off, her fan dropping to her side in defeat.

"I've done nothing of any significance in ages. I learned of him last year," Victoria said, but her gaze didn't meet Isabelle's.

Isabelle chose to ignore Victoria's most unladylike inclination to gamble for the moment, her attention circling back to the man who had just slipped from the room. "You met St. James…last season. Then he's often in London?"

"We haven't been officially introduced, but I'm certain he has a home here. He's a well-known gentleman around town, in certain circles anyway," Victoria hedged, signaling a footman for another glass of champagne.

"That's disappointing. I thought him a pirate."

When Victoria turned back with a glass in hand, there was a look of resigned concern in her eyes. "Isabelle, someday your dreams are going to lead you into trouble."

Isabelle didn't want to cause her sister to worry over her, but Victoria was rather quick in her judgment of people. People in London were primarily good at heart, probably even that intent man who'd left the ball a moment ago. If she'd only spoken with him, she was certain she would have discovered the reason for his scowl. Perhaps he simply needed to practice his heartfelt smile as well. Isabelle grinned at the memory of Mr. St. James's tense attempt at a happy face before relaxing back into what was clearly his normal look— watchful consideration.

"There's no need to worry. If I ever find trouble, I'll be rescued by my true love." Isabelle smiled at her sister, knowing how such statements annoyed Victoria and enjoying every second of her torment.

Victoria raised an eyebrow in her direction. "Mr. Brice?"

Isabelle said nothing in response.

Yes, Mr. Brice.

Two

Isabelle Fairlyn's Diary
January 1817

I spent this afternoon at the museum. When I'm within those grand walls, I can't seem to contain my smile—of course that's also true of when I sketch in the garden, shop on Bond, take a walk in the park, or attend a ball. Walking through the upper rooms of the British Museum, however, brings me even more happiness than usual.

The principal librarian seems to truly appreciate the pieces on loan from Grandfather's collection. I told him of the grandness of the family's gallery before the fire all those years ago. I wish so many pieces hadn't been lost that awful night, but it only makes me appreciate the remainder that much more. The hillside chateau piece seems to be in fine condition. I oversaw its installation, and today I got to stand in for the under-librarian and explain the history behind the piece to a group of ladies. It was wonderful!

I'm thankful that I get to spend a few afternoons

every week looking after the family's pieces displayed in such an elegant setting. I think Grandfather would approve of the location. I feel closer to him when I'm there with the art he loved so. One day I hope to have a gallery of my own, where I will stroll past familiar paintings and say good morning to them like they're old friends.

—Isabelle

THE WORDS ON THIS PAGE DREW REGINALD GRAPLING in more than the previous entry, the information calling to him like a siren's song. His pulse quickened with the possibilities held there in feminine script. He'd read the page twice already, as the details of a new plan strung together in his mind.

He'd come here seeking knowledge. Either of the Fairlyn girls would have suited his needs, but only one girl had written out her every thought as if baring her soul for him. On this cold winter night, he'd found more than what he'd been looking for—he'd found the perfect path forward. Soon the weather would warm and the season would draw the last of society from their country homes. It was too perfect.

"This diary is a treasure trove," he mumbled to himself as he stroked his fingers down the page in admiration. "My most sincere thanks, Lady Isabelle."

By coming here, he'd hoped to discover one of the girl's interests, where she might be found alone, what he could use to lure her away from her family, anything that might help him turn the tables on their father, Lord Knottsby.

"*Knottsby*," he breathed. "Even his name reeks of entitlement and arrogance." *Soon*, he promised himself, focusing instead on the looping, ornate lines of text in front of him.

These sweetly written words changed everything.

❧

Spring 1817

Fallon took the stack of old files from the shelf in the corner of his library and turned back to his desk. Although he could remember every detail of the Westminster boardinghouse incident far too well, even four years after the awful event had occurred, he needed to read his own words on the matter once more. Whether he liked it or not, Grapling was back. The knowledge made his heart speed up even as his footsteps slowed on the thick rug that covered the floor.

"Revenge or unfinished business? Perhaps both?" he asked the portrait of the kind-eyed man on the wall between the towering bookcases. He wasn't certain who the man was other than a predecessor in this house he now called his home and headquarters for the Spare Heirs Society, but he found his presence somewhat comforting nonetheless. Paintings were the best friends a man could ask for. They had the ability to listen to one's musings, yet never divulged a single secret—a quality he admired.

"I'll discover the truth," he assured the painted man as he clutched the files tighter in his hand.

Crossing the remainder of the room, he tossed the packet to the top of his desk, reached for the teapot that always resided on the corner, and tipped it up. Empty. "Mrs. Featherfitch!" he called out, knowing the housekeeper was just outside his library door.

"Never in my days have I witnessed such cater-wauling over picking up a few hats," the older woman said in exasperation as she stepped into the library, dusting her hands on her skirts. The woman never gave up her stance against household clutter, yet her efforts only thinned the amount of hats, notes on scraps of paper, and miscellaneous debris from twenty different gentlemen's pockets that landed in the main hall. The housing of the Spare Heirs who needed rooms was a constant at headquarters, and something his housekeeper grumbled over at every opportunity. "And I overheard a few of them laying wagers on how long it would take to drive me mad with the mess. You would think I'd asked them to ship off for war!"

"Apologies," Fallon said as he moved around his desk to take his seat once more. "I'll speak with them." He added the item to the ongoing list in his head.

"Dear me. Are you out of tea?" she asked, crossing the room. The rectangle of early-morning light that spilled from the front window farthest from the hall illuminated his desk in its corner.

"It's bone dry," he confirmed with a thin smile.

"That won't do! How are you to keep all of society from turning on each other with no tea?" She lifted the tea service from his desk but didn't leave.

She was studying him, as she often did. Waiting for his armor to crack, he supposed. If she wanted them to share some sentimental moment that involved a long talk about loss while dabbing at tears with a handkerchief, it wasn't going to happen. Especially not today, no matter the date on the calendar.

Pearl may have been gone ten years today, but it was a lesser-known loss he was concerned with this morning—that of a common prostitute whose only crime had been coming too close to Mr. Reginald Grapling four years ago.

Mrs. Featherfitch swallowed and blinked away the mistiness in her eyes, the teapot rattling against the silver platter she held. She could always be counted upon to be emotional when no show of the heart was required, but in an odd way, he liked that about her. It reminded him that ingrained loyalty—not to a cause but to an individual—still resided somewhere within the walls of his home. That, on some level, this was a normal house, even if sentimentality only existed belowstairs.

"Would you like a bite of something while I'm off to the kitchen?" she asked as she shifted the tray in her arms to steady the rattling china.

"No." It was the same answer he gave her every morning. It wasn't going to change, yet she always asked.

"One day, I'm going to get you to eat before noon. Or after, for that matter," she tossed over her shoulder as she moved toward the door. "It isn't good for you to go about on an empty stomach."

He remained silent. Mrs. Featherfitch didn't need to be reminded of his reasons. Fallon hadn't eaten before noon in ten years, and he wasn't going to begin today. Mornings had once been filled with laughter, and now he had no choice but to work until the morning was behind him. He would eat later, when there was more time.

He glanced down at the documents on his desk. Tea wouldn't dull the ache of knowing what he was about to read, what he could have stopped from happening. If he'd only seen Reginald Grapling in a clear light. He'd been preoccupied, and it had taken only a moment for details to slip past his attention. That's all that had been necessary for theft and ultimately tragedy. And he wouldn't allow it to happen again.

Suddenly anxious to delay, he pushed his papers aside and stood from his desk. It was nearly nine o'clock in the morning—surely some of the gentlemen would be about by now. He moved to the door and stepped into the hall, spotlessly clean aside from the large table piled high with coats, hats, and random bits of twenty different men's lives.

Fallon gave a small nod to the cherubs in the mural on the ceiling, as he always did. Their dark, round eyes had watched over the lives of the inhabitants of this home for as long as anyone could remember. Those cherubs knew enough secrets to bring an end to the entirety of London high society, and as such, they deserved his respect. The other gentlemen didn't understand his attachment to the merry little fellows, but as long as he was the head of things around here, those cherubs wouldn't be covered over with a single fleck of paint.

The sound of voices reached him as he neared the

main room of the Spare Heirs Society's headquarters. The constant hum of activity brought him comfort this morning, as it often did. When he'd first received the house from Lady Herron—Pearl, as he'd known her— this had been an oversized and seldom-used drawing room. Flowers had been the primary theme here, as they had been everywhere in her house. Fallon's lips twitched in an effort to smile before he recalled himself. Nowadays, this room served a purpose. The floral draperies had been stripped away in favor of something more masculine, and extra armchairs had been added over time. With each passing day, there were fewer reminders of Pearl, replaced by evidence of the gentlemen he'd drawn into his circle. Life had moved on, and Fallon was in the lead, just as she would have wanted.

Fallon moved around the billiard table in the center of the room so as not to disturb the early-morning game taking place, and headed for his usual spot in the corner. He liked this vantage point to view the day's activities. From his chair here he could watch the goings-on of the society, keep a close watch on the members while still maintaining a view of the street outside. Nothing escaped his notice—not an occasional woman slipping from the front door in the early hours or an argument after too many drinks at night.

Drumming his fingers gently on the table, he watched. He'd always been perceptive—the skill that had once made him an awkward child now served him well.

"Sir," his butler offered as he neared.

"Togsforth," Fallon returned, still watching his men across the room.

The butler followed his gaze to where Wentwood and Lawson were playing a hand of cards. "They seem to be on friendly terms again."

"It seems so." Last week's disagreement appeared to have ended. Fallon stood behind his decision to add a man to their team, overseeing the protection of the gaming hells in the east end of town. It allowed for work to continue at all hours—not to mention it prevented corruption. He ground his jaw at the reminder of corruption from long ago and looked away from the men, absentmindedly watching Togsforth continue on about his daily routine.

If the presence of the Spare Heirs Society was known across the country, most would find issue with their dealings. Living on the murky side of the law as they did, influencing and quietly profiting from society and keeping the seedier side of the city running safely, didn't sit well with those of a fragile temperament. Those who knew the true nature of the gentlemen's club that Fallon had founded, however, understood the need the group filled and were thankful for its existence. Fallon had built an army from the gentlemen society often overlooked—younger sons of the nobility.

Without the Spare Heirs, those men—*his* men—had few options in life. Fallon gave those gentlemen purpose, a wage, and in many cases a roof over their heads, and London was better off as a result. There had been only one gentleman who had fallen prey to the lure of more funds than St. James could provide through the Spare Heirs Society. And that man had now escaped prison and was back.

Somewhere in the city, Grapling was milling about, no doubt hatching another plan to serve his own interests. What was he after? Fallon had eyes at the prison. How could the man have possibly slipped past their notice? And yet he had.

Men like Grapling didn't simply visit town to enjoy the sights. The entertainments he sought weren't so entertaining to those around him, and now it was up to Fallon to eliminate the threat Grapling posed everywhere he went. Fallon was sitting and staring out the window at the movement of carriages up and down the street when someone dropped into the chair at his side.

"You should have come with me to the card room last night," Brice said, already reclining in his seat and still in his clothing from the night before.

"You're up early," Fallon said with a wry smile.

"Just a nightcap before bed," Brice said, lifting the half-empty glass in his hand.

"You're staying the night here? Difficulties with your father again?"

Brice shrugged and looked away. For a man who was ever eager to share a tale, he'd always been surprisingly quiet when it came to his family.

Brice was the fourth son of Lord Dillsworth, a man known all over the country for his keen eye for numbers and, as a result, his vast wealth. Dillsworth was not known, however, for being a jolly fellow or adoring father. Fallon didn't know much else of the man, but Brice's silence spoke volumes.

Fallon had wondered for years if he should inform his friend that he had such an obvious tell, if not for the sake of his cover in town, then to improve his bluffing skills in cards. But he had—like Brice—remained silent on the uncomfortable subject.

Instead Fallon simply ensured that one of the rooms upstairs was always kept open for Brice for those occasions when he'd rather not return to Dillsworth House.

"Any word on Grapling?" Brice asked around a loud yawn. He stretched his arms and almost knocked the tea tray from Mrs. Featherfitch's hands as she approached.

"He escaped…again," Fallon said, giving the house-keeper a nod of thanks as she set the tray down and left. She had the knack for finding him. Of course, there was a rather short list of places he could usually be found, even within the sizable home.

"Sorry he got away, but it was a brilliant night at the tables."

"That's a comforting consolation with a madman on the loose."

"I am feeling rather comforted at the moment," Brice said with a grin as he patted his pocket. When Fallon only scowled, Brice added, "I'm only having a go at you. I might have lost sight of the bastard last night, but I'll continue the search today after a bit of a rest."

"I've already sent a few men to scout his former haunts." Poor sods. Fallon had divided a list of the worst taverns and brothels between them and sent them off at first light this morning. Constant watch of Grapling's family's home had been in place since last night. And still he wished he could do more to find the man.

"Don't leave me out of the fun just because I need

a bit of sleep now," Brice complained, leaning back farther in his chair to stretch his legs beneath the table.

"I wouldn't think of allowing you to miss the reunion." Fallon ignored the plate of breads and the paste-colored bowl of porridge his housekeeper had included on the platter and poured a cup of tea.

"You haven't worked out why he's back yet, have you?"

Fallon winced and took a drink of the searing-hot liquid. "I'm going to go to the Swan and Pony in a bit. The man must eat at some point, and he was always prattling on about the food there."

"That shabby little spot in front of the museum? I think it was the barmaids who held his attention, not their soggy meat pies. Made the mistake of going there once. It's a wonder the nobs at the British Museum haven't forced them to clean up their establishment. *Its very proximity might soil the curiosities!*" Brice fairly screamed in a false voice clearly meant to impersonate some museum official as he leaned forward to take a piece of the bread from the platter. A few men looked over but only shook their heads and continued their daily activities.

"Even so," Fallon muttered.

Brice ripped off a bite of bread with his teeth and asked, "You're off to the Swan and Pony then?"

"After I wrap up a few things here." He needed to read the notes he'd abandoned on his desk. Instead of standing, he drained the last of the tea in his cup as if it could drown the troubles he was having. He poured another cup, intending to take it with him back to his library. He'd sat here too long already.

"We'll find Grapling in no time. If he'd been in the card room, he would have witnessed quite the game. You should have come with me." He pointed to Fallon with the half-eaten piece of bread in his hand. "There I was, simply filling in for Lord Turnwell so play could continue, and…"

Fallon couldn't remember the last time he'd sat down to a hand of cards without the intention of discussing business. A hand of cards as sport was as foreign to his life as sipping rum in island heat in the shade of a palm tree. What was the point of sitting about and chatting when that talk didn't further some strategy for the Spares?

While Brice had relaxed last night with a hand of cards, Fallon had met with one of his men and a lord in town to discuss their mutual interest in a piece of legislation currently before parliament. Then he'd moved on to meet with another and receive an update on the investment in Crosby Steam Works that Claughbane had brought to the table. That was how an evening should be spent—productively.

Move ever forward.

That had been the mantra of one of the gentlemen he'd respected the most at the Spare Heirs Society. He might have been Fallon's subordinate, but he'd always offered guidance when it was needed—and in those first few years, guidance had been in short supply. Now Fallon had built an empire and his friend was no longer with the Spares, but his words still resonated through everything Fallon did. He was always moving forward. By midafternoon he would have Grapling in hand and all his other plans could proceed without incident.

"I look down, and I'm holding the winning hand of cards," Brice said, leaning back in his chair with his arms folded across his chest. "Granted, it was originally Turnwell's to play, but he should have thought of that before he stood to get another drink and told me to keep an eye out for him. Anyway, some things happened, and now I owe Lord and Lady Winslow a new table. Quite a win, though, so it balances out in the end." He shook his head and took a sip of the whiskey in his glass. "You really should have been there."

"Things outside the card room were equally inter-esting last night," Fallon mused before he could catch himself. Clearly this issue with Grapling had him at odds if he was offering unsolicited information. He truly needed to leave now.

"You spotted Grapling in the garden after all? I thought you were still looking for him. Didn't give the all-powerful St. James the slip, did he?"

He had indeed, only not in the garden. Fallon had looked back at Lady Isabelle Fairlyn for but a second. She had been standing there in the ballroom, bathed in soft candlelight, and Grapling had vanished from the front doors. "I saw him from a distance but no more," he muttered.

"You need to put down the work and get out more, St. James. Seeing someone from a distance isn't the definition of excitement."

"Perhaps." His encounter with Lady Isabelle Fairlyn had been invading his thoughts more than he would ever admit. He hid the amusement that tugged at his lips over the memory of her laughter. Would he see her at the next grand society event? He should make it a point *not* to see the lady again...

"I meant no insult, St. James."

"Insult?" He looked up from the steaming cup of tea in his hand.

"About you having a bit of fun from time to time," Brice explained. "You look like your favorite pudding was stolen from you without a bite."

"You know I don't eat sweets. They—"

"*Extend the dinner hour beyond what is necessary and don't provide enough nourishment to justify the time wasted in their consumption.* You've mentioned it on occasion. But I know the look of stolen sugary treats in a man's eye. I'm the youngest of four. I had to fight for my share of such things. It's why I'm so mean today." Brice flexed his arm with a grin.

"Yes, you're terribly angry. If you'll excuse me, I need to see to some things before I leave for the Swan and Pony. Perhaps Grapling likes sweets and will be enjoying an extended meal there."

"Go on, then. If you find him, send for me. I want a piece of that one for the trouble he's put us through."

"If I find him, I'll serve him up...like pudding," Fallon promised.

❧

The Swan and Pony was the sort of establishment that held many secrets—what was actually in the stew for one. But Fallon was in search of only one secret today: Had Reginald Grapling been seen here since his escape?

Fallon gave a nod to his driver to circle the area as

they'd discussed, opened the door, and walked into the dimly lit tavern. The pungent scent of countless glasses of whiskey burned his nose, and he blinked in the low light of the open room. There was a layer of grit on the floor that had been scrubbed to a lighter shade of dirty by countless boots scraping across the entrance. The walls were yellowed from a century's worth of pipe smoke. The same smoke still seemed to hang low over the tables as if trapped there. Fallon scanned the room, focusing on every shadowed corner before he turned to the barkeeper.

"Pint?"

"Not today," Fallon said, moving closer to the well-worn edge of the countertop. "I'm looking for someone."

"A friend?"

Fallon didn't reply, only slid a few coins across the wooden surface toward the older man.

"A good friend of yers, I can see," the barkeeper muttered as he pocketed the coins.

Fallon watched him, gauging whether the man would tell him the truth or fill him with lies, even with money involved. "Have you seen Mr. Grapling since his return?"

The barkeeper's eyes grew wide for a second, then he looked down to get an empty glass, taking his time to pull it from a shelf below the counter. His hands shook, rattling the glass against the wooden surface of the bar top. Then the man's gaze cut to a closed door on the far wall. It was a tiny movement, but Fallon saw it.

"I don't know a Mr. Grapling. Sorry to disappoint ya," the barkeeper finally stated.

"I have all that I require. Thank you." Fallon slid two more coins across the counter. "For your troubles."

"I don't want any trouble 'ere."

Fallon gave the man a nod and moved toward the closed door. He didn't want this trouble either. Talk inside the tavern continued on around him, but all Fallon heard were his own footfalls as he neared the door.

Then in one swift motion, he flung the door open and stepped inside. He barely registered the single table, empty chairs, and still-steaming plate of food in the center of the room. His gaze went straight to the open window. Grapling had been here when he arrived. Pushing chairs from his path, Fallon rounded the table and climbed through the window.

The walls of an alley surrounded him with only one means of escape, back toward the street where he'd left his driver circling.

Setting off at a run, Fallon dodged abandoned crates and debris that littered the ground. He reached the corner and slid to a stop with his hand on the cool stone wall. Which direction?

He turned to look toward the wide street that separated Montague House from the surrounding businesses. And that's when he saw someone running across the open courtyard in front of the British Museum. The man leapt over a bench and pushed off a tree, not slowing even for obstacles in his path.

"Grapling," Fallon growled as he set off in the man's direction. Slipping in between carriages, ignoring the curses of the drivers around him, he reached the courtyard and increased his pace. Grapling was now running up the steps to the museum, where no windows stood open for an easy escape.

The gap between them was shrinking. Fallon had always been quick on foot, a skill he now used to his benefit. His breaths came out in heavy puffs, and his coat billowed out behind him.

He was gaining ground on Grapling. Just a bit farther. Fallon hit the bottom of the steps and kept going, taking them two at a time. He would finally have the bastard. And unlike last night, there was no Lady Isabelle here to distract him!

❧

Isabelle moved down the hall, offering a smile of greeting to both the museum patrons and the portraits alike. The portraits deserved a bit of kindness too after the way she'd heard some gentlemen criticize them only a few minutes before.

"*Simple swirls of paint…* Don't listen to them for a moment," she told the painting of the lady sitting with a bowl of oranges as she passed by.

The people depicted in these portraits were part of something wonderful. Their beauty and spirit would live on forever in these *simple swirls of paint*. She ran a gloved finger over the corner of the nearest frame and nodded at the young boy in the portrait.

She'd only just left her reticule, pelisse, and maid, for that matter, with the under-librarian, a kind man, in the back work area where repairs were made. The two seemed pleased with the idea of chatting while he mended a frame, so Isabelle had left them there. Now she had the entire afternoon to wander the halls of the upper rooms of the museum. She almost twirled at the thought but collected herself in time. It wouldn't do to spin about in public, as she'd been told many times by her mother, even if in her heart she was turning with her arms stretched wide. The only thing that could make this day better would be if she could catch sight of Mr. Brice while on her walk home. There was a hop to her step as she neared the end of the gallery.

The large front doors of the museum banged open at the bottom of the wide marble staircase, and Isabelle flinched at the echoing sound.

"You have to sign in," the porter called after someone.

Isabelle peered around the corner and through the legs of the giraffe diorama on the top landing of the grand staircase. Perhaps it was an art thief, known around the world for his rapid escapes, fleeing museum after museum with priceless stolen works to fill the galleries in a lavish home on some foreign coast. And now he'd come to take spoils from this museum during her volunteer hours! What a boon!

She moved forward, unable to resist the lure of such excitement. He would wear black, naturally, and have a mask of some sort. He'd have to have a large sack in which to stow his loot. Would he sport a mustache? Carry a knife? Would she have to defend her paintings?

Isabelle slipped down the stairs to find out. After all, a portion of the museum was under her watch between the hours of one and four. This was prefer-able to yesterday, when Lady Smeltings returned to continue her complaints about the lack of benches. Poor Mr. Jasper, the principal librarian, had been overwrought with anguish at her badgering. If the man couldn't manage Lady Smeltings, he could hardly handle a thief in the museum. It was best to leave him be and deal with this herself.

Isabelle moved in silence down the stairs. Her friend Roselyn wasn't the only one who was well suited for spy work. She smiled at the thought and slipped around the corner, into the main entrance to the museum. The large entry to the building was empty when she entered, and she caught only a glimpse of the porter disappearing down one of the halls. The doors stood open on their hinges, and she frowned at the sight. She'd taken only a step toward them when someone bounded over the top of the stairs and ran inside. The gentleman slid to a stop on the polished floor and whirled around as if looking for something he'd lost. Stopping his chase, his gaze raked over the room, dismissing her before he'd really seen her.

She stood staring at him. He ran his hand through his dark hair where it was disheveled from his quick entrance and shook his coat back into place. Mr. St. James from the ball last night? How odd that she would see him again so soon. Of course, that was marginally less odd than the way he'd run into the museum as if fleeing for his life.

"You know most gentlemen simply *wander* through museum doors," she said as she moved to close those same doors behind him.

"Do they?" he asked as he stepped farther into the building, craning his neck to see down each hall that led off of the main lobby. "I'll try that on my next visit."

When the doors were secured, she turned and

followed him to the center of the room, watching as he took in every detail of the museum entrance. His gaze seemed to linger on the shadowed corners where large plants flanked the casement opening that led deeper into the building before he spun on his heel back in her direction. He still didn't seem to have really *seen* her.

"Are you…" She swerved her head from side to side to gain his attention. "Are you looking for someone, Mr. St. James? An international art thief with an exotic home on a cliff overlooking stormy seas?" She should be searching for the one who had caused the scene with the porter instead of talking to St. James, but curiosity held her captive.

When he didn't respond but continued to look around, she filled in his clear response. "No, I suppose that's not the case at all." Her imagination must have gotten well away from her this time. An art thief—ha! "Your dog then? You've lost your dog. How awful that must be for you."

"No, I'm…" He blinked at her as if just realizing with whom he was speaking. "I'm here…to look at art. And you? Why are you here? Did you see—"

"I'm here for the art as well." She lifted her arms out to the sides and glanced around at the spacious first floor, which housed the museum's collection of ancient drawings. "I have volunteer responsibilities in the afternoons from one o'clock to four."

He took a few steps away to peer down one of the long halls before returning to the center of the room. He watched her with a sharp gaze as if the answer to some great riddle rested with her. "What are you voluntarily responsible for in the afternoons?"

"I watch the art."

"You watch art," he repeated, his brows now drawn together. He shook his head and stepped back to look down the opposite hall. Then he moved to her once more, running a hand through his hair again, clear agitation showing through his serenely asked questions. "Is that eventful?"

"Oh, quite," she confirmed with a smile. What had St. James so wary this afternoon? He was acting oddly—even for him.

"The art doesn't need to be watched in the mornings?" he asked with a raised brow.

What an absurd question. She laughed and nudged his elbow with her own. "Of course it does."

"Of course…" He looked dazed as he stared down at her.

"And I ensure the lemonade served in the lobby remains in the lobby. That's terribly important. Lemonade could be doused all over a book older than we are or, heaven forbid, a portrait that could never be replaced. You don't require a drink while in the lobby, do you?"

"No, I don't."

"Good, then you may come with me," she said, indicating the grand staircase. "This is the third part of my responsibilities: leading tours."

"Do you lead tours for any gentleman who walks through the doors?" Though he was talking to her, Isabelle had the distinct impression that St. James was listening to every noise in the museum at the same time.

Her theory was proven true a second later when a door shut somewhere out of sight and he lunged to the side to get a view of the action. She couldn't imagine that a dog on the loose inside the museum would be this quiet. There would be shouts and barking…

St. James must be thinking the same because a second later he sighed and turned back to her, giving her his complete attention. Poor man. She hoped he found the furry scoundrel soon.

"I'm not a librarian, but I am allowed to assist on occasion." She reached out and grabbed his arm, forcing him to escort her. A walk around the museum would do him some good. Together they started up the stairs to the upper rooms, where she worked. "I usually get the older ladies who can hear only half of what I say, but I'm making an exception for you."

"For me? Why?" He paused and studied her, his hand on the ornate metal stair rail.

"Because we're going to be friends, Mr. St. James. It's already been decided. And the librarian is in the workroom with the under-librarian, a footman, and my maid, so no need to worry over my reputation." She tugged on his arm until he moved again, ascending the stairs at her side.

"Why would you wish to be friends with me?" he asked, as if friendship was the most foreign concept of which he'd ever heard.

"We've already survived potential scandal together. Really, what further test of friendship does one need beyond being set upon by a giant display of cakes?"

"*Friends*," he said, appearing to test the word on his lips.

"Come this way," she insisted as they walked through the door at the top of the stairs and were instantly surrounded by her family's paintings. She spoke over her shoulder as she pulled him with her to the far side of the room. "I want to show you the pieces of this collection, and you have to start at this end of the room and walk to the right. Always walk to the right. You're traveling through time with the paintings instead of moving past them. It makes a remarkable difference. Do you see? Begin here." She smiled up at the first painting and squeezed his arm, unable to contain her excitement over the artwork all around her.

"How long have you volunteered at the museum?"

"Only since the beginning of the season."

"That's all? How do you know the works so well?"

"Oh! I didn't mention that, did I? This collection was my grandfather's. It's on loan to the museum. My favorite visits with my grandfather were the days spent among his paintings." She sighed over the memory. "And not because my sister was always busy elsewhere," she laughed.

He shook his head as if trying to remember some memory that had long since faded away. "Is she older than you are?"

Isabelle drew him along a few steps to the right and admired the next piece in the collection. "Only by minutes. She's my twin sister, Victoria. She's... You would have to meet her to understand."

"A twin sister, exact likeness to you, but this art that you watch in the afternoon is your own, your responsibility. I believe I do understand."

He studied her with eyes so dark they reminded her of black oil paint. Yet unlike the paint, they held a warmth that she couldn't quite define. If he were still and contained within a gilt frame, she would stare into those eyes for hours, complimenting the artist on the fine work with warm, dark tones, the way his gaze heated the skin and followed the viewer. But she couldn't stare at Mr. St. James in such a manner. He was her friend. Perhaps he was a pirate, perhaps not. But she knew with all certainty he was not made of paints. Isabelle blinked and looked away.

"Friends always do understand," she said a moment later after she'd collected herself.

"Do they?"

"Certainly," she said, chancing a glance back at him. "You have other friends. Only last night you were with—"

"Brice," he supplied. "I *have* known him for many years, I suppose."

"Yet you don't consider him a friend?"

"Of course I do. My friendships are just a bit more complicated than—"

"A shared disastrous event at a ball?"

"Disastrous?" He quirked a brow at her, and his gaze seemed to lighten with amusement.

"Well, we did have to run from the scene of a crime covered in evidence."

"Delicious evidence," he murmured. His voice was deep and smooth, the kind of voice that washed easily over one, all the while hinting at the danger of diving in any deeper. Even when speaking of cake, he sounded like a delightfully villainous character from a novel. It was marvelous! She could listen to him speak forever.

"Are you a pirate?" she blurted out before shaking

off the question. "I'm sorry. I'm sure that even if you are a pirate, telling me would be against some sort of code of secrecy." She turned to look at the painting of the young boy in the field. Her cheeks were burning. This was why her cousin, Evangeline, always said she should examine her words before they rushed out of her mouth. Perhaps she *was* the complete ninny Victoria had called her only that morning. "There's no need to answer my question," she muttered.

"You sound rather hopeful at the idea."

She glanced up at him, instantly comforted by the lack of irritation on his face. Instead of the usual eye roll and laughter that she seemed to receive from everyone, there was what she could only define as interested curiosity. Mr. St. James was indeed different from anyone else of her acquaintance—a fact she was quite enjoying. "I've never befriended a pirate before."

"It's true, pirates aren't usually the friendly sort."

Her eyes widened as she watched him. "Then you know from experience."

He chuckled.

"I see you don't deny it. I'm sure you're one of the good pirates, always searching for treasure yet taking the time to give a bit of it to help those who require assistance. A fine leader of men. You're a Robin Hood of sorts!"

He turned and looked at her as if she were a fortune-teller whose prediction had hit the mark. Mr. St. James seemed the type of man to carefully protect his thoughts, but just then she could see some truth shining beneath his carefully brushed-smooth surface.

She'd stood in awe of paintings like him before,

wondering at the meaning behind the images. What emotions lingered behind each stroke of the artist's brush? And just like a silent portrait, St. James didn't divulge any further information. She would have to form her own view of him. And to her, he was the very image of treasure-hunting Robin Hood, commanding men by day and saving ladies in distress by night.

"Come along, my piratical friend. There's a small collection of paintings inspired by the sea I think you'll enjoy."

"You know I'm no—"

"Shh. Don't destroy the illusion."

"Very well. Tell me who you are, then. If I'm not simply a gentleman who resides in town and occasionally visits the museum, then neither are you a lady making the rounds of the season. Are you a siren on a cliff perhaps?"

"No." She recoiled at the thought. "I wouldn't wish to harm your crew or your boat."

"Ship," he corrected.

"Oh, quite. A mighty ship with a large crew under your leadership."

His brows drew together as if her words were true indeed, but he said nothing more. They fell into a companionable silence as they rounded the corner into the next room. But his silence revealed more than words. He was comfortable with the idea of managing a large crew and navigating dangerous waters. That much of St. James's life story must be true.

Isabelle broke the silence at last. "If you are a pirate, then I'm a poor fisherman's daughter in search of my family who were lost at sea. Or perhaps I'm the one lost at sea. Yes! I'm a lady lost at sea."

"How did you meet such a fate?" he asked, looking up at a marble statue as they passed by.

"An evil lord. All such tales can be traced to an evil gentleman at the root of the problem."

He turned to look at her, studying her as if she held great wisdom. "I agree completely."

"Do you?" No one ever agreed with her. It was rather disconcerting to have it happen now, with him. He must share her love of fables and myth. "Do you enjoy the theater? Books?"

"I usually read with purpose, to gain knowledge on a subject," he said, shifting to continue their stroll past the works of art.

"Pity. And the theater?"

"I've conducted meetings there from time to time."

She gazed up at a painting of violent waters and a small boat being tossed about. Sympathy rose within her, both for the small vessel and the man by her side. "Meetings, knowledge—my dear pirate, when do you become lost in a story for pleasure?"

"Is that not what I'm doing now?"

Isabelle shook her head and gave the back of his hand a pat as they moved down the hall of paintings.

"I'll take that as a no."

"I'll provide you a list of books and theatrical productions you must experience."

"I do enjoy lists," he hedged.

She made the clucking sound with her tongue that she'd often heard from her old governess before Victoria's and her first season. "Lists you have time for but not tales of knights, valor, and the ongoing battle between good and evil?"

"Ongoing battles between good and evil require meetings, knowledge, and lists."

"And which side of the battle are you on, my pirate friend?"

"You best hope the good side. You are a lady lost at sea and without the benefit of familial relations after all."

"Indeed." She glanced up at him again only to find she couldn't look away. Some strange tension held her gaze there on his, pulled to him as if by magnets. How odd. She'd never experienced such a thing. Of course, she'd also never strolled through the museum on the arm of a gentleman.

Having a friend with whom to peruse the pieces housed in the grand building was a matter of much excitement. Art did have the ability to intoxicate the senses, and they were surrounded by beautiful works collected from around the world. That was what was filling her stomach with butterfly wings and her mind with downy clouds—the art.

How long had they stood here? She wasn't certain, but when he finally spoke, his voice seemed to come from a long distance, as if she were waking from a dream. "I'll see you safely back to shore now. Or, in this case, back to your paintings."

Clearing the haze from her mind, she took a step forward. "Let me guess—you have a meeting to attend?"

"Something like that." His eyes darted to the doorway on the far wall that led to the main staircase. Did his meeting have something to do with his speedy entrance to the museum? Whomever the porter had chased away must be involved with Mr. St. James in some capacity.

"He was a rival pirate," she declared. "You followed him in pursuit of a treasure you're fighting over."

"What?" he asked, but a second later his thoughts must have caught up with hers. "No…but the analogy is a bit close." He shook his coat into place as if it were a suit of armor. Any openness she'd seen in his eyes vanished as he turned to look at her. "How do you do that?"

"Sometimes friends can understand what others can't, remember?"

"Friends…" He stared at her for a moment, his expression unreadable. "Thank you for the tour, Lady Isabelle."

Just then a flash of movement dashed across the open door, drawing their attention to the top of the stairs. And in the next second, St. James was gone.

"Just as quickly as he arrived," she muttered, staring after him. One day she would discover who he really was. Friends always discovered secrets long buried. And Isabelle Fairlyn took her responsibilities as friend very seriously.

Three

Isabelle Fairlyn's Diary
February 1817

Mother and Father are at odds again. There was peace for three whole days while Father acted as if Mother didn't exist, but she pressed for his attention, as she always does, in the fashion that she always does. Unfortunately she received quite a bit of his attention when she batted her eyes at Lord Hornsby right in front of Father. She only wants Father's love. I wish he understood that. Or is he capable of love? I'm unsure, even after nineteen years in his company. Today I'm in the garden to escape the harsh words being screamed inside. It will go on like this for a few days yet before Father returns to ignoring Mother and the whole cycle begins anew. I wonder if they ever had happiness together. Perhaps before Victoria and I were born they were content together. It saddens me to think that Mother will live an entire life without knowing love. I wish I could change circumstances for her, that I could make them love each other. All I can *do is vow that an unhappy marriage won't happen to me.*

I want a marriage like the ones they sing about in Italian verse at the theater, the ones that inspire books and poetry. That's the only kind of life I want. I won't take anything less than an honorable knight with flowers in hand who is prepared to lay down his life for mine. I know it's a great deal to ask for, but I've seen too much sadness in matrimony to accept a marriage of convenience. I will find love with a good-natured gentleman, and he will be the knight of my dreams—perhaps at tonight's ball. If only Mr. Brice would look in my direction.

—Isabelle

❧～❧

"Brice. Ha!" He released a humorless bark of laughter and turned the page in the diary, searching for more information.

But he'd yet to start the next entry when footsteps sounded in the main hall and voices echoed up the stairs to where he stood. He'd have to take the diary with him and risk Lady Isabelle noticing that it was missing.

Stuffing the book into his pocket, he turned and looked the room over to ensure he'd left no other evidence of his presence. Only the candle remained, washing the bedchamber in faint, flickering light. And with a quick exhale, it was dark.

He was out the window and securing his hold on the stone sill when the door inside was thrown open.

Two identical ladies stepped inside, the first carrying a lantern, the second a fan that she flipped about in her hand. The fan was covered in flowers, as was her gown—the clothing of a true romantic.

Reginald knew who she was in an instant. He was watching Lady Isabelle.

⤚

Spring 1817

Isabelle turned at her dressing table but didn't make a further movement. She eyed the bouquet of flowers that was currently obscuring the butler's face from view—a large bundle of roses from yellow to red and every variation in between were trapped in that crystal vase. The size of the arrangement was rather impressive…and unexpected. She watched for a moment in awe as the butler set the vase down on a table near the door before recalling herself. "And they just arrived?" Isabelle asked. Her surprise was the only thing keeping the squeal of delight that was rising in her throat from erupting and echoing off the walls.

Who would have sent her such a gift? Certainly she'd shared a quadrille or two here and there with gentlemen, but no one among them seemed likely to have sent such a beautiful arrangement. *It could be from Mr. Brice*, a small, hopeful voice said from the vicinity of her heart.

"You're certain the bouquet was intended for me?" she asked, still staring at the colorful blossoms. "It wasn't for Victoria? Mother?"

"It's yours, m'lady," the butler confirmed with a

small nod of his head. "It was left on the doorstep just moments ago with your name on the note."

"There's a note?" She almost yelled the question in her excitement. The yellow gown she'd already put on for tonight's ball flowed around her ankles as she bounded across the room with a complete lack of decorum. There was a time to be ladylike—being presented with mysterious flowers before a ball wasn't that time. She needed to know more.

Inhaling the thick, sweet scent of roses, she leaned closer to investigate. There, wedged in between the stems, was a small lumpy envelope. She reached in and pulled the parcel from the flowers in a heartbeat, her fingers shaking with excitement as she read her name in bold black ink.

Lady Isabelle Fairlyn. Her name was a lovely sight when viewed on a note accompanying flowers from a gentleman. And the parcel seemed to hold something of slight weight.

Everything she'd hoped for, all of her dreams, seemed to begin here. She grinned and turned the small parcel over in her palm.

"If you don't require anything further from me, I'm needed back in the parlor," the butler said from the door.

"Of course," she replied, but she couldn't look away from the note. "Return to your routine."

When she heard the door close behind her a second later, she ripped open the letter. This was it. She was about to discover the identity of the gentleman who had cared to send her these lovely roses. But as she unfolded the letter, the weighty item fell from the paper and landed on the rug. Light from the fireplace reflected in its surface. Was that…jewelry? Who had sent her jewelry? Certainly no gentleman would do such a thing. It would be scandalous if anyone knew of it.

She glanced to the closed door. Her good fortune was boundless today, it would seem, for who would know of this but her and her mystery gentleman? Crouching low, she scooped the piece from the floor—a locket in the shape of a heart with a tiny golden butterfly perched on the surface. It couldn't have been more perfect if she'd designed it herself. She clutched the necklace in her hand and unfolded the letter, anxious to discover who knew her so well as to give her such a well-thought-out gift.

Could it truly be from Mr. Brice? Her heart sped at the thought. Her dreams were coming true! She smiled at the locket, savoring this shining moment. Had Brice finally noticed her? Perhaps so… But even if this gift was from some other gentleman, he could be just the gentleman for her. The flowers and the locket showed that he knew her quite well, whoever he was—and anyone who knew her well would be *sure* to bring the sort of joyful peace, the escape she yearned for. She took a breath, vowing not to make judgments until she knew who'd chosen to brighten her day. Spreading the paper flat, she read.

Dear Isabelle,

When I look upon your comely face, my world is brightened by the glow of my love for you. Though I

*have yet to spend time in your company, I knew when
I first saw you that our lives would be forever linked. I
can see kindness in your eyes and an appreciation for
the lovely things that grace this world that I also hold
dear. We are surrounded by strife at all sides. Escape
it with me. Live with me surrounded by my love.*

*I saw these flowers and knew they belonged with
you. One day I hope to gather some myself from a
field while I think of you, but since London has no
such lands, I hope these are to your liking. The necklace has been in my possession for some time, waiting
for the perfect lady. If you are open to the possibility
of love, wear it and I shall know your heart.*

—Your admirer

When Isabelle entered the ballroom later that evening,
Fallon couldn't pull his gaze from her. She was a vision
in yellow. Her blond hair trailed in soft curls down her
neck, melting into the deeper hue of her gown and
giving her the look of the sun setting over a field in
autumn. And just as with the sunsets of his youth, he
found he couldn't look away. Every second possessed
magic, and he couldn't miss a moment.

She moved closer, gliding on a wave of kind
smiles for everyone she passed. She wasn't ambitious
or grasping, like other members of the *ton*. So many
doled out kindnesses like game chips to be collected on
later. Not Isabelle. The honesty of her well-meaning
gestures shined in her eyes. It was rather refreshing.

He wasn't certain how long he'd been admiring her as she moved through the ballroom, but he knew he should look away. Then she turned, the light glinted off something at her throat, and his heart gave an unfortunate sudden jolt. The necklace she wore…

Fallon knew it all too well.

It couldn't be. How would she have acquired that specific piece? And just when Reginald Grapling had reappeared?

Panic pulsed within his body as he watched her—beautiful, guileless, and alive.

Narrowing his gaze, he studied the locket that hung from Isabelle's neck. Perhaps he'd only imagined a similarity. He was across the room from her. It couldn't be. He began moving closer, hoping he was wrong. There was more than one gold locket in the world, after all. But as he got closer to her, that small bit of hope died. He'd only ever seen one pendant in the shape of a heart with flowered scrollwork covering the surface and a tiny golden butterfly perched on the top, and that golden necklace was now draped from Isabelle's throat.

Nothing would remove the image of the last time he'd seen the piece. The gold had been splattered with blood, as had the body they'd found. That had been the night he'd learned the depth of Grapling's deceit and how he'd abused his place within the Spare Heirs. Prison had been kind compared to what Fallon had wanted to do to the man. Now, he'd escaped, and Isabelle was wearing a dead girl's necklace at a ball. It was all too familiar.

Fallon wanted to rip it from Isabelle's neck so the

cold of death wouldn't touch her skin. He could hardly go about ballrooms taking ladies' jewelry and tossing it into the garden outside. In the absence of that option, he was left to wonder at how the piece could have come into her possession. Wouldn't it have been locked away somewhere with old memories? It should have been. He couldn't recall what had happened to the locket after all was settled that day, but he couldn't imagine it had been left lying about. Did her family know Isabelle wore it tonight?

He shook off the panic that had taken hold of his body and focused on Isabelle. History would not repeat itself tonight. He'd moved from his position in the shadow of the stairs. A silent plea warred with the truth he didn't want to acknowledge.

Forcing his eyes up from Isabelle's jewelry as he rounded the group of ladies who separated them, Fallon worked to keep any wayward emotion from showing on his face. It was a skill he'd practiced for years. Isabelle didn't have the same inclination, as far as he could surmise. She displayed every emotion, spoke every thought that crossed her lovely mind. But then, there was something pleasing in the honesty of her expressions. Honesty, forthright thought, and her particular flights of fancy were rather foreign to him. She was a curiosity, just like the artwork she watched over at the museum. And just like a painting that captured the light and emotion of a perfect moment in time, when he was in her presence, he couldn't look away.

Tonight she was bright and merry, clearly unaware of the history of the necklace she wore. He pushed his own harsh memories away, determined to focus

on her. With beauty like hers, she didn't deserve to
have the evening tainted by his dark ruminations on
the past. She deserved wildflowers and real butterflies.
Delicate things of great beauty should remain in like
company, after all.

"Are you following me?"

"I try to make a point *not* to follow ladies about
town."

"And yet here you are, following me. Any other
lady might get notions about your interest," she teased
with a punishing swat of her fan against his arm.

"I wouldn't stop to speak with any other lady,"
Fallon stated in a rare moment of honesty. She must
have been rubbing off on him. "I'm here on a business
matter."

"As am I." She lifted her chin and flicked her gaze
out across the crowded floor beside them.

His eye was drawn once more to the blasted necklace at her throat. Business matters... Was there some
chance she knew of the history of the piece? Had she
worn it in some misguided intention this evening? But
he shook off the thought as soon as it occurred to him.
Isabelle wasn't involved with the hunt for Grapling.
There was no way she could have known the details.
And she wouldn't have been so cheerful if she did.
"What business do you have this evening?"

"Isn't it obvious?" She beamed up at him and
shifted her hips back and forth to make her gown swirl
around her in blithesome swishes.

"You're on the hunt for a husband?" he asked,
already relieved that his instincts were correct. The
last complication he needed was for Isabelle to get

involved. She was an innocent lady—albeit with regrettable taste in jewelry this evening.

"Not just any husband—the ideal husband. I have standards."

"Yet your standards include Mr. Brice?" Something about her quest to conquer his friend grated on him. "Those are rather low standards, my lady."

"You only say that because you're a gentleman."

"Really?" He'd thought it bordered on ungentlemanly to comment at all.

"Of course. You don't know what attributes ladies hold higher than others. If you did, you would wear a bit more color. And you wouldn't attend a ball while intent on a business matter. Balls are for dancing. Could you be convinced to dance?"

"Never."

"I didn't think so," she said with a pitying look in her eyes. "You must dance if you're to find love, you know. Love is everywhere, even if we don't realize it's present." She cast a quick glance around the room as if looking for some long-lost love and turned back to him, smiling.

"My business here tonight is quite different from your business," he confided. One of the best places to hold meetings unnoticed was in the crush of a society gathering. Tonight he'd come here to meet with two lords about some recent work the Spare Heirs had completed and to ask a few key people about Grapling. The man had once had friends. Fallon's chase wouldn't be any easier if the man renewed his old friendships.

"What is your business? My father has investments.

He used to travel into London for meetings until he acquired his title and lands a few years ago. I always asked to accompany him on his trips, but he said it was no place for a young lady. I disagree. London is the perfect place for a lady."

"I doubt your father was attending balls while here," Fallon said cryptically. He knew exactly why her father had come to town, and that situation had indeed not been ideal for a lady.

"*You're* here on an official matter," she countered.

"I am."

She watched him for a second before he could see an idea light her eyes. "Ignore your clearly dull business and dance with me. Friends do dance."

"This one does not," he said, dismissing her plea. "You believe my work is dull? There is bit of excitement involved."

"Pirate dealings or not, you're always on your way to a meeting of some sort. Meanwhile there's dancing," she stated with a wave of her fan toward the ballroom floor, nearly colliding with a lady waltzing past in the process. "Do you twirl while in a meeting?"

"No."

"That settles things, then. You are entirely too focused on what must be done. Gentlemen should enjoy their leisure time as well. Come with me." She wrapped her hand around his arm before he could offer it.

"Where are we going?"

"To enjoy a leisurely pursuit. If you refuse to dance…"

"On the terrace?" He would wonder at the type

of friendship she had in mind for him, but then he glanced at her. No lady would smile so broadly and walk with a bounce in her step on her way to a rendezvous. Thinking of dark terraces—and certainly him—in those terms didn't seem in Lady Isabelle's nature. And that was a relief—truly it was. The last thing he needed was for a lady to set her sights on him. She desired Brice, which was as it should be.

Once on the terrace, Lady Isabelle turned to him. "Isn't it magical?"

"It's dark. If our hosts added more candles, they could entice more guests in this direction, thereby gaining larger occupancy for their entertainment and the possibility of enlarging their guest list."

"St. James."

"What? Isn't a mad crush what all of these societal types want for their events? I suppose if one were looking at it from the standpoint of profitability, then the expense of candles—"

"Shh. The magic is in the starlight."

Fallon fell silent for a moment as he stared off into the black of the back garden. He should question her about the necklace, take it from her to aid in his investigation, and return to hold his meetings in the light of the ball.

The terrace really was quite dark. Candles weren't free, but they certainly were a necessity. The Spare Heirs incurred expense every day, yet the venture was profitable for all involved. "Some expense can bring about the optimal conditions for business dealings," he mused aloud.

A small finger touched his chin and lifted his gaze

upward. Thousands of stars were scattered across the sky on the cool spring night. It wasn't often that one could see the stars while in London. He had to admit it was a beautiful sight.

"Pirates should appreciate the stars," Isabelle stated. "Weeks at sea with no entertainment and all."

"We can't all live aboard ships," he muttered.

"What does that mean?"

Fallon turned to look back down at her. He owed her no explanation of his thoughts. He shouldn't even be lingering on the terrace with her, not for a moment. His schedule would be rushed for the remainder of the evening because of this diversion. This situation would be easily resolved by ripping Isabelle's necklace away from her and continuing on about his evening.

But the innocence of her question held him still. "Sometimes the mighty kings and knights from the books you enjoy are drunken idiots in reality. And sometimes the pirates everyone fears are truly good men making the best of life on land."

She lifted her face to the night sky once more. "St. James, that doesn't make any sense at all."

"Perhaps not." He chuckled.

"Thirty-four," she announced a moment later.

"Are you guessing my age now? You've already pegged me as a pirate," he teased.

"That's how many stars I've counted thus far. You're far older than a mere thirty-four."

"I am not. How old do you think me?"

"Forty…or perhaps older than that?"

He gaped at her. First his smile and now his age? "You were closer with your count of the stars."

"Really?"

"Really!" He didn't know why he was so insulted. How was this nymphlike creature able to get to him? To the rest of the world he was a solid wall, the guardian and watchman for an army.

"It's because you work too hard. I've heard it ages one's looks. I suppose it's true. Gentlemen of leisure enjoy dancing and looking at stars—"

"Let me guess. They have heartfelt smiles as well?"

She shrugged but didn't turn to look in his direction. "I meant no offense. There's good in everything, even growing old and having an insincere smile. It allows you that stern look of decisiveness you so enjoy displaying."

The wood nymph was correct in a way. He shouldn't care about smiles or age. He was St. James, and he had a society to oversee. He was stern, decisive, and always in control—he had to be. This was the path he'd chosen, and he enjoyed his life.

He shifted a fraction closer to Isabelle without her noticing his movement. He had a job to do this evening, and it didn't involve staring at the stars, no matter how diverting his current company was proving to be. His gaze dropped to the necklace once more.

"Where did you get this?" he asked, lifting the locket from her warm skin to hold it in his fingers.

She flinched at his glancing touch, and her gaze flew to his. Her eyes were wide as she watched him— or was she waiting for him to release her? He wasn't certain, but he didn't move. With a swift yank, he could remove it from her throat. He could finish this encounter entirely. But he didn't.

The moment hung between them. He stood,

grasping the chain around her neck, and she stayed, clearly stunned by his sudden movement. He should have known better than to lift the piece from her body, and now she stood far too close, her chin raised as she watched him. But there was no going back now.

Fallon could easily blame his lapse in good judgment on his surprise at seeing this locket, of all pieces, hanging around Isabelle's neck, but that would be a lie. The effort not to touch her skin was growing more difficult every time she was near. It could only be likened to the need to place one finger upon the petal of a perfect rose blossom when it was spotted in bloom in the garden.

If only for a moment, he wanted to be part of something this beautiful. The heat of her skin warmed his fingers even though he was only close, yet not touching her.

He had no right. If anyone should be so close to her, it should be Brice. She was enamored with him, after all, and only wanted Fallon in the role of friend. His grasp tightened about the locket. Was this how friends acted toward one another? He knew the answer but didn't back away. He never backed away from anything.

But this was Isabelle—sweet, innocent, and now looking at him like perhaps he was the villain of the story in her mind and not the faithful friend after all. Her breaths were shallow. A mix of confusion and curiosity now lived in her eyes.

"I found it among my father's things," she finally answered, but her gaze shifted away as she spoke. She was lying. "I believe it's my mother's."

"Is it? It's unusual." Where had she gotten the blasted thing, and why was she lying to him about it? His suspicions were growing by the second. But as every part of the sordid tale involved the Spare Heirs Society, he could hardly discuss it with her. He forced his grip on the piece to loosen, his fingers brushing over hers for a second as she took the locket from him.

The tension in her gaze eased as she shifted half a step away from him, her eyes returning to their usually sunny gleam. "Isn't it lovely? I don't think my family even noticed I'd added it to my ensemble, but I think it really..." Her words drifted away as she watched him. "What's the matter?"

"Nothing." Damn. He'd been a child the last time he'd allowed someone such easy access to his thoughts. But ever since he'd met her, his guard had been slipping away. What was it about this girl that had him forgetting every carefully honed skill he possessed? Perhaps it was simply the presence of that locket and the memories it held inside its heart-shaped enclosure. "It's...nice."

"I thought so too, although I've yet to be able to pry it open," she said, now looking down at the locket.

"That may be for the best," he returned. The less she investigated the necklace, the better. His mind raced to create a list of ways she could have come into possession of the piece. She could have found it among her father's things. But Knottsby wouldn't have been so careless as to leave the damned thing lying about. Fallon hadn't even thought the man had kept it. Which left Reginald Grapling...

"It may contain someone's true identity or the name of a secret love. I wish I knew—"

"Once seen, you cannot unsee, no matter how much you wish it to be otherwise."

"Do you think it contains a scandalous miniature?" she asked, laughing. "That would be quite the shock."

"Perhaps." Or it could contain an image of the woman to whom it had once belonged, which would raise more questions. That blasted locket needed to remain closed. Then Isabelle would lose interest and move on to her pearls or some other accessory next time.

Isabelle shrugged and dropped the locket back to rest against her body, clearly still curious about what she would find inside the piece of jewelry. "I hope it isn't something awful. That would be quite disappointing."

"Return it," he said, hoping she would heed his words.

"I...I can't."

"If you discovered it among your father's things, simply put it back where you found it."

"It...isn't that simple. And I rather like it."

"Not all treasure is worth the price involved in its possession."

"Is that the warning posted on treasure maps beside the large X?" she asked with a grin.

"Unwritten wisdom. Disappointed?"

"I am a bit." Isabelle elbowed him in the arm and laughed again. "I've quite lost count of the stars, and it's entirely your fault, sir."

"Thirty-four."

She turned to look at him. "Was that the number? Do you recall all facts with that speed?"

"Only the important ones."

"How do you decide which are important and which are rubbish?"

"Your words are all important."

She blinked in shock as she looked up at him. "Do you think so? You're the only one. I'm told I need to remain focused on reality if I'm to find a husband."

"But you prefer the gentlemen in stories to the ones in that ballroom…aside from Mr. Brice, of course."

"Is it so wrong to want the sort of love that's written about in books and portrayed in paintings? The kind of love that inspires song in an opera? I don't want a marriage to a lord only to gain his title for my family's connections. No. I want a worthy knight with armor that gleams in the sunlight. He would rid the kingdom of all our enemies, then gather flowers from a field, smile warmly to all around him, and lead his lady in a dance— that is all I want. And I know I'll find it. Perhaps soon."

Fallon knew the true nature of gentlemen better than most, and he'd yet to meet a man who both slew enemies and showed any interest at all in flowers and dance steps alike. Isabelle's quest was horribly flawed. And the very idea of Brice fitting that description was laughable. Brice had his skills, and Fallon was thankful for them, but the main skill his friend had honed since his youth was the art of fooling everyone around him—Isabelle included, it would seem. If she knew Brice at all, the spell would be broken.

Was that what kept her hiding behind cakes and not speaking to the man? She kept the world at bay, choosing to live within her dreams instead. Her actions made complete sense and yet at the same time no sense at all—just like Isabelle. He fought back a smile.

"I want to live my life in happiness. Marriage without gifts, longing looks, and laughter every day from an honorable gentleman will only lead to sadness. And sadness breeds anger. I don't like fighting."

"I don't believe anyone enjoys fighting."

For as opposing as Fallon and Isabelle were in how they viewed the world, their childhoods were remarkably similar. Her parents held no great affection for each other. Everyone who had eyes on society knew there was no love lost between the Fairlyns. But Fallon had never considered the effect that Knottsby's discontent had on his own family. He should have. Isabelle's life mirrored Fallon's own in many ways.

"Many homes aren't happy ones."

"How did you know?" Her eyes were wide as she watched him. "I only said I want to be happy in marriage. I didn't intend to say anything against my family."

He shrugged and moved to the terrace wall. He braced his hands on the low top cap and stared out into the darkness. "My mother died when I was young. I'm unsure if my father's drinking began then, or…perhaps it had always been his weakness. It was a private matter, and at one time I thought it to be the usual thing.

"When I was eleven, my father came home from the local tavern particularly foxed. Even for him. He fell in the hall, sprawled across the bottom of the stairs. My older brother was no stranger to drink either and found Father's state amusing. I spoke up, took charge of the situation. Called for servants to be awakened to assist him. Coffee to be made. Then I told him what I thought of the mess he was making in our home, and by that point around town as well. A blackened eye later, I vowed that I wouldn't become like him. My brother followed in my father's footsteps. He has wealth, the title, the estate, and he spends his life in a tavern."

"And you don't partake in liquor at all," she finished for him. "Always the responsible one in control of the situation. Always on to the next meeting, the next item on a list."

Fallon swallowed. He'd never told anyone that story. What was he doing with this lady? It was as if the binding on all of his personal thoughts unraveled in her presence, yet there was something he quite liked about the freedom. "I understand your wish for happiness," he said, turning to look back at her. "Fighting is your bottle of spirits. You should have a happy life. You deserve that."

"Only I'm a lady." She looked down to her hands where they were entwined together on the wall. "I'm not allowed that kind of control over my life. I can only hope for the best."

"And this is why you escape your life, living in stories instead."

"Is that such an awful thing?"

"No. It's enchanting." She was enchanting, from her oddly perceptive eyes to her dreamy view of all the world had to offer. He shifted to lean a hip against the wall, lowering himself a bit to meet her gaze. "I've never met anyone like you, Lady Isabelle. Just don't let this life pass you by while you're dreaming of another."

She grinned at him, a smile intended for a friend—only a friend. "Point life out as we go. Then I won't miss it."

"Friendship. That's why you keep me about," he muttered, wishing for a moment that she would really see him right in front of her.

But it was for the best that she didn't. Nothing was possible between them. He could never offer her the life she wanted, not the one she deserved. And anything between them would be an added complication when he had plenty of official matters to be getting on with at the moment—at every moment. What was he thinking even lingering here with her?

"I'll put your keen pirate eyes to good use," she teased.

"It's for a noble cause," he replied, but he was already focused on the ballroom behind Isabelle, where his responsibilities awaited him. And that was when he saw movement just inside the terrace doors. His worst fear was in a moment realized.

Reginald Grapling was standing there, his eyes fixed on Isabelle.

The necklace. He glanced back to Isabelle. The blasted locket that hung around her neck fairly called Grapling to her. Had the man planted it in Knottsby's library for Isabelle to find? Was this simply some sick coincidence? Had he somehow given the damned thing to her?

There was no time to think about that now. His only concern was for the lady who stood before him, oblivious to the danger at her back. Steeling himself against the icy chill that sliced through his body, he worked to keep his breathing steady. This was a mission like any other. *It's just a job for the Spares*, he told himself. Isabelle just happened to be present for this one.

First Fallon had to get her to safety, only there was no place to take her other than straight toward the very man who'd killed the locket's previous owner. If Grapling knew what was good for him, he would remove his filthy gaze from Isabelle's perfect fair skin…now!

Fallon forced his pulse into a steady beat while staring down his enemy. A cruel sneer appeared on the man's face. He raised a brow a fraction, as if pleased about seeing Fallon there with Isabelle. Self-serving… but he wouldn't get anything from them tonight. Fallon gripped the edge of the wall at his side, tamping down his desire to lunge across the terrace and pummel the man. That would only cause talk in town, something Grapling clearly knew. Fallon had to get Isabelle away from here.

"Let's return to the ball," Fallon suggested, his gaze never leaving Grapling's. "You have dances to enjoy, I'm certain."

"And you have your meetings and other such dull activities." She gave him a pitying sigh as she took his arm. She was looking up at him, still unaware of their audience, and Fallon was grateful for it. She didn't need to even lay eyes on someone like Grapling.

They were mere steps away from the man. Under different circumstances, Fallon would have dragged the bastard into the dark garden and apprehended him right then, ended this chase. But keeping Isabelle safe won out.

Fallon put himself between the threat beside the door and Isabelle. Tensed for potential battle, he moved closer with Isabelle on his arm.

One step. Then another. Closer to danger. And all the while with Isabelle unaware of the trouble she was walking toward.

But in the next second, the crowd shifted and Grapling was gone. Fallon sped as much as he could with Isabelle in tow, but the man had vanished—just as Fallon had taught him to do all those years ago.

The only thing that remained was the look Fallon had seen in the man's eyes when he'd spied Isabelle's necklace. Like a bull spotting red, the pistol fire at the start of a horse race… Fallon knew that look and what it meant.

The game was on.

Four

Dear Lord Knottsby,

I hope this note finds you well. You asked long ago to be advised if there ever came a situation that might affect your new title or family. While I am investigating this unfortunate matter myself to ensure the safety of everyone involved, you should know that there is a potentially dangerous situation at hand. Please be on your guard. Your vigilance is appreciated and will be remembered in the future.

—St. James

❧⚓❧

THERE HE WAS, BLOND HAIR BLOWING IN THE BREEZE. His eyes danced across the crowd gathered in the garden. Sunny strands of his deliciously overlong hair whipped across his tanned skin even as he smiled into the face of the unfortunate weather. After such a clear evening, today was bringing quite the change.

The brisk wind that had blown in was doing nothing to calm the nerves of Lady Marksby, their host for the outdoor gathering today. But it suited Mr. Brice perfectly. This must be what he would look like atop a horse as he raced across a field on his way to save a small child from harm.

Isabelle adjusted the locket at her throat, sighed, and stared. Had he sent her the locket to wear? Thus far, her mystery gentleman was just that—a mystery. And all she could do was wait. Somewhere behind her, conversation continued over her friend Roselyn's new shoes and moved from there to news of her cousin Evangeline's outing to the park earlier, in the company of some gentleman. Normally Isabelle would have jumped upon the retelling of such a romantic event, but not when she was deep in a dream of her own romance. At any moment Mr. Brice would look in her direction and their eyes would meet across the lawn. He would see the locket at her throat, and he would know that she wore it for him. He would sweep toward her and meet her just like the wind on this blustery day. Then they would—of course—be married, since his love for her was so grand. Unless it was another gentleman who had sent her the necklace… But she would worry about that later, if necessary.

Mr. Brice was sporting a blue waistcoat today. Not dull gray like the one Mr. St. James was wearing at his side. "St. James," she muttered to herself. He knew nothing of fashion, not like Mr. Brice. Everything about Brice was perfection. And he would be the perfect husband for her, if he would ever look in her direction again.

Just then Brice turned, apparently sensing her gaze on him.

One should be careful what one wished for. Now he was certainly noticing her existence, but there was no accompanying violin music like in her dreams of this moment. How odd. Where was musical accompaniment when it was needed? Why wasn't he sweeping in her direction like the wind?

She needed something to do to look collected at such a pivotal moment. *Remain calm and allow him to sweep in your direction, you ninny!* Her fan! Thank heavens she remembered the piece she held in her numb fingers. She'd forgotten it entirely in her excitement.

Flicking the fan open, she nearly dropped it, to land in the grass at her feet. But just in time, she caught it in midair and gave it a wave. She was the picture of wifely elegance. She smiled and gave it one more wave.

"Must you carry a fan?" Victoria asked, leaning away from her. "Someone will no doubt lose an eye with all that flapping about. It's as if we're socializing with a flock of angry birds, and it's windy enough as it is."

"Roselyn told me I ought to practice after you ripped my last fan to shreds for *apparent* misuse," she replied without looking in her sister's direction. Eye contact with Mr. Brice was far more important than conversing with Victoria, although the man's curiosity must have been satisfied just then, since he turned away mid-bat of her lashes. St. James, however, was watching her every move. Isabelle huffed and turned to face her sister. "Anyway, I thought today was the perfect occasion to heed Roselyn's advice."

"Really, Roselyn?" Victoria mumbled. "You know she requires no encouragement."

"I said she should practice," Roselyn hedged with a shrug of her shoulders, her dark brows drawing together in concern. "I suppose I should have included *in the privacy of her home* to my instructions, but it's no matter. I think she's quite getting the measure of it now."

Isabelle glanced over her shoulder to see if Mr. Brice was looking her way and noticing her skilled fan work but saw only St. James's eyes on her. What did he know about fans? Not a thing. Although he had been interested in her locket last night. There may be hope for him yet.

She turned back to the ladies in front of her with a flourish of her fan that almost hit Victoria in the nose and made Evangeline draw back a fraction to avoid contact. "Thank you, Roselyn, for your kind words. I'm following your example."

"And a fine example that is this season," Roselyn said with a laugh. Tiny ringlets of dark hair had escaped on this breezy day and circled her rosy cheeks. But it wasn't the constant struggle with her hair to which Roselyn was referring now. Their friend had spent the first few minutes of the garden party telling them of her first, somewhat-disappointing attempt at spying on the new Lord Ayton. Roselyn's original plan to wear black and stick to the shadows had somehow changed yesterday to dressing in a footman's clothing and attending a pugilism exhibition at Gentleman Jackson's. It sounded like quite the adventure, though Isabelle was certain there were details of the day her

friend was omitting. It still struck Isabelle as odd that
Roselyn would put such effort into spying on a man
she claimed to despise. She would have to pry for
more information later.

"Better than Evie's example," Victoria said.

"I'm not certain what you're implying, Victoria,"
Evangeline retorted, but Isabelle noticed her blush as
she returned her gaze to the gathering around them.
The shadow of the Marksby's stately graystone house
kept Isabelle and her group in the shadiest corner of
the lawn, but no shadow was strong enough to hide
Evangeline's rare look of guilt.

"I don't imply. I state fact. Were you not on a
clandestine ride through the park with a mysterious
gentleman only hours ago? And now that your mother
is about, you appear to be carved of stone. Would you
like me to distract Lady Rightworth so that you might
breathe? You haven't inhaled in at least ten minutes in
an effort to hold that pose."

"I'm quite comfortable," Evangeline said with her
chin raised against the wind.

"Did anyone else notice that Evie didn't refute
the claim that her ride in the park was clandestine?"
Victoria asked as she took a sip of her drink, which was
no doubt hiding something stronger than lemonade.

"It was all quite aboveboard," Evangeline said, still
unmoving from her pose. "He collected me in that red
phaeton that belongs to—"

"Mr. Brice!" Isabelle cut in with her eyes wide on
her cousin. "How did he manage such a thing?"

"The gentleman who escorted me is acquainted to
some degree with Mr. Brice."

"Are we to discover this gentleman's name or simply guess at it?" Roselyn asked.

"I could venture a guess," Victoria said with a smirk from behind her glass. "If any of you would like to take a wager…"

Isabelle swatted her fan at Victoria's arm at the mention of gambling. "Never mind that. What was it like to sit atop such a fashionable conveyance?"

"Never mind you. Don't hit me with that thing," Victoria challenged as she rubbed her forearm.

"We're supposed to admonish people with a flick of a fan. I'm only doing as Roselyn suggested," Isabelle said in place of an apology. Victoria simply needed to become used to London life and the prominent use of a fan in conversation. Isabelle turned her attention back to Evangeline to ask, "Now, what was the ride in the phaeton like?"

"Tall."

"Evie, you must tell me more than that," Isabelle begged, taking a step closer to her cousin.

"Very well… It was quite enjoyable, perhaps too much so." Evangeline blushed a dark pink, and her mother started in their direction, her eyes narrowed.

"Evangeline, darling," Lady Rightworth called to her as she neared. "We must leave at once. This dreadful wind will have your cheeks raw from exposure. You're growing red as we speak," she added in a desperate whisper. "I should have known better than to attend an outdoor event. You know I dislike the weather."

"Yes, Mother," Evangeline said in a soft voice, giving the others a nod of farewell before she turned to follow her mother away. Evangeline always did as her mother wished. And as honorable a quality as that was in a daughter, it was unsettling to watch when it involved Lady Rightworth.

"I would love to see Evie tell that woman no just once," Victoria muttered as she watched them leave.

Isabelle hit her sister with her fan once more. "Shh! *That woman* is our aunt and she could hear you."

Victoria jumped back, rubbing her arm again as she stared Isabelle down.

"Who do you think Evangeline's mystery gentleman could be?" Roselyn said, stepping between them in a clear attempt at ending a sisterly squabble. "She's being so secretive about him."

"I know," Victoria boasted. "It's terribly obvious, just like Isabelle always is."

"What have I done that's obvious?" She adjusted the locket at her neck, hoping her sister hadn't noticed the sudden appearance of her new piece of jewelry.

"The eyes you've been making at Brice hide nothing, Isabelle."

"Oh, that. Well…I don't know what you mean," Isabelle lied, glancing across the open lawn to the man in question and sighing the second her eyes made contact with him.

"You're correct, of course. Your infatuation isn't obvious at all to everyone who sees you. Look, you're even gaining the attention of his friend with all of your longing looks in their direction."

Isabelle flicked her fan closed and hit her sister's arm with it. "That is Mr. St. James. We're…"

But her words drifted away as Victoria grabbed the fan from her fingers and snapped it in half.

"...friends. St. James and I are friends," Isabelle finished, staring at her second broken fan in a week's time.

"Right. Well, you may have this back now," Victoria said in a chipper voice.

"My, what is the time? Is that Lily calling me? On my way," Roselyn called out and scurried away from the corner of the garden where they'd gathered.

The wind whipped a strand of Isabelle's hair from its confines, and she tucked it behind her ear as she glared at her sister. Polite chatter surrounded them, but Isabelle said nothing.

"I'll go to Bond and buy you another fan tomorrow," Victoria said after shifting on her feet and heaving a sigh.

"Is that a promise?" Isabelle asked.

"Of the most sacred sort."

"Good. I don't want to forget all that I've learned by lack of ability to practice," Isabelle stated.

"Yes, none of us would want that," Victoria muttered at her side, but Isabelle was already looking across the garden to where Brice still stood talking to St. James.

Brice seemed to be telling some tale. Isabelle wished she could hear him. She liked elaborate stories. She was sure she could listen to his stories forever, and someday she would. St. James, on the other hand, stood in silence, watching the event, the people chatting, the movement of the crowd as if looking for something or someone. Then their eyes met, and he gave her a nod. He wasn't smiling, but there was a heartfelt quality to the warmth in his eyes. It was an improvement at any rate.

She smiled and adjusted the locket at her neck. And for a fraction of a second, she saw something quite different in St. James's eyes than she'd ever seen there before: worry.

❧

Fallon should have gone to her yesterday at the garden party, but the lawn between them might as well have been a canyon. He'd watched Isabelle chat with her friends while the wind billowed her dress out behind her. His hesitation to go to her wasn't for the social implications involved with crossing the grass to speak with a lady but what he would have said once he reached her.

She was happy, a true innocent in a dirty world. Yet Isabelle was still wearing that necklace, unaware of its dark history. He needed to tell her. Truth could be cleansing or some such, couldn't it? He was certain he'd heard it claimed somewhere, just not within these walls. As soon as he told her about what hung around her neck and the danger she was in while wearing it, the innocent light she possessed would dim a fraction. He couldn't do that to her yesterday, but he needed to soon.

He braced his hands on his desk and stared unseeing at the documents strewn across its surface. Fallon had always strived to be in control of every situation he encountered, but there were times when keeping everyone around him safe was a difficult task.

He needed only a bit of sleep or another pot of tea or two. But he knew no amount of sleep or tea would make this problem solve itself. Reaching for his cup, he drained the warm liquid inside, but his mind was no clearer on the subject of Isabelle than it had been a moment before. Straightening the papers on his desk, he glanced at the clock on the mantel across the room. He would need to get dressed for tonight's ball soon. But before he'd taken a step away from his desk, Ash Claughbane banged the door open as he flew around the corner into his library.

"There's a problem."

Fallon stared at the man—his newest recruit to the Spare Heirs and a young con artist selling investments in the future of steam. He was crossing the room, out of breath from running. "Is it Rightworth? I told you to be careful there. If you need to leave town—"

"It isn't investments for my steam works that are in jeopardy. It's Brice." His eyes were wide, and he was clearly shaken by whatever he knew. "There's a fire."

"Where?" Fallon asked, already rounding his desk, hoping the conclusion he'd jumped to was wrong.

"Bond Street. He was in—"

"Ayton's family's jewelry store," Fallon finished for him. Brice had gone in search of documents that could help in Ayton's brother's murder investigation. But there had been a fire? How had that happened? Fallon had to help; he had to fix this. Brice was one of his oldest friends and associates, as was Ayton. "How much damage? Is Brice all right?"

Claughbane tugged at the untied cravat that hung loose around his neck. "He was escaping the flames when I left. St. James, you should know, there was a lady with him."

"A lady?" Brice would never take a lady along on

a mission, no matter how many of them filled his free hours.

"One of the Fairlyn twins, I believe."

Isabelle. Fallon had to reach her. Had she followed Brice again? And she'd trailed him right into a fire this time.

But Fallon didn't know that it was her. It could be her sister. Either situation was terrible, but Isabelle couldn't be hurt. She just couldn't be. He took a breath through an ever-tightening throat and ground out, "Which one? Which twin? Isabelle or Victoria?"

"I don't know, mate." Claughbane shuffled his feet and sighed. "But this is bad business. Is there any way I can assist?"

"No." Fallon was already moving toward the door. "Informing me was the right thing to do." He paused to clasp a hand on Claughbane's shoulder in appreciation, then kept moving. He had to get to Bond.

❧

Isabelle had been safe at home when Bond Street was ignited, a fact that should give him peace of mind, and it did. Yet the result of the fire yesterday was a waking nightmare no matter which sister had been present for it. Brice, Lady Victoria, and two charred London shops...

Fallon braced his elbows on his desk and fought to keep the grimace from his face, but it lurked just under the surface of his expression. If someone had told him earlier this week that Brice would soon burn down a portion of town, he wouldn't have believed it.

Yet somehow that was exactly what had happened.

He stared down the two men across the desk from him. "Now that we're not standing in a pile of ashes, you have the next ten minutes to explain to me how you managed to incinerate a portion of Bond Street."

It was late afternoon, a full day since the damned fire began, and these two were only now appearing at headquarters for an official report. Fallon hadn't slowed since he'd heard the news, and he'd yet to hear an apology from his men for his inconvenience. Though the two men before him did look a bit worse for wear as well. Brice still wore yesterday's clothing, and Ayton, though clean, had a dazed look about him that brought even more questions to mind.

Fallon had known both men since their school days. The Spare Heirs had been only a vague notion then. A dream, really. Fallon had just acquired their head-quarters and needed younger sons to help in the club's establishment. Kelton Brice and Ethan Moore had been just the gentlemen to assist him. He'd relied on them then. Now? Fallon sighed. He still relied on them, but the two men were in rather unfortunate situations.

Then again, weren't they all?

Ethan Moore—now Lord Ayton—had recently returned from a long stay on the continent and inherited his brother's courtesy title and a pile of trouble along with it. He was tracking a killer, and though he wouldn't admit it, the lady whose name had been tied to his brother's held a great deal of importance to him. Fallon would be more concerned about the murderer on the loose, but if anyone could handle himself in a London alley, it was the large-framed boxer.

Then there was Brice, who'd been given the simple

task of retrieving some documents from a jewelry shop on Bond as part of Ayton's search. And now that shop and the one beside it were smoldering ruins.

"There were lots of hats," Brice began before Ayton stopped him with a raised hand, his dark head shaking to keep his friend silent for once.

"We have the documents Brice went to the shop for," Ayton said, trying to place a positive light on the incident even though he must have been furious. His family's inventory had been destroyed with the jewelry store, along with the milliner's next door. "I know it wasn't a perfect mission…"

"Do you remember the Hinklebent fiasco?" Fallon asked, leaning forward over his desktop to grab the teapot. There was not enough tea in London for all he was left to repair today. He'd been in his fair share of near misses and tight situations but had always navigated the group to safety. Now he must do it again.

The two men winced at the mention of one of their higher-ranking failures.

"Lord Fistershot?" Fallon continued as he refilled his cup.

"That's hardly fair," Brice cut in. "We were young, and he—"

"This is worse," Fallon confirmed. "You started a fire on Bond Street."

"I didn't intend to burn the place." Brice leaned back in his chair, somehow managing to look uncomfortable even as he lounged and stretched his legs. "It was that damned lady, Lady Victoria Fairlyn. She spotted me and…"

"Go on then. Tell him." Ayton groaned as he

scooted his chair away from Brice a fraction. Clearly he didn't want to be cooked in the same pot as his incendiary friend.

"She threw hats at me," Brice ground out with his brows raised as if his explanation said it all.

Only it didn't explain a thing.

Fallon abandoned his cup and stood from his desk. Turning away from the two men, he looked out the window. Bracing his forearm on the window frame, he watched a carriage roll down the street below. There was nothing to be done about the fire except assist in the repairs—and do so without attracting London's notice. The Spares may have quiet hands in most profitable endeavors, but they didn't leave destruction in their wake. He'd spent last night in meetings to begin the process of covering up their involvement, and that was only the beginning. He would have to meet with more than a few gentlemen to set this fire business right. Not to mention the matter of Victoria Fairlyn.

On top of Ayton's murder investigation, Claughbane's steam investments, and any number of other orders of business he was overseeing, there was now a fire to clean up, and a lady's reputation in serious danger thanks to the Spares.

And even with all of this, the image he couldn't shake from his mind was a different lady—Lady Isabelle Fairlyn with that blasted locket hanging around her neck.

He needed to repair the damage quickly before it was beyond even him.

If Fallon could distract society for a while—give them some splendid show to keep them away from the

sleight of hand that was occurring at the same time—
the Spare Heirs and their involvement in the fire
might slip by unnoticed. Much could be learned about
manipulation of a crowd by watching a magician.
Claughbane, resident swindler of the *ton,* would be
pleased with him. Though Fallon would never tell the
man. His head would swell to twice its normal size.

What Fallon needed was a diversion—a bright,
shining, beautiful diversion. To cover the scandal of
a fire on Bond, it had to be big. Something happy.
Something the people would be excited to see.
Something that involved Brice…

There was one clear option, of course: a wedding.
One lady and one gentleman happened to be involved
in this scandal, which meant the participants were
already in place. Everyone always enjoyed watching
a confirmed bachelor fall to the trap of marriage. And
Lady Victoria was beyond beautiful in looks—she was
Isabelle's twin sister, after all. Brice would complain,
but in the end it wouldn't be a terrible burden.

Fallon had always believed that the straight and
clear path to resolution should be plan A. All of
the numbers added up—Kelton Brice's marriage to
Lady Victoria had to be this first option. As for plan
B… There wasn't time to consider a plan B. Not if
there was any hope of saving the Fairlyn family from
potentially irreparable harm. More than that, he had
important things to do—beginning with finding
Reginald Grapling before he could do anyone harm.
If he hadn't already.

He had to protect Isabelle on both fronts. She
would be devastated by the news of the wedding, of

course, but her life was more important than temporary pain. As long as this issue lingered, he couldn't
devote his time to catching Grapling. Fallon had seen
the way that man had looked at her. She wouldn't be
safe while Grapling was roaming London's streets.

Friends don't do things like this to each other, a voice
that sounded an awful lot like Isabelle's accused him.
But his *friend*, Brice, had left this problem on Fallon's
doorstep. When presented with problems, Fallon
solved them. He would do what he must.

He turned back to face Brice and Ayton. They
were looking to him for direction. Everyone looked
to him.

Shaking his coat into place and steeling himself for
what was to come, Fallon stared back into the seeking
faces of his men. "Brice, I'll need you to do what you
do best."

"Beat a man until he sees reason? Or break in
somewhere to steal papers?"

"I wouldn't claim that stealing documents was what
I do best just now," Ayton mumbled under his breath.

"Neither. Today I need you to make the rounds in
society. Act the hero. Talk of how you rescued Lady
Victoria from harm."

"You want him to call attention to this madness?"
Ayton asked.

"Yes. Like I said, I need him to do what he does
best—talk."

"Which would further associate my name with
Lady Victoria's… St. James, you can't be considering
what it seems you're considering. I know that look on
your face."

Fallon didn't say a word. There were no words. He was asking his friend to give up his freedom to save a lady's reputation and the future of the Spare Heirs. It was a heavy price to pay and one that couldn't be coated in sugar to make it more palatable.

"Absolutely not! You know what that would mean for me...for her!"

"I do. But is marriage a worse fate than allowing her to face this scandal alone? You have the ability to fix this situation. I can see that the repairs are made quickly, but the talk of it... Brice, you know as well as I how long that will linger."

He hesitated, clearly wanting to argue...then slumped back, decision made and fate sealed. "I suppose it was blasted honorable of me, carrying Lady Victoria out of that fire like I did," Brice finally conceded with a sigh. "It appears that, in the end, I won't be as unsuitable as my family has always believed. All right: I'll marry the girl, for her sake and the Spares'."

Ayton clapped a hand on Brice's shoulder. "Whiskey?"

"A damned leg shackle. Yes, I'll take a whiskey, Ayton. And I'll have yours as well."

Fallon eyed his friend with more than a small amount of sympathy for a moment before standing and murmuring, "Thank you."

With the final words on the subject spoken, Fallon left the men to drown themselves in spirits and moved toward the door. He had a wedding to orchestrate with Lady Victoria's father. It had been some time since he'd paid a visit to Lord Knottsby. It seemed today was the day to call in an old favor.

$$\mathcal{Five}$$

BACK IN THE SAFETY OF HIS BLACK CARRIAGE THAT resembled every other carriage on the streets of London, Reginald pulled the diary from his pocket and tapped his fingers on the cover as he stared out the window into the icy winter evening.

"Quite respectable these days," he mused as the Fairlyn home disappeared from view. The lord of the house, Knottsby, had built a good name in society since they last met. A lordly name, a lordly home… Even the shrubbery in his garden had been pruned just so.

"After everything he stole from me," Reginald said, his grip on the small diary tightening.

Life for Knottsby was about to suffer a devastating blow. He would do well to enjoy his lordly reputation today, for soon it would be gone.

St. James would attempt to stop events from happening, of course. That man must always place his nose where it didn't belong. St. James had a need to control everyone and everything around him, was willing to do anything for the sake of protecting the innocent and his precious Spares. He always had. They lined his pockets, after all. But he wouldn't be able to keep these plans from happening.

"Go mad from trying, St. James." With a grin, he descended from the carriage and started up the steps to his accommodations, anxious to read yet another entry in Lady Isabelle's private journal.

Isabelle Fairlyn's Diary
February 1817

I read Sir Tristan de Lyones's story from Malory's "Le Morte d'Arthur" again last night. The pages of my copy are well worn with curling corners, creases, and dots of tea from years of enjoyment. I wish I could recount the number of times I've read the story, as I'm certain it would be an impressive number, but all I know is the truth I'm always left with on the last page of Tristan's tale. I want to know a love like the one he had for Isolde, and someday I shall.

With that in mind, my qualifications for my future husband are as follows:

1. Blond hair
2. Polished appearance and keen sense of fashion
3. Drive a festive red phaeton or ride a powerful steed
4. Be a skilled dance partner
5. Admire flowers and other beauty in the world
6. Friendly smile with even teeth
7. Honorable and upstanding in society

Gentlemen who embody every ideal listed above and are therefore under consideration for marriage:

1. Mr. Kelton Brice

—Isabelle

❦

Spring 1817

Isabelle loved her sister. And that was what made today so terribly difficult.

She wasn't certain how long she'd been standing in her bedchamber with her arms wrapped around herself as she shook. The large brass key to her door pressed jagged lines into the palm of her hand, but she made no move to ease the pain. She'd been betrayed.

"Isabelle Fairlyn, open your door this instant!" her mother shouted from the hall.

"No," she whispered to the empty room.

"If you don't, I will find the housekeeper and allow myself entry!"

"Do what you must," Isabelle replied, though she didn't believe she could be heard through the paneled door that separated them.

Two years ago, she'd asked her cousin Sue to paint vines and flowers on the walls of her bedchamber. She'd always thought them cheerful: their various shades of pink and purple, sweeping around her, full of life and the expectation of blooming in the sun. She preferred the idea of living in a garden rather than within the four walls of a house. Gardens were happy. No one argued in a garden. In a home, however…

"Isabelle!" her mother bellowed, punctuating her thoughts on home life rather well.

Now the garden walls closed in and choked her with thoughts of how wrong she'd been. She'd always believed in the good in everyone and everything around her—until now.

How could Victoria have betrayed her so?

Victoria observed proceedings in her life like a watchful owl on the topmost branch of a tree, always surveying and looking for her next move. She wouldn't have allowed this to happen unless she'd wanted it. She'd been in control in that milliner's shop with Mr. Brice, in control when she'd allowed him to rescue her, and in control when she'd agreed to Father's bargain that she become his wife.

Victoria only cared for Victoria. Isabelle had overlooked all her sister's faults, believing the small shreds of good were what truly held her together beneath her jaded exterior. Isabelle had been wrong.

Victoria had done this to her on purpose, and Isabelle would never forgive her for it.

It would seem her sister wasn't good deep beneath her jaded facade, as Isabelle had always believed—she was actually quite evil. Isabelle shook with the knowledge and pulled her arms tighter around herself.

"Isabelle, your sister has been through quite enough of an ordeal. You will come out from behind this door and give her the comfort she deserves."

"Comfort her?" Her voice cracked as she spoke. After what Victoria had done? She'd stolen away the only man Isabelle had ever loved. *They* were to be married, not Victoria and Mr. Brice. It was supposed to be Isabelle. "I'm the one who needs comforting," she called out louder than before, her voice strengthened by the anger that surged within her.

"Your sister is the one who has survived a fire. Don't be dramatic, Isabelle."

"I'm not…" she began, but there was no use arguing with her mother through a closed door.

Her entire life she'd been accused of overdramatizing events. Perhaps in the past it had been true, but it wasn't true today. Today was all too real. Today she'd lost her hopes and dreams. She should be allowed time to mourn the happiness she could have had in her life. The love she would have experienced. The laughter they would have shared. The flowers he would have brought to her. She scowled at the blossoms that covered her walls, mocking her with what could have been.

Was she to stand by while her twin sister took her future from her?

"And I'll have to watch," she whispered. It was like some horrid image in a mirror playing out the wrong future. She squeezed her eyes shut.

Isabelle had to find a way through this, or she would surely perish from a broken heart. That was all very well on some later day, but just now, she refused to give Victoria the satisfaction. If she avoided her sister, if she avoided everyone involved…if she could survive their wedding, then…

She grew weak at the thought. Their *wedding*. How had this happened to her?

Isabelle sank to the floor and hugged her knees to her chest. She'd wanted a life with Mr. Brice for so long. And now, in an instant, that life was gone.

Victoria's name would be listed on the banns with his, their lives forever linked.

What do you plan to do? a voice whispered through her thoughts.

She didn't know the answer. But she couldn't very well sit here and pine over a man betrothed to her twin sister. They would have children and a home together. Isabelle might live through the wedding vows, but their life together beyond that day she could not take. Those were *her* dreams; she'd written of them in her... She needed her diary. She needed the comfort of the words written there—her words. Everything had become so distracting, now that the season was in full swing, that she hadn't written in the small book in more than a month, but she needed it now.

Scrambling to her feet, she went to the table beside her bed, but the drawer was empty. She opened the drawer farther and searched the back corners. Empty. When had she last seen it? She knew she had left the book here. Now the one place she could pour out her soul without judgment was gone too? Isabelle sank to the top of her bed. It mattered little anyway. Her thoughts were so scattered just now that they would be no more than scribbles on the page. Everything was lost.

When one dream was stolen away, could another dream take its place? Or was she destined to live the rest of her life in this despair?

"*For-ev-er,*" Isabelle drew out the word on a whispered breath and fell back on her bed.

Victoria and Mr. Brice would have a family together, and Isabelle would be the spinster aunt who gave the children sweets. She would be alone to ponder what could have been. No, that would not do at all. Seeing them together day after day, year after year, while Isabelle remained unattached sounded dreadful. She would have to find another gentleman to marry, set her sights on someone else, someone just as appealing as Mr. Brice. Perhaps someone even better awaited her.

Kindness had been what drew her attention to Brice in the beginning. Surely he wasn't the only gentleman with a good heart in the city. Could she replace him? She tried to remember the list of perfect qualities from her missing diary.

"Red phaeton, talented dancer," she whispered to herself. But dancing abilities and the type of conveyance a man possessed didn't seem to matter as much now as they once had. The longer she lay there on her bed, the more she wondered if she'd truly known anything of value about the man of her dreams.

Perhaps it was time for a new list, one that looked beyond the color of a man's hair. She trailed a hand over the locket that still hung around her neck. The right gentleman, a gentleman who would love her, was hiding somewhere in the shadows. Perhaps he was waiting for her, for this moment.

Perhaps she might escape after all.

She sat up, dropping the key on the bedspread and crossing the room to the small writing desk. Throwing open drawer after drawer, she searched once more for her diary. She'd left it here somewhere, she was certain! But she didn't wish to dig about her rooms all afternoon—not today. She grabbed a piece of paper, slapped it down on the desktop, and began scribbling a list. She would mark down her requirements for the perfect husband—truly the perfect husband this time—and search for those qualities. She would lure the right man from the shadows.

Victoria could keep Mr. Brice. He still held a special place in Isabelle's heart, and as her first love, he likely always would, but she needed to move forward and find her way through this mess. The quill tightened in her hand for a second as she thought of her sister smiling up into that cheerful face, but then she banished the image. Hanging on to what could have been would only lead to more sorrow. She would find love again. She would find someone who could take her from her father's home to a place where no one ever yelled, where there was always peace and joy and sunshine. She had made lists like this dozens of times before in her diary. She shook her head. It was just as well she couldn't place the journal. This time she would look beyond any one man and let go of the dreams of him that had filled the pages there.

This time she would find *true* love. She had to believe that.

The perfect husband must…
Possess a jovial spirit.

She paused to brush a tear away with the back of her hand. With a sniff, she pulled the paper closer and continued. Nothing would stop her from this mission.

Have a noble and honest heart.

She sniffed again. There were other good men in existence. There had to be. All people had some goodness at their core, didn't they? It was the one truth she'd leaned on her entire life. Now she wasn't so certain. If Victoria could hurt her this way—and she was Isabelle's sister!—what did that mean for the rest of society? Were there good people in the world at all, or had that been the delusion of a lady who'd never had her heart broken before? Her aunt had always claimed Isabelle had delusions of grandeur. Perhaps she was right after all. Isabelle's entire world seemed to shake with the thoughts coursing through her mind. "There has to be a good gentleman out there," she whispered.

Be willing to protect me from harm.
Never utter cross words.
Love me.

She would not end up in a loveless marriage like her parents. She would find her brave knight. A hero in armor that gleamed in the sunlight, someone who would happily scale tower walls for her, someone who would love her. Her search would begin at tomorrow night's ball.

Isabelle stood from the desk, clutching the list in her hand, and crossed the room to retrieve the key to the door. If her mother required her presence, she would be there. After all, supporting family during difficult times was what good daughters did.

❧

"Well, I'm *Lord Hardaway* now. Are you pleased? What do I want with a blasted title, St. James? I only want to be Brice! Only Kelton Brice. Damn this entire season!" Brice—or Hardaway now—fell into the chair in headquarters and buried his head in his hands.

It had been only a few days since the fire, but that had been all the time Fallon needed to fix most of the problems in London. *Hardaway* had certainly done his part of acting the hero—perhaps too well, since yesterday he'd been awarded a title for his bravery. Fallon had winced at that unexpected turn of events, but there was no turning back once they'd begun repairing the damage done by the fire. Plans were now well in motion to make the entire "burning of Bond" incident vanish from the memories of the *ton*.

Fallon, along with his begrudging friend, had spoken to Knottsby and arranged for a marriage contract to be signed. His poor friend, now Lord Hardaway, would be bound for life to Lady Victoria. Fallon's involvement was something Isabelle could never discover, or she would seek the first opportunity to kill him for his intrusion in her life and destruction of her plans. Of course, a desire to kill him seemed to be common among his friends as of late.

"Apologies, but you know—"

Hardaway stopped him with a raised hand and a small shake of his head, clearly not interested in receiving condolences. Fallon shifted in his chair, looking out the front window to avoid seeing the look of agitation on his friend's face. The man sitting across the small table from Fallon might possess a powerful punch, but it was Isabelle's anger that gave him true

concern. Fallon had had a difficult time not thinking
of her the past few days—of her and what she must
be thinking. But he'd made the correct decision. Her
infatuation with Brice had to end eventually, and
Fallon had only helped things along. Even still, he
would seek her out at tonight's ball—he would make
time between his meetings. He was certain she could
use a friend just now.

Anger and heartbreak aside, Fallon's plan was working to perfection, as he knew it would. The grandness
of the upcoming wedding was already being discussed
over every cup of tea in the country—neatly replacing
the fire the honorable Lord Hardaway had caused.

*What a hero that brave gentleman was to save Lady
Victoria. And to be awarded a title for his valor is the perfect
addition to the story. How wonderful that love grew from
such a nasty start.*

Fallon almost smiled.

Meanwhile the Spare Heirs Society would survive
another day. If only all problems could be solved so
easily. He'd throw half his men into leg shackles if it
would help him find Grapling, but engineering marriage proposals would do no good where that man was
concerned. The same tricks wouldn't work with that
sort of adversary. Though the man had turned out to
be rather unstable and driven by his own greed, he was
a worthy opponent—unfortunately.

Fallon had trained the man personally, had taught
him how to blend into shadows and look for opportunity in every situation. Damn his own thoroughness!
Now finding the one who'd gone rogue and returning him to prison where Fallon had sent him once

before was proving to be difficult. He hadn't spotted the man since that night on the terrace with Isabelle some days before. He could continue his search later today. Now, however, Fallon needed to discuss matters with his friend. Surely a wife and title weren't the end of the world like he was making them out to be…

"I did tell you to play the hero. Clearly you were successful with your mission," Fallon said, weighing his words so as not to make matters worse. The title hadn't been part of his plan, but it must be dealt with now that it had happened.

"All for following damned orders." Hardaway leaned forward, a concerned look crossing his face as he looked at Fallon. A tense moment of silence lingered between them before Hardaway finally asked, "I'm not tossed out, am I? The rules…this title. I don't want it. If I could give it back…"

"If only I could be rid of you that easily."

"Of all times, this is when you joke? St. James, what am I to do about this?" Hardaway pushed away from the table and grabbed a decanter of whiskey and a glass before falling back into his chair. Once there, he poured and mumbled, "A wife and a title? I only went in to get some damned papers." He tossed back the contents of the glass and continued. "This is all her fault, you know. That opinionated woman with her blasted hats. And now I'm stuck with her at my side for life? How will I work? How will I enjoy anything ever again?"

"Perhaps once you know more of the lady—"

"I'll learn she's worse than I believe her to be at this moment? It would be a difficult feat to be a less appealing wife, but I think that one might be up to the task." Hardaway refilled his glass.

"Her looks are passable," Fallon hedged, not wanting to reveal to his friend how lovely he found the lady's sister.

"I suppose I should be grateful I didn't rescue some hag with sharp teeth, claws for fingers, and a bony arse. How fortunate I am."

His friend might have been disappointed with the dish he'd been served in life—and Fallon sympathized, truly he did—but Fallon only had the next few minutes to console Hardaway and end things in some kind of positive light. He needed to return to his work before tonight's ball, or he would be buried until morning and unable to attend. He needed to say something. He had to pull his man up from the muck. "You've survived worse," he finally offered.

"Have I?"

"Yes, remember that time you burned down Bond Street? How everyone spoke of your villainous ways and you were shunned from all entertainments in society for the remainder of your life? The Spare Heirs Society was discovered to be involved, and it was forced to disband. You were left with no work, no income."

"I—"

"Not to mention what your family thought of the scandal," Fallon said, knowing he'd thrown down the winning card.

"You believe that you're clever," Hardaway accused.

"I am clever."

"Bollocks. I have to accept that the title is mine in addition to agreeing to marry that woman, don't I?"

"You do."

"But I can keep my membership to the Spares?"

Fallon nodded.

"To unwanted marriages and titles." Hardaway raised his glass and tipped the whiskey into his mouth.

Fallon stood, preparing to leave his friend to drink the whiskey, the day, and his problems away, and surveyed the room. His men were either conversing amicably or relaxing after some job. For the moment, all of his problems resided outside the walls of this house. And tonight he would meet those problems head-on.

Would he see Isabelle at the ball tonight as well? He hoped he would at least catch a glimpse of her. Though if she'd somehow discovered the truth about his meddling, he should stay well away from her. Wood nymphs were dainty creatures, but he would imagine they grew quite violent when pushed to anger. And if Isabelle ever discovered the truth, her anger would put the worst of the classical gods to shame.

Six

"STOP ADMIRING BLASTED BRICE! I'M ILL FROM READING this syrup-covered drivel!" Reginald bellowed, tossing the diary across the room.

It landed with the pages splayed open on the worn floor in front of the door of his rented room. A second ticked past while he settled his breathing and stared at the small book. Then he moved to retrieve it.

Anger wouldn't help him now. Calculation, on the other hand, was just what he needed. He would use every drop of knowledge he gained of this lady to end her father—and St. James by association. And with the season now gaining momentum, he was almost ready to make his move. He pulled the old necklace from his pocket and ran his thumb over the golden surface before returning it to his side for now. Opening the diary once more, he turned to the next entry written in Isabelle's hand.

"Soon, Isabelle. Soon. And then your father and St. James will regret ever placing a finger on me."

Isabelle Fairlyn's Diary
February 1817

I'm worried over Victoria. She's across the parlor even as I write this. She's shuffling a deck of cards over and over. It's a soothing sound against the cold winter rain pattering against the window, but is she practicing for something in particular? I don't mind her enjoyment of a wager, but Father said he would send her back to our estate if she gambled again. I love the London season—the balls, the excitement of city life—but I don't want to be here without Victoria. She may push me over my limits at times, but I adore her. She's my sister. I hope she never reads this. She would taunt me with my words of love for weeks if she knew what I was writing.

Tonight is the first ball we will attend this season. We've scarcely been in town long enough to put down roots, and already I suspect that Victoria is sneaking out of the house at night to find a card game. I know I can't stop her gambling, but I will hide her secrets to the end just as she would do for me. How do ladies survive life without a sister? I'm thankful I don't have to discover the answer to that question.

—Isabelle

❧～❧

Spring 1817

"I'm fine. Quite fine. Thank you for inquiring," Isabelle mumbled once the lady's back was turned and she was moving away into the crowded ballroom. The evening thus far had been nothing but questions about Victoria—and only questions about Victoria.

How is your dear sister?

When will we see the lucky lady at a ball again?

We hear there's to be a wedding—is it true? Since your sister isn't in attendance, you must tell us all the details.

Her mother appeared to be answering their questions as well a ways down the side of the ballroom. The only difference was how excited she seemed over every answer she gave. Isabelle took a steadying breath under the guise of adjusting the heart-shaped locket at her throat and searched the ballroom for Evangeline and Roselyn. Or anyone she knew, really.

Victoria had always been at her side at these events, filling any silence with biting commentary about the festivities around them. Isabelle didn't realize how awkward standing on the side of a ballroom was until now, but she'd best grow accustomed to it. She must. Roselyn and Evangeline couldn't remain with her forever. They would busy themselves with their husbands and families one day. And here Isabelle would continue to stand, without even her sister for company.

No. Isabelle would carry on with her own path, as Victoria had chosen hers. With her eye on the crowd gathered around the perimeter, she took a step backward, closer to a row of potted trees that lined each side of the ballroom. Away from the surrounding groups of people, she could now observe and perhaps spy her secret admirer. There was such a crush—perhaps a bit farther. She took another step back.

"When you asked me to point out life with my

keen pirate gaze, I didn't think you intended on walking about without looking where you were headed at all."

Isabelle spun around and looked up at St. James. Finally she'd found a friend this evening. She could throw her arms around him in gratitude. She didn't, but in her mind she did. St. James! She wasn't alone—she had *him*! And with his refusal to dance, he wasn't likely to be married anytime soon, not like her other friends. She was saved.

"Being your lookout seems a great deal of work, now that I think about it," he added when she greeted him with only a relieved smile.

"Not up for the job? And here I thought you liked any type of work. How disappointing."

"Someone told me I worked too much," he countered, warmth lighting his dark eyes as he looked at her.

"And you listened to her advice? She sounds like a ninny."

"Nothing of the kind."

She paused, studying him. He might be dressed for a ball in his dark evening wear, but he was here in some official capacity. She could see his intent in his occasional glance to the main doors and the tight set of his jaw. "You didn't truly heed her advice, did you?"

"No." He almost grinned. "I'm meeting someone here in a few minutes about a business matter."

"Spare minutes in your day? Whatever shall you do with the time? Take up some sport? Perhaps read a book?"

"Why were you backing out of the ballroom?" he asked, ignoring her taunts.

She supposed she should have known this topic—the blasted fire, Victoria, the wedding—would be an inescapable talking point. It was the only conversation she'd been able to have all evening. "I was getting a better vantage point to see the available gentlemen. I…don't know if you're aware, but there was a fire."

"I know," he stated, removing the need for her to delve into matters once again.

"Well, then…I suppose Mr. Brice, or Lord Hardaway rather, told you of it. He must be…quite pleased."

St. James didn't reply, only watched her with an intensity that made her glance down at her hands.

"Anyway, it seems I require a new choice of husband. If it can't be—" She broke off, not wanting to continue the conversation. Isabelle could always be counted upon to chatter on about any topic offered up in conversation. But not about this. The subject was simply too painful. She looked away, watching a lady in the opposite corner of the room laugh at something a gentleman had said.

"Have you seen anyone of interest thus far?"

She looked up, meeting his gaze. His brows were drawn together in what she assumed was concern. What a kind friend she'd found. No one else at the ball mattered just now, not even the gentlemen she was supposed to be scouting, because she was here with St. James. He somehow understood without words. He knew her secret and her heartbreak, and he was here to comfort her. She blinked away tears of gratitude and smiled up at him. "Are you offering to help me look for a replacement?"

"A replacement husband? Not up to your usual romantic standards, is it?"

"A replacement for my interest," she clarified with a small sniff she hoped he wouldn't notice. "The husband part will come after I've met him, of course. I can't sit about for the remainder of the season. I need something to do, a project of sorts. I have a list of qualifications."

His brow quirked up in question, and he almost smiled—almost. "You're referring to it as a project, and you have a list of qualifications as in an advertisement for employment? Now who is overly interested in business matters?"

"That is still you, Mr. St. James, but that's why this task should suit you." He would help her, wouldn't he? She didn't want to be alone in this just now.

He crossed his arms over his chest and settled into a businesslike stance, studying her. "Tell me your list."

"I knew you would assist me!" She raised her hand and began ticking off items on her fingers. "My future husband must be jovial in spirit. A bright smile that lights the room and a booming laugh wouldn't be remiss, but that part doesn't matter as much as the meaning behind it."

He nodded in understanding. "You want your future husband to have all his teeth. That should be manageable."

She glared at him for a second. "It has nothing to do with teeth, St. James. Haven't we discussed this already?"

"Of course. How could I forget? Heartfelt smiles displaying inner joy. Good to know I've already been eliminated. Do go on."

"He must have a noble and honest heart." She ticked off another finger on her hand.

"Should the gentleman in question leave his shining armor with a footman when he arrives tonight? What of the sword he used to defend the honor of that maiden in the last story?"

"He would never wear something as inappropriate as armor to a ball," she replied with a grin. "But if it helps narrow the field, I do prefer brightly colored ensembles. Though I'm making an effort to look beyond such things."

"A Sir Lancelot with large, protruding teeth and bright clothing. He should be easy to find, even in this crush."

"Perhaps I was wrong to trust you," she threatened, not meaning a word of it.

"No. You can trust me." Any good humor St. James possessed vanished in an instant. "A good-natured, honorable gentleman... Someone who will make you laugh, care for you—it's what you deserve."

In a sea of unfair words spoken about her sister's much-deserved happiness this evening, St. James's comment was a raft that offered rescue from drowning. This conversation with him, these few minutes spent together, was returning life to her limbs and joy to her heart. St. James was truly the most sympathetic and kind pirate she'd ever met.

Roselyn and Evangeline had consoled her over the past day in their own ways, and it had helped. They'd offered promises that life would move on and the sun would still shine, but this conversation was different. This man somehow knew what she needed to hear: that she deserved to feel the sunshine, that she deserved laughter. And just now in the glow of candlelight, it actually seemed possible.

St. James was watching her warily, as if he'd just told his darkest secret and was waiting for a reaction. It was a rare peek into his true thoughts, yet she didn't understand them. His statement had been about her life, not his. Why would he feel exposed by those words? Whatever his thoughts, this moment between friends was touching, and she found she couldn't look away.

"Thank you," she finally said to break the silence.

"I suppose he should have blond hair like Hardaway," St. James murmured.

"My only true wish is for a good man, an upstanding gentleman with a positive disposition who is in a position to marry. Do you think he exists?"

"Not here," he said in a low voice, glancing away for the first time in a few minutes to check the door. Likely for the arrival of the lord with whom he was to meet.

"Am I too far in the shadows of the ballroom? Perhaps you're correct. Mother has warned me that only scoundrels lurk about in corners."

"You should listen to her," he said with a meaningful glance at their shadowed surroundings. "The other side of the room seems to hold promise." He took a step away from her, suddenly looking more sullen than business minded. "I must attend to the matter that brought me here tonight. Will you excuse me? Perhaps I'll find you later."

"I could be married by then if I find the right

gentleman. Marriages seem to happen rather quickly as of late."

St. James nodded uncomfortably at her jest and moved away through the crowd.

"I thought it was rather lighthearted, considering the situation," she mumbled to herself as she watched him leave. At least now she could allude to Victoria's wedding without speaking around a lump in her throat. She considered it a marked improvement, and it was because of St. James.

She smiled after him and set off for the other side of the ballroom in search of the perfect gentleman to marry.

Isabelle had only been on the edge of the ballroom floor for a minute before her mother caught up with her, with a halfhearted setdown about wandering about alone. Lectures from her mother always began the same way, with a reference to another lady who had been offended by Isabelle's behavior. In this case the affronted party had been Lady Smeltings.

"Lady Smeltings saw you move to this side of the ballroom and was so concerned…"

Despite giving birth to children of her own, her mother had never seemed certain of what a mother was intended to do, at least to Isabelle. Always looking to those around her to gauge whether she should be outraged by her daughters' behavior had made her mother a rather inconsistent chaperone. Isabelle supposed everyone had strengths. Her mother's strong suit was what she supposed it had always been—her youthful looks and ability to bat her eyes over the rim of a wineglass. Her skill had served her well in her younger days. After marriage, however, it had not served her well at all.

Which was why Isabelle would find a marriage where no one fought, a marriage where every day was filled with complete happiness. But she couldn't find it standing here, being berated by her mother.

Isabelle tossed out a quick apology for wandering away without an explanation or an escort and turned away from her mother to begin her study of the gentlemen who were milling about the area. Leaning around a group of ladies, she ran her fingers over her necklace as she scanned the room for gentlemen.

"In search of a better view of the room, Lady Isabelle?" Lady Smeltings asked as she joined them. Her usual air of judgment turned her question into quite the put-down, but Isabelle didn't flinch under her scrutiny. At least it wasn't personal—Lady Smeltings acted that way with everyone. "Striding off that way alone had us quite concerned," she added.

"I should have told my mother of my plans. Apologies if I worried you."

"Has a certain gentleman caught your eye?" the woman pressed. "You and your sister could share a wedding breakfast. Wouldn't that be lovely? Everyone present would enjoy that, I'm certain."

"That would be quite the event." Isabelle almost choked on the words.

"Who is the lucky gentleman who has caught your eye?"

"I'm not certain just yet." Isabelle put aside her misgivings about the lady at her side. If there was one person who knew the details of society's doings, it was

Lady Smeltings. Well-known busybodies and gossips were usually also authorities on available gentlemen, which at the moment was rather convenient. "Perhaps you could assist me on that front."

Five minutes later, after Lady Smeltings had imparted the high points of those standards she held in perfect regard, Isabelle was rewarded with a full dance card. Perhaps her ladyship was correct and Isabelle would be married soon. Though a joint wedding breakfast with Victoria and Lord Hardaway was utterly out of the question. This evening had certainly turned in a positive direction since she had seen St. James in the crowd.

Or perhaps not...

Only a few minutes later, she was dancing the most rigid version of a waltz she'd ever experienced and on the arm of a rather severe-looking gentleman. According to her ladyship, Lord Erdway was the most generous-hearted man in town, having just returned from some charitable endeavor in the countryside. He might have a sterling character, but he'd yet to smile.

Wouldn't benevolent gentlemen be predisposed to cheerful things like smiles? Perhaps he was only con-templating his next gift to the community. Meanwhile Isabelle was contemplating that this would be how armies waltzed if they were to dance into battle. *Left, left, march, march, and take that hill with a twirl!*

She smiled to herself. There would be less war if the military had dance instruction from this gentleman. No one who danced was angry enough to fight. One simply had to look around a ballroom to know that statement was true. Dancing was happy and romantic. St. James should try it sometime. And she should focus on her own dance partner, not waltzing armies, the ball around her, or her businesslike friend.

"Lady Smeltings tells me you're only recently back in London," Isabelle led in to begin some conversation with the man.

"That is true," he stated as they rounded a corner of the room with a jerking motion. "I spent the past year converting one of my estates near the Welsh border into housing for children in need."

"An orphanage?" She drew back in surprise. He cared for children who had no home of their own. She would have never guessed it of the stern man before her. "How wonderful. You have a large heart to do such a kind thing."

"I didn't have a choice in the matter."

"I agree," she replied with a smile. "Once you know that someone is in need of your assistance, you could not turn your back. But the donation of an entire estate is quite the gesture. The poor dears will be well cared for now. You must be pleased."

"Quite. Like I said before, I didn't have a choice in the matter. But all is settled now."

"You saw the orphanage project to completion, then? How kind you are." Perhaps he would be a good fit for her after all. They would travel the countryside establishing charitable establishments and spreading goodwill.

"The project is ongoing," he corrected, cutting into her thoughts. "Or perhaps it isn't. I haven't an idea. I sold my interest in the estate and returned to town as soon as possible."

"Oh." He sold his interest. But what of the children? "Is the orphanage still to open on schedule?"

"That is no longer my concern." His harsh words about children's welfare were the end to any musings she'd had about marriage as far as *he* was concerned.

"I see," she muttered.

The remainder of the dance passed with comments about how nicely lit the ballroom was tonight, what a fine turnout there was for the event, and, for Lord Erdway's part, how everyone should be forced to learn the proper steps to the dances or not be allowed on the floor.

When the dance ended and Isabelle was returned to the side of the room, she realized how straight her spine had been in an effort not to offend her dance partner. Not only was his giving spirit not as generous as had been portrayed by Lady Smeltings, but Isabelle also had no desire to stand like a soldier for the entirety of her marriage. She allowed his lordship to walk away as quickly as he wished. Lord Erdway, as it turned out, was not a suitable replacement for Mr. Kelton Brice, Lord Hardaway, after all.

By the beginning of the next dance, Isabelle was once again filled with hope. Lord Hempshere was said to be quite the upstanding gentleman in town. With him at her side, she would host only the most respectable of events, and they would base their relationship on honesty with each other. Honesty and trust would be a strong foundation for their marriage.

They had just come back together for a time after circling the other couples on the floor when Lord Hempshere asked, "Do you enjoy the quadrille?"

"It's my favorite," Isabelle said honestly. "I always make a misstep and dissolve in laughter by the end of it."

"That doesn't cause you embarrassment? How curious," he mused, just before they separated once more.

Isabelle spent the entire time she circled the lady opposite her justifying his comment. It was simply a forthright question, and she wasn't accustomed to such talk when it didn't come from her sister. By the time she returned, she knew he was only attempting to speak with her in earnest. She should explain herself, allow him to know her and understand her to a greater degree. "I learned these dances when I was older than most, when my father inherited his title. I suppose the steps didn't sink in as well as they ought."

"Don't concern yourself with how off-balanced you look doing the steps. I don't think anyone has noticed," he said with a smile. With a blasted smile! Was he unaware that he'd insulted her?

She'd always enjoyed the lively nature of this dance until now. She glanced around, suddenly very conscious of the proper direction she was to take after this curtsy. "Thank you for that reassurance."

"I meant no offense. Only offering a bit of honesty."

"Honesty is an admirable quality," she hedged, now wondering how high a priority a noble character was on her list. Apparently it was possible to be too honest to suit her.

Lord Hempshere deposited her back at her mother's side a moment later and nodded as he left.

Isabelle was fairly certain that as lovely as this ball was, even with everything bathed in candlelight and scented by the flower arrangements, there was no romance to be found here tonight. It was quite the sad thought, and it had her turning to search for a footman with a tray of champagne glasses. Her mother had a glass—surely more existed around here somewhere.

As she turned back to the ballroom floor, a man was standing in front of her. She almost jumped back at the sight of his bright-green waistcoat but caught herself after only a quick blink. He was looking at her as well, his focus moving from her face, over her gown, and back up her neck before meeting her gaze once more.

"Good evening. I didn't see you approach. Do I owe you a dance?" Isabelle's eyes darted to Lady Smeltings, unsure of what the woman had arranged for her. But her ladyship was turned away chatting with Isabelle's mother, leaving Isabelle to wonder at who this gentleman in the brightly colored evening wear was. There was something familiar about the build of this man or perhaps the intensity in his gaze, but she couldn't quite add up the pieces enough to place him in her memory.

"I saw you from across the room and knew I must come speak with you." He flashed a wide smile as he looked at her. "If you have room on your dance card…"

"My dance card is a mystery at the moment. A friend of my mother's was determined to see it filled and has taken over all control of it. I fear my feet may fall off by the end of the evening."

He laughed openly and tossed his white-blond hair back as he did so. It was an unusual hair color. It was as if he'd dipped his head in snow and didn't look quite natural, but it somehow suited his sharp features. "Perhaps you could use a break from the dance floor, then." He signaled someone behind her and a second later produced two glasses of champagne and handed her one.

How did he know she was thirsty? She studied him as she took a sip. Perhaps it wasn't the grandest of gestures, but offering her a drink and the option to sit out a dance seemed rather heroic, noble, and good at the moment.

He took a drink before indicating the bustling ballroom floor at his back. "I must confess, though I would enjoy a dance with a lady such as yourself, I prefer other entertainments. Books and art are more to my liking, but these events are never held in a library or a gallery. What's there to see in a ballroom—other than you, of course?"

She blushed at his compliment even as her mind clung to his previous statement. "You enjoy books and art?" He was rather ideal, down to his emerald-green evening wear. "What a wonderfully small world we live in. I volunteer at the British Museum."

"We were destined to meet one another, then," he said with another wide grin.

"Perhaps so." Her heart was still a bit bruised from the recent betrothal news, but if this was destiny, she should at least be receptive to it. It was almost unnerving how well he embodied her list of qualifications—the old list and the new—like she'd somehow wished him into existence. She looked up in wonder at this man. Was he her secret admirer? Could it be?

"I apologize for keeping my distance before tonight," he confided after a moment's hesitation. "I've wanted to talk to you for longer than I'd care to admit."

"Have you?" Her hand flew to the locket, her fingers sliding over the metal surface as she watched the man who stood before her. "Why did you delay?"

"Timing…but none of that is important now. I see you received my note." His grin returned, even wider than before.

"I did. I very much liked—" She broke off with a glance at her mother to ensure they couldn't be heard. "The gifts. They were beautiful."

"It will be our secret. We could keep every word spoken between us a secret. I confess, I'm a bit of a romantic."

"What's your name? Or is that to be a secret as well?" she asked in a low voice, captivated by the excitement of it all.

"For only you to know, I'm Mr. Reginald Grapling."

Seven

St. James,

I hope you're enjoying this little game of ours. You must have known when you ended the last round by placing me behind bars that it wasn't the end. That was too easy. This competition between us will never be over. Having me thrown in prison only interrupted our fun. And now our game continues. The move is mine, and I've selected a lovely pawn. I believe you know her.

Her name is Lady Isabelle Fairlyn. I'm certain you remember her father. I know I do. It was interesting to watch you with his daughter on the terrace that night. Quite enamored with her, aren't you? That should make this game entertaining to say the least—for my part anyway. Does her family know of your interest in her? What a mess that would be. They couldn't possibly approve. You should know that gentlemen like us don't get the girl. Or do we?

As you may have already pieced together, I've decided to pursue Lady Isabelle. She's a beautiful *lady, and her company is tolerable enough. For some time now, she's thought of me as her secret admirer. How did I manage such a feat and keep it from your notice? It was simple, really. I sent her flowers and jewelry, and she told me her secrets—all her secrets. The lady is simply in too valuable a placement on our game board for me to overlook.*

That she's Fairlyn's daughter was enough, but when I saw the way you looked at her, I knew what I must do. Of course she's hasn't any idea about this contest of ours, but she's certainly going to be fun to toy with while you watch. You, Fallon St. James, great protector of the land, can do nothing to stop me. And I will know of any attempt you make. Just like you, I now have eyes and ears everywhere. Can you guess where? How close to home? I would warn you to be careful what you say, but you always have been the silent one.

Do you see the perfection of my move yet? Allow me to elaborate. If you warn her away from me, she dies. If you warn her father of my plot, she dies. You will watch while I destroy Fairlyn's lovely daughter and the man himself in one move of one perfect pawn. I hope you weren't too fond of her.

Best of luck. You'll require it.

—RG

❧～❧

FALLON DROPPED THE LETTER HE'D PRACTICALLY MEM-orized to his lap with numb fingers. He couldn't look at the words written there any longer. Of course, he also couldn't look away. The carriage pulled to a stop, but for a moment, he didn't move.

Fallon had thought he was making the correct decision last night when he allowed Isabelle to seek happiness with a gentleman in a position to marry. He'd meant what he'd told her about deserving such things. And from across the ballroom last night, he'd watched her try on men like shoes. All had been as it ought to be, no matter how he wished he could talk to her a bit longer, hear her laugh, see her eyes light up at some idea. He'd convinced himself that she must move forward, away from him. But he'd had a vague sense of unease that lasted the remainder of the night.

He'd dismissed it, knowing the emotion that surged through him was an irrational one. This morning, however... This morning was a different story. He swallowed and stared at the words on the paper. If he warned anyone, she would die? There was always a countermove to be made. Always. And until he discovered what that move was, he would be following Isabelle...everywhere.

∽

A brightly lit museum wasn't where Fallon would have thought to find Grapling, but that was indeed where the man was this afternoon. Strolling. Perusing the art. And the part that made Fallon want to commit murder was the man's attention to Lady Isabelle Fairlyn. The only thing missing from the scene before him was damned dancing and laughter. Was there something he could have said at some point to stop this from happening? But Fallon knew Isabelle wouldn't listen when it came to her dreams of romance—she never had. And now that beautiful quality was being exploited by the worst sort of gentleman. Fallon shouldn't have left her alone at the ball last night.

Grapling had called her his pawn. But what exactly was the man after? What torture did he have in store for Isabelle? Fallon had to do something to stop this, but he couldn't risk Isabelle's life. Every unanswered, feverish thought pulsed through Fallon's brain with a painful thump against his skull.

Fallon stepped behind a tall marble statue, waiting for Isabelle and Grapling to pass by. Flaxen hair created from boiling lye? He let out a harsh breath at the lengths Grapling would go to in order to escape capture. Fallon should have alerted his men to potential changes in Grapling's appearance. He ticked off another shortcoming on the great list in his head. This entire situation was Fallon's fault.

His blood boiled with the knowledge that this villainous man, a man who had committed murder and theft, was just beyond Fallon's reach, both literally and metaphorically. Strolling through the museum, chatting with Isabelle as if he hadn't a care in the world. His Isabelle! Granted, she wasn't *his* Isabelle. But she was a damned sight closer to Fallon's than blasted Grapling's.

"This is where you spend your days?" Grapling asked Isabelle with a wide smile. Too wide, in Fallon's opinion. "It suits you. I've always enjoyed places where the rooms are swept clean of the city's dust and good society can stroll about...and appreciate art, of course."

Ha! Amusing for a man who reveled in getting his hands dirty. Fallon shifted so that he could continue to hear their conversation without being seen.

"I hadn't considered the cleanliness of the museum as a benefit to volunteering here, but there are maids on staff," Isabelle replied as they moved deeper into the maze of the upper rooms of the museum.

"A building this size would need a sizable staff to function. Who works in this area with you?"

Fallon nodded to an older gentleman who passed, but on receiving the man's curious glare, Fallon was forced to move. Slipping to the opposite side of the room, he clung to the wall beside the open door, listening for anything he might have missed.

"It depends on the time of day. It's quiet in the mornings from what I hear. In the afternoons, I assist Mr. Jasper, the librarian. There's a nice man who services the wobbly frames in the back workroom. He makes tea for me on occasion and tells me stories about his family."

"They are fortunate to have such a giving lady in their employ," Grapling stated. Fallon could almost hear the sickening smile in his voice. He held himself back from vaulting out to knock the false look from the man's face. *Giving*—Grapling had no interest in charitable endeavors. He never had. What was he after besides taunting Fallon with his closeness to Isabelle? Murder again? But in the letter he used the word *destroy*. A scandal that involved Isabelle? Perhaps, but what scandal? And when? Fallon had to understand the man's intentions if he was to protect Isabelle.

"I'm a willing volunteer. I'm the fortunate one, to be able to spend my afternoons amid such beauty,"

Isabelle returned. Her voice was closer, as if they were looking at the painting on the other side of the wall.

"Your own beauty exceeds that of these paintings."

Fallon closed his eyes and forced himself to remain still. This was the worst part of gaining information. There always came a point when it became difficult not to rush in with fists raised. But information could be just as valuable as an enemy with a bloody nose. Often more so. Fallon knew that, but with Grapling leering at Isabelle on the other side of the wall, he was having trouble remaining still.

"Oh. Thank you," he heard her gush, most likely smiling and blushing. Fallon released a harsh breath.

"I'm honored to have you give me this tour."

"We share a love of art," Isabelle replied. "A tour is the least I can do."

Fallon shook his head. Of course Grapling had convinced her that he appreciated the pieces here; he was trying to use her. He was Reginald blasted Grapling! He used everyone. But there was nothing to be done for it now. All Fallon could do was listen and wait for some piece of information that would turn the tide in his favor.

"How long will this collection be on display?"

"For the remainder of the season, then it will return to our home. For a time anyway," Isabelle replied, her voice growing distant as she and Grapling moved farther from the open door where Fallon stood.

"It belongs to your father?" Grapling asked, making Fallon tense and listen more carefully. He would need to move in a moment to get closer.

"For now. He's a custodian, really."

"Meaning?"

Fallon tipped his head around the corner into the next room and spotted a display of ancient pottery. He ran for it and came to a stop behind a raised display featuring bowls and pitchers of various sizes. He could now catch glimpses of the two as they perused the artwork.

"It was my grandfather's collection," Isabelle was saying. "One day soon, once my sister is settled, it will be displayed in her home as part of her dowry. All but this one painting." She pointed up to a large painting of a castle on a hillside that hung on the wall. "For now, it's here for all of London to enjoy."

"Only one painting will go toward your dowry? That hardly seems fair. Your family is unjust."

"It's the centerpiece of the collection," Isabelle cut in with obvious affection for the painting of the distant land. "I don't mind that I can keep only this one. It's my favorite anyway."

"Even still…"

"They were catalogued and divided when I was only a baby. Father didn't have his title then. It was all he had to give us for us to marry well. Things change, though. Father inherited unexpectedly, and then there was the fire at my grandfather's home. Most of my portion of the art collection was destroyed. But that only increases my appreciation for what remains. These paintings survived. I like the beauty of that."

The circumstances of Isabelle's childhood were ones Fallon knew well—ones many younger siblings with families had to overcome. He'd spent the past few years ensuring that his men could provide a stable life for their families. Without an inheritance and with a social inability to delve into trade, gentlemen like

Isabelle's father didn't have many options. For Fallon, everything always came back to the Spare Heirs.

Further resolve to take Grapling down and stop whatever game he was playing in town seeped into his bones. Enough watching. That was what Grapling wanted him to do. Fallon was done giving Grapling what he wanted. This man was constructed of lies. Nothing Grapling told Isabelle today would help Fallon be rid of him for good.

Fallon shifted, and a piece of the pottery clanked against the display.

"Survival can be difficult at times." Grapling's eyes flashed to where St. James stood behind the pottery, having just become aware of his presence.

Fallon straightened to his full height and moved forward, his focus on Grapling. He was so close. Fallon could grab him now and end this mad chase around London. But the thought of Isabelle in danger stayed his hand. However, nowhere in Grapling's rules of this game did it say Fallon must make it easy for him to win. Fallon edged closer. Isabelle's back was thankfully turned, or she would have seen the menacing gleam in his eyes. Her pirate fantasy had come to life.

"Have you had perilous adversity you had to over-come?" Isabelle asked Grapling. "Perhaps a fearsome foe or a fight to near death?"

"Yes, Grapling," Fallon added. "Have you a fear-some foe while playing your little *parlor games*?"

"St. James!" Isabelle exclaimed as she turned to greet him, surprise widening her eyes. "What are you doing here? You two are acquainted? I wasn't aware…"

Fallon stepped closer under the pretense of greeting

Isabelle, but should things become violent, he could pull her from harm's way. He gave her a polite nod. "I was in the area and thought I would take some time for a leisurely stroll and enjoy the art like my old friend Mr. Grapling."

"You? A stroll through a museum?" Isabelle asked with a smile.

Apparently"—his gaze slid back to Grapling as he spoke—"I'm interrupting. I believe Mr. Grapling was about to tell us of the troubles of his unfortunate life."

"*I* have no troubles." There was a tense moment in which Fallon was reminded of the look in an opponent's eye just before pistols were drawn at dawn.

"No? How odd. The last time we met, you seemed to be in a bit of an unfortunate circumstance." Fallon could remember it quite well. The sadness at the situation. The sense of betrayal that one of his own had turned on him. The relief at having him placed behind bars.

"That was quite a long time ago, St. James," Grapling said with a false levity that didn't reach his eyes.

"A shorter time to some than others," Fallon returned.

Isabelle let out a nervous laugh, clearly sensing something was off between the men. "Have either of you seen the exhibit from the plains of Africa? Truly extraordinary."

"Mr. Grapling's expertise is in other areas. He enjoys displays of weaponry, knives in particular… Or that's what I hear."

"You're misinformed as usual, St. James. Where *do* you get your information? It's quite flawed."

"Oh?" Fallon mused. "It has been some time since

we've caught up. Where have you been, and what brings you to town after such a long absence?"

"It's London. You know I simply can't keep away from its charms."

Charms. Fallon had heard the man describe a woman in such terms before, mere days before she'd learned too much of his plans and he'd killed her. The present day was four years too late to save one woman's life, but he could certainly save Isabelle's now.

"The city is charming, isn't it?" Isabelle smiled and clasped her hands together.

The motion was one of such pure happiness that it made Grapling look that much sourer by comparison. He didn't deserve to be anywhere near this lady. Yet the man was here at her side as if he belonged there. The thought brought Fallon's anger to the surface in an instant. Grapling wouldn't turn his filthy gaze on Isabelle while Fallon was present. He wouldn't allow it.

"I love the life this city has, both day and night," she added, clearly unaware of the tension surrounding her.

"As do I, Lady Isabelle," he murmured. Fallon would not allow this man to harm anyone of his acquaintance, especially not Isabelle and her family. He would not allow this man to cause havoc in the city he called home. And he would not stand here for another second and watch that smirk on his face grow larger. In that moment Fallon—always aware of his actions and thinking five steps ahead—didn't think. He swung.

His fist collided with Grapling's jaw in a manner that would make Ayton proud. Grapling staggered backward, shock mixing with pain in his eyes.

He heard Isabelle's sharp intake of breath over his shoulder. "No," she called out. "What are you doing? Please don't fight. I don't... I can't..."

"He has misgivings about my presence here with you, my lady," Grapling stated as he turned to look at Fallon with an amused gleam in his eyes. "Are you the jealous type? Interesting."

"Jealous?" Isabelle drew back in more surprise than she'd shown when he'd punched Grapling. "You have it all wrong. We're only friends."

"Apologies, my lady, but—"

Anything Fallon would have said was cut off when someone grabbed his shoulder and hauled him backward.

Grapling watched, his reddened lips twisting up in pleasure as he mused, "Close call, there. I'll be watching, as will you."

"You got him. That's the one. I knew when I saw him creeping about the place he was up to no good," a man said from the door to the next room. The gentleman from earlier must have alerted someone downstairs. Fallon glanced up to see the giant of a footman who was dragging him away from Grapling.

"Let go!" Fallon commanded as he watched Grapling move steadily toward the opposite door, abandoning Isabelle with a quick bid of farewell. He would lose the man. This game with Isabelle. That look in his eyes... Fallon couldn't allow any of it to continue. He couldn't let him get away. Not now! Not ever! Fallon cocked back an elbow that made the man grunt but not release him, and the heels of his boots only scraped the wooden floor.

"Unhand him," Isabelle cried out at his side, hitting

the man on the arm to no avail. "This is all some sort of misunderstanding. Isn't that right, Mr. St. James?"

"St. James? This is Mr. St. James?" The large footman pushed him upright in an instant, St. James's coat falling back into place on his shoulders. "Terribly sorry, sir. I meant no disrespect. Misunderstanding... Will never happen again."

But it was too late. The damage was done. Grapling was gone.

Eight

Dear Lady Isabelle,

I know my words pale in comparison to the writings of such great works as the tale of Tristan and Isolde, yet I must write to you nonetheless. The scarce hours I've spent in your company are a treasured gift. Thank you for agreeing to see me again after my quick departure from the museum last week. Our time together in the park on Tuesday will remain in my heart forever. The light of your smile that day rivaled the sun. Next time I hope to be able to walk you home. You have my apologies for the business matter that called me away just as we were to return to your family. Soon I hope such things won't hinder our days together. Until then we must cling to the moments we have to ourselves. I shall keep all thoughts of you close.

Yours,
Mr. Reginald Grapling

ISABELLE SHOULDN'T HAVE COME HERE, AND CERTAINLY
not alone. But the museum was silent this time of day,
and Mr. Grapling had been correct—the still and quiet
of the artwork were just what she needed today.

She'd slipped out of her home amid the chaos of
flower arrangements and preparations for the wedding
breakfast on Victoria's big day. Victoria herself had
been shut away in her bedchamber along with their
mother and every available maid. It was just as well
since Victoria had had nothing but cross words for
Isabelle since the engagement had been announced. In
their last conversation, Isabelle had consoled her sister
with how lovely her wedding dress was. It had taken
great strength to offer such a compliment, but it had
taken even more to strength not to strangle her sister
a moment later when Victoria offered her the gown
in jest. With a sigh, Isabelle had walked out the door
today without anyone's notice.

Now Victoria's wedding was just over an hour
away. Her family was no doubt still racing around and
calling orders to scrambling servants, and Isabelle was
here. The silence of the museum pressed in around
her, her only comfort during the storm of her life.
From the museum it was only a short walk to the
church. She would meet everyone there, calm from
her time spent here alone, and the day would carry on
without issue.

Her sister would soon walk into that church Lady
Victoria Fairlyn and walk out Lady Hardaway. Isabelle
swallowed hard and focused on the painting in front
of her. None of that mattered. She had moved on.
Mr. Grapling was taking her mind from her troubles

for now. Perhaps something would come of her time spent with him. Though she wasn't planning their wedding just yet, he had been a fine distraction thus far, almost as if she'd dreamt him into creation herself. Victoria could spend a lifetime listening to Lord Hardaway's hearty laugh. Isabelle would be fine—better than fine, in fact.

Even if St. James didn't approve of Grapling, had even gone so far as to hit him, Mr. Grapling knew her, understood how much she needed to gaze upon these paintings this morning. His letters proved how much he cared for her. And being cared about was all she really wanted just now. She smiled at the memory of yesterday in the garden. Sneaking out of her house to meet him amid the roses had been enough to tell her how genuine he truly was, no matter what St. James might think. Mr. Grapling had insisted that she come here today, and his advice was spot-on. The artwork at the museum did bring her peace on an otherwise-hectic day. He really was a kindhearted gentleman.

Could St. James truly be jealous of the time she was spending with Mr. Grapling? Surely not. But it would explain why he was finding fault with such a pleasant man. St. James would understand in time. Isabelle needed hope at a time like this. She was fortunate that she'd found her secret admirer before Victoria's wedding, or she would have been more devastated than she was already.

Smiling up at the paintings, she moved down the hall toward her favorite one. Simply walking past the pieces in her grandfather's collection reminded her that the day would turn to night, the seasons would change, and yet here in the scenes depicted in paint, every detail would remain the same. Paintings could be counted upon. Maybe they didn't seem like such sturdy objects to others, but to her they were stability—beautiful scenes of calm.

She studied the way the artist had created the waves on the ocean in the piece before her. Even the wind was held still. Nothing could move on or begin anew. Here every toss of that ship remained, held steady for eternity for all to look upon in awe. This single moment in time would be preserved forever more—if the paintings were well cared for—and she'd dedicate her days to ensuring that was the case.

She strolled to the next piece, already feeling better about her life. She had these beautiful works to look after. She had a gentleman in her life who had been so considerate of her mental state on her sister's wedding day. And friendships she treasured—she had plenty of those with Roselyn, Evangeline, and now St. James. She smiled up at the painting of a young girl posing beside a bowl of fruit. She was going to get through today without any troubles.

In another moment she would leave. She couldn't very well miss her sister's wedding because she was busy strolling through the upper rooms of the British Museum. No one would understand that reasoning at all.

Moving to her favorite piece in the collection, that of a tumbling-down castle standing alone on a hillside, she smiled. She often wished she lived there—

Clunk!

She was knocked to the side, and a sound seemed

to echo inside her head. Blinding, sharp, slicing, silencing pain. The room swam before her eyes, then went black.

Her knees buckled beneath her, and she was falling. Falling. Falling.

The last thing she saw was the castle, standing proud against the sky, calling her to come inside and stay within its walls forever.

Nine

Spare Heirs Society
Report of Events
30 September 1813

*It's now known that Mr. Reginald Grapling
has been taking funds from the Westminster
Boardinghouse for more than two years, beginning
when he was first assigned the task of its protection
in June 1811 under the authority of the Spare Heirs
Society. The discovery of the missing amount (for
exact accounting, see appendix C) was made by
Mr. Henry Fairlyn while conducting an audit of
the Westminster Boardinghouse books for Madame
Molloy, proprietor of the house. The audit was
administered after allegations against Mr. Grapling
were raised by one of the women residing at WBH,
Miss Maggie Redmond. This information was
presented to Mr. Fallon St. James dated yesterday,
29 September. At Mr. St. James's instruction, a
full investigation was launched. The missing funds
were retrieved after a raid of Grapling's home led by*

Mr. Kelton Brice. Grapling was not present to be apprehended at that time.

At eleven o'clock this morning, Mr. Grapling was found having tea in the drawing room of Madame Molloy's establishment. Minutes later, Miss Maggie Redmond was found unresponsive on the floor of her room at the same location. Miss Redmond's body was bound, gagged, and covered head to toe in shallow wounds from a knife. When she was found, she wore only the locket that witnesses claim Mr. Grapling gave the woman as a gift months prior—a token of his affection. The depth of Miss Redmond's wounds suggests that she was allowed to bleed out for most of the night. Mr. Grapling had the murder weapon in his possession downstairs where he waited for her passing...

Spring 1817

"ALL OF LONDON SOCIETY IS HERE," HARDAWAY hissed through clenched teeth.

Fallon scanned the church, attempting to count in rough terms how many were in attendance. "I would estimate it at half of society," he murmured a moment later. "Of course, there are many who don't come to town who I'm also taking into account."

"I meant *why* are so many people here?" Hardaway asked in his version of a whisper—which was more of a low rumble that the first pew of people in front of them could surely hear.

"It isn't often a lifelong bachelor and *ton* darling is finally chained to a lady." And Fallon had called in a few favors to make sure there were strong numbers present. There was no point in holding a wedding as a diversion from recent disasters if no one came to the event. He didn't want his friend to marry without reason. Guilt already plagued him over the necessary ruthlessness he'd had to use in sacrificing one of his oldest friends' bachelorhood. For that high a price, the wedding had to be worth discussing for weeks on end.

"I'm not some spectacle to be viewed in the park, and don't call me a *ton* darling."

Fallon glanced to Hardaway at his side with a suppressed smile. His friend needed to lash out at him to relieve his anxiety over waiting for his wedding to begin. It was the least Fallon could do to rib the man into a fight to distract him. "Today you are both of those things. Isn't it a beautiful occasion?"

"Shut it before I hit you, St. James." Hardaway drew back at his own words and turned to stare at him. "You're far more loquacious as of late. It's odd. I like it, but it's odd."

Fallon didn't respond. It was true. He'd spoken more in the past few weeks than he had in a year. There was only one change to his schedule where he could place blame for such an oddity: Lady Isabelle Fairlyn.

The woman and her excessively cheerful nature had somehow crawled under his skin, and the situation got worse every time he saw her. Now he found he was talking more often than before. The worst of it was that he wasn't speaking of anything of importance; they were…almost leisurely discussions. He gave an inward shudder and adjusted his stance at the front of the room, his gaze sweeping the crowd.

Where was Lady Isabelle this morning? He'd yet to catch even a glimpse of her. She must have been keeping her sister company. Or perhaps she was too upset by the wedding to sit about and wait for it to begin. It was taking quite a while to get started.

Fallon resisted the urge to pull out his pocket watch and check the time, knowing many eyes were upon him while he waited at the altar. He wasn't accustomed to being at the front of a crowd of people, much preferring to rule from the shadows, where he could check the time if he chose. He spotted Ash Claughbane and his new wife, Evangeline, chatting quietly with each other. Claughbane hadn't seen marriage on the horizon until it happened either, and to his lifelong enemy's daughter no less. Everything was changing, but the happiness he saw on Claughbane's face gave Fallon peace of mind about that fact.

"Where is my bride?" Hardaway hissed at his side, drawing Fallon's attention back to the event at hand. "She should be here by now."

As should her sister. Yet Isabelle was nowhere to be found. The crowd was growing louder as the people gathered grew impatient. Then Victoria appeared in the back doorway of the church, music played from the balcony above their heads, and the rumble of the crowd died down. The lady's eyes darted around the room, searching. Isabelle... She hadn't been with her sister then. Which raised the question: Where was she?

Looking out across the faces of those in the

church, he saw that he wasn't the only one to notice Isabelle's absence. Her name was mouthed in wordless whispers by quite a few people while others craned their necks, looking for her. Something was wrong. Isabelle knew enough about society to know she couldn't abstain from this event. She would know of the reality of society expectations. Everyone would talk. She must have been more distraught by this day than he'd imagined. If she wasn't here, where was she? He needed to find her.

But gasps pulled him from his thoughts. Victoria had stopped moving when she was only halfway to the front of the church. She stood rooted to the floor for a moment, and her eyes darted around the room before landing on Hardaway with a wary look.

"What..." Hardaway breathed at his side, his body going rigid with tension as if preparing for a brawl in an alley.

Lady Victoria looked to be preparing for the same eventuality. She parted her lips as if she was about to say something; then in the next second, she picked up the bottom of her gown, turned, and took off at a run.

Fallon turned to ask Hardaway what had happened between them, but his friend was already running after his would-be wife. "Victoria!" he bellowed just before he disappeared at the rear of the building.

Fallon blinked. This was certainly one way to divert attention from the recent fire.

He wouldn't have recommended this course of action, but now that it had occurred...it wasn't an altogether bad outcome. Everyone would certainly discuss this over tea for a long while. He should be pleased, but all he could think about was the one end of the rope left to unravel.

Where was Isabelle?

❧

The front doors of the museum rattled beneath his hands as Fallon pulled on the handles. Locked. The museum wouldn't be open for another hour yet. But Isabelle must be here. He pushed off the thought once again that Grapling had taken her, that she was in danger. This was simply Isabelle mourning her sister's wedding. There were no games here, no pawns, only Isabelle. He took a breath. If not the museum, where would she go? He'd already asked after her at her home, and any friend or family member she would think to visit had been present at the almost-wedding. Stepping to the side, he lifted his hand to shield his eyes from the sun. He peered in the window, unwilling to walk away just yet.

A shadow of movement caught his eye beyond the main hall of the museum. Perhaps Isabelle was here after all.

He turned and descended the steps, scanning the sides of the building for a secondary door. Rounding the corner of the large stone structure, he moved down the narrower side street, toward the door that Isabelle must have used if she was in fact here. A moment later, he threw it open with a nod of satisfaction before charging up the service stairs that led to the upper rooms. The area was for the use of the librarians who worked in the building, but that didn't slow Fallon. He was no stranger to clandestine trips into service areas.

Within seconds he'd reached the upper floor, where Isabelle had once given him a tour. He would surely find her here, staring at a painting, forlorn over her lost love. Or had she truly moved on to Grapling just as the man had planned? Perhaps he could offer her some comfort in the fact that her true love was still today an available bachelor. If he told her about the failed wedding, would she run to fawn over his friend? Some selfish part of him wished he could keep the information secret a bit longer. Then he could keep her to himself—if only for the afternoon.

Fallon had built an empire upon secrets and omissions of details, but he knew he must tell her the truth about her sister's failed wedding. At the same time, he knew she only wanted friendship from him. And he had no room in his life to have her as more than a friend. It was fact, reality, no matter how much he wished it were not.

His booted feet fell in silent steps on the thick rug that ran the length of the room leading to the main gallery. It was rather eerie to walk the halls of the museum with the building this silent. Many painted sets of eyes watched his progress as he wound his way toward the area with Isabelle's family's collection. It was odd, though… He'd seen movement through the front window, yet all was quiet inside. There were no light footsteps as Isabelle moved around the room, no chatter as she talked to a maid—only silence.

He quickened his pace, unsure what he would find after all. When he reached the opening to the large gallery where Isabelle's family's art collection was housed, he finally understood the silence.

He paused for only a heartbeat as the shock of the scene before him tensed his muscles for battle. Then he was running.

"Isabelle?"

The walls where the paintings had been displayed were bare, the room empty. Isabelle was on the floor, limbs in disarray as if she'd fallen and hadn't moved since. She was bleeding. The scene was all too familiar. Not again. Not Isabelle.

"Isabelle," he tried again, sliding to his knees beside her. Silently begging for her to be alive, he turned her head to see her face. He braced himself for the sight of whatever damage had been inflicted on her to bring her to this state.

Her eyes were closed but not blackened. He cupped her cheek in his hand and brushed a stray curl from her forehead. She was still warm. He could now see a cut in her hair above her left eye from the blow that must have brought her down. The hair around the wound was matted, dark red, and growing worse by the second. He pulled out his handkerchief and pressed it to her head to stop the bleeding, but she needed more assistance than he could offer her. There was blood everywhere. He had to help her. He leaned over her, pressing his ear to her breast. Her heartbeat was steady. But her breathing was already faint. God, how long had she been here? He should have come faster. He should have known she would come here.

"Isabelle!" He shook her gently by the shoulder, but she didn't rouse. She needed a doctor. He had to go for help. Was there no one else in the building? There must be...

He leaned back on his heels, looking around the room more warily than before. She'd been left here like this on purpose. It was a message. He scowled down at the locket around her neck for only a fraction of a second before he ripped it from her throat and stuffed it into his pocket, unable to revisit the familiar scene in his mind.

He scanned the floor around her for the object that had caused her head wound, partially to understand how it had happened and partially to arm himself against a possible unseen foe. But the room was empty except for a piece of paper at her side. Picking it up, he quickly scanned through the words.

Dear Father,

Everything has been stolen from me. I've lost my love to my own sister, and today I lose my sister as well. You should have seen that my heart belonged to Mr. Kelton Brice long before he became Lord Hardaway, just as you should have seen that my interest in this art collection would lead to this day. I've arranged for the paintings to be sent somewhere you will never find them. And I remain as a constant reminder of what you lost. Now we've both been stolen from. This is a small theft in the face of what you've done to me, but it's a start. My sacrifice today will show the world who you truly are. Enjoy the outcome of your selfish concerns.

—Isabelle Fairlyn

Was this simply coincidence?

His mind had jumped to Grapling as her attacker, filling in the gaps as necessary to make the man guilty of this crime. Had Isabelle set out to steal from her family and had something go horribly wrong? It couldn't be.

Then he saw the minutely printed string of letters and numbers along the bottom of the page. Anyone else would dismiss the line as scribbles, but not Fallon. He scanned the line, once, then twice, his heart racing with the information he found there. Between the code and the last line of the note, he knew he'd been correct in the beginning. This was Grapling's work.

"Enjoy the outcome of your selfish concerns," Fallon whispered as he dropped the note to his knee and looked down at Isabelle where she lay on the floor as he pieced together all that he knew. There was something familiar about those words—as if he'd heard them before. Were they from a well-known book or a line of verse? He shook his head and stuffed the note into his pocket. He would have time to consider that riddle later. Right now Isabelle's well-being was a larger concern.

He couldn't risk raising the alarm or have her seen to by a doctor here. He was the only witness. The code he'd seen in the bottom corner of the note was even more concerning. He was one of the few men who could read such a message since he'd invented it as a means to give orders in writing to his men. He hadn't used it in years, but he remembered it.

Four copies. Can you find them in time? No more or it wouldn't be sportsmanlike.

There were four copies of this blasted note, and he was in possession of only one? Where were the other three? Where would he start? Questioning the *Post* and finding known forgers to prevent additional copies from being made to begin with, but those steps would have to wait. Right now he had Isabelle to deal with. Even if he concealed the copy he'd found here, others placed all blame for the theft on her shoulders. Even if no one believed their claim, the scandal was enough to ruin her. Isabelle had nothing to do with this. She was as Grapling had claimed: a pawn.

Fallon's brows pulled together, making his head ache. There was no way around it. Until such time that the other notes were accounted for and the artwork recovered, Isabelle would be in the thick of a scandal— another one, considering what her sister had just done.

The Spare Heirs, however, had a doctor. The situation could be kept quiet.

Fallon was already scooping Isabelle up in his arms. He'd known Isabelle's father for years. This was a matter of protecting a lord's daughter. Fallon was simply doing his job. Help a friend in need, gain an owed favor...

But this was Isabelle. This wasn't about business, future gain, or future debts to collect on.

Her thin frame draped over his arms like a coat on a cold day. Shifting her so her head rested against his chest, he looked down into her pale face. Ever the wood nymph who now haunted his dreams, luring him into brightly lit clearings, her cheeks still held the slightest hint of rose. He clung to the sight of her color-filled cheeks. She would live.

"You're going to be fine, Isabelle."

He wasn't certain which one of them he was reassuring, but he continued talking anyway, all the way through the museum, down the stairs, and into the street.

"Everything will be all right. I'm going to take care of you. I'll sort this out in no time. I'll fix it. It's what I do. I care for an army of gentlemen. I have a doctor on staff. If anyone can retrieve paintings, it's me. I'll make this scandal disappear for you. I know you would prefer it if a knight saved you, but there were none available today. I'll have to do. You'll be all right, Isabelle. You're safe now."

When he turned the corner, his driver spotted him and jumped down to open the carriage door. He asked no questions, only watched Fallon grow near with wide-eyed concern. His men knew better than to ask. It's why this would work. He could care for Isabelle at headquarters, hide her there until matters were solved.

No one would pry. No one would find out. And if they did…he would have to put a contingency plan in place. He glanced down at the lady in his arms. Her father wouldn't like any of this, but he could be made to understand. The gravity of his actions weighed on his shoulders even more than the woman in his arms. It must be done.

"Back to headquarters. She needs to be seen by Dr. Mathers. Tell no one else of this."

"Yes, sir," his man replied as Fallon climbed inside the carriage, still holding Isabelle against his chest.

As the carriage began to move, he wrapped his arms more tightly around Isabelle. Holding her as one might hold a sleeping child, he cherished every faint beat of her heart against him.

"Not much farther now," he murmured into her hair as he pulled her close. "You can make it. Stay with me, Isabelle. Please stay with me."

Ten

Dear Lord Knottsby,

I know this has been a troubling day, but I must inform you of your daughter's current state of health. I found Lady Isabelle unconscious at the British Museum and brought her to a safe place. There was a theft. The artwork is gone, and a letter of confession was left behind. Worry not. I have the letter in my possession—one copy of it at any rate—and I'm already tracking the others. The man behind this action will pay for his crimes. Mathers is seeing to Lady Isabelle now. He says all we can do is wait for her to wake. I'll inform you when I know more. Apologies if this is brief, but I must return to your daughter now.

—St. James

❧⟶⟶⟶❧

ISABELLE STRETCHED HER FINGERS AND TOES AGAINST the soft bedding and curled onto her side. Why did her head ache so? Had Victoria forced an entire bottle of champagne down her throat? No, that wasn't right.

She hadn't seen or spoken with Victoria in more than a week. She'd gone to the museum...

The sound of a thousand door knockers as something hit her head. Everything had gone black. Victoria's wedding. She had to get to Victoria's wedding! What was the time? She blinked her eyes open and tried to sit before falling back into a pile of pillows, her skull pounding, threatening an imminent explosion. What began as blurry shapes slowly sharpened into focus.

Where was she?

She stared up into the canopy of a large bed, but it was not her own. As she turned her head to the side, her cheek pressed into soft fabric. It was the color of red roses after the heat of the summer sun had faded their blooming color to the deepest pink imaginable. Her mind careened through every bedchamber decor in her family's home, her friend's homes, but she had no memory of seeing this place before. She wasn't sure of the time of day, but judging by the presence of a lamp turned low beside her, the rest of the room in darkness, it was nighttime. But that couldn't be.

Floral-printed draperies were drawn over the window at her side, falling into puddles on the flower-covered rug. In fact, everything was covered in flowers. Floral upholstery, walls... She ran her hand over the surface of the bed, which was—of course—also covered in tiny embroidered flowers. It was lovely but entirely unfamiliar.

Her gaze settled on the glow of the lamp, seeking

answers from the light of the glass-encased flame. That was when she noticed the cup of tea still steaming on the table and the empty chair pulled close to the bedside, as if someone had been watching over her as she slept and had just stepped away.

Was someone here with her? What was this place? The last she remembered was the pain in her head and falling to the hard floor.

"Am I dead?" Her voice croaked as if she'd never used it before.

"No. Thankfully not," came a male voice from the far side of the room.

She gasped and pulled herself up a bit against the pillows. Why was there a man with her in a strange bedchamber? Had he hit her on the head and brought her here? Her mind reeled with questions, each punctuated by the pain in her skull.

Coals from a near-dead fire sprang to life in the grate across the room, lighting a tall silhouette. The man dusted his hands off and turned toward her. "You did have me worried there for a bit though."

Blinking into the haziness that was the other side of the room, she forced her eyes to adjust to the light. There was something familiar about his deep voice, the confidence in his movements, but she couldn't make sense of any of this. "Whose bedchamber am I in?"

"Mine." St. James came into focus as he moved to her side, but his answer was no answer at all.

This room couldn't belong to St. James, and she couldn't be lying within it. None of this was real. It was all a dream caused by the bump on her head. She must have hit it quite hard to envision herself in such a place, with St. James of all people. It was rather amusing, really, aside from her throbbing head. That part wasn't amusing at all. But the setting she'd placed St. James in did bring a smile to her face.

A large bedchamber filled with plush furnishings and covered in busy floral patterns—ha! And in her mind she'd made her most stern—and only male—friend claim he lived there. Dreams were entertaining at times. St. James's chosen place to sleep would be on a dark cot beside a desk, wouldn't it? Or perhaps he never reclined to the prone position at all; he only caught a quick nap in a chair between meetings. She giggled, which only drew him closer. A look of concern made him look more serious than ever as he stood surrounded in flowers.

She scowled back at him and laughed. "St. James, I'm in your bed—your overly feminine bed," she whispered up to him. "Are we married in this dream? Don't you want to kiss me, have your way with me here on our wedding night?"

"Devil take it, you're delusional. I'll have to have the doctor return," he muttered. He leaned against the bed, next to her, and lifted a hand to check something on her forehead.

"Oh, a doctor! Yes, I'll need one of those. I *am* injured. Horribly injured! Save me, St. James. The only way I'll live is if you kiss me." She reached up and grabbed the fabric of his waistcoat, pulling him closer. He braced a hand on the bed on the other side of her body, smoothed her hair back from her face, and watched her. The fabric of his waistcoat was textured by the pattern of gray threads stitched into it and was rough under her fingers, drawing her attention from the intense look in his eyes. How odd to have such detail in a dream.

"Your clothing feels so real."

He'd removed his coat and cravat. His waistcoat hung open, and his clothes were rumpled, as if he'd slept in them. She'd never seen him in such a state of undress. She moved her hand to his shirt and splayed her hand across his chest. The heat of his skin warmed her fingers as his heart beat beneath her palm. Dream St. James had a broad chest and muscles that twitched at her touch. She lifted her hand to his shoulder, her other hand skimming up his side. His breath hitched in his chest. It was odd that she'd never noticed the real man's fit form, never before caught the look in his eyes that was one part caring concern, one part intense desire.

He moved his hand over her hair, the pad of his thumb caressing her cheek. The real St. James was her friend, only a friend. She wouldn't be able to face him for a week once she woke from this scene, him sitting so close, her touching him. "This dream…"

"Isn't a dream," he said, not breaking the contact he had with her. Instead he searched her eyes and continued to touch her cheek, her temple, in soothing, gentle caresses, as if she might break.

It took a moment for his words to sink into her aching skull. "It isn't…" She froze in her exploration of his body, her gaze dropping to her hands that had been roaming over his chest for well over a minute. "What?"

"You aren't dreaming. I found you on the floor of the museum earlier today."

"And you brought me here? Where are we? Why?

Wait… *Earlier today?*" She had to leave. She had to find her family. She tried to push St. James away to sit up, but he didn't budge.

"You were unconscious. I know you're confused, but you're safe now…in my home, my bed."

"Your… No, truly. Where am I?" She ripped her gaze from his to scan the room beyond him, looking for anything that made sense of the past few minutes. This room could not be Mr. St. James's private quarters. It didn't fit what she knew of the man. And why was she in his private anything? She couldn't be. Her reputation. Victoria's wedding. She needed to gather her things and leave this place, wherever it was.

"You're in my bedchamber—truly."

"How? What?" She stared up at him, taking in the sympathy and, unfortunately for her, honesty in his expression.

"You need to rest," he said in a tone that would command armies but not Isabelle on her sister's wedding day.

How had she made such a blunder of things? She shouldn't have gone to the museum. It had been a foolish idea. Blast Mr. Grapling for suggesting such a thing. And then she'd gotten hurt. But this really wasn't his fault. She shouldn't blame him. It had been an accident of some sort. What *had* happened? She didn't know, but now was not the time to seek answers. She had to get to the wedding. If she were late, everyone would talk. There would be scandal.

"I have to leave," she stated as she pushed against his unyielding chest in an effort to sit up. "I'll miss Victoria's wedding."

"Everyone missed Lady Victoria's wedding," he said, keeping Isabelle still on the bed with a hand on her shoulder.

"*Missed*," she repeated, looking up at him. "You said *missed* in the past tense. How long have I been here?"

"Here?" He shifted away from her to pull out his pocket watch and check the time. "Almost seven hours. I don't know how long you were unconscious on the museum floor before I found you."

"Victoria!" She leapt to her feet while St. James was distracted placing his watch back in his pocket. "I have to…" But her words dwindled into nothing as her ears began to buzz and everything turned black once more.

"You need to rest," St. James said somewhere close to her ear as his arms surrounded her.

As much as she wanted to stand her ground against him, she gave in to the strain of the day and rested her head against his shoulder as he placed her back on the bed and settled her against the pillows.

"You took a nasty hit to the head," he murmured.

"I recall. Pieces of it anyway. But my sister's wedding…"

"There was no wedding. Your sister fled the church."

"Victoria fled her wedding?"

"She didn't marry Hardaway," he confirmed.

There was a tension in his jaw as he watched her reaction to the news, but she wasn't certain what she thought of this new development. Kelton Brice and Victoria were not married. Perhaps it was the hit to the head, but she found herself more concerned for her sister than pleased that the gentleman she long admired was once again a bachelor.

"Poor Victoria," she muttered, and she saw the tension leave St. James's gaze in an instant. She knew he didn't approve of her interest in Lord Hardaway. He must have been relieved not to have to listen to her talk about his friend. Fortunately for him, she had far too many things to think about above a former love interest's availability.

"When your sister ran out the doors, I left to find you," St. James continued.

"How did you know where to find me?"

"I know you," he said simply, looking into her eyes.

"I'm glad you do," she finally whispered. They both fell silent as the oddly intense moment wrapped around them. Her heart was pounding as she gazed up at him.

What was happening? She was overwhelmed from the events of the day. That was all.

She was supposed to take Mr. Grapling's advice and find serenity in her favorite pieces of art this morning. Victoria was supposed to wed Lord Hardaway this morning. Instead, Isabelle had hit her head. She still didn't understand anything that had led up to this moment, and now she was here with St. James. He was looking at her, and she couldn't pull her gaze from his. Everything was at once warm, soft, and compelling her to stay.

"I'm so confused," she muttered.

"I'm afraid that's your head injury." He eyed a spot on her forehead as he spoke. "You were seen by my doctor while you slept. You may need to be seen to again tomorrow if there isn't any improvement. As it happens, I have some experience with such things. It should heal nicely."

"You have experience with wounds?"

He didn't answer, only examined her forehead.

"Was it bad? It hurts like the devil." She lifted her fingers to the spot that ached and encountered soft linen covering her hair. Apparently she'd been hurt badly enough to warrant such treatment.

"You were bleeding when I found you. It was…" He paused, watching her for a second before he released a sigh and reached for the bedside table, producing a folded piece of paper. "I'm glad you're awake."

"What is that?"

"The note I found on the floor beside you at the museum."

"Does it explain what happened? Things are a bit foggy in my mind. Is it an apology note from someone for accidentally hitting me over the head perhaps?"

"No." He tapped the folded piece of paper against his thigh as he watched her. "I need to know if you had anything to do with it."

"No. I didn't." Even with an addled mind, she knew she hadn't written the note. "What does it say?"

"You haven't looked at it. I already suspect what occurred, but I need to be certain, without a doubt, before I proceed any further."

"Proceed with what?" Why was he looking at her with a wary eye like that? "What does the note say?"

"It's your written confession to the theft at the museum."

"Theft? What theft? St. James, what are you talking about?" She tried to sit up but couldn't find the strength.

Why was he asking her about a confession? She hadn't taken anything. She would never… Someone had stolen from the museum and claimed she'd done it? The entire situation threatened to swamp her there in the pile of feather pillows.

She took a breath, then another, focusing on St. James's face. His dark-brown eyes were the color of rich soil, the kind that would grow multitudes of flowers. His jaw was covered in the stubble of his unshaven beard. Seven hours. The tea and chair at her side. He'd looked after her while Victoria was somewhere in town not married and a thief escaped with artwork. She'd been looking at the painting of the castle on the hillside when she'd collapsed. Her head pounded as she forced herself to breathe. She needed an anchor as life stormed around her, and right now that tie was him. She reached for him, her fingers curling into the fabric of his shirt where it covered his forearm.

"Settle down," he said, placing his other hand on her shoulder and soothing her nerves. "You're all right now. I'll get this sorted. I shouldn't have upset you. You need to rest. You took quite the blow to the head. It's too much for you just now. Perhaps in the morning…"

"St. James, what was stolen from the museum?" she asked, somehow already knowing the answer. She needed to hear it all the same.

He watched her for a minute, clearly gauging his words and choosing how to handle her. "Your grandfather's art collection was gone when I arrived."

Gone, just like that? She'd likely been the last one to see it, to enjoy it. She closed her eyes, trying to remember the morning. She'd been standing in the largest of the upper rooms when a blinding pain split her head. Her knees had buckled, then nothing. She opened her eyes and looked at him, needing him to understand, to believe her. "I didn't steal my own grandfather's art collection. I cared for those pieces. I volunteered there. I had a duty to look after those paintings. I would never take them. And for what reason, money?"

"Revenge against your father," he corrected, studying her as he spoke. "The note makes a convincing argument against you. It claims you arranged the theft…that you wanted to be caught to destroy your family's reputation."

"I thought you knew me," she muttered. She stared up at him, her eyes beginning to pool with tears.

"I do. But that hardly matters with this information written in ink in a hand that could easily be yours."

"It does matter." She relaxed a fraction. He believed her. She would hold on to that one small shred of hope in this mess. She had St. James. He was on her side in whatever battle she now found herself in, and together they had better odds than her facing this alone. "It matters to me that you believe me," she clarified.

"What I believe is there are three more copies of this note that aren't accounted for. Others don't know you." He held the paper up for her to see. "You could be taken to prison over this. If the handwriting matches your own… You aren't safe as long as the other copies exist."

"Sniff it," she demanded with every bit of strength she could summon.

"Excuse me?"

"Smell the note in your hand."

St. James raised the paper to his nose and breathed in. With a questioning look in his eye, he glanced at her, sniffed it once more, and shrugged.

"What does it smell like?"

He glared at her as if her head wound was far worse than he'd imagined. "Paper."

"Exactly. I keep dried lavender in the drawer with my correspondence to give my notes a pleasant fragrance. Those who receive my correspondence appreciate the effort."

His cheek twitched as if he wanted to smile but couldn't quite make a full go of it. "Unfortunately, I doubt your name will be cleared of all wrongdoing based on scented paper. For now, you should rest."

"I should return to my home," she countered. She'd been inside his bachelor residence for a damning amount of time already, without adding spending the night on top of it. "My family will be concerned for me already. I have to let them know I'm safe. And I have to find who stole the paintings. I have to speak with Victoria to be certain she'll survive. There're a great many details to see to."

"No."

She shifted on the bed beneath his arm. "I must have misheard you. It sounded as if you said no."

He met her gaze with a businesslike stare. "I did. You can't leave."

"Why not?"

"Because it isn't safe for you to go. I knew when I brought you here how this would have to proceed. I knew you wouldn't be pleased, but it had to be done."

She was in his home, in his bedchamber, and she

couldn't leave? What did that mean? "I'm sure I'll be fine once I arrive at home," she said, searching his face and trying to understand.

"No. I won't allow you to do that. If you leave here, you'll be in danger, and I can't...I can't allow that to happen."

"You won't allow me?" She drew back as far as she could while reclined against pillows. "Are there locks on the doors and bars covering the windows?"

"Yes." He gave her a severe look, his eyes narrowing in warning. "The door is locked and will remain so. And so you're aware, you're on the fourth floor of my home, quite a distance from the ground. There's no escape from this room. Therefore, I suggest you don't attempt it."

"What?" She looked up at him in disbelief. "I must contact my family. They'll already be in a state of worry. I can't stay here."

He couldn't be serious. He'd locked the door? He was her friend. Friends didn't do this to friends. He was going to hold her here against her will? That was... There was a word for it. But it couldn't be. Not him. Not her friendly pirate. "Mr. St. James! Have you... Did you kidnap me?"

"That would appear to be the case, yes."

❧

Heaving a heavy breath, Fallon stared at the letter to Lord Knottsby he'd just penned, the words swimming on the paper. "Blast!" he bellowed to the empty library as he leaned forward to brace an arm on his desk. The back of his hand brushed against the heart-shaped locket he'd pulled from his pocket earlier. He'd fallen for it—a classic distraction he should have seen for what it was weeks ago—a lie. And all the while Grapling was working on a plot of revenge. Fallon slid a drawer open, threw the blasted trinket inside, and slammed the drawer.

This day had been among the most tormenting he'd ever known, as he'd waited, unsure if Isabelle would live. He hadn't left her side while she slept aside from the brief meetings he held in the hall outside the room to send a message to Knottsby, begin the search for the other letters, set extra guards around headquarters, and track down all known forgers. He should be thankful. Isabelle was alive—beaten, angry, and in his bed with her life torn apart while he sat here making arrangements with her father, but alive nonetheless.

He blinked away the image of her collapsed on the museum floor that had haunted his thoughts all day.

Fallon had made the correct decision, hadn't he? He'd acted on impulse to be sure, but he'd done the only thing he could in the situation. No plan. No organization. Thankfully it looked like Isabelle would survive, but would he? Three floors above his head, an angry woman was in his bed. And he must somehow continue on as he always did, solving the problems of those in his care. Only this time the one in his care was Lady Isabelle Fairlyn.

Duty, responsibility—he would focus on the ideals that had been at the center of his life for so long. Everything else would sort itself out, if he could only remain in control.

Fallon stared down at the last sentence of his letter

for a moment before he folded and sealed the paper, stamping his signet ring into the wax. Other such rings indicated a title passed down from father to son for generations, but Fallon's was different. He enforced order from this desk, and his signet ring, unlike others, was earned, built from determination and a certain disregard for how society should be run. "Responsibility," he whispered to himself. "This is what you do."

He could survive caring for Isabelle, and he would. Looking at the seal on the letter, he gave a nod of satisfaction to the stamped *SHS* that now made the document official. He rose from his desk, scooped up the letter, and moved toward the door, making a mental list that he would write down later: find the other copies of the confession letter, recover the missing paintings, haul Reginald Grapling from the shadows, and make him pay for what he'd done to Isabelle.

Finding and destroying the copies of the letter would be the first step in all of this mess, right after he fed the lady he'd "kidnapped." He almost laughed. She *would* view their situation in those terms, not that he could blame her for her interpretation.

He'd had to step away to get some air after the kidnapping conversation. The pain he'd seen shining in her eyes when he'd told her she couldn't leave had cut him to the bone. And before that, when she'd touched him... Even now she was lounging in his bed. He climbed the stairs, attempting to banish that last thought with every step. He'd given her father his word. He owed it to Knottsby to keep that word. *Duty, responsibility, maintain control.*

He would care for her, spending far too much time with her in his bedchamber in the process. If it were necessary for him to step away for a few minutes in order to keep his sanity, that's what he would do. Fallon had made his choice nearly twelve hours ago when he'd scooped her up off the floor of the museum. Now he must see it through.

I will do what I must, he repeated to himself. They were words he lived by, but today, scratched out on the paper by his own hand, they held more meaning than ever before.

He'd already made use of the few minutes he'd stepped away to update Isabelle's father on her condition, but Fallon needed to get back to Isabelle now. Was she safe even here? Grapling's network was larger than Fallon had originally assumed. Fallon could well have a security leak within his own home. Until Grapling was captured, the extra guards he'd stationed around headquarters would remain in place, Isabelle would remain in his bedchamber, and the fewer details she knew about the danger she was in, the better. Grapling's threats of violence if Fallon revealed the man's identity could still be in play, and Isabelle's life couldn't be risked—not again.

Of course, none of his efforts would matter if he allowed her to starve, and she hadn't had a bite since before her ordeal began this morning. Had she eaten at all today, or had she been too busy grieving for Brice on his wedding day?

He was halfway down the hall that led to his bedchamber when he spotted Mrs. Featherfitch leaving the service stairs, a tray piled high with various foods.

"Excellent timing," he said by way of greeting the woman. He took the heavy tray from her hands and replaced it with the letter. "Have Smithwick take this to Lord Knottsby. He knows where his home is. And tell him to wait for a response before returning to head-quarters. Knottsby will want to send over a package."

"You're taking dinner in your suite of rooms instead of at your desk in the library as usual. At rather a late hour as well. Not to mention the amount and variety of foods you requested *including a dessert and wine*," she mused, appearing to watch him for some sort of clue.

"Was there a question hiding in that acknowledgment of my dining preferences this evening?"

"No, only an observation." She brushed her hands on her apron but made no move to leave and clear the way for him to unlock his bedchamber door.

"Observe if you wish. So long as nothing you see is repeated to the other staff members."

She waved away his comment on silence, eyeing the tray between them. "At least you're eating. And with sweets no less."

"Men can change, you know," he returned in an attempt to alleviate the woman's suspicions.

"Ha! If that were true, I'd have you eating every morning and sleeping a bit more. All the work you do isn't good for the soul, you know."

"I appreciate your concern. See that Smithwick gets that letter out this evening. It must reach its destination tonight and in the usual fashion."

"No passing it off to a footman. I know. I have been suffering you gentlemen for a few years now."

"That you have."

"But you still aren't going to share with me what all that food and your change of schedule is about, are you?" She raised a brow at him and waited. "I didn't think so."

"Good evening, Mrs. Featherfitch."

"Same to you."

Fallon shifted the tray of food in his hands and unlocked the door, slipping inside before his house-keeper could spot Isabelle inside the room. Kicking the door closed with the heel of his boot, he braced himself for the evening to come. By the look of Isabelle, sitting in the center of his bed with crossed arms and an even crosser face, it was going to be a long evening indeed.

He glanced down at the tray in his arms. "I wasn't certain what you usually prefer, so I had my cook gather several options. It's late. You must be hungry."

"Are kidnapping victims not to be starved to ensure their compliance?"

"Only if I were attempting to get information from you," he replied, moving to place the tray on the small table beneath the window, where he'd once taken his meals. Turning back to her, he asked, "Do you have any information that would require interrogation?"

She fell silent, and her eyes lifted to the side in a clear effort to think of something of importance to tell him.

"My lady, you have no information," Fallon said, cutting into her thoughts. He crossed the room, prepared to help her to the chair at the table. She shouldn't be up and about with a recent head injury.

"And your compliance is a hopeless thing to wish for anyway. I've seen you stalk gentlemen in ballrooms and flee after dropping cakes on the floor. You might as well eat."

She grimaced in resignation and crawled to the edge of the bed to take his arm. "As long as I'm not forced to eat beets. I can't abide beets."

He forced back a grin. "I can't abide kidney pie, but I believe we're both safe with what's here."

He led Isabelle slowly to the table already arranged with two chairs and pulled her seat out for her. He hadn't eaten here since his last days with Pearl. When her ladyship could no longer use the stairs, he'd had some furniture moved in so she could continue to live as she once had. Once she was gone, Fallon hadn't had the heart to dismantle her private quarters. It seemed disrespectful to the dead. So here the room sat, ready for a private meal for two. It was rather convenient at the moment since only his driver and Dr. Mathers knew of Isabelle's presence. The quieter this situation remained, the safer she was from danger and from talk in town.

Isabelle leaned forward to peer under a cloth that covered a bowl before taking only a piece of bread. He'd never thought this to be an intimate setting, but with Isabelle curled up like a cat in the opposite chair as she picked at the bread, he realized just how alone they were. How was he going to manage this situation?

Everything Fallon dealt with on a daily basis was with intention and careful execution. Everything he was involved with had to be carefully orchestrated if he was to keep all the wheels spinning. Until Isabelle.

From the second he'd met this lady, he'd been thrown from his normal course.

A series of rash decisions later, and here he was eating with her—the beauty whose company he found refreshing, her spirit honest and enchanting. Every moment with her was like venturing into a foreign land, with spontaneity and unexpected sights around every corner. And his duty was to find a way to consider her as nothing but another mission to complete. He cleared his throat and took a large gulp of water. They were alone, but he didn't have to dwell on the pout of her lips as she considered every bite of bread.

"I've written to your father to ease his mind about your whereabouts," he informed her.

Her gaze snapped to his. "And you told him I was here? Locked in your bedchamber with you? Sharing a quiet dinner without proper dress or even a cracked door for propriety?"

"I neglected to mention that part. I thought it best to keep that between us."

"I should be the one to write to him. He doesn't know you. He'll want to hear from me."

"You're in no condition to write letters. And your father does know me. You must trust me for now. You can write to him soon."

She nodded but said nothing for a moment as she reached for a piece of meat from the tray, then took a small bite of the pheasant with a bit more force than was required. When she looked up at him, it was with the doe eyes that made him want to dive in and swim around for the evening. "I'm quite ruined, aren't I? Will we be forced to marry?"

"Not if I can help it. No one knows you're here save the two of us, my driver, the doctor, and your father. Not even my household staff are aware of your presence here." He had to protect her reputation. If word got out that she was here… She was right, he would have to marry her. And that couldn't happen. He wouldn't allow it. No one wanted another wedding meant to solve a problem, least of all him. "I'm quite good at keeping secrets."

"I'm awful at it, but since I have no one to talk to, I think we're safe for the moment." She attempted a smile as she sifted through the small bowl of fruit and retrieved a strawberry, twirling it between her fingers by the green stem.

"I'm sorry it must be this way," Fallon offered.

"I read the note while you were gone," she admitted a moment later, still looking down at the strawberry spinning back and forth in her hand.

"The one on normally scented paper?"

She looked up, meeting his gaze with sorrow-filled eyes. "The one written in a hand far too similar to my own. Everyone will think I stole from the museum, from my own family."

"It was a forgery. I'll find the other copies and have them destroyed," Fallon promised as he stabbed a piece of meat with his fork.

"How?"

Didn't she understand? That was the simple part in all of this. He'd already begun the process the second he'd returned to headquarters with her unconscious in his arms. Orders had been given hours ago, and even now they were being carried out. *This*, sitting here alone with her and trying to maintain a business demeanor, was the difficult portion. *She views you as a friend and now her kidnapper,* he reminded himself. *Nothing can come of this time spent together, and nothing should.* "You need to worry only about resting. You have a head injury. You shouldn't be concerned with—"

"The things it said about my father... I don't like discord. This could be the start of a battle that will rage within my family. You don't know how he can be. He could believe I wrote those awful words."

"He won't." Fallon almost reached across the table to grab her hand and comfort her, but he caught himself.

"He believes the worst of my mother. Why not believe this as well?"

"Lack of scented paper." Fallon couldn't explain further. Isabelle couldn't find out the truth about the Spare Heirs or her own father's past dealings with Reginald Grapling. Not only would those answers lead to questions he couldn't answer, but Isabelle could be killed. He couldn't bear the thought that Grapling's reach could extend as far as this bedchamber, but there was too much at stake to dismiss the man's threats. As much as he would like to destroy any affection she might harbor for Grapling, Fallon must keep silent. The image of Isabelle's limp form on the museum floor filled his memory, no matter how he wished he could banish it. "You simply have to trust me."

"It was shameful to read...as if I'd voiced the worst of my thoughts about my family. Whoever wrote it... How did the thief know all of that? The penmanship truly did look like my own. Perhaps I am responsible for the theft and I simply struck my head and can't recall. I could be mad. It happens to people on occasion."

He leaned forward, studying the trouble evident in her eyes. "You didn't write that note. Those weren't your thoughts. You know what's true and what isn't."

She nodded and stared down at the table between them for a moment. "I would never say such things aloud, much less write them in a note someone could find and read. I would never steal from my family." She looked up at him, unshed tears pooling in her eyes. "But I did think something similar when I first learned of Victoria's wedding. There was some truth there."

"There was no truth there," Fallon countered. It was only after the words were out of his mouth that he heard the harsh edge to his voice and sighed, leaning back into his chair. It was a commanding voice meant to cease an argument between men. This was different. "The person who wrote that note tried to kill you. That same person stole the artwork you look after and left you for dead to be blamed for the theft. There is no truth in anything there, my lady, only deceit."

Isabelle fell silent for a minute as she finished her glass of wine. "Isabelle."

His fists clenched and unclenched beneath the table, and he stared at her. While he wanted the use of her name, wasn't that yet another layer of proper social conduct vanishing from between them? She was already dining in his private quarters and confiding her secret thoughts.

He shouldn't encourage anything that diminished his control over the situation. He had the Spares to oversee. She was a distraction from everything he should be focused on. He couldn't allow himself to feel anything for her. She would imprint herself on his life simply by existing here in his world. If he succeeded and solved this scandal for her, she would be returned to her father's care. All would return to normal for both of them, and the light she brought into his life would be extinguished. Though it was his job to protect her, in the end was he not the one who needed to be protected?

What would be left of him when she was gone?

If keeping her here wasn't wise, using her given name while doing so was lunacy. In spite of all of that, he parted his lips and murmured the most beautiful word in the English language. "Isabelle. You may call me Fallon."

"Once a pirate kidnaps you, I believe using given names is acceptable," she mused, returning her wineglass to the table as she spoke.

"You know all of this is for your own protection."

Isabelle waved away his comment, a hint of a smile brightening her face as she studied him. "Fallon St. James."

"Yes?" He wasn't certain, but he was taking this sudden lack of sullen glares to mean she was becoming resigned to this arrangement. If he were wise, he would welcome her cross statements and sadness as a way of keeping distance between them, but where she was concerned, his usual wisdom didn't exist. Instead he leaned forward, basking in the warmth of her sunny disposition.

"This is your bedchamber," she stated.

"We already established that, but then you *do* have a head wound."

Lifting her hand to touch the upholstered panel on

the wall beside her, she traced the edge of a flower depicted in purple thread. "This room with the flowers. Is where you reside."

He sat back in his chair, knowing where her curiosity was leading the conversation. "Do you have a question about it?"

"No." She looked around, studying every detail of the room. "It's only that you don't seem the sort to have such an abundance of flowers around him. You don't even dance."

"What does dancing have to do with the decor? Are you feeling well? I can send for the doctor again."

"I'm as well as I could be under the circumstances, I presume. I'm surprised is all."

"That a gentleman who doesn't dance and lacks a heartfelt smile has flowers in his bedchamber?" he asked, filling in the gaps for her.

She returned her gaze to his. "This is a bit more than one arrangement on a side table, Fallon."

"The room wasn't always mine, I admit. But I chose not to change it when I had the opportunity." This was a subject he never spoke about. Of course, he never allowed anyone inside his bedchamber to see the decor either. "It's like being in a garden," he mused in a rare moment of honesty.

"And gardens are peaceful escapes from life," she murmured, completing his thought. "I understand, quite well actually."

"Good." He glanced away from her and rubbed a hand over the back of his neck. The discomfort of having exposed so much of his private world to her in such a short period of time made him anxious to move. He couldn't allow his guard down any further, or things would get uncomfortable between them during her stay. He should go. He had responsibilities. Pushing back from the table, he stood. "Do you need anything before I—"

"You're leaving? Where will you sleep? Am I not to stay here...in your bed?"

"You are," he replied as he moved to the fireplace to stir the coals. He couldn't look in her direction while she was discussing staying in his bed, not if he wished to keep this a business matter. "There are adequate accommodations in my dressing room."

"It can't be that adequate. It's your dressing room, after all."

"Don't concern yourself with any of that." He couldn't stay here with her now that he'd completed his task of supplying her food. He'd felt his guard slipping already while they dined together. He needed to leave.

"I can't allow you to—"

"I've slept there many nights," he cut in, already halfway to the door.

"Why?"

"If there isn't anything else I can get for you, I'll go," he said, ignoring her question. He'd placed enough details of his life out for her examination tonight without adding more to the list. "I have a few things to see to this evening. I should allow you your privacy. I'll see myself back in later to go to my dressing room for the night."

"I don't want..." she began, but her voice trailed away when he didn't stop to argue with her.

"Try to get some rest." He paused with his hand on the doorknob, turning back to look at her for the first time since their discussion of his bedchamber. She looked lost and small across the room in that sea of flowers. But across the room is exactly where she needed to stay if he was to continue on as he was. "Good evening, Isabelle."

He turned and left the room, not slowing his pace until he'd reached his desk in the library—the one place where his life made sense. On some level he knew nothing could distract him from what he'd left behind in his bedchamber, but the faster he could repair Isabelle's situation, the faster he could return his life to its usual patterns. No matter how empty his home would be once she was gone.

∽

Isabelle wasn't where he'd left her. Reginald Grapling smiled as he listened to the man who'd delivered the news to him. "And the confession note?" he asked.

"Gone. We didn't see a sign of her or the note, sir. Did we?" The young man turned to his fellow, who stood turning his hat around and around in his hands as if it were his job to do so.

"The place was empty when we went back for the statue you said you wanted."

"All is going to plan then," Reginald mused as he turned to admire the artwork that now leaned against various walls in the small rented room. "Did you load the statue into the carriage?"

"We were unable to move it through the side door of the museum…sir."

"It's neither here nor there. Leave it." The statue had been a fleeting desire to increase his take in the heist anyway. That wasn't what mattered just now.

What mattered was his bait had been taken.

Only one man swept in and took control of any situation, repairing every detail for those around him. It could be counted upon like clockwork. So predictable. "St. James," he muttered with a chuckle.

He'd pull his men back now, increase his watch wherever he'd put the girl. And while he could have hidden her away anywhere, he wouldn't place Isabelle in some safe house on the outskirts of town. She was inside headquarters. And if his ranks were thick in that section of town, they'd be thin elsewhere.

Fallon St. James didn't rule London—not anymore.

Reginald turned back to the room. The two young men were still standing in front of him, awaiting his instruction. "Are you ready for the next move in our game?" he asked them. "Because I am."

Eleven

Dear Lord Knottsby,

I have new information regarding your daughter's condition. Apologies if my earlier missive was concerning to you on an already-troublesome day. Lady Isabelle is awake now and is as well as can be expected after surviving a strike to the head. Fear not, as I am seeing to her safety. I hope that you will see to your other pressing issues from the day and allow me to handle this situation in your stead.

I had her head wound looked after and now have her hidden from any prying eyes. She will remain safe here until the danger has been eliminated. I will have word spread as best we can that she left town to visit family in the country in order to protect her reputation given the events of the week. Her stay is comfortable, but a few dresses wouldn't go amiss. You may send her things with the gentleman delivering this note; he's been instructed to wait. Further information to follow in the morning. Rest assured, I will do what I must.

—St. James

FALLON SIGNED THE BUNDLE OF DOCUMENTS IN FRONT
of him and handed the stack off to the man waiting
at the corner of his desk. "See that this reaches Lord
Elandor with the treasury," he stated, watching as one
of the newer members of the secret society stuffed the
papers into his pocket and turned for the door.

The young man had been filling in where necessary
until Fallon could fully assess his strengths. It was one
of the many roles Fallon filled for the Heirs—that of
assessing people for proper utilization. Some men were
an instant fit, like Ash Claughbane, his new partner in
the steam engine industry, but others required some
guidance. If only he hadn't failed so miserably years
ago at assessing Grapling's character, Fallon's current
situation would be quite different. Isabelle wouldn't be
upstairs in his bedchamber. He wouldn't be considering returning to check on her at this very moment,
nor would he have been thinking about it every other
moment thus far today…

He shook off the thought and focused on the young
man now leaving his library. Soon Fallon would have
to find a more permanent position for the man. Fallon
could tell by the sharp look in his eye that he could
take on more for the organization. Hopefully this time
Fallon wasn't being deceived. His mind returned to
the woman three floors above him, unable to return to
her home, injured, stolen from, and all done as part of
some sort of revenge against the Spare Heirs—against
Fallon. He grimaced to himself as he scrawled out a
note to follow up with the young man who'd just left

the room and another about taking Isabelle some food as well as the trunk her father had sent for her that now sat in the corner of his library.

Fallon had slipped past Isabelle last night and again this morning while she slept. He hadn't had as much good fortune as she when it came to rest last night, but his lack of sleep had given him more time to set his plan against Grapling in motion. He was already receiving updates on the search for the man, the art, and the other copies of the incriminating letter. The search had proven fruitless so far, but his team was only hours into the job.

There were fewer men than he'd like stationed around London, but with constant communication with them, Fallon was free to manage the operation from headquarters—and check in on Isabelle through-out the day. It was customary to check in frequently on someone suffering from a head wound. At least that was how he justified his actions to himself today. Tomorrow was another story.

He read through the report in front of him. He should take Isabelle some tea at least. She would surely be awake by this time of day.

A second later, the door opened amid the sound of heavy footsteps. Fallon didn't have to look up to know who had entered—even his boots were loud against the floor.

Fallon tensed at what he knew awaited him once he looked up from the reports on his desk. He owed the man some type of condolences for the mire his wedding had become. But what was there to say? Fallon didn't know where to begin. His friend hadn't even wished to marry and was now the center of the talk in town after that wedding hadn't happened. And Hardaway was enduring it all for the sake of a lady's reputation and the future of the Spare Heirs. This couldn't be mended with a simple *Sorry, ol' friend. Tough break, that.* It was best to keep the man distracted until the scandal settled down. Hardaway was always happiest when he was busy with work.

Fallon sighed and glanced up at Hardaway. "Have you had any luck at all finding Grapling's known associates?"

Hardaway sat down hard in the chair and glared at Fallon from across the desk. "No 'How's your day? My, my, Hardaway, my friend, you were left at the altar in front of most of London society only yesterday morning. Are you certain you're ready to return to your work?'"

"Was that supposed to be me?" Fallon asked as he shuffled the pile of papers in front of him into a stack and set them aside for something to keep his hands busy. "I would never say 'my, my.'"

"Nice to know you care, St. James."

Fallon eyed his friend. Fallon *did* care, but he also knew what Hardaway most needed. It hadn't slipped Fallon's notice that his friend had stayed the night at headquarters.

Hardaway stayed in his room here only when he was having difficulties with his father. It was an easy bet that he'd stay tonight as well. It couldn't be pleasant to have everyone whispering your name as you passed.

"This outcome was never my intention," Fallon stated. Public humiliation wasn't an easy thing to endure. On the other hand, he'd known Hardaway for years, and the man was made of tougher material than what town talk could rip apart. Still, he didn't like seeing his friend in such a situation. "What can I do to help matters?"

Hardaway batted his question away without a reply and tilted his chair back on two legs to prop his boots on the edge of the desk.

"I hear you're still up to terrorizing the local taverns. Wild time of it last night?" Fallon asked, changing the subject.

"All to mend my broken heart," Hardaway said with a hand clutched over his chest.

"I wasn't aware that barmaids had that ability."

Hardaway chuckled. "I'm back today, ready to focus on a proper job."

"I thought you might feel that way. We have a mess that needs to be sorted quickly and quietly."

"My specialty." He lowered his chair to the floor with a loud thud and leaned forward.

Fallon raised a brow at Hardaway's claim that he could ever be quiet about anything but didn't contradict him. He needed his friend's expertise just now. "It's Grapling."

"Right you are. It doesn't sit well with me that such a weasel of a man is still evading our men. If we don't find him soon—"

"He resurfaced yesterday during your—" Fallon broke off, searching for less painful words than the obvious ones.

"Go ahead, then. Say it. During my blasted wedding."

Fallon worked to choose his words, eyeing his friend as he considered the consequences of every line of conversation from this point forward. "He stole a roomful of art from the British Museum. There was a lady involved," he finally said.

"A lady?" Hardaway asked in alarm. "Was it as it was before? Did she live? St. James, how are we to cover up the murder of a lady? We can't. We shouldn't, at any rate. And with the authorities involved...there goes the secrecy of the entire Spare Heirs Society. A title, a public laughingstock, and now my club? My work? Damn, I need a drink." He rose from his chair and stalked across the room to the decanter Fallon kept filled for his men.

"Calm yourself. The Spares hasn't seen its last day yet. She's alive, and we're avoiding the mess of authorities. For the moment, anyway."

"Who is she?" Hardaway asked, returning with a glass in his hand. "How the hell are we supposed to keep a—I'm assuming—horribly injured lady quiet? Not to mention hiding a heist at the blasted British Museum? Ladies talk, St. James. They aren't like you with your secrets and glares."

"I need you to retrieve copies of a letter. I put Haperly on inquiring at the *Post*, but—"

"But I'm better at document retrieval?" Hardaway asked, the recent fire clearly still on his mind.

"You're the best we have. Check with the usual publications first to stem that issue, then question everyone involved with daily activities at the museum. Remind Mr. Jasper of our continued patronage and convince him in any way you can to keep the theft quiet. He's the head librarian—it's his reputation at stake as well."

"That should be an interesting conversation, seeing as how you had that brawl there only last week," Hardaway cut in.

Fallon ignored the reminder of his moment of impulsive behavior and continued. "The copies of the letter we're searching for…they'll be forgeries. How many skilled forgers do we know?"

"Five, counting Sims and Gordon."

"There are three copies of this letter that are unaccounted for at the moment. We need all of them and to keep more from being written."

"What's this letter about? Something like that hardly seems important in light of the circumstances. Grapling, an injured lady, and a theft—and you want me to spend the day finding copies of a letter?"

There were things Fallon could hide from everyone, and then there was what Fallon could hide from everyone but Hardaway. He should have known that from the beginning. Simply because he couldn't tell Isabelle or her father about Grapling didn't mean he needed to keep silent with Hardaway. He had to tell someone the full story, and Hardaway should know it. If Fallon sent his friend in search of the evidence against Isabelle, Hardaway would discover the truth anyway. "These are Grapling's words, not Lady Isabelle's," he said passing the letter over the desk to his friend.

"Grapling's words… Lady Isabelle? My former intended's sister?" Hardaway grabbed the note and unfolded it. A mixture of emotions crossed his face as he read the words, but the last expression matched Fallon's own: determination. He tossed the note back onto the desktop with a low whistle. "*Enjoy the out-come of your selfish concerns*...those were the last words the authorities said to him at his sentencing before he was imprisoned. That conniving bastard. We have to find him. Art theft is bad enough. This?" He nodded toward the note on the desk. "This is personal."

"Indeed." It was more personal now for Fallon than it had been just a few days before, though he would never admit it.

"She was almost my family, St. James. And her father... I'm certain he isn't pleased."

"He doesn't know that Grapling is responsible, and we must keep it that way. Word is being spread that Lady Isabelle left town yesterday. The family is blaming her absence on a visit to an ill aunt. But we need to find the other copies of that letter, wherever they may be."

"No one will be suspicious of her sudden disappear-ance as long as they're all still talking about the giant blun-der that was my damned wedding," Hardaway grumbled.

"Good."

"Good? Have a heart, man."

"It's good if the gossip stays focused on her sick aunt and your wedding as opposed to getting closer to the truth." The truth would end in either Isabelle's imprisonment or her marriage to Fallon, and neither were good options.

"She isn't consoling her sister somewhere, then, is she? Is she terribly injured? Don't say near death. Grapling is a right nasty piece of work. She could still be in danger if he can get his hands on her, not to mention the potential of being hauled off to prison for theft."

"Lady Isabelle is safe."

Hardaway narrowed his eyes on him. "What have you done with her? Not some moldy safe house, I hope. I had to stay in that one in Bath last year. You remember? I'm still trying to forget the experience. It had rats, St. James, *rats*! Large ones. I think one crawled on me while I slept. Little claws… That place isn't fit for a lady. I know the wedding didn't go through, but we were almost family. I won't stand for her sitting alone or worse, with the likes of one of the Spares, while we investigate this mess."

"She's quite well."

Hardaway eyed him in a way only a friend since childhood could do. "You didn't."

"What?"

"You brought her here, didn't you? You never have trusted the men to do their jobs. Damn. St. James, you know you can't do everything yourself."

"I couldn't allow Grapling to get that close to killing her again," he answered honestly.

"Then we better find that bastard. She can't stay in the guest rooms here forever. The men will find out. This is a bachelor residence of the worst variety."

A moment passed, and Fallon said nothing. What was there to say?

"St. James, tell me you put her in one of the guest rooms."

"As opposed to…"

"Some dungeon beneath the kitchens you've never told us about, complete with bars on the door to keep your enemies at bay."

"She's well cared for, Hardaway."

"It doesn't matter how many cherubs you have painted on the ceiling, it's still a dungeon. She's a lady! I know you don't care for such nuance, but—"

"Stop your yelling. I saw to the matter myself. She's well settled abovestairs."

"Oh." Then a moment later his eyes widened. "Oooh. Is she now?" Hardaway chuckled.

Fallon stared his friend down across the desk. "We need to get those letters, Hardaway."

"Very well. I know you're fond of your secrets. At least she isn't pining over me, her lost love."

"I'm not above hitting you."

"Hmm, a sensitive subject, I see." He laughed and stood, leaving his empty glass on Fallon's desk. "I'll get your confession notes, and then we can sort out Grapling for good."

Fallon watched him leave before returning to his work. Isabelle was simply another mission for the organization, a matter to handle. His friend had the wrong idea entirely with his laughter and knowing looks. Five minutes later, when he'd read the same line of text over seven times without knowing what it said, he sighed and stood from his desk. "Blast you, Hardaway. What the devil do you know about it?"

He went to the corner and hefted Isabelle's trunk from the floor. If he couldn't focus on work at the moment, he could take the opportunity to feed and clothe his newest responsibility. Slowly he made his way out of the library and up the stairs, to where she waited for him.

Dropping the trunk in the hall outside his door, he sank to the top of it for a moment. What had Knottsby sent over for Isabelle's stay, a large box of stones? After three flights of stairs, he needed a moment to catch his breath. Whether the need for a rest was from carrying her trunk or because he had to walk inside this room with it as soon as he stood was debatable. "She's a job, nothing more," he whispered to the empty hall.

Standing, he unlocked his door and pulled the trunk inside. What he found on the other side of the door, however, stopped him cold.

Isabelle was leaning against the windowsill and staring back into the room, barefoot and rumpled from sleeping in her dress from the previous day. She'd removed her own bandage, and the look on her face was one of the deepest sort of agony. He crossed the room to her in an instant. He shouldn't have left her alone, even to rest. "Is it your injury? I'll send for Dr. Mathers immediately."

He was already lifting a hand to the wounded area when she replied, "My head isn't aching like it did yesterday. I believe it's healing."

Fallon pulled back, his hand falling to his side as he studied her. "What's troubling you? Is your stay that unbearable already? I had some of your things brought around. I want you to be comfortable while you're here."

She looked up from her intense study of the rug at her feet, meeting his gaze for the first time since he'd stepped into the room. "Happiness grows from love, doesn't it?"

"I don't know that I'm an authority on the matter," Fallon hedged. He knew Isabelle to be a lady quick to fall in love, but it couldn't be with him. Suddenly uncomfortable with standing so close to her while alone and discussing love, he moved to one end of the sofa and sat, facing the fire. That would surely be a safe distance.

Unfortunately Isabelle followed him and sat down at his side to continue their conversation. "Love hasn't brought me happiness." Pulling her feet up beneath her, she wrapped her arms around her knees and continued. "I thought I'd found love, Fallon. I thought… but I'm far from happy. It brought me only heartache and bitterness toward my sister."

He shifted beside her, unsure what to say. Of all the confrontations and discussions he'd had successfully over the years, nothing prepared him for chatting about love with Isabelle.

"If one finds love, one will find happiness," she continued on, unaware how out of his depths he was. "There will be no fighting, no hurt. But I'm hurt. Horribly hurt." She leaned her head against his shoulder and stared ahead into the dying flames of the fire.

Against all he knew was wise, he adjusted his position and wrapped an arm around her shoulder. He couldn't sit by and allow her to be in pain, physical or mental, and do nothing to offer her comfort. She'd called him a friend, hadn't she? Surely this was within the realm of friendly behavior. Only a second later, she leaned into him as if she'd done so a thousand times before. And he grazed his fingers over the soft skin on her upper arm just beneath the short sleeve of her dress as if it was the most natural, easy action he'd ever made. It was so simple, so easy, and that made it that much more dangerous.

This is not the way to keep her at a safe distance, Fal. But he ignored the warning.

"I always thought love would be the golden light that daydreams are made of. It would shine all around me, and my days would forevermore be filled with joy. But I find I'm left rather empty—after Hardaway and then my attempt to be open to finding a new love with Mr. Grapling."

"You love your sister," he countered.

"I do. And she betrayed me. My heart aches from it." Isabelle sniffed and curled even closer to his side.

Had her sister truly betrayed Isabelle? Ladies were expected to do as their families required of them. And Fallon had made certain that her family had required Victoria to marry Hardaway. It had been the best solution to his problem at the time. It was his job to keep the Spares operational, and he didn't regret his actions. Now, however, sitting with Isabelle, hearing how deeply the matter had hurt her, was…less than ideal.

Guilt assaulted him, making him glad Isabelle wasn't looking up at him just now. But even if he hadn't forced the marriage to occur, she still wouldn't be with Hardaway. What hold did the man have on her? And more irritating still, when would that hold end? The entire subject filled him with the restless need to get up and pace the room or stir the fire, but he didn't move. Perhaps if Fallon could help mend things between Isabelle and her sister, it would ease his mind. Finally he asked, "Did your sister have a choice in the matter?"

"I would have refused to marry the man I knew she loved," Isabelle murmured.

A muscle near his eye twitched at her continued proclamation that she loved blasted Hardaway, but he didn't otherwise react. Instead Fallon shifted to meet her gaze. "She did just that." Aside from believing herself in love with his most unsuitable friend, Isabelle had the wrong of the situation where her sister was involved. Victoria hadn't betrayed Isabelle at all. "Isabelle, she didn't marry Hardaway. It only took her time to come to the same conclusion as you. She was doing what your father required her to do in the beginning, but in the end, she couldn't go along with those plans."

"Hmmm, I hadn't considered it in that light. But that would mean… Am *I* the reason why she fled the church? I'd assumed…knowing Victoria's opinion on marriage…"

Fallon didn't answer, since he didn't know the truth behind the lady's actions, but he rather suspected Isabelle had something to do with Victoria running away.

"If that is true, it's a rather large weight lifted." She released a heavy sigh and sank back against him once again.

Fallon stroked the outside of her arm and stared into the fire. Her cheek pressed to his chest as she leaned against him, her legs curled up beside her. How long had they been here? It was the middle of the day. His men would be looking for him. Yet he didn't make a move to leave.

"He should have demanded my hand instead, come to my rescue," Isabelle said as if it were part of an ongoing conversation, seemingly unaware that they'd been sitting together in companionable silence.

"Who?"

"Hardaway," she explained, sitting up just enough to meet his gaze. "The lady's true love always comes to her rescue in the end, but he didn't even put up a fight about marrying my sister."

"He certainly drank himself into a stupor over the news," Fallon recalled.

"Did he mention me?"

His answer would only cause her further pain. He wanted to take her hurt away. But perhaps it would be like a piece of metal being taken from a wound. It hurt like the devil as it happened, but it allowed the wound to heal. Fallon watched her, debating the issue for another moment before answering. "No. He didn't mention you."

"Oh." She frowned up at him, her cheeks growing pink with the knowledge. "He didn't think of me when he arranged to marry my sister," she confirmed, her words thick with emotion. "He didn't think of me at all."

Isabelle was worthy of all the happiness life had to offer. She should never be made to feel less than perfect. She was full of life and was everything bright and beautiful in the world. He would do anything to take that look off of her face.

"I thought of you," he offered, wanting to help her, to fix this. He never spoke so openly to anyone. What was happening to him?

"What did you think?"

"I considered how hurt you would be," he admitted, keeping to himself the part where he was responsible for setting everything in motion. "I knew you fancied yourself in love with Hardaway."

A fine line formed between her brows as she looked up at him. "You don't think my love was true?"

"Do you love him still?"

She studied him, saying nothing.

Had he offended her? Honesty was somewhat new to him, certainly where ladies were concerned. Perhaps she was correct and he was in the wrong. He'd only had one example of love in his life, but he knew it had been love. He missed her even today. "I loved someone once. Not in a romantic fashion, but love nonetheless. I love her still. It doesn't end. That's love."

"Perhaps I never had love to begin with. It seemed so close at the time. Do you think there's a chance I could still find it? Perhaps with Mr. Grapling? My notions on the romantic sort of love apparently aren't as clear as they should be."

He tensed at the mention of the man's name. No, there was nothing that even resembled love between Isabelle and Reginald Grapling, but Fallon remained silent on the subject. "My notions aren't as clear as they should be either," he said instead.

"Will we figure it out one day?"

"You will," he promised, stroking his fingers down the back of her arm as he spoke. "You desire love in your life."

"You don't? Of course you don't. That would complicate your businesslike bachelor life, wouldn't it?" She gave him a playful nudge and smiled at him.

"It would indeed."

But a second later, the smile slipped from her face. "I've complicated your life. My stay here—"

"You have. But it isn't your stay that's complicating things," he said, unable to resist the pull of her warmth, the comfort of her weight as she pressed into his side. Everything with Isabelle was unexpected, unplanned, and terribly easy. The way she wore her heart on her sleeve and the depth of her goodness called to him, begging for him to place every one of his closely held cards out on the table for her to see. Friendship…was that what this was? This need to share, to be open? He never shared with anyone.

"You came to my rescue," she said, pulling him from his questioning thoughts. Her round eyes were wide as she studied him, a new liveliness making them sparkle. "You thought of me, and then you saved my life."

"I suppose I did," he hedged. At least he'd scooped her from the floor and brought her here.

"Fallon…"

He fixed problems. That's what he did, that's what he always did. And friend or not, she was simply another problem to fix. She had to be. "Don't," he commanded in a soft voice.

"Don't do what?"

"Look at me with stars in your eyes. It's the same way you looked at Hardaway when you were hiding behind those blasted cakes."

"He wasn't worthy of stars, as it turned out," she said with a sheepish smile.

"Neither am I. You deserve all the stars in the sky. But this is far too complicated, as I said before."

"What is so complicated, Fallon? Is it so wrong to lov—"

"No. I mean yes. It is wrong." He shifted away from her, ran a hand though his hair, and pushed to his feet.

She couldn't decide she was in love with him just like that, like she had with Hardaway. She was staying in Fallon's bedchamber. He'd put excuses for her absence in place, was doing everything he could to protect her reputation through this mess, but not marrying her would become that much more difficult if she went and fell for him. Blast it all, marriage to him was not going to happen. Everything with her was already so...

Damn. Perhaps he needed to visit one of the brothels he oversaw if he were to survive this day, let alone this week. He wanted everything about her, and she was looking at him like he was the hero of one of those blasted stories in her head. He was no hero. "I...I have to go see to my work. I'll have food sent up for you. My housekeeper will have to be trusted to know you're here."

Mrs. Featherfitch, that's whom he needed. If he had some distance from Isabelle, he would see the other side of this in no time.

"You wouldn't have kidnapped me if you didn't care about me. You don't have to return the sentiment, but don't leave. I don't want you to go. Surely you can see it too. Now that my eyes are open to it, I understand. It's real this time. Fallon, I lov—"

"You're in my bedchamber, Isabelle," Fallon cut in before she could say more. "I can't go far, can I?"

He didn't stay to hear her retort, but he was certain it would have something to do with her being kidnapped and his prisoner. He, on the other hand, was beginning to wonder: Between the two of them, who, exactly, was holding whom prisoner?

❧

Isabelle had fallen back on the sofa with an unladylike thud, and that's where she'd been for the past twenty minutes. For the first three minutes, she'd been concerned with appearing tragically abandoned for the occasion of Fallon's return, but he hadn't come back. The next seventeen minutes had stretched out as she studied the subtle rosebuds painted on the ceiling above her head.

"Fallon St. James," she whispered to herself. He wore subdued colors and refused to dance at balls. He certainly didn't meet the qualifications on her original list. Except that he'd rescued her. He'd thought of her feelings. He was always kind to her. Their conversations flowed unlike any that she'd ever had with a gentleman, in the ballroom or over tea. Perhaps that was why she'd never considered him for her list.

With him there were no nerves, only an odd peace and easiness she'd never experienced before. Wasn't a nervous inability to speak a requirement when in the presence of love? Not that any of this mattered since he clearly did not want to be listed among her potential husbands. *Far too complicated*, he'd complained. What about this was so complicated?

At the squeaking sound of the door opening, Isabelle bolted up from the sofa. "Fal…" she began, but her voice trailed away. It was a woman filling the doorway, a shocked look on her face. She was a sturdy-looking older woman in a dark ensemble that had seen better days. Was this Fallon's housekeeper?

"Oh! There is someone here." The housekeeper jumped, almost dropping the tray in her arms. "I thought he was teasing. He's not one to do such a thing, always so serious and quiet, but it caught me so off guard, you know. But here you are in his bed-chamber." Her eyebrows rose a bit, clearly offended on some level by the impropriety of the situation. "Forgive my surprise."

Isabelle uncurled her feet from beneath her and stood to greet the woman. "We can be surprised by this news together since I hadn't planned on being a houseguest. I'm Lady Isabelle Fairlyn."

"A lady…here." The housekeeper's face flushed for a moment before she collected herself. "How…interesting."

Interesting? This was the most activity Isabelle had experienced since her arrival, other than Fallon's company. And she was trying to put that from her mind for the moment, to concentrate on the housekeeper. "It isn't interesting at all, to be quite honest."

"I'm sure it isn't. I'm Mrs. Featherfitch. I have the run of things around here. Well. The house part anyway." She turned away to place the tea tray on the table where Isabelle had shared dinner with Fallon the previous night.

Isabelle had cleared the table last night and placed everything beside the door, where it was still piled high now. At her home, someone would have cleared the dishes away when the fire was stoked for the night, but the oversight was easily explained by the locked door and her current imprisonment. Perhaps now that the housekeeper knew about her, Isabelle could have someone attend to a thing or two.

"It's a pleasure to make your acquaintance," Isabelle offered with a smile as she tugged at her dress to straighten it. "My stay will hopefully be short. I won't be too much trouble."

"A short stay? Only for a night or two, then?" she asked with her back turned and poured Isabelle a cup of tea.

"I'm not certain. Mr. St. James may be able to better answer that question."

The housekeeper busied herself for another moment moving plates around on the table unnecessarily all the while grumbling under her breath, "If Lady Herron were here…disgrace…her very bed, I'm sure."

Isabelle couldn't hear all of her mumbled words, but she heard enough. Mrs. Featherfitch had the wrong idea about Isabelle's presence, but it was the mention of another lady that caught her attention. "Lady Herron? Did she live here? Was this her home?"

Mrs. Featherfitch trailed a hand down the floral draperies with the reverence one would have for a fallen queen. Yet Isabelle couldn't help but notice the dust the woman released with her touch. "This home now belongs to Mr. St. James, but Lady Herron's spirit lives on."

"Does it indeed?" Isabelle hung on every detail of the housekeeper's story. "A true apparition? I suppose you've heard the doors opening and closing at all hours of the night? Voices in the halls? Last night I thought I heard singing, and I wondered then—"

"Of course not!" the woman said, glaring at Isabelle.

"I only meant that Lady Herron lives on in these walls, breathing through the flowers she loved so."

"Really?" Isabelle lifted an embroidered pillow from the sofa and examined it. "Is she ever seen though? I heard once of a spirit who would warn all guests to leave the home at once, but I always thought it rather unwelcoming. It must have been terribly disappointing for the owners of the home to always have their guests fleeing into the night. But if she's the friendly sort…"

"A lady of her standing in society would never stoop so low as to be an apparition."

"Hmmm. I see." With the noise Isabelle had heard at all hours last night, she would be the judge of that. "Who was she, if you don't mind? I'm sleeping in her former room, am I not? It would be nice to know something of the history."

Mrs. Featherfitch thawed a bit at her question. "Lady Herron was a vibrant lady, well respected in town. She lost his lordship early in her marriage, the poor dear. She made the best of things, though. She was strong of will. But after many years, her ladyship grew lonely. She longed for companionship, a gentleman in her life."

"I quite understand her plight. I'm searching for love in my own life."

"Indeed." The woman's eyes flitted to the bed with a judgmental gleam before looking back to Isabelle. "She looked about for a husband, but by then she was of an age."

"Oh, how devastating." Isabelle couldn't imagine the horror of proceeding with life knowing that her time to love had spoiled in the sun—like that time when the groom had left a pail of milk sitting near the garden gate. She wouldn't wish being spoiled milk upon anyone, especially not someone with a love of flowers like Lady Herron.

"Then along came Mr. St. James." Mrs. Featherfitch paused to smile over some memory. "He was far too young for her, of course, at barely nineteen. And untitled."

"What does that matter?" Isabelle bristled.

"It doesn't, my lady, except to those who wish to have a piece of the world you live in. Suffice to say, St. James became a large part of Lady Herron's life."

"They were married, defying society's demands otherwise?" Isabelle asked, her heart clenching at the romance of it all even if she couldn't envision the man she knew being happy with a woman so much older than he. Still, she supposed, age was only a number where the heart was concerned. "I didn't know St. James was once married. That would mean he's a widower. He's never mentioned—"

"No. He remains unwed. Mr. St. James and her ladyship were friends of a sort. He lived here. At first we were all a bit dismayed at the arrangement. But they were so happy together. Soon, Lady Herron was no longer keeping to her room but was taking walks with St. James. They attended balls again, things she hadn't done in some time. He helped her live again, fixed her right up."

"That's beautiful," Isabelle murmured. He'd helped an elderly lady to regain her strength. He'd fixed that lady's problems, just as he was doing for Isabelle. He was truly a kind man.

"It was a lovely thing when he came to live here. Talk in town made it seem tawdry, and in some ways it was. He did stay with her night after night, right here in this room."

And suddenly everything clicked into place in Isabelle's mind, filling a space she reserved for unromantic things that Victoria told her and memories she'd rather forget. "In this room—"

"Yes," the woman confirmed. "As close companions."

Isabelle narrowed her eyes at the housekeeper. There had to be something she was missing. Fallon wouldn't do such a thing, would he? "Companions still require their own accommodations," she tried to argue. "My aunt has a companion, Lula. I'm unsure of her true name, as that's what we've always called her. What I do know is that my aunt put Lula in the servant's quarters belowstairs and my mother called it shameful. I'm quite sure if that is shameful, then not providing a companion any sort of room is unspeakable."

"Lady Isabelle, pardon my phrasing, but as I'm quite certain you're seasoned to such things given our current surroundings, your St. James was a kept man."

"He isn't my... We haven't. I mean to say, we are not... A...kept man?" After attempting to argue the various misconceptions in her last statement, her mind could only focus on the one: Fallon had been a kept man. Was that how he gained this home?

None of this could be true. She knew Fallon, didn't she? Or had she dreamt him into becoming the version of the man that now resided in her heart? She sank into one of the chairs at the table, not the least interested in the food placed there.

"They were quite close despite the vast difference in their ages," Mrs. Featherfitch continued. "I believe he still blames himself for not being at her side the day she passed. He left to attend some meeting. Even in those days he would slip away for such things on occasion. Her ladyship was reading a book in the garden, and...well, that was that." She dabbed at the corner of her eye with the back of a finger. "God rest her soul. The house was in a frenzy over what would become of her legacy, until we learned she'd left it all to Mr. St. James. Every coin, including the house. He's lived here for some time—in mourning, although he won't say a word on the subject. Of course, a few changes occurred as soon as her ladyship passed, but that's not for me to discuss."

"This is all quite the secret. He's never mentioned anything of this to me."

"Nor has he spoken of you to me until I was instructed to bring tea here for a guest." The housekeeper indicated the tea growing tepid in front of her as they spoke.

"My...visit was rather abruptly planned," Isabelle tried to explain, looking over the food on the table and not finding any of it appealing.

"These things usually are."

"Are they?" she asked, looking up. "I must admit this is the first instance for me."

"That is at least pleasant news. Lady Isabelle, you should know that I look after this house and its inhabitants to the upmost of my ability. And though

I regularly turn a blind eye in favor of love when it comes to the affairs of others, this circumstance is quite different since St. James himself is involved. If you expect me to fill the role of lady's maid…"

"Oh, that won't be necessary, Mrs. Featherfitch. I don't plan on attending any balls during my stay. Mr. St. James is rather insistent that I stay right here, in fact. I know how busy our household staff remains at my home, and I wouldn't want to be a burden on you."

"Good. Because between us, I do not approve of this arrangement. Not in the least. I will accept all else that that man does with her ladyship's home, but this…"

Isabelle was sad that this woman thought so little of her, but then Fallon's housekeeper had only just met her. Isabelle would endeavor not to be a burden to the woman. She smiled the broadest smile she could muster in the situation. "I'm not terribly pleased with the arrangement either, but I'm in no position to leave."

"Quite, my lady. Quite," She glared at Isabelle one last time and moved toward the door.

"It was a pleasure to make your acquaintance, Mrs. Featherfitch," Isabelle offered after her. "You can take the"—the door shut—"dishes from last night away."

She frowned at the closed door for a moment, absorbing everything the woman had said. Isabelle had decided that St. James would be her friend, and he was now her captor, but she knew nothing about him. His home had been a surprise and now his past… Nothing matched up to the man she'd thought she'd known. If she was to stay here—and with a locked door there didn't appear to be much option in her accommodations——she needed to know more about Fallon.

Her eyes raked around the room. All at once it didn't seem at all like the man but at the same time expressed everything about him. "Secrets. So many secrets," she whispered. At this point, she wouldn't have been taken aback if wild horses were kept in the dressing room where he had slept last night. She glanced across the room at the closed door on the far wall. The dressing room... That was where Fallon kept his personal effects.

She took a step in the direction of his private dressing room. Was this wrong? She'd always had trouble resisting the mysteries of closed doors and shut drawers. Exploring things that were hidden away was a weakness that had landed her in hot water with her family more than once. But she wasn't with her family now. Her cousin Evangeline would call her curiosity an invasion of privacy. Victoria would have already stormed inside to discover all she could. Roselyn would at least peek inside the door. But none of them were here. And her group of ladies tended to push across the borders of proper conduct anyway. "They would approve in the end," she mumbled to herself with a shrug as she crossed the room.

Isabelle grabbed a lamp from a nearby table and went to the closed door. Placing a hand on the doorknob, she cast a quick glance over her shoulder, pausing for a heartbeat before she slipped into Fallon's dressing room.

She set the lamp on a side table, casting a hazy light over the rectangular space. Wardrobes flanked the corners, and in the center sat a narrow bed, a table with a lit lamp, and an armchair. Judging by the tattered blanket that had fallen in a heap on the floor, it had been a fitful night of sleep for Fallon. "You took his bed from him. Of course it was fitful," she muttered stepping over the blanket.

Tugging on one of the wardrobe doors, she cringed at the loud creaking of the hinge. With a glance over her shoulder, she quickly pulled the door the rest of the way open and looked inside.

Coats were stuffed in every available crevice, and his cravats were wadded in a pile on a shelf. It was a wonder he was able to dress every day without looking a sight. A valet must be beyond his means. He did lack a title and therefore a guaranteed income, after all. She sighed. Poor Fallon.

Perhaps his desire for a proper valet was why he was always so busy with meetings. He was saving for the additional expense. But as soon as the thought occurred to her, she started laughing and had to take a minute to recover. Fallon would never care so much for his wardrobe that he would desire a valet in the first place. This was simply neglect on his part. She lifted a few of the coats, inspecting them, but they seemed to all be the same. An entire wardrobe filled with copies of the same gray waistcoat—of fine quality but then poorly cared for. She shook her head. Some things about Fallon were not a surprise at all.

Closing the door, she moved to the other cabinets and confirmed her suspicion—their contents were all the same. He owned the same trousers many times over, all disheveled in their storage, the same coat, the same waistcoats, as if he woke every day and donned a uniform that required no thought. It was all so terribly Fallon—the friendly pirate version that she'd thought she'd known before she came here.

If that version of the man were true, what of the floral decor and being a kept man for a much older lady? She cringed at even thinking of him in that light. Sinking into the chair opposite the narrow bed, she sighed. The palms of her hands trailed over the threadbare arms of the chair, the simple dark-green fabric all but worn away. The cushion was broken in beneath her from years of daily use, only the proportions were more fitting for someone taller than her. Someone like Fallon.

Straight ahead of where she sat was the plain wall behind the bed where he'd slept last night. Chips in the paint and occasional scuffs marred the plaster, almost as if the bed had been there—and used regularly—for quite some time. But this was Fallon's dressing room. She looked around in confusion and caught sight of a stack of books beneath the table on a variety of informative—and to her quite dull—topics. A well-used chair and books, a bed that had seen many nights of sleep, and a blanket on the floor that had holes worn in it. Why would there be more evidence of Fallon's use in this place than his main bedchamber?

She leaned forward and narrowed her gaze on the space beneath the bed, a cot that was more fitting for servant's quarters than a gentleman's dressing room. Boxes were stacked side by side, and a lap desk stood on edge wedged between them.

I've slept there many nights. His words drifted back

through her head in Fallon's deep timbre. It looked as if he'd spent more than a few nights in this room. He'd lived here at some point. But why not live in the main room with the lady Mrs. Featherfitch said he loved so?

Slumping back in what she now realized was Fallon's chair, she picked up the book on top of the stack beside her and placed it in her lap. It was the only book that had any sort of adventure within the pages. *Travels into Several Remote Nations of the World. In Four Parts. By Lemuel Gulliver, First a Surgeon, and then a Captain of Several Ships.* She'd read this story one summer.

It had been the summer when she'd found that spot in the woods near their former home, the one with the moss-covered boulders by the lake. She'd spend every day that summer sitting on those rocks, reading books, hiding from everyone. It made her smile now, knowing that Fallon had read the same tale. They'd arrived on different paths, but at some point long ago, they'd shared the words in this book. They'd both lived the lives printed on these pages, and that created a bond between them.

Fallon might have more secrets than the depths of the black lake that summer, but this was special. She ran a hand over the worn cover. Whoever Fallon St. James truly was, she knew one thing: she wanted to know more.

Twelve

Dear St. James,

I appreciate your daily updates on Isabelle's health. Her mother is quite distraught over this whole ordeal, so your ongoing news of Isabelle's recovery is welcome indeed. We've spread the false tale to cover her absence, just as you asked, even when speaking with Isabelle's sister. Do you have any new information on the artwork? I received the note with Isabelle's forged signature upon it just as you warned me I might. Dreadful business, this. I enclosed it with this note for your safekeeping.

If you were not working to solve this matter on my behalf, I would be in severely troubling times. I will owe you for the remainder of my life for seeing to my daughter's safety as you are doing. I wouldn't trust anyone else with such a task. If I can assist in the search for either the artwork or the two remaining letters, do not hesitate to ask. Pass along our concern for Isabelle, if you will.

—Knottsby

❦ ～ ❦

THE SUN WAS SETTING BEHIND THE BUILDING ACROSS the street, casting long shadows at their feet. He'd arrived only a few minutes before, meeting Hardaway in the alley behind a row of shops, yet Fallon was already anxious to be done with their business here.

There was nothing wrong with the area. It was a rather respectable section of London in terms of typical Spares work, but he was away from headquarters, and that had him tapping his fingers against the outside of his thigh in impatience. He'd been avoiding his bedchamber and its current occupant for two days now, but this was his first time outside of the house's walls since he'd brought Isabelle home with him. Somehow being a carriage ride away left him anxious to return even though he would keep his distance once he was back under the same roof.

She'd tried to claim she loved him. Fallon took a steadying breath and surveyed the opposite side of the street. He was certain if he stayed to hear the words two days ago, *I love you* would have been said. That couldn't happen. Isabelle—in a general sense— couldn't happen.

He forced his mind back to his current mission, leaning out to glance farther up the street. Grapling couldn't be staying in an area this respectable, could he? He was on the run from Fallon's men. He would be easily discovered in such a place. And this was no location for an underhanded sale of any sort. Looking over at Hardaway leaning against the alley wall at his side, Fallon questioned him. "You're certain this is where he's reported to meet with potential buyers to be rid of the art?"

"I already told you it was," Hardaway said without taking his eyes from their target. "At some point, you need to learn to trust me—or anyone, for that matter. I have reliable sources in town. I've been at this awhile."

"I know you have," Fallon conceded, turning back to the brick building where the deal would supposedly happen moments from now. Meat hooks still hanging in the window suggested the place had once been a butcher's shop, but a layer of dust and empty counters inside indicated the shop had long since closed its doors. And now Grapling was using the location to meet potential art buyers? It was the wrong location for such an activity—far from the harbor and surrounded by too many homes where someone could take notice. Experience told Fallon that they'd followed a false trail, but he said nothing more. They had to follow every possibility until they found what they were looking for. Thus far they had only two of the four confession notes—the one left at the scene and the one sent to Isabelle's father. She was still in danger, and the artwork was still at large.

"We'll find him, St. James," Hardaway said a moment later.

"Any luck finding the last two copies?"

"We'll find those as well." Hardaway shifted beside him, bending to pick up a rock from the ground. He tossed it back and forth between his hands. "How many jobs have we pulled since we started the Spares?"

Fallon had never counted. It was a statistic he

should know. He made a mental note to look it up later tonight. "I'd have to search through figures, check my files... Even counting the few from the early days before we had headquarters?"

"You and your details and exact numbers." Hardaway shoved him in the shoulder. "An arse load! A fuck ton. More than the number of barmaids I've winked at over a pint." Hardaway turned back to their watchful vigil. "St. James, we'll sort this out as well. Enjoying your time with the lady involved at least, eh?"

Fallon shrugged, focusing on the far entrance to the brick building, making certain they missed nothing. He hadn't enjoyed his time with Isabelle as much as he would have liked. Having her near him was driving him steadily toward madness. They could have no future together. Starting anything with her wouldn't end well. But keeping things businesslike between them was killing him at a rapid pace.

Even his men could sense that he had been a bit off these past few days, and that was a suggestion of weakness he couldn't allow. He had to get his head straight again. Perhaps they could once again be friends—at least once she wasn't sleeping in his bed and lounging in various stages of undress in his bedchamber. The only solution was to find the man responsible for all of this and send Isabelle home to her father. So he was here, chasing a false lead.

"No wonder you're as jumpy as a frog on a fire," Hardaway accused. "You're playing this all wrong, St. James."

Fallon swung his head back around to Hardaway and raised a brow. No one had ever accused him of not playing the proper angle in a game. He always thought five steps ahead of everyone around him. He thought too much, which was the bloody problem now. He was too wise to allow Isabelle into a compromising situation and imagine they would both walk away unscathed.

"Don't look at me like that. I'm not the one being driven to the edge by a woman—not at the moment anyway. Last night was another story. She was tall, long legs on her—legs that could wrap around a man twice."

"A mental image I don't need, but thank you."

"I get that you're doing the gentlemanly bit with this lady."

"I'm doing the 'I can't marry her when this goes wrong' bit with this lady. Can you imagine trying to run the Spares with a wife? She would want a sedate home life and me there to participate. I don't have time for country life, and she deserves that and more. I'm sure she'd force me to move from headquarters."

"Would she?" Hardaway asked, eyeing him skeptically for a second before shrugging off his pondering. "Anyway, in typical fashion you've thought this out ten years ahead of schedule. All I'm saying is you should enjoy this time for what it is. The poor lady is trapped in your bedchamber with nothing to do. A little romance might brighten her days. And we both know you aren't going to take a holiday—ever. That's what this is—a holiday—only you get to keep working, which also makes you happy. You do everything for others. Do this for you.

"I know I was against it at first, but St. James, I've never seen you like this. As long as you don't get her with child, no one will ever know. You've already made certain the tracks are covered. She's already in your blasted bed. Look up from your responsibilities with the Spares and live life. The lot of us will survive your lack of management for the…" Hardaway looked him over for a second, scrutinizing him before continuing. "We'll survive the three minutes it will take you to regain your sanity," he finished with a grin.

Fallon punched the man hard in the arm. "Perhaps that's how long you took with Miss Legs last night."

"It was a glorious night. At one point I had her—"

Fallon held up a hand to stop his friend. "If I promise to *consider* furthering things with Lady Isabelle, will you promise to never tell me this story? Contrary to your belief, some tales are better left untold."

"A fair deal."

Fallon would consider enjoying his time with Isabelle more. He'd been *considering it* every second since he'd met Isabelle. *Considering it* was what kept him in his library attempting to work at all hours of the night so he wouldn't have to be near such temptation.

A few minutes later, Hardaway sighed. "Grapling should have arrived by now. I think I received some bad information."

"Or intentionally misleading information. Have us follow a trail on this side of town to conduct the true meeting in the logical location."

"By the harbor," Hardaway supplied.

"He can't sell art that was stolen from the walls of the British Museum to a local," Fallon added.

"A damned diversion. I'll check the usual places across town, and then I think a visit to my informant is in order." Hardaway flexed his fingers into a fist, a menacing gleam in his eye. It was rare that anyone saw this side of his friend, but those who did regretted it immediately.

"I'll be at headquarters if you find anything." Fallon pulled out his pocket watch to check the time in the fading daylight. If he hurried, he could get a report from the men ending their day in the field and speak with those going out for the night before they left. He had to keep all his men focused on their tasks, especially with Grapling on the loose. "I'm sure my presence has been missed by now," he muttered.

"I'm certain it has," Hardaway said with a chuckle.

Fallon ignored him and took a step back toward his carriage, which was parked on the next street over. "Don't enjoy your work too much tonight. I know your love of cracking skulls."

"Don't forget to enjoy your work all night tonight," Hardaway called after him. "We have a bargain."

Fallon raised a hand in farewell but didn't turn back. He knew from years of experience that Hardaway liked to have the last word in any conversation, and Fallon was happy to let him—on this occasion.

No matter the bargain his friend thought he had, Fallon couldn't take advantage of Isabelle's trusting nature like that. She was searching for love from a gentleman who had time to devote to her, someone who wore garish colors and had nothing more to do in an evening than dance at a ball.

The truth was no lady in society would ever mix well with the lifestyle he'd chosen. But as Fallon climbed into his carriage, a question Hardaway had asked tapped at the edges of his already-frayed thoughts. *Would she?* Would Isabelle force him to move away from headquarters and give up everything he'd built if she knew the truth about him?

No lady would fit well into the life he'd carved out for himself, but Isabelle was no average lady. He would never admit that Hardaway of all people had been right, but perhaps by closing Isabelle off and keeping his distance he'd undersold her. After years of assessing gentlemen to discover their talents, he had to admit that he hadn't given her the same courtesy.

Perhaps the connection between them would break on its own. Perhaps she would grow weary of his company. Perhaps a million things, but Isabelle was worth the risk of discovering the answer.

He opened the door to his carriage and braced his boot on the step. With a glance up to his driver, he called out the one place he wanted to be more than anywhere else. "To headquarters."

❧

"I don't require anything further, Mrs. Featherfitch," Isabelle called out when she heard the door open. "Enjoy your evening."

She'd played more hands of solitaire than she could count over the past few days, just as Victoria had taught her to do on long rainy days at home. Unfortunately the game appealed to her sister more than it did to her. She'd even lost interest in the book she was now reading, but with nothing else to occupy her time, she didn't look up. She enjoyed a good story, but one could only read so many books in a day without conversation with a real person before losing one's mind altogether. Mrs. Featherfitch was thawing to Isabelle by minute degrees, but she still wasn't someone Isabelle would want to spend the afternoon chatting with. She wanted to see Fallon.

He hadn't come back to see her in two never-ending days. Was telling a man you loved him so terrible a thing to say? And she hadn't even gotten the words out. Imagine if she'd finished her sentence. Then he would burn his own home to the ground with her in it just to avoid seeing her.

She sighed and ran a hand through her loose hair, cringing at the thick weight of it around her wound. She hadn't been able to wash it since the day before Victoria's wedding, and she didn't want to think about what might still be matted above the slowly healing cut. "Rapunzel's hair must have been positively filthy," she mumbled to herself. Her own hair hung in a thick clump down her back. She twirled it into something resembling a braid and shifted it to lean back on the sofa.

"I would think so." A deep voice rumbled from across the room. "After years of a witch's dirty feet and hands dragging against Rapunzel's hair as she climbed the tower…"

Fallon! She grinned and sat up. He hadn't left her forever! "You've forgiven me? I shouldn't have said—"

"I've been busy," he cut in. "I shouldn't have left you alone so long. Have you turned into Rapunzel in my absence?"

"Unfortunately I have her hair… In condition, not in length," she clarified.

"Do I have a witch to kill?" he asked with a wry grin.

His steps seemed lighter as he crossed the room to her, the expression on his face more pleasant than when he'd abandoned her days ago. But she was so grateful he'd returned, she didn't question the change.

"I hadn't even considered the grime the witch would have added to her flowing tresses." She tossed her book aside and turned to look up at him as he neared the back of the sofa where she'd spent the day. "Poor Rapunzel. She must have longed for a lady's maid if only for her dirty hair. You've only had *me* locked away for near a week."

"This is hardly a doorless tower, Isabelle," he said even as he glanced back to the closed and locked door and winced.

"Nevertheless…this cut isn't becoming any cleaner with time."

"I could have Mrs. Featherfitch bring a bath. She's no lady's maid, but I'm sure if pressed, she could assist you."

"No!" Isabelle scrambled to her feet.

"Did something happen with Mrs. Featherfitch?" he asked, moving closer. Concern drew his brows together as he studied her.

How did she explain that though the woman was pleasant, Isabelle didn't want to spend the evening listening to stories of Fallon's love for the previous owner of this home? She could handle the woman's misconceptions about why Isabelle was here, but conversations with the housekeeper always ended with tales of Fallon's great love for another lady. She looked down at her hands as she muttered the only thing to be said in difficult situations—the truth. "I don't like the stories she tells."

He rounded the sofa, nearing her with slow steps. "You have her reading to you? I underestimated your boredom. I should have come sooner."

"No." Isabelle forced herself to look up and meet his gaze no matter how difficult it was. This was Fallon, her friend. And no matter who still held his heart, for her part, she loved him. "She tells me… She talks of the past, the history of your home."

"Oh." He had the good grace to shift uncomfortably on his feet for a moment before he said more. "I apologize for that. She should know not to speak of such things." Some emotion crossed his face for only a fraction of a second, but Isabelle could have sworn it was disappointment mixed with frustration.

She couldn't allow there to be a dispute in his home because of her, not after the inconvenience she'd been to him. "It isn't your housekeeper's fault. Please don't be angry with her. I asked questions. I'm sure I'm to blame. Isn't there anyone else who can wash my hair? I would do it myself, but I've always had a maid. The cut on my head is healing, and…I suppose I could try if I had a pitcher of water."

He fell silent for a moment, the corner of his mouth twitching up slightly. She'd noticed it was the face he made when he was deep in thought, so she didn't interrupt him, only met his gaze in the quiet room.

"I'll do it for you," he finally said, closing the gap between them and lifting a hand to her hair where it fell over her shoulder. "I want your stay here to be enjoyable, Isabelle."

"You…" She should have taken a step away from him at the shock of his offer, but she didn't. After all, she'd never been one to sidestep an adventure. "That seems…" *Wonderful, delightful, dangerous,* and *exciting* all collided into a mangled pile of words in her mind. The man she loved was going to run his hands through her hair. She blinked up at him, eyeing his weary eyes and the stubble of beard starting to appear across his jaw. He looked every bit the pirate tonight. "All right."

Isabelle saw only a glimpse of Fallon's slow smile before he turned away and went to work. But that smile—there had been some secret, entirely male thought behind it, she was certain. Just the brief sight of it as he looked at her made her knees weak. She sank to the sofa, staring at the fire as her heart pounded. This was a very poor idea indeed. Evie certainly wouldn't approve. But Isabelle was already locked away in Fallon's bedchamber and had been for days. She might as well enjoy her imprisonment with clean hair not matted with dirt and blood from the museum. That's all this was.

A moment later, Fallon instructed her to go behind the screen in the corner and to stay out of sight until everyone was out of the room. She sat quietly on the small stool, hidden from view of the servants, and watched through a small crack as footmen brought bucket after bucket of water into the room.

Fallon watched over the process as he did every-thing else in his life, with great attention to detail and a commanding presence. If only he looked after himself with such care. But for Fallon, she was learning, everyone else's needs came before his own. He was even seeing to her needs when he must have been exhausted. He hadn't returned here to sleep in some time. It was already early evening now. Had he eaten? Someone needed to look after him as well as he looked after others.

Perhaps that was what Lady Herron had done for him when she was alive. It wasn't Isabelle's place to take up the task. She was here for only a short time. If he didn't wish to hear about her love for him, he certainly wouldn't wish her to fuss at him about his eating habits and lack of proper sleep. He wanted only her friendship, and she would have to be content with that, sad though the fact might be. Perhaps unrequited love was simply her plight in life. She shook off the melancholy thought and watched Fallon check the temperature of the water.

Even with such a simple task as having water brought in, he oversaw the operation as if they were on the front lines of battle and this was the most important mission in a great war. She couldn't look away. When the last jug of water steamed in a pitcher before the fire and his staff had left the room, he turned toward the screen. "Come here, Rapunzel."

Isabelle rose from the small stool and moved toward him with hesitant steps, but there was a confidence in Fallon's stance that pulled her forward. Perhaps having one's hair dealt with by a man wouldn't be odd at all. She did trust him. And for his part, there was only friendship between them. It was only the new experience that had her body filled with butterflies.

"You'll want to change into this so your dress

doesn't get wet," he instructed, handing her a slightly wrinkled piece of linen.

"One of your shirts?"

"It should hang to your knees at least, for modesty." He was already removing his coat and tossing it onto a nearby chair. "I'm a bit larger than you are."

She watched as he removed his waistcoat as well and then his cravat. His shoulders were broad beneath all that clothing. He was indeed larger than her, and she couldn't keep from staring. He was looking down as he rolled up the sleeves of his shirt, exposing muscular forearms. She cleared her throat, trying to collect herself. "Is this terribly wrong?"

"Not at all." He glanced up at her, his expression one of completely businesslike efficiency. "Once you've changed, sit on the floor where I have the towels covering the rug. I'll give you some privacy."

She moved back to the floral dressing screen in the corner and pulled her day dress over her head. It was odd. Even if it had been for only one short second, he'd looked at her earlier in a way that made her heart race. Now he seemed to be disconnected from the situation, guarded. "You act as if you've done this before."

"I have."

"Oh." Her dress fell to the floor behind the screen, followed shortly by her petticoat, stockings, and stays. She should have been expecting such a response, it should even put her mind at ease, but it didn't. "I don't suppose you've rescued other ladies from art thieves."

"No. You're my first prisoner here."

"That's what I thought." She suppressed a sigh and pulled his shirt over her head. Even though it had been laundered, it still smelled like Fallon, clean yet with some mysterious scent that made her pick the fabric from her neck and sniff it. She looked down, noticing that he'd been right—his shirt did fall just below her knees. He was the sort of man who knew everything at all times, she was beginning to discover.

How did he anticipate the correct outcome to any situation? Perhaps he would teach her. It was a skill that could save her from further heartache in life. She would have known of Victoria and Lord Hardaway's engagement. She'd have seen ahead of time the threat posed by going to the museum alone even if the visit had sounded lovely when Mr. Grapling had suggested it. And she'd have been prepared to encounter Fallon's already-claimed heart.

An uncomfortable silence grew between Isabelle and Fallon that for the life of her she couldn't find a means of breaking. She stepped out from behind the screen and moved to the area of the thick rug where the towels had been spread out for her, not daring to look up and meet Fallon's gaze where he stood before the fire. But once she'd settled herself on the floor, pulling the shirt down over her knees, the quiet of the room began to close in on her.

The seconds were counted in the sounds from the fire at her side, every crackle of burning ember, another moment passed. Then Fallon closed the distance between them.

He knelt beside her, and his thigh brushed her side through the thin shirt. It occurred to her for the first time just how intimate washing a lady's hair could be. But she seemed to be the only one unbuttoned by the experience, as he set to work gathering her hair in his hands. There was still a silence hanging between them, but it grew steadily more intense as he slid his hand to the back of her neck. He held her head in the palm of his hand as he guided her to lean back against the side of the tub. She blinked up at him, trying not to think of how his arm curved around her, holding her steady, or the warmth of his fingers against the back of her head.

"I cared a great deal for her," he said and settled her gathered hair in the water with his free hand.

"Oh." Her heart was pounding. She really did need to get a hold of herself. This wasn't the makings of one of her dreams. This was Fallon washing her hair. Her friend Fallon. *Her friend*, she repeated to herself.

He ran his fingers up the back of her neck to make sure no strands had escaped his grasp, and she shivered. His touch was gentler than that of any maid she'd ever encountered. She was trying not to think about the fact that a man was caressing her skin, even out of perfunctory need. Unfortunately, their current topic of discussion was unsettling as well.

"You don't have to tell me about Lady Herron. Really. It must be difficult for you to discuss her, and I don't need to know. Just know that I'm...glad for you that you had her in your life." Those last words almost killed her to say, but she'd done it and now it was over, dealt with. They could discuss something else now. Fashion? The weather? Anything was better than conversing about Fallon's lost love. She exhaled.

The movement of his hands over her scalp stopped, and he looked down, meeting her gaze. "I'm glad she was in my life as well, but she wasn't in my life the way you're thinking of it."

Isabelle's eyes went wide. She almost sat up straight to have this conversation without distraction, but then he poured warm water over her head, and she found herself sighing into the firm hold he had on the back of her head. Even her back, rigid a second ago, settled against his thigh. She rested against him as warmth trailed in rivulets over her scalp. "She wasn't your lady? I mean… I wasn't thinking of anything so…"

"Scandalous?"

She opened her eyes—they had drifted closed with the soothing effect of the water—to see he was smiling down at her.

"Pearl liked scandal, enjoyed the talk, even encouraged it."

"She sounds like Victoria."

"Perhaps she once was," he mused with clear fondness ringing through his words as he applied soap to her scalp. "When I met Pearl, she was in a very different stage of life than your sister."

"Mrs. Featherfitch told me she was a widow, that she was much older than you are now. She said your position here was that of a…" She couldn't bring herself to say the words.

"I was many things to Pearl," he began to explain as he massaged the lather with his fingers. His strokes somehow managed to be firm and gentle at the same time. Isabelle sighed into his touch, like a cat begging to be scratched. Her eyes drifted shut, and she simply listened. Fallon's deep voice washed over her like the warm water that steamed around her.

"She gave me guidance in life when I was lost. She housed me, clothed me, and in exchange, I cared for her."

Cared for her sounded like an entirely different relationship than Isabelle had been led to believe. "How so? I'm sorry. I shouldn't ask. Whatever happened between you and Lady Herron is none of my concern. It's your private business. I have no place to ask—"

"Pearl was above all else a proud woman. When she became ill…she couldn't have society guessing the reality of it. She needed a companion to look after her medical needs without anyone discovering the truth of her condition. She had a specific list of requirements for her companion that included being muscular and quick witted." He broke off with a thin smile and shake of his head.

"She found me—young, taking dangerous chances with my life and walking a thin line toward destruction—and she took me in. The first ball I attended with her, she clung to my arm the entire evening. No one knew it was due to the weakness in her legs. People see what they wish to see—she taught me that—and they saw an elderly widow together with a gentleman a quarter her age, chatting, laughing… I enjoyed my time with her. My own mother died when I was a boy. Pearl…Pearl was special."

His mother—had he just compared Lady Herron to his mother? This was entirely different from the tale she'd been told. She opened her eyes and tried to catch his gaze beneath the constant motion of his arms, arching her neck up to catch his attention.

He paused, sliding both hands around until her

head was cradled there in his hands, and looked down at her. "Relax. I have you."

Isabelle stilled and let her shoulders sag back against his thigh once more. She stared up at him in awe, unable to look away. He focused once more on her hair and set back to work rubbing away not only the dried blood from the wound in her hair but also the tension from her entire body. Her heart was pounding at the intimacy, but his confidence allowed her to simply feel. "You were her companion and care-giver?" she asked a moment later. "Why would Mrs. Featherfitch, your own housekeeper, have such a poor view of your past?" She knew her hair would soon be clean, but she didn't want him to stop. She'd never felt such longing to have someone continue to touch her, to stay draped across a man's lap while he talked to her.

"Mrs. Featherfitch doesn't know the truth. No one does…except for you." His gaze dipped to meet hers. His dark eyes usually hid every inner thought, but now they simmered with a desperate need for her to understand what he was saying.

Only her. She didn't understand anything about their situation, but she knew one thing for certain: this moment of truth between them was special. She reached up and placed her hand against his jaw, the rough surface of his beard abrading the palm of her hand in a pleasant way. "Why? Why me?"

He tilted his chin into her touch for a second and exhaled a small ragged breath. "I needed to tell you the truth."

"Truth is a noble virtue." The heat of a blush flooded her cheeks as she looked up at him. "Sorry. I

won't romanticize this. I know you don't want that."
She dropped her hand and squeezed her eyes shut.
"Why not tell your staff the truth as well?"

"They were her staff first." He poured warm water
over her head and trailed his fingers through her hair
to rinse the soap from her scalp. "And we made a
bargain. She left me her home for use as I saw fit, and
in exchange, I agreed to keep her secret."

She opened one eye and quirked a brow up at him as
he continued to rinse her hair. "But that paints you as a
kept man who took advantage of an old lady as a result."

"So be it."

"You don't wish to clear your name?"

"No." He looked down at her, his honesty resonat-
ing in his words. "Only yours."

"Fallon…" She was at a loss for the appropriate
response. His sacrifice for the sake of the dignity of
a widow who had passed away long ago was straight
from a tale of brave knights laying down their lives for
their ladies fair.

He said nothing, only continued to stroke his
fingers through the long strands, loosening any tangles
that had formed. Although she knew her hair must be
clean by now, he seemed in no rush to have her move,
instead running his thumb with a featherlike touch
around the wound in her hairline where she'd been
hit. He narrowed his eyes on the injury for a second
before smoothing her hair back and looking down
at her. His other hand was still wrapped around her,
holding the back of her neck steady. If she could stop
time, she would want someone to paint this moment,
exactly like this, with Fallon looking at her like she

was an exotic flower, his hands on her, holding her before him. It was a beautiful moment she would hold on to forever—if not in paint, then in her memory.

With a rueful smile, he let his free hand slip back to brace it on his hip. "This is the life I've chosen, Isabelle. And in truth it isn't at all like one from the pages of some great story, even though that's the way I know you're painting it in your mind. I can see it in your eyes."

"You're heroic whether you like it or not, sir." Lifting herself up a fraction, she poked one finger at his chest in accusation. Water streamed from her hair, pouring into the tub behind her.

But instead of allowing her to drop back once more and continue on as she'd planned, he held her there, studying her. "I thought to you I was an old pirate lacking a heartfelt smile."

She searched his dark eyes for a second. Did he not want her to view him in those terms? They weren't particularly flattering descriptions, but he'd made it clear that he didn't want her to be more than friendly with him. "I'm unsure what you are," she hedged even as she thought, *My friend, my love, the unlikely man of my dreams*. She'd already scared him away once when she spoke from her heart; she didn't want to do so again.

"I see you aren't taking back your insults."

"Perhaps I misspoke when I claimed you were old." She didn't think of the strong man who was holding her as old at all. The only sign he showed of age, after all, were the crinkles at the corners of his eyes on the rare occasion when he smiled, and she found that rather endearing. Surely there was some middle ground to be found between professing her love and having him believe she thought the worst of him. "I only meant… I meant that you…"

"You don't even have a good excuse," he said in mock dismay as pulled her upright, released her, and threw a towel over her wet head.

"You act responsible for the world," she tried to explain as she attempted to wiggle away, only to have him pull her back to where he now sat on the thick rug, facing the opposite direction. "And you're wise, which makes you seem old, but clearly you're quite young."

"Now you're making up stories." He chuckled as he reached around her to dry her hair.

The position put his bare throat just in front of her. It was a commonly overlooked part of the male body. She'd devoted pages to bums in her diary, but now, sitting so close to him, she found herself entranced with this exposed piece of quality male flesh. His shirt was splayed open at the neck, revealing a most intriguing part of him that was usually hidden away from view.

With the towel disguising her exact actions, she angled her face forward until she could feel the heat of his skin just a heartbeat away from her lips, quietly investigating. "You like my stories," she murmured, her voice coming out rougher than usual.

She thought she heard a mumbled curse, but with his hands holding a towel over her head, who could tell? "I do like your stories."

"Do you want me to tell you the one about the

sour old pirate who never smiled?" she asked, straightening her back even more to inhale the scent of his skin just below his jaw.

"Only if he meets a wood nymph who insults him at every turn." His deep voice rumbled through her, setting her nerves on edge.

He smelled of worldly man, one who had seen adventure and lived to tell of it. Her lips almost brushed a spot at the base of his throat, and she saw him swallow. "They became great friends," she continued, forcing her mind to remain on their story, but her voice came out just above a whisper. "In an odd twist, he kidnapped her."

"To rescue her from danger," he supplied, his movements slowing, though his muscles stayed tensed around her.

"Mmmhmm." What would he taste like if she dared to stick her tongue out and try? She couldn't, obviously, since they were only friends. Fallon didn't want...

"And then he kissed her because he couldn't take her curious breaths against his neck anymore."

She could feel the heat rise in her face before his words fully registered in her mind. "He did?" she began, but she fell silent when Fallon pulled the towel from her hair and tossed it aside.

The firelight danced across his face, illuminating the strong line of his jaw and catching the waves of his hair where it curled ever so slightly around the rim of his ear. She looked into his eyes—dark and hot as he watched her—for the space of a heartbeat. Every muscle in her body went tense. His thumb traced the top of her cheekbone as he slid his fingers into her hair. The rough touch of his fingers dragged against her smooth skin. Would his kiss be the same?

Her gaze dropped to his lips and the secrets they held. This was it—the magical moment when Fallon would kiss her. The fire crackled beside them; flowers were all around; he was holding the side of her face in his palm. It was perfect. All there was left to do was actually survive the kiss without shattering like the fragile glass she felt she was made of at the moment. Her heart pounded in her chest as anticipation spun her stomach into knots in her belly.

"Isabelle, you're shaking," he whispered. In the next second, his hand was on her waist. He pulled her closer to his side until she was leaning back against his angled knee, his other hand still in her hair. He studied her as he ran his hand up and down her side, skimming over her body with only the simple linen shirt between them. His movements were slow and methodical. Thorough, just like Fallon. His palm slid around the outside curve of her breast before slipping back down into the dip of her waist and over her hip, then back up again. His eyes never left hers. Her breaths were shallow as tension built within her. She leaned into his body, her limbs turning liquid. He was so close, surrounding her, invading her senses.

She'd curled her fingers up into a fist as she waited to be kissed, but she relaxed now and reached for him, sliding her hand up his chest to slip around his shoulder. Where his shirt left his skin exposed, the heat of his body soaked into her fingers. All of Fallon she'd experienced so far was hot, strong, and inviting. She tilted her head into the hand that still held her cheek, his fingers in her hair, as she stretched her own fingers out, reaching, wanting more.

"Better?" he asked, one corner of his mouth tipping up in a hint of a knowing smile.

She couldn't look away.

She tried to answer, but only a faint sound came from her throat as she studied the tempting curve of his lower lip. Her eyes drifted closed, their connection taking over her body.

He brushed his lips over hers, and she found herself leaning forward as he held her suspended in that moment with him. With every press of his mouth against hers, he drew her in. His touch was unhurried, as if they had forever to be like this. Yet something had sparked between them, and his slow and steady movements only made it burn bright and hot. She delved her fingers into his hair with one hand and reached up to brace herself against his shoulder with the other, wanting to soak up all that he offered. He was holding back, she could tell. Barely restrained power—she could feel it in his gentle hold on her head and the drag of his palm up her side. She dug her fingers into his arm and pressed her lips to his, pleading for whatever he was keeping from her. She wanted to know everything.

Only he pulled back a fraction, breaking their kiss to study her with heavily lidded eyes. He slipped his hand from her hair, tracing the line of her jaw with his fingers as his thumb passed over her bottom lip and tugged it down. She watched him, waiting.

She had no experience to lean upon. Certainly she'd flirted plenty, but that's all it had ever been: innocent flirtation. She wasn't like Victoria. She couldn't command men about. She was just Isabelle. Kisses for her had been the sparkly, rose-scented clouds that dreams were made of. But Fallon was real. How did she tell him what she wanted?

He must have read her muddled thoughts somehow because a second later his mouth was back on hers, more commanding than before. She leaned into him, wanting more, and he bit at her bottom lip, the place that he'd toyed with only a second before with his thumb. Her lips parted as she allowed him access to her mouth.

He made a noise deep in his throat at her surrender, one that rumbled through her body with delicious tremors and pulled her closer in his embrace. Then he tasted her, his tongue tangling with hers. She roamed her hands over his back, his shoulders, as she arched into him.

He smoothed his hand up her side and cupped her breast in his palm, tracing hypnotic circles around the peak with his thumb all while plundering her mouth like the pirate she'd accused him of being. Taking. Demanding...but giving back more than she could handle.

That was when she realized all of her dreams of romantic kisses with handsome knights hadn't prepared her for the reality of Fallon. Her head spun with desire. She slid her hand around the thick column of his neck to where his shirt gaped open, and she slipped her hand inside. The muscles in his chest flexed beneath her grasp.

He broke their kiss but didn't pull back from her.

Resting his forehead against hers, he murmured, "Isabelle, you were supposed to stop me."

Her breath was ragged as he continued to tease the sensitive peak of her breast through the linen of his shirt. "Why would I stop you?"

He chuckled. "Right now, I haven't a clue." He moved to the side of her neck, and her head fell back to give him as much of her as he wished.

The stubble of his jaw abraded her skin even as his soft lips trailed down to the base of her throat. He caught the pulse that beat wildly for him there and tasted it with his tongue. Moving his lips over her collarbone, he dipped his attention to the breast he'd palmed earlier, grazing his teeth over the peak through the thin fabric of the shirt. The sensation sliced through her body, and she was reaching for him in the next second.

She pulled at the linen that he still wore, wanting to feel him, to taste him as she'd imagined doing earlier this evening. She didn't have any idea what she was doing, but as long as she was with Fallon, nothing else mattered. She knew now that she didn't have to fear the unknown with him. He held her steady in the palm of his hand, leading her with every touch, every press of his lips, and every flick of his tongue. Every soft murmur against her skin guided her forward.

He paused to study her, a question in his dark gaze, but in the next second he was reaching up to rip his shirt off over his head. She watched as the white linen slid up his body to reveal tightly corded muscles, a broad chest with a smattering of hair covering the surface, and powerful arms that returned to her before the shirt had even hit the floor.

She trailed a hand over his chest. He would rule the seas with ease just like this. Leaning forward, she touched her lips to a spot on his shoulder. His skin was hot beneath her mouth, and she inhaled the warm air that surrounded him. Unable to resist, she darted her tongue out and tasted him. Salty skin—the most masculine and delicious concoction she could have imagined. She smiled against his neck as he roamed a hand down her back and over her hip to grab her bottom. Her eyes widened at his touch, but she didn't move away, only moved her mouth over his shoulder, breathing in everything about him. Learning. Memorizing.

When she lifted her head from his neck, he kissed her again with a thoroughness that left her disoriented when it ended. She blinked at him and saw him smile. It wasn't the wry lift of the corner of his mouth she saw often on his face but a true smile. It was a smile just for her, and she knew it came from his heart— even if he would claim otherwise if asked. There was a truth in his smile, one that didn't require words. He was happy here with her. He may have walked away two days ago when she'd tried to tell him she loved him, but tonight he was hers, she was his, and this was what he wanted. The magic that surrounded them was what stories of love were made of, and she wanted to hold on to it forever. Nothing beyond this room mattered.

"Our tale is one of pirates and wood nymphs," he mused as he brushed his lips over hers again. "Kisses were always bound to happen. Untrustworthy fellows and all…"

"Fallon?"

He raised a brow in question but didn't reply.

"I trust you."

His hands froze on her as he looked into her eyes.

"I do. I've never been with another like this. And...I...wouldn't want to. Only you."

His eyes narrowed on her for a second, his question clear even though he said nothing.

It was true, she'd recently claimed she loved his friend, then had been on the path toward love with another before he'd brought her here. And really, she'd done the same over Fallon before she'd learned about his past. She'd been the ninny that her family often accused her of being, but so much had happened since she came here, even if it had been a short time. Now, sitting here in Fallon's arms while her hair dried by the fire, she was in a different world, one she didn't want to leave. He was the true noble and trustworthy gentleman of her dreams. She knew his deepest secrets and loved him all the more for what they revealed about him.

What she felt for him was larger than the color of his coat or his ability to dance the quadrille. She *knew* Fallon, and she loved him.

A knock sounded at the door, making her jump. Fallon didn't flinch but smoothed her hair from her face and placed a kiss on her forehead. Releasing her, he grabbed his shirt with a sigh and pulled it over his head.

"Remain here, out of sight." And with that, he left her.

She wrapped her arms around her knees and

watched him answer the door. He leaned an arm against the opening above his head, blocking all view into the room with his body. She smiled at the disheveled look of his untucked shirt and rumpled hair. He appeared as if he'd been enjoying exactly what he had been before the knock at the door. She bit her lip and admired his tall, lean form from across the room.

A low male voice came from the hall. What was the nature of Fallon's relationship with his staff? Now that she knew his great secret, it made her curious.

"…He says he can only meet with us tonight. Parliament will be in session tomorrow and… Otherwise the deal… The profitability of the job will…"

Fallon glanced back to her for a second before nodding and murmuring something to the man. A second later he shut the door and moved to retrieve his discarded clothing from the chair. "I have to go take care of some business. I don't know when I'll be free to return. I know we were…" He looked down at the cravat in his hand for a second before his gaze met hers. "I apologize for leaving you like this."

He was going out now? At this hour? "You haven't eaten. It's late as it is."

"I'll have something sent up for you," he offered as he gave his hastily tied cravat a final tug and stuffed his arms in his coat.

"I'm fine. I was thinking of you," she countered.

"I'll survive. It's what I do." He shrugged his coat into place, ran his fingers through his hair to push it back out of his eyes, and gave her a quick nod of farewell. "Get some rest."

She stared after him for a second wondering what

that footman had said to make him leave so quickly. "What about you getting rest?" she asked, but he was already gone.

The man *survived,* as he said, on little food, even less sleep, and not even an evening to himself. What kept him so terribly busy? Why was a footman alerting him to a business matter in the dead of night? Although he'd told her some of his secrets, apparently Fallon St. James was still a mystery.

❧

"Come live with me and be my love." The words floated into the dark room and Isabelle sat straight up in bed, her eyes wide open.

Singing. She'd heard distinct singing. It had *not* been a dream this time. Fallon wasn't the sort to even hum, let alone belt out a verse in the dead of night. "Fallon?" she asked anyway. Staring at the flickering light visible beneath the door—the only light in the room—she waited for an answer that she knew wouldn't come. Fallon had yet to return.

"Shut it!" came a bellow from somewhere beyond the locked door, making Isabelle gasp and pull her knees tight to her chest. Who had that been? A servant? Surely not, yet Fallon hadn't mentioned any other houseguests to her.

The presence of another live person should bring her peace at such a time, but it also proved that the voice she'd heard was real. She wasn't alone.

"Who's there?" she called out, pulling the blankets closer around her in defense against the unknown.

"And we will all the pleasures prooooove." The deep

voice sang out again, striking and holding a rather high note at the end of the verse.

Isabelle raised a brow at the closed door. Whoever was singing seemed to be quite deep in their cups. Had Fallon brought friends back to his home? It didn't seem likely. "He left to attend a meeting. He's still out," she murmured to herself.

"*That hill and valley, dale and field,*" the singer in the hall continued.

Isabelle could now hear laughter in addition to the singing—a woman's laughter. She drew a sharp intake of breath and strained to hear more. "What is happening in your home, Fallon?"

"*And all the craggy mountains yield.*" Another chirp of laughter accompanied a distant thud.

Isabelle could barely breathe. There was someone else in Fallon's home, and he wasn't present to see to it. Would he have mentioned a scheduled houseguest to her? Or they could be intruders! Someone was here to steal from Fallon while he was away.

"*There I will make thee beds of roses. And a thousand fragrant po-ooosies.*" The last word was drawn out in a poor attempt at opera.

Falsetto? "Get a hold of yourself, Isabelle," she muttered as she watched the gap of light under the door for movement. It was only an unfamiliar house, new surroundings… There were no intruders, only foxed houseguests of Fallon's that he'd neglected to mention to her. Yet she pulled the blankets up to her chin all the same to hide from whatever was making such a racket.

A door slammed shut somewhere in the house, and

Isabelle jumped. Then all was silent. She sat, waiting, listening, and wondering if she was safe here after all. But the longer the silence extended, the more she grew irritated with herself for fearing Fallon's friends. She was certain whoever was in the hall earlier wasn't the violent sort.

"Intruders with a plot to steal from Fallon," Isabelle whispered as she fell back onto the pillows behind her and stared at the ceiling. "I've been reading too many of the books Mother sent for me," she muttered. "I require something else to help fill my idle hours, or I'll never sleep again." Surely there was something within the walls of Fallon's bedchamber that she could do—a project of sorts. With a gasp and a smile, she knew just the thing.

Thirteen

Kelton glanced up and down the hall. His information had led him to these rented rooms, meant for those who were only passing through London or, in this case, those who didn't wish to be seen while here. "Grapling," he whispered, knowing he was getting closer to finding the man.

Kelton took a step back, then shoved the door open with a great heave of his shoulder. Stumbling inside, he searched the room. Empty. Only the furniture that would have come with the room remained. Grapling had already left.

Just when he'd turned back from throwing open the single drawer on the only table, he spotted something lying on the dusty wood of the floor.

"Careless of you," he whispered, moving toward what appeared to be an envelope. "Perhaps too careless." He bent and picked up the abandoned parcel, eyeing it. A string of letters and numbers were written in small, precise handwriting across the surface. It was a code—their code, the one they'd used in the early days of the Spares. Was he meant to find this, or had it been slipped under the door after the room was emptied? He scowled at the envelope for a second and began translating it as fast as he could.

Delivery Instructions. Open Immediately Upon Receipt.

Then he tore it open, anxious to read the only piece of evidence that Grapling had left behind, even if had been left behind with the intention of taunting or misleading the Spares in some way. Right now, aside from endless questions around town about forgeries and the exporting of stolen art, this trail was the only one they had to follow.

The enclosed confession letter needs to reach the Head Librarian at the British Museum. A hack will be waiting for you in the side alley beyond this building. Instructions have already been given to the driver. You will arrive at the museum via the side entrance. Ascend the stairs and make your way to the workroom at the end of the hall. Between the hours of one and two, the staff will be called away on an errand. If you are seen, keep moving. Place the letter on the oak desk in the corner. Your payment will be made in the usual fashion.

—G

It was nearly evening again, and Fallon had yet to return to Isabelle or the miserably narrow bed in his dressing room. He nodded to one of his men as he left the drawing room and moved toward the stairs.

He was always moving. He hadn't stopped since he'd left Isabelle last night, and he hadn't stopped thinking about her either. He'd thought about her while he discussed the Spares' interest in the upcoming legislation with the Marquess of Elandor until early morning. He'd remembered what she felt like in his arms while he sat alone in his carriage for the ride back to headquarters. And when he'd returned, he'd kept her in mind while discussing Grapling with the men who'd just come back from searching the city.

Fallon had to find that bastard—not only to save Isabelle from certain ruin but also for the men who had been involved from the beginning years ago. He shook off the continuing irritation that the man had vanished again so easily in Fallon's town. His own blasted town! He controlled more of London than anyone outside of the Spares suspected. The fact that Grapling was still on the loose, here where Fallon was strongest, pointed out that he still had weaknesses in his network even after all of these years. At least Brice had turned up with another of the confession letters this morning. One left, but it was one too many.

His eyes narrowed on the stairs ahead of him as his boots fell hard on each step. He'd examined and refined every one of his processes and mapped the entire city searching for holes in his defenses. He'd even met with his key men until early afternoon, cross-referencing their reports for possible oversight. And while the problem with Grapling persisted, day-to-day activities within the Spare Heirs continued, all requiring his attention. He enjoyed his work, truly he did. But there were times when the burden of it weighed heavy upon him. This was one of those times.

He paused and released a harsh breath, gripping the stair rail at his side until his knuckles turned white. He couldn't allow this situation with Grapling to destroy every life it touched. Fallon had worked so long to ensure security for the men of the Spare Heirs Society and the longevity of the organization itself. He would keep on as he always did, and somehow he would see this situation resolved. The gears on this club would continue to spin and whir just like Claughbane's steam machine. Life would go on. Isabelle would once again be safe to attend events and be seen in public without risking her freedom. And then she would be…gone from his home.

His speed increased as he moved down the hall toward his bedchamber. By the time he reached the door, he had the key already in hand and threw the door open. She sat at the small table by the window, surrounded by papers and small plates of food. Her back was turned as she studied something in front of her.

Isabelle's hair still trailed down her back in soft blond waves, as it had since he'd washed it last night. He'd spent the better part of the morning thinking of the silken sensation of her hair against the palm of his hand, the softness of her skin beneath his fingers, the curious gleam in her eye just before their lips met. He turned back to close the door with a soft click, tamping down the fire that burned hot with every thought of her.

The waters with Isabelle needed to be carefully tested. Even if she had kissed him last night, she was here for her own protection. She shouldn't need protection *from* him, no matter how he wanted to rush into things, to savor every second he got to spend with her alone in this room. He had to move forward with caution, or she could get hurt. She was beautifully idealistic, innocent, and perfect when compared to his soiled life. If she suffered as a result of all of this, it would be the same as if he'd harmed a baby chick or perhaps a fluffy rabbit.

But when she looked around, saw him, and smiled, the last of his control over the situation vanished. He crossed the room in an instant, sinking into the chair opposite her at the table.

She reached for his hand across the table and squeezed his fingers. "You were gone all night. It's nearly evening again."

"Meetings," he murmured in an attempt to explain as much as he could about the secret society he ran out of his drawing room. Perhaps it hadn't been wise to come here when he was so weary. His defenses were down. He twined his fingers with hers, unwilling to let her go.

"What's all this?" he asked, staring down at the table top between them. Pages of scribbled notes blocked the wood grain from view with small dishes containing ten different foods sitting on top of the papers.

"Try a bite of this one. It's divine." She pushed a plate toward him with her free hand.

He eyed the food and then glanced up at her, waiting for some sort of explanation.

"I'm certain you haven't eaten," she pressed.

"I had…a cup of tea a few hours past."

She glared at him, pulled her hand free of his, and grabbed a fork from the table. Lifting a cut of meat to his lips, she held it there, forcing him to take a bite.

It was covered in some sort of sauce, and his eyes must have rolled back in his head at the rich, buttery taste that practically melted on his tongue because she smiled and said, "See? Isn't it delicious?"

He hadn't realized how hungry he was until that moment. Taking the fork from Isabelle's fingers, he began to eat the variety of foods on the table. Although he only ever ate what was required to keep from growing faint, this was… "Incredible," he murmured between bites.

"Your cook is French," Isabelle said with a nod of her head as if sage wisdom had just been imparted.

He knew Madame Chabois had been born in France. She'd been the cook in this household for years before he'd even arrived. But he'd never tasted anything like this from his kitchen. Her food had always been bland. It was sustenance, which was all food needed to be; therefore, he'd never complained. But this… He took the last bite of the dish closest to him and looked up from the now-empty plate to meet Isabelle's gaze. How was it that Isabelle was so well advised about his cook when she'd been here since he left her last night? "You met my cook? Not in the kitchen, I hope, or I'll have words with Mrs. Featherfitch. It isn't safe for you to leave this room. Someone could see you."

"Madame Chabois came here. She's an interesting woman. Her stories about her childhood in the French countryside make it sound so beautiful. She described it as if it could be a painting."

"She came here and saw you? That isn't safe, Isabelle. The more who know of your presence…"

"Your cook can be trusted. I'm an excellent judge of character, I'll have you know. I knew you were a kind pirate, didn't I?"

"And the food? She brought you all of this when you met with her for the first time?" He raised a brow, knowing the selection in front of him had to have taken all day to prepare.

"These are samples of her work," Isabelle said, clearly excited by the artistry of the food displayed on the table. "She mentioned pastries and tarts as well. Such talent. Did you know this represents her true ability?"

He liked seeing the sparkle in Isabelle's eyes. It was the same look she'd had when she'd shown him around the museum. Her question, however, was a punch to the gut. When was the last time he'd been to the kitchen in his own home? He let his housekeeper handle such matters.

"She's quite talented. It's sad to see her abilities overlooked. Any cook can heat toast, but this…"

"Madame Chabois is unhappy in her employment here?" If he'd allowed the needs, artistic or otherwise, of someone who lived under his own roof to be neglected, it was a concern. The woman had always prepared food in a certain manner. He'd assumed that was simply her preferred way of doing things, but he'd never once asked.

He looked down at the table covered in servings of various dishes, fine foods, things he'd never seen served here before. The truth of the situation in his kitchen landed hard enough in his mind to rattle the china that sat before him. "Pearl couldn't eat certain spices, rich sauces… She's still cooking as if she's feeding a lady who is ill," he murmured, leaning back in his chair and running a hand through his hair. It had been years. How had this slipped beneath his notice? First Grapling, now his cook? He had to fix this. He had to fix all of it.

"I first met her this morning when I…" She glanced down for a second in clear discomfort before meeting his gaze once more. "I refused the food that was brought up for me. I appreciate your hospitality, Fallon, truly I do. I know that this is your home, and I have no place here."

"You most certainly do have a place here," he countered. Isabelle's care was on his shoulders, and if she wanted to live on nothing but tropical fruits, he would see that it happened. "I have no desire to starve you during your stay. Anyway. You have no information I require, so torturing you does me no good, remember?"

"You don't mind, then?" she asked, indicating the plates on the table with a nod of her head.

"I'll set up a meeting with my entire kitchen staff first thing tomorrow. *This* problem I can solve rather quickly. And I shall. I never intended to neglect anyone who looks to me for guidance and care."

"I…put together a menu with Madame Chabois earlier today." She handed him one of the pieces of paper on the table, her eyes darting between the menu and his face. "There are no kidney pies."

"Or beets, I see." He glanced up at her. She'd put this together with his cook? It seemed fine, but he would still need to speak with the woman. It was a change that would affect the gentlemen, his staff… He had to oversee something of that magnitude. Everything about this place had to be successful, even what he fed the men who lived here. He would see that the change was properly handled.

"She brought up these samples. The menu would allow for some variety and interest while not being wasteful with the budget. By repeating some key ingredients within short spans of time…"

He watched Isabelle speak about the menu as if giving a report from some mission for the Spares. Had he underestimated her once again? She was just as passionate about this as her paintings or stories from her books. He could listen to her talk forever. "Go on," he prompted when she stopped.

"You're looking at me as if I'm mad."

He rose from his chair and gave her what he hoped was a reassuring smile before moving to stoke the fire in the grate. "You're insightful, not mad, but I've always suspected that to be the case. The way you look at paintings, you see them as individuals, as living creatures. I simply wasn't aware that your expertise extended beyond books and art."

"I *am* a lady."

"I've noticed," he retorted with a wry smile as he turned back to her with the fire poker still in his hand.

"Meaning that I know how houses are to function. Fallon, your home—aside from the flowers—is a normal bachelor residence, just like any other."

That was debatable, but he didn't argue her point. Instead he leaned the poker against the hearth and went to the sofa, beckoning her to join him. The day was catching up with him. Perhaps it was his own weariness, but if Isabelle wanted different foods, so be it. He never took time to sit down to a proper meal anyway. He would talk to his cook about the changes Isabelle had proposed in the morning. Above all else, he wanted Isabelle to be happy here.

A second later she joined him on the sofa, still going on about his "normal bachelor residence."

He would have to tell her the truth about that at some point, wouldn't he? That was a topic for another day. His mind was already turning fuzzy from lack of sleep. The room was warmer now with the fire stoked, and Isabelle was at his side. Her voice was a soothing sound to his ear.

"Your bachelor residence is also either haunted, or filled with a large number of guests or thieves, since I regularly hear voices at night, but that's a subject for another time."

"It isn't haunted and no one steals from me," Fallon stated, silently cursing Hardaway and his booming voice. It would be him echoing through the halls as he returned to his rooms in the wee hours of the morning.

"You clearly didn't hear what I did, but we're discussing the menu at the moment. Ladies are trained in such things, you know. My training in dance steps began a bit late, but the part about homes and family is long ingrained in my mind. Families...children are what's expected, after all."

Fallon straightened, instantly alert, his drowsiness

gone. She couldn't be serious, but then this was Isabelle, who tried to confess her undying love before he'd ever touched her. "Children? Isabelle! I…" He wouldn't ever be able to have a family with her—not here, not surrounded by all that the Spares were involved with. He was mad for even encouraging a relationship beyond friendship with Isabelle, and now she was discussing children? How had they gone from French food to a family in a heartbeat?

"I'm not suggesting we have a child," she said, shoving him in the arm. "Heavens! I simply planned a menu…among other things." She mumbled the last bit, but he heard her all the same. "I don't wish to have discord with you. Perhaps this was a poor idea after all. I only wanted…" She scooted away from him a fraction, her eyes focused on the rug where they'd kissed only last night.

He was an arse…and now he'd scared her away. Reaching for her, he said, "I'll meet with Madame Chabois tomorrow morning. I'll review the menu with her and see that some changes are made."

"Fallon…do you trust me?" She looked up at him, uncertainty pulling her brows together above her eyes.

He studied her for a moment before nodding. Oddly enough, considering he'd only met her this season, he did trust her.

"Then allow me to do this. I want to help you."

The sentiment behind her statement was one he'd often heard from his men—Hardaway being the most vocal on the subject—but he'd never equated controlling a situation to not allowing anyone to assist him. Not until now. Isabelle wanted to help him. It was touching that she'd stepped forward to make him such an offer. He couldn't deny that some assistance would be a welcome change. And perhaps allowing her to help would fill her days and bring a smile to her face. He would do anything if it made her smile. "Very well."

"Thank you." She beamed at him and slid back to his side with a sigh. "I also asked Mrs. Featherfitch to send a maid here earlier this afternoon to organize your clothing."

Well, perhaps he wouldn't give her *anything* simply to make her smile. His clothing? A maid? He sat forward and turned to look at Isabelle. What fresh hell was this? The maids tended to talk, especially Molly. How did Isabelle know which one could be trusted? "Which one?" he asked, with every other question piling high in his mind as if in a long queue waiting for answers.

Isabelle winced before cautiously replying, "Mrs. Featherfitch recommended Emily. I...had her put order to your clothing as well as see if you had any pieces that required replacement."

"I will not have you replacing my clothing with some garish ensemble that Hardaway or blasted Grapling would wear," he grated a bit louder than he'd intended.

"Of course not," she said, her voice getting smaller the larger her eyes grew. "That wouldn't suit you at all."

"You instructed Emily in organizing my clothing," he repeated, wondering what had brought all of this on. Was Isabelle that lonely during the day?

"You're angry," Isabelle said. "I'll go make a mess

of your shirts and try to put everything back where I found it. I can tell Mrs. Featherfitch to cancel the order for the new staff uniforms and to ignore the new cleaning schedule I put in place. I thought after last night that you wouldn't mind, but I can see that I was quite wrong there." Her words were rushed, as if she were using them as a vehicle to run away from their conversation. "You can find me another room to stay in while I'm here, I'm sure. There won't be any way to tear apart the blanket I mended from your bed though. But if I leave you be…" She looked down as sorrow seemed to fill her expression. "Clearly this isn't right, whatever is between us."

"What?" What was happening? She wanted to distance herself from him? She'd taken over his life, changing things without warning, and when he reacted, she changed her mind? Only Isabelle had the ability to turn his life on its head in one day.

He sighed and pushed to his feet, unsure how to proceed. He always had a plan of action, yet all he could do was stare at her in confusion.

"I apologize for my work on your blanket. I found a needle and thread and mended it while Emily sorted the contents of your wardrobes. I didn't want you to catch a chill." She crossed her arms over her chest and drew back into the corner of the sofa. "Other than the blanket, I'll take the rest away, cancel all plans. If you would be so kind as to find me another place to sleep for the evening, you can have your bed back."

"You'll be sleeping here tonight, tomorrow night, and the night after that," he commanded in the same voice he used when he had to end a quarrel between men. He should soften his tone with her, but he was so rattled he couldn't make himself do it. "Until such time that it's safe for you outside this room, you'll remain here."

He didn't understand anything that had occurred in the past hour. He'd chosen a fine time to go multiple days without sleep. If he only had a moment to put his thoughts together, but that didn't seem likely while he was getting threats and sullen glares. He needed to find the solution to this mess, to regain what little control he had over the situation.

"Good night, Isabelle." He turned and went to his dressing room, shutting the door behind him.

Once alone, he took a breath and ran a hand through his hair, blinking into the small, candlelit room. Eyeing the tidy space, he reached to the side and opened the nearest wardrobe. Inside, his shirts hung pressed and ready for the day. They marched in a blasted row, and damn if it didn't look orderly. It was something he should have seen done long ago, yet it irritated him. Isabelle had made changes without involving him.

"Surprises," he grumbled to himself. The sensation of surprise was quite overrated in his experience. Sinking to the bed, he lifted the folded blanket in his hands. *I didn't want you to catch a chill.* Isabelle's words repeated in his head. He found the hole that Isabelle had mended and ran a finger over the small lines of thread. She'd wanted to help him. Her intent had been noble. He'd only questioned her methods and timing, and then everything had tipped sideways.

There must be some rationale behind the way she'd

pulled away. She hadn't even allowed him time to understand what she'd done before she'd announced her desire to leave.

Facts—those were always a good place to begin.

One. Isabelle had stepped in as if she were the lady of the house and begun ordering things as she would have them. He'd witnessed her hurry to fall in love with three different men in the span of two months. In hindsight, he really should have seen this issue on the horizon. It was like her to rush into her life here as well, even if it was temporary.

Two. She'd changed the manner in which his home was run within a day. If she'd discussed it with him or involved him in some way, he wouldn't have reacted as he had. He liked knowing what was happening in his own home, after all. Was that honestly too much to ask? But he also knew from his men's complaints that he tended to take his oversight to the extreme. Was that so bad? He only wanted to make sure they succeeded in all their endeavors. And he was the only one suited to such a task.

Three. Isabelle had become irrational the second he'd voiced an opposing opinion. From the moment she'd declared that he was angry…

He sighed and climbed from the bed, finally understanding what had upset her so. Her aversion to disputes, her insistence on happiness in marriage.

This was about her parents. She'd thought she and Fallon were fighting, and she'd retreated. But no one agreed all the time. His pressed shirts weren't so terrible now that he'd seen them. And the food she'd selected was delicious. He had to admit, for the first time in ages, he no longer had the gnawing ache of hunger in his gut. Damn. He had to fix this.

He opened the door a crack, but everything was dark. Had she found his key and left? He moved forward into the room, panic seizing him, but then he saw the Isabelle-shaped lump in his bed and stopped. He watched her chest rise and fall and her face relaxed in slumber.

"I like the changes you made," he whispered. "I like your company. I like you." Someone he might say those words when she could hear them. For tonight, he was relieved that he'd managed to keep her here— his beautiful captive. If only she could stay.

❦

There were certain activities most ladies would try to avoid. Whistling, for one. Doing it while teetering precariously on the window ledge of a single gentleman's bedroom, while her legs flailed about inside, more so. But those ladies lacked determination.

Isabelle whistled again, reaching her arm out toward the pigeon on the tree branch. Only a bit farther. The bird tilted its head in study of her but stayed firmly just beyond her reach.

"Come along now. Hop onto my finger." She worked to keep her tone encouraging and cheerful— the sort of voice she would wish to hear if she found herself a bird on a tree branch.

She stretched farther still. Her gaze darted to the grass three stories below where she hung, and her one-handed grip on the windowsill tightened. But she was almost there. *Don't dwell on thoughts of falling now—that simply wouldn't do.*

If she could use this bird to get a message to her family, she would be rescued from this place. After much consideration this morning, she'd come to the conclusion that this was her best—and only—option. She'd agreed to stay in Fallon's home for the duration of her ordeal, but any contentment she'd had in the arrangement had ended last night.

There was no anger involved with true love, only happiness.

As much as it hurt to admit, she'd been wrong about Fallon. She'd been disappointed by love before, and she wouldn't make the same mistake again. And now she needed to leave—a necessity Mrs. Featherfitch apparently did not understand, since the woman refused to post any letters from Isabelle. But Isabelle had vowed to herself long ago that her future would hold happiness and love, and now it was clear that she had to venture forth to find it.

With an exhale, she lifted her eyes to the bird again. She shimmied out the window a bit more. Her fingers almost grazed feathers before the pigeon hopped to the side and just out of her reach once more.

As she stretched out as far as possible, her feet kicking about behind her in an effort to find balance, the warmth of hands suddenly surrounded her waist and fingers bit into her sides. "Oh!" she gasped as she was lifted from her precarious perch and the bird she'd been enticing flew away.

Arms slipped farther around her, dragging her back inside—strong arms that could only belong to one man. Fallon. The same man she had no wish to see.

A moment later her feet found the floor, but he

didn't release his hold on her. Instead he spun her about to face him and pulled her close. "Isabelle," he rasped as if horribly upset. He moved his palms up and down her sides and around her back, clearly searching with his fingers for damage as his eyes searched hers for answers. "There's no escaping this room through the windows. Are you trying to end your life? We're on the top floor."

"Of course that wasn't what I was doing." Although she was certain the sensation of flight would be one to be remembered, she didn't want to end it all that way. She tried to take a step away from him, but he didn't release her.

"When I saw you hanging from the window…" He ran his hands up and down her spine, pulling her even closer until her cheek pressed against his chest. His heart was pounding in her ear.

As much as she wished to leave now that she knew there was no love between them, she hadn't meant to concern him. She should move away. She was supposed to be keeping her distance. But she had been hanging out the window such a long time, her skin was chilly and muscles sore from her positioning on the sill. His touch eased all of that discomfort. Horribly wrong though it might be, it was comforting to have his hands on her, to feel the strength of his arms surrounding her.

Instead of moving away as she should have, she rested against him, allowing the blood to return to her limbs under his gentle touch. It was true that he wasn't the one for her—that had become clear with their quarrel last night. But for some reason, she still longed for him. What she needed was to capture that bird, send the perfectly worded message, and be gone from this confusing place for good. "Next time I'll use leftover toast. That would do the trick."

"Next time?" Fallon pulled back to ask, his arms still looping around her. "And what trick? Falling with a splat in the garden below?"

"Luring the pigeon from the tree branch," she said in complete confusion.

He studied her for a second before he spoke. "If you would like a pet, may I suggest a dog?"

She tried to push away from him, but he didn't let her go. "Don't be silly."

"I wouldn't dream of it. Isabelle, if this is about last night—"

"We don't need to discuss that," she rushed to say. The last thing she wanted was to argue with him again today. She'd been so relieved to see he'd left the room before she woke this morning, and now here he was.

"Yes, we do need to discuss exactly that. I returned weary last night only to find that you changed my home all about while I was out for the day. I'm not someone who enjoys surprises. I plan and implement change on my terms. I always have."

Oh no. No, no, no, she would not participate in this disagreement. Where was a garden to flee to when she needed one? "I told Mrs. Featherfitch to cancel the changes first thing this morning." Her heart was pounding as she looked about for any escape, but there was none.

"I know," he said, standing firm in front of her even though she was shaking now. "I met with her and the rest of my staff after that and approved everything you set in place."

Approved everything... Her mind raced to catch up with his words. "What?" She stilled and looked up at him. "You didn't have to do that."

"I *needed* to do that. The adjustments were long overdue. I should have seen the issues before now."

"I don't understand. You're angry over this...aren't you? We fought."

"Do either of us have blackened eyes?"

"No."

"Then it wasn't much of a fight, was it?"

"I suppose not." Even her friend Roselyn could throw a punch, from what she'd heard. But Fallon had been stern with her. That was always how these things began. She'd seen it over and over with her parents. Father would get stern, then came the shouting, and it would end with both parties finally retreating into separate rooms in silence. But their fights never ended like this.

She stared at Fallon for a second and saw only concern in his eyes. Had she been wrong to demand a change of rooms? "You never truly screamed," she muttered mostly to herself.

"Raised voices aren't productive, in my experience, and I've settled a great many disputes. Please don't jump from the window to be away from me, Isabelle."

Even if he did wish to make amends, he wasn't entirely to blame for this. "I shouldn't have met with anyone about changing things, Fallon. You keep everything here just as..." She sighed. "You keep things just like Lady Herron left them. It was wrong for me to—"

"Isabelle," he cut in as he moved to brush her hair from her face. "You mended my blanket so I wouldn't be cold at night."

"I did." And she'd used what she suspected were Lady Herron's sewing supplies to do so. That had been clearly wrong on many levels.

"I neglect my clothing, and you had it put in logical order and pressed. You planned out a menu for the cook to adhere to. You arranged for uniforms and a schedule for my staff."

"And all of that was wrong. I shouldn't have over-stepped my bounds so. I got carried away. I often do that." She stared at his cravat, unable to meet his gaze. Her family had often told her she was too excitable. She'd seen a means of helping Fallon while she was sitting about doing nothing. It would occupy her mind during the day so that she might sleep without visions of ghosts or thieves. She'd leapt onto the idea with full force. He wouldn't mind, she'd told herself. He'd kissed her, after all. She'd thought that had meant something to him. Love was a confusing game.

"Isabelle, no one has ever cared if I was cold at night." He tipped her chin up with a finger until their eyes met. "Only you. The uniforms needed to be updated, and the cleaning... It had been on my mind to see to, but I..."

"Have been preoccupied with an art theft?" she asked with a thin smile. What was happening? The heat she'd seen in his eyes two nights ago was back. This wasn't like any argument she'd ever witnessed. This was different.

"I never considered that my cook might be

unhappy in her employ here, that she would find it helpful to set a menu."

"You're not angry with me," she stated, finally realizing what he was saying.

"No. I'm…" His lips were on hers as if he couldn't stop himself, and all of his usual restraint was cast out the window.

She melted into his kiss, grateful that they were friends once more. Friends—perhaps that term wasn't quite right. She slid her hands around his waist as he deepened the kiss between them.

But at the sound of a bird's song outside the open window behind her, Fallon pulled back to look at her. "I shouldn't ask, but why, exactly, do you want a pigeon in the room?"

"I know you've written to my father, but my family must want to hear from me… Don't they? Perhaps not after that confession note." She sighed and looked into his eyes. "They haven't written to me. And I'm not allowed use of the post to send them correspondence. I thought… I wanted to send a note to my family."

"How would that work?"

"Messenger pigeons. I might attempt it still, though for a different reason than before," she explained. She cringed at what she must now admit to him, but it must be done. "In truth I didn't simply want to contact my family. I was going to seek assistance with my escape. I know I must stay, though. It isn't safe for me. I could still be blamed for the theft. And…I want to stay, but I do miss the companionship of my friends. But being so long with no word from anyone has me at loose ends.

"Not that I'm unhappy with you," she rushed to assure him. "I enjoy your company. Actually a great deal." Her heart slammed against her ribs with the admission. She was especially enjoying his company just now, even after their argument, with his arms around her. "It's only that I miss my female friends. Their company is quite different from yours."

"I would think so." He smirked.

"Then you understand. When I'm with them, I don't feel…"

His hands stilled on her back. "When you're with me, what *do* you feel? Wait, don't answer that. I don't want to hear the answer."

"Is that because I attempted to tell you that I lo—"

He kissed her again, halting the rest of her question. "This is already complicated enough. I shouldn't have asked."

"I wouldn't dare say *that* again," she muttered. Her announcement of her love had pushed him away the first time. She didn't want to do that when things were only just mended between them.

Did she, though? Did she truly love this man? What she felt for him was too complicated to explain to herself, much less to him. He was her friend, her captor, the man who had his hands on her in the most exciting fashion she'd ever experienced, and the man with whom she'd quarreled only last night. He was hardly the man she'd envisioned as her ideal husband. And soon their time together would come to an end. This wasn't forever. She would do well to remember that.

She stepped away from him and cleared her throat. And for the first time since his arrival, he released her. She turned back to the window, focusing on the leaves of the tree just beyond reach, not the man at her back. "If I could attract that pigeon, I could send a note to Roselyn or Evangeline. They wouldn't tell anyone of it. If the bird could go as far as France, I could reach Sue. The secret of my stay here would be safe with my cousin in France, wouldn't it? I wonder if pigeons travel that far. Do you know how far pigeons fly in a day?"

"I'm not certain. However, you know that isn't how messenger pigeons work, don't you?"

"I have a ribbon for its leg," she said, holding up the hair ribbon she still clasped in her fingers for him to see. "I wouldn't write a long note, nothing that would weigh the poor creature to the ground. Can you imagine? I don't have much to tell, trapped as I am. The scenery doesn't change from day to day, but this is quite the adventure."

"Did you read a book where messages were sent via bird?"

"I did!" She turned back to him, feeling it was safe to look at him once more. "That was how the castle siege was ended. How did you know?"

"I know you miss your life, but can't you be content here with me a bit longer?" He slid his hands down her arms, the look in his eyes luring her a fraction of a step closer to him. "I'm working to fix this mess, and releasing birds into my home isn't going to hurry that process along."

"I wasn't going to have it flapping about," she murmured in defense. "I have the ribbon."

"You would have to have a bird trained to a

particular roost, which would return only to that place when it was released. You can't instruct a pigeon to simply *find Roselyn*."

"Perhaps *you* can't," she countered.

He didn't say anything, only looked at her, a hint of a smile lingering on his lips.

"Very well. No pigeons."

He laced his fingers with hers and pulled her away from the open window. "You'll have to suffer through my poor excuse for company for now."

Didn't he understand? He was perfect company! If only he wouldn't leave her here alone so long. She gazed up into his warm brown eyes.

He was trying to assist her out of friendly concern for her welfare. It wouldn't do to get lost in those eyes when he'd made it clear he had no interest in love. His feelings where she was concerned were far simpler than her own, no matter how complicated he claimed things might be.

Looking away, she asked, "Any news on my grandfather's art collection?"

He led her to the sofa and then moved to stir the fire in the grate. "I'm making inquiries and getting closer to finding the man behind the theft. Two more letters have been found and are now in my desk for safekeeping. That leaves one *confession* letter unaccounted for, but until we find them all… It's only a matter of time before the culprit is apprehended and you can return to your life."

"You have an idea who he is then?"

Fallon was taking a great deal of time stoking the fire, especially for such a warm afternoon. "I do."

"I don't understand why someone would do this," she mused, voicing the confusion she'd been struggling with from the start. "I've never harmed anyone. Last year I nursed a squirrel back to health at great protest from both my family and the squirrel. Yet this man sought me out to cause me harm. Why?"

Fallon's shoulders seemed to sag under a great weight as he turned from the fire and crossed the rug to sit beside her. "The man who did this is a bad person. He isn't like you." He reached up and slowly tucked away a lock of her hair, his fingertips grazing the rim of her ear as he moved. "He doesn't see the world through these beautiful eyes, doesn't see the promise of hope—only what could be his if he presses his luck."

"You think my eyes are beautiful?" she asked, taken aback by his statement.

"Not just your eyes, but the way they view the world. You're a lovely person, Isabelle. A lovely person who was assaulted and left at the scene of a crime for the sake of the price of some paintings. You simply stumbled across the wrong path. This was not the result of anything you did or didn't do."

"I'm not perfect, you know. I once climbed through a window to attend a masquerade ball on my neighbor's estate."

"Not a crime worthy of a head wound."

"I shoved my sister quite hard a month or two ago and made her drop her wineglass on the parlor carpet. And then I moved a chair to keep my mother from noticing the stain."

Instead of being shocked as he should have been,

Fallon laughed. "What had your sister done to anger you so? I can't imagine you in such a rage."

"I thought she'd stolen my new fan. My skill with a fan is a bit of a sore spot between us, but I searched her things after that and didn't find it. See? Yet another fault. I get curious and look through drawers. I can't seem to stop myself. I see a closed door and think of all the mysteries it must conceal."

"What did you think when you looked through my belongings?"

"That you don't give a care for your appearance," she teased. "And you have no personal possessions other than a few books. I've never seen someone live with so little evidence of that life lying about. You're a mystery, Fallon St. James. A man full of secrets."

"So they say," he mumbled. Though his gaze met hers in the quiet room, it was as if he'd placed a great wall between them in an instant.

The longer they sat there, the more Isabelle wondered if there were more secrets about him that she'd yet to discover.

Fourteen

Dear Victoria,

Though I can't send this letter to you, I need to write it. I have so many things to tell you, yet I don't know where to begin. I realized this morning that this is the longest we've ever been apart. Remember that time when I was sick and Mother wouldn't allow us to spend time together lest the fever spread in the house? We wrote notes and created that guessing game. I'm still surprised our maid kept that a secret. I miss you.

I tried to send you a message by pigeon earlier this week. It wasn't successful, though I'm certain you would have guessed as much. I wish we had that maid to pass notes between us now. I don't like that we parted at such a straining time. I heard that you didn't go through with the wedding. My feelings about Hardaway have changed a bit since I've been here. Many things have changed during my stay, in fact. But I'm pleased you didn't marry him—not because of me but because of you. I can't imagine you married to a man not of your choosing. I know you don't wish *to marry at all, but perhaps truly knowing someone and sharing your life with him every day would suit you if you met the right gentleman.*

I met someone. Well, I'd already met him, but things are different between us now. I can scarcely explain it since I don't quite understand it myself. But know that I am happy and I am happy with whatever choices you make in your life. I'm sorry I was so angry with you. Forgive me? I hope to see you soon.

—Isabelle

P.S. Solitaire is a horribly boring game, and I don't know how you can abide it.

FALLON WALKED INTO HIS BEDCHAMBER AND BLINKED at the abundance of color that assaulted his eyes. He was used to the flowers that covered every surface, but there were quite a few additions to the decor now.

"I see you received the canvas and paints I sent up this morning."

"My captor has returned! You didn't abandon me to wither away like a flower past its bloom!" Isabelle exclaimed, twirling around to greet him with a brush laden with pale-green paint still dangling from her fingertips.

He chuckled at her comment but didn't respond to it. Since he could barely leave her long enough to complete a single task, withering was hardly a problem. And he didn't think Isabelle capable of fading in the sunlight anyway. She would simply bloom brighter. Focusing instead on the four paintings that were leaning against various surfaces around Isabelle, Fallon moved forward. Colorful blobs of paint danced on fields of green and blue. Were they garden scenes? Surely she wasn't quite finished with any of them. "Were my private quarters lacking in flowers?"

"No, you have walls full of those," Isabelle countered as she placed the brush down on the palette of paint colors beside her. "I thought with these you would have some variety."

"Indeed." Fallon moved farther into the room, looking down at the closest canvas leaning against the legs of a side table. "They're all quite…cheerful. I like this one with the roses the best."

Isabelle moved to stand beside him and appreciate her work. Leaning her head on his shoulder, she studied the piece for a moment before she said, "Those are apples."

He winced at his mistake. "But they're in a garden, growing under a tree."

"For sale in a basket at market," she corrected.

"Of course they are. I can see that now. All of your time spent with great works of art has clearly influenced—"

He broke off at the sound of Isabelle's laughter.

"I meant no insult. Your paintings show great enthusiasm."

Her laughter increased until she was clinging to his arm and tears gleamed in her eyes. "Enthusiasm," she repeated on a cackle. "I don't believe any museum showings are in my future."

"Perhaps not, but I enjoy your paintings."

"You, sir, may keep my precious works of art to grace the walls of your fine home."

"An honor to be sure. Should I hang the blobs of red in the main hall for everyone who visits to admire or the blobs of blue? The red, I think." He smiled and shook himself out of the coat that had been overly warm all afternoon. There was no need for formality with her. There was no formal nature to anything between them anymore. Ever since they had put an end to their dispute earlier in the week, an easiness had settled around them, luring Fallon deeper into what he logically knew were dangerous waters. Hang logic. Isabelle was fresh air after a lifetime of enclosed spaces.

Fallon had only the next ten minutes to see that she had everything she needed before he must leave again—that's what he had told himself in the hall, anyway. But then he'd entered the room, and every inclination to return to his desk had crumbled. To say that she was distracting was an understatement. For the moment, the Spare Heirs Society disappeared from his thoughts, and all that existed was her and her truly awful yet somehow endearing paintings.

She cleaned the paint from her fingers with a cloth and moved to investigate the bowl of fruit left on the small table, taking a strawberry. "The painting worked to keep the ennui at bay from too much time spent alone—it helped me today anyway. Tomorrow I'll be lost once more now that I know my skill with artwork ends at viewing it." She gave him a dramatic sigh that would have been more effective if not for the twinkle in her eye. "You have me at quite the disadvantage, you know. Keeping me locked away in your bedchamber while you go about your day, only coming to visit when it suits you to do so." Her voice was wistful as she painted the picture of her captivity. And in the next second, she punctuated it by taking a large bite of the berry in her hand.

He watched her lick sweet red strawberry juice from the corner of her mouth and abandon the stem on the table. "Now you make it sound like you're a kept woman. That's hardly the case. You're clearly an artist."

She gave an excited gasp and looked at him with wide eyes before taking a few steps backward with her arms out to the sides. "This *is* what it's like to be a kept woman! I'm trapped here alone waiting for you to return and entertain me while I gaze at the world outside my little window, lounging about in dresses you bought for me." She threw herself onto his bed in a dramatic display of what she must assume was mistress-like behavior. "Funny, I always envisioned it being more scandalous than this. I wonder how such women fill their days."

"This *is* scandalous. As you pointed out, you're locked in my bedchamber with me. Which is why you can't send notes to your friends via pigeon or the post for that matter. If anyone discovers that you've been hiding here…" *You'll be forced to be my wife*, he finished to himself.

Isabelle might think it dramatic to be a kept woman, but she deserved the kind of grand love match to a passionate lord that she'd always dreamed of. He couldn't steal that away from her.

"No one will find out." She absentmindedly twirled a lock of hair around her finger and stared up at the canopy above her head.

There were thousands of reasons why he should not take another step toward her, but just now all of the grounds he had to stay away sounded like cause to hold her close. She was beautiful, had claimed love toward him, and was here alone with him. Perhaps she was right, and no one would find out the details. He'd kept her presence a secret already. What were a few more secrets added to the stack at this point?

When he remained silent, she added, "You've kept my stay quiet. I only converse with one maid, the cook, and your housekeeper."

Once again she was right. He took a step toward her, unable to look away while she was sprawled across his bed. "I should go," he murmured, not truly meaning his words.

She sat up to look at him. "Don't leave."

He reached for her, tucking a lock of her hair behind her ear. "I'm fairly certain captors don't lounge about dungeon cells with their prisoners."

"And what about gentlemen with kept ladies?" There was a curiosity in her gaze that made him want to throw open all of the doors and show her every secret he knew.

"That's quite different," he murmured.

"Is there any role to play in between captor and keeper-of-a-mistress in which you're my friend and you stay to keep me company during my confinement? Any proper gentleman would do so."

"A proper gentleman wouldn't bring you to his own bedchamber and then remain locked away *with* you, but I've never claimed to be such."

"You'll stay then?"

"For now." He only had a secret society to govern. He could disappear for a few minutes. He'd never neglected his work before he met Isabelle, but now he found he couldn't walk away just yet. Of course, neither could he loom over her, staring as if she were a piece of meat on a platter. He wanted to dive into everything that passed between them and swim about in the warmth of her happy heart. Her kind spirit would wash over the blackness of his soul, and in turn he would satisfy the curiosity that rippled through her eyes every time she looked at him.

Seeming to read his thoughts—which was a bit concerning, considering the pattern they took where she was concerned—she tugged on his fingers and smiled up at him. "Come. Sit with me."

Every gentleman in town knew Fallon wasn't someone who took orders from others well. Fallon was always the one in control. Isabelle, however, didn't see things that way. Even now she was wiggling back to rest against the headboard and patting the empty spot at her side. With a grin over the fact that this thin-framed, blond, and doe-eyed lady had that sort of sway over him, he climbed up to sit beside her as she had decreed he must.

Somewhere downstairs his men sat about lacking his direction. Tasks would not be accomplished. Things that required his attention were waiting for him, lest without his mark of approval, the Spare Heirs came to a screeching halt. Yet he couldn't make himself get up from the bed where he sat beside Isabelle.

"What did you want to do with your life when you were a child?" she asked as she leaned her head against his shoulder. "You have no title. You must have had some idea, some dream for your future."

"I wanted to be the pirate that I am, of course," he answered as he laced his fingers with hers. "I'm pleased that worked out for me."

She elbowed him in the ribs for his cheek. "I'm asking a serious question, and you're teasing me."

"Very well." Fallon hadn't thought of his childhood dreams since, well, since he'd been a child. His life had been set on a path years ago, and he hadn't looked back since. He was head of the Spare Heirs Society, and he was living his dream. Or so he'd thought until he met Isabelle. Between her talk of dreams and her heartfelt smiles, she'd forced him to stop and look about for the first time. He was always left with a sense of loss when she wasn't near.

He traced the delicate lines of the backs of her fingers as he held her hand in his. "I recall wanting to be a sheep farmer for a time, overseeing my flock, caring for their needs by day and relaxing in the comfort of my cottage at night."

"I assume your dreams of sheep farming were dashed at some point, since we are not sitting in your cottage in the country but your home in London."

He smiled at the thought of having Isabelle to himself with no threats or distractions, settled in a cottage surrounded by sheep. Perhaps in another life, they could have been married. They would live out their days together in a peaceful pastoral existence. He would bring her wildflowers from the field every day, and they would sit together by the fire each night.

"Were no farms available for sale when you came of age?" she asked as she curled further into his side, resting her cheek against his arm.

"By the time I was of age, I'd set my sights upon overseeing something a bit larger."

"Cows?"

He leaned his head back against the wood of his bed and stared up at the canopy above his head. "Have you ever wanted to change the way things are? To find a place within the chaos people cause and put it into order? To make room for those who have no purpose and are left out in the cold?"

"No one should be left out in the cold. I don't enjoy the chill of winter at all. Mother always got angry with me when she would see me sitting too close to the fire. The house I lived in until Father inherited was rather drafty. But there was always a fire burning in the kitchen for dinner that night. The winters in that house were harsh, but not when I was there on top of a mountain of blankets and so close to the embers. I was quite warm, waiting for the thaw of spring."

"And imagining yourself in the book you were reading?" he added, filling in the gaps of her story.

"The worlds held within those pages were better worlds than the one in which I lived."

"Reality awaits me downstairs, and I find I prefer the world here, chatting with you. Yet we live where we must." For the first time, he truly understood her desire for a few selfish moments to call her own.

She shifted to look up at him. "Even hardworking pirates require a break from time to time."

He lifted one hand to her cheek. Her skin was soft beneath his palm. She looked at him, and he was lost, trapped there in her eyes. "People depend on me. I have to take care of them, answer their questions, see to their needs."

"Like your sheep?"

"Something like that." His gaze dipped to her lips.

"And who takes care of the sheep farmer?"

"I have you," he murmured. He didn't truly have her, but he couldn't think about the end of things just now.

"And before I came here?" She whispered the question.

"I never realized until I met you that I might need to be cared for as well."

He kissed her before she could respond. It was a slow and tender kiss meant to savor every touch of her full lips against his, embracing everything sweet and good about her. But then she kissed him back, and all thoughts of an innocent embrace were banished. He released her hand, shifted to his side, and tugged her down onto the bed beneath him fast enough that she drew in a surprised breath.

Deepening their kiss, he skated his hand down her side, over the soft curve of her breast, the dip of her waist, down to her rounded hip. He shifted further over her, dragging his hip up over the apex of her thighs. It was a bold move, but he'd lost control of what was happening between them, and he wasn't about to fight to regain it. Instead he took more, tasting her while grinding his hip against her. She made a beautifully needy little sound against his lips and slid her hands up his back to press every one of her gentle curves against his body. His hand roamed over her arse as he held her close. Tension built in her, and every flinch and shimmy of her body beneath his reverberated through his hands as he held her. Trailing his mouth down her neck, he continued to move against her body and tugged the sleeve off her shoulder with his teeth.

Having her shaking with need beneath him was glorious, but it wasn't enough. He shouldn't push his luck. Surely there was a line where, once crossed, she would pull away. He glanced up at her between placing kisses on every bit of skin he could access.

In the next second, any question of lines or pulling away was answered when she shook her arms out of the short sleeves of her dress and returned her hands to his back. Her grasp tightened on him as she arched her body from the bed, seeking more. Her fingers delved under his shirt to pull at his sides. Allowing more of his weight to press down against her, he watched her for a second as confusion, surprise, and pleasure all warred with one another in her eyes.

Dipping his head once more, he pulled her dress down with his mouth. She wore no stays—why would it matter, since she couldn't leave the room to be seen, in any case? He was glad he hadn't asked one of his maids to assist her with such things since her lack of undergarments now put her within his reach. Her skin smelled of some flowery concoction that embodied everything about Isabelle—light and fresh yet intoxicating and dramatic. He followed the curve of her body with his lips, allowing his breath to heat her skin as he moved. Moving his hand up her side to cup one breast, he teased the tightened nipple with his fingertip.

"Fal…" she breathed, unable to complete even the one word. Her hands tightened on him in the same second.

He grinned as he swirled his tongue around the peak of her nipple, pulled it into his mouth. He gently dragged his teeth against her, and she bucked her hips into his body. He looked up, wanting to watch the passion in her eyes as she found her release, but he didn't stop touching her. He ran his mouth across her other breast even as he twitched the nipple he'd just abandoned between two fingers, tugging her over the edge.

She breathed out a harsh breath and clung to him. Her gaze met his for an intense second before her head fell back on the pillows. He peppered kisses over her now pink and heated skin up to her shoulder, and rolled to his back, taking her with him.

"What just happened?" she asked a moment later, laying sprawled across his chest. "Did we—"

"No." He pulled her closer into his embrace, not wanting to let her go just yet. He was still hard as a rock, but he could ignore the discomfort. "That was only a bit of pleasure."

"It was… I…" she tried, but her words tapered off.

"Shh." He slid his hands up and down her spine. "You're perfect. You don't have to say anything."

"My bloodthirsty pirate," she whispered. "I'm glad you took shore leave with me today."

"Is that what we're calling this?" He chuckled.

"You need a first mate, so we might do *this* more often."

"A first mate?" She was the only one he needed, no one else. His mind drifted back to the dream of having her to himself in a country cottage. "Perhaps I'm more of a sheep farmer than a pirate after all."

"No," she said a moment later as she propped her chin on his chest to look at him. "You're not a pirate or a sheep farmer. What are you, Fallon? What business keeps you so busy?"

This was it—his opportunity to tell her the truth. Then he would know for sure if she would hate him—once she knew who he really was and the sort of work he was involved in. He opened his mouth, but old habits were difficult to break. He shifted uncomfortably beneath her on the soft bed. "Business is what I should be seeing to. I ought to go."

"Wait." She grabbed his arm before he could move away. "I shouldn't have pried. I'm sorry. Please don't leave me."

He smoothed her hair back from her face and held her to his chest. "I want to stay. You have no idea how much. But I truly do have things awaiting me. I shouldn't have stayed this long."

"It's already dark outside, and I hear things at night," she pleaded.

"Isabelle, you're safe here. No one will attack you while you're in my company, I promise you that. I protect a great many people, and I'll protect you."

"You mean your staff," she stated, watching him. "You offer protection to your household staff? Is that who I hear at night? Last week there were voices in the hall, and at one point I heard rather boisterous singing. I thought you had houseguests since thieves don't sing."

"Hardaway," Fallon muttered under his breath.

"What?"

"No one will harm you as long as you're here. You have my word."

"Even still. Stay with me."

He sighed and wound his arms farther around her. "A few more minutes."

"And tonight?"

He had meetings scheduled. At least five of his men would need instruction, or everything he'd built would begin to slip through his fingers. That was how trouble always started—with the shift of a single grain of sand. Before long, one side of a mountain would slide away into the valley below. He contemplated the mountain he'd claimed as his own. Then he tossed aside that metaphorical grain of sand, reached up, and held Isabelle close.

"I'll stay the night."

Fifteen

Knottsby,

In response to the note you sent this morning, I must insist that you keep your head clear of this and allow me more time to handle the situation. It isn't safe for you to make inquiries on your own. Hardaway delivered the copy of the confession letter to me just days ago that was intended for Mr. Jasper at the museum, so there's no need for you to pry into matters there.

Along with the letter you received the day after the theft and the one left with Lady Isabelle, there's but one missing before that ordeal at least is behind us. We have assurances from the forger responsible that he will never pen another letter in that hand. I know your daughter is anxious for things to return to normal, and I'm working as quickly as possible toward that day. We must be patient, however. I checked with my contacts at the papers, and it appears the last confession letter is still at large. I have people looking for it—quietly, of course. We

*certainly don't want to create a larger scandal with
the investigation than the original crime was able
to do.*

*I'm also having all known art buyers followed
in an effort to find what was taken from you. This
will soon come to a satisfactory ending for everyone
involved, I'm certain. I ask only for your patience and
your silence until that time.*

—*St. James*

❧～❧

"DELIVER THIS TO LORD KNOTTSBY," FALLON SAID AS HE
handed off the quickly written note to one of his men.

What he'd told the man was true. He'd simply
omitted the part about Grapling being the man
behind it all. Isabelle's life couldn't be risked.
Although Fallon had questioned everyone who
walked through his door over the past few weeks,
he still didn't trust…well, anyone. Not when it came
to Isabelle's well-being. He'd claimed in his note
that he was growing closer to a resolution, but with
Grapling, one could never be too careful. Grapling
was still beyond the Spares' reach even now, though
the damage he'd done with his vengeful plot was
getting smaller by the day. It was only a matter of
time before one of the men known for having a
hand in art acquisitions led him to Grapling and the
missing paintings. He'd had men trailing the every
step of such individuals for weeks. But could he trust
his men? The words of Grapling's note about their

game still ate at him, but Fallon forced his lingering doubts away.

Only one letter remained, and the forger had been removed from play a week ago. Then there would be only the missing artwork, but Isabelle would be safe. The one outstanding letter would keep Isabelle in his home for a time but not forever. He cleared his throat and shifted some papers around on his desk, seeking order in the midst of troublesome thoughts.

"Should we question the art dealer we found? It appeared to be a promising lead since he has access to a ship," one of his men asked.

"Of course. Get the answers we need," Fallon replied, knowing this could be the order that brought everything to an end with Isabelle. But it was the right thing to do. "Will you excuse me," he muttered as he rounded his desk and headed for the door.

If the hours were indeed limited in which she would remain under his roof—and they very well could be—Fallon didn't want to waste another second away from her.

He didn't run from his library in his haste to see her, but in his mind he did. He took the stairs two at a time before striding down the hall in her direction. His hand paused on the doorknob as he forced himself to wait for a second to keep from racing into the room and sweeping her up in his arms. No matter the sense of urgency, no matter the need that pounded through his body, he couldn't run at her like a schoolboy determined to claim some prize.

But she was a prize. Every smile, every uncensored laugh that tripped from her lips, every sleepy sigh she made as she drifted to sleep in his arms, every curious touch of her fingers bestowed on him a gift.

He let out a telling, ragged breath and opened the door. Spotting her in her favorite place to read—the corner of the sofa by the fire—he crossed the room, careful not to rush.

She was curled up like a cat on a lazy afternoon. A book was open in her lap, and she looked up at him, disoriented, as if he'd just pulled her back from a far-away land. He wondered briefly what exotic life she'd inhabited this afternoon. He was about to ask, but then she smiled in that manner she had that made him wish he could join her inside those fanciful daydreams for even a moment. In her eyes, the world must glitter as if perpetually caught by the setting sun. When she turned her round-eyed gaze on him, even he felt a bit shinier than before. He wished he could be the man she clearly perceived him to be, but he was mortal, flawed to his core, and he wanted to enjoy the little time they had left together.

"Come with me," he said as an idea took root in his mind. She'd been locked within these walls too long. He wanted to share his home and his world with her. That wasn't possible, but there was still one place he could take her. He took her hand and pulled her to her feet. Glancing down, he smiled. Isabelle was barefoot, as had become her habit in the past week, but there was no need to delay for the sake of stockings and shoes. She didn't need shoes tonight. He remembered the day many years ago when the large smooth stones had been added so Pearl could walk across the surface more easily. Isabelle would be comfortable there tonight. The sun had been bright in the sky today; the rocks would still be warm this early in the evening.

"I'm leaving?" she asked as they reached the door, her hand tightening on his.

He stopped and turned around to face her. Was she sensing the same impending end to things that he was? He'd been so wrapped up in his own thoughts on the matter that he hadn't considered Isabelle's concerns at all. "You're leaving my bedchamber. That's all." He lifted his free hand to her upturned face, caressing her cheek and brushing his lips against hers in a brief kiss. "I want to show you something."

Relief flooded her eyes, making his heart clench. "I thought perhaps it was over."

"Do you think I release my prisoners so easily?"

She bit her lip and lowered her lashes as a blush spread across her face.

He tilted her chin up until her gaze met his. "You're not going to leave my sight."

"Where are we going, then, my captor?"

"I have a garden," he said as he led her through the door and into the hall.

"Someone could see me if I'm outside," she whispered at his side. She had a slight skip in her step as she moved down the hall, her clear excitement showing through her wary words. "Isn't that why I've been imprisoned with you these past few weeks?"

"No one will see you," he promised. He opened a door at the end of the hall and ushered her inside the service passage. This hall must not get regular use—not a single candle lit the way—but he remembered the path well. Securing her hand in his, he led her deeper into the dark.

"I can see the garden from the window. It doesn't look very private," she mused.

"That isn't where we're going." He turned to the right and pulled her along behind him.

"You have a private garden I could have visited instead of being locked away all day?"

"I forgot it existed, to be quite honest," he admitted. They reached the door to the stairs, and he pulled it open on creaking hinges. "I haven't visited in years. No one has."

"Does it have high stone walls that are covered with vines preventing anyone from finding the gate?"

"We're in London, not the countryside somewhere on the Continent, but it likely is overrun with vines. It hasn't been tended to in ages." He took a step up and turned back to her. "Mind the stairs."

"Where is this garden?"

"You certainly have a list of questions this evening."

"If you were locked away for weeks on end then suddenly allowed a glimpse of the outdoors, wouldn't you have questions?" she asked from behind him on the narrow stairs.

He really had imprisoned her. She teased him with good humor over the loss of her freedom, but he had kept her locked well away for longer than was ideal for anyone's happiness. He wanted Isabelle to be happy. He would give anything, do anything... "I am sorry this happened, that you've had to remain hidden away from sight."

"I'm glad I've been hidden away with you."

Her softly spoken words caught him like an anchor tossed into his heart, almost causing him to stumble. He turned back to Isabelle as he reached for the knob on the narrow wooden door, only seeing her silhouette in the dark. "I know it hasn't been pleasant all the time."

"Being locked away in your bedchamber has its advantages."

He couldn't see her blush, but he imagined it was there, blooming in her cheeks like flowers in spring. "If you're talking about having time on your hands to learn to paint or read a book, I'm going to be quite disappointed."

"This morning I was reading one where the heroine was sent to live in another country, away from everyone she knew. And I found myself thinking, 'Did she survive a blow to the head? Was she saved from certain imprisonment by a dashing gentleman? Did he kiss her?' For once the reality of my life is more exciting than the fantasy."

"Dashing?" His hand tightened around the doorknob, but he made no move to open the door.

"Yes, dashing. And unlike the lady in the story, I *was* bashed over the head, rescued, held prisoner, kissed… My life is better than a story."

"Only you would consider surviving an assault to be better than attending balls or taking tea from the comfort of your home." He smiled and opened the door, stepping out into the moonlight.

"It's quite dramatic—" She broke off as she stepped over the threshold and onto the roof of his home. "Oh! What is this place? It's lovely, Fallon!" She moved out onto the stone floor and dropped his hand. "See? I told you my life was better than a book now."

"And I told you no one would see you here except me." He watched as she began to explore the abandoned rooftop garden, unable to take his eyes from her.

She walked forward, inspecting the flowers one by one. The plants that had once been meticulously cared for had gone wild, creeping out of the pots they had been planted in. Vines clung to the parapet wall that surrounded the area, closing them into a starlit room, alive with green leaves. In this long-forgotten portion of his home, the garden had grown together into a riot of flowers that made the roof seem like another world hanging in the night sky. The effect was quite becoming and somehow matched the barefoot, loose-haired lady he'd brought here. This was where she belonged.

"You never come here?" she asked as she moved to the parapet wall to peer over to the street far below.

He would climb those stairs every day if it meant seeing Isabelle. He could see her spending her days here, picking blooms in the afternoon sun. But it would do no good to allow his mind to linger on that future. He'd done too good a job at hiding her whereabouts, and there was no need for him to save her reputation with a quick wedding. Everyone thought she'd left town. His life wasn't suited to such sedate domestic life anyway. This was never meant to be a lasting situation. Soon Isabelle would return to her home, safe to live out her life however she chose. Which meant this night was precious, one of the last few he would spend alone with her.

Turning back to him, she trailed her hand over the

glossy leaves of the plant at her side. "I would live out my days in this place and never leave."

"You know it rains quite a bit here. You thought my bedchamber was bad, try being relegated to my roof on a rainy London day," he teased in an attempt to toss off the thought.

"It's not raining now. It's...perfect." A warm breeze lifted her hair from her shoulder for a second, as if even the wind agreed with her words.

It seemed that tonight was planned by the fates and approved by the same deity who had sent Isabelle down from the clouds to live among men; the evening was indeed perfect. Overhead the stars glinted against the black sky, matching the starry-eyed look Isabelle was giving him right now. "All the stars in the sky. All shining for you. Just as it should be," Fallon mused.

"No, this is as it should be." She stepped closer to him and wrapped her arms around his neck.

"I take back what I said about your smiles. I like that your smiles are mine, like a secret only I know," she murmured, making him aware that he was grinning at her.

"You make me smile," he said as he wound his arms around her waist.

"Thank you for all of this. Truly, Fallon."

"I should have thought of it earlier. You can come back here anytime you would like, even during the day. I'll make arrangements with Mrs. Featherfitch to escort you. You're in no danger here."

"I meant bringing me to your home. You found me, rescued me, and protected me."

She looked up at him as if he'd done a great thing,

but all he'd been thinking about through any of it was her. It was hardly heroism.

"No matter how dramatic and exciting I find imprisonment with you, I know having me underfoot has been difficult. *Complicated*, you called it, I believe."

Unable to keep from touching her more, he splayed his hands over her back, holding her within his embrace. "I was wrong when I said that."

"I know my stay hasn't been ideal for you. I've turned your quiet bachelor existence on its ear. You've only just started sleeping in your own bed again, and even then I'm taking up space there." Her cheeks turned pink, and her lips curved up as she looked at him.

He ran his hands up her back, her hair tickling his fingers as the breeze blew around them. He wasn't going to argue that she'd turned his life on end, but he liked the space she inhabited in his bed. Last night, while holding Isabelle close, he'd experienced the most restful sleep he'd had in years. And his home was functioning better than it ever had before. His life was better because she was in it. And soon she would be gone.

"I was the one being difficult," he said. "Being with you is quite simple." As he spoke, he ran his hands up her arms. He paused to unlace her hands from his neck before tugging one sleeve of her day dress down her arm. Lowering his lips to meet her soft skin, he kissed the top of her shoulder.

"What's difficult is that I want to soak up every second I'm allowed with you. I want to savor you and give attention to every patch of exposed skin I see. How to choose…" His words trailed away as he gave her shoulder a playful bite and soothed it with his tongue.

She let out a harsh breath and tilted her head to the side, allowing him better access to her neck.

He moved at a brutally slow pace to the base of her neck, memorizing every curve of her body to look back upon later in the long hours ahead when he would sit alone. This was a dangerous game, one he might not survive, but he wanted to live every second of this night. They were together now. Future plans didn't matter. Isabelle was his only concern in the world.

Her skin was soft, like flower petals brushing against his lips. The taste on the tip of his tongue was sweeter than the finest candy, only with an earthy, salty edge that suited Isabelle to perfection. She was a wood nymph at heart, and tonight he wanted nothing more than to ignore the reality all around them and roll about on the forest floor with her.

"You see how difficult this is for me? Such a trial." he murmured as he followed the line of her neck with his mouth. Her hair brushed against his forehead as he pressed his lips to her delicate collarbone. She trembled beneath his touch, and he moved his hands to her waist, needing to hold on to her for as long as possible.

"Fallon," she whispered, her fingers digging into his arms as she leaned into him.

Guiding her to move with him, he took slow steps toward a garden bench that sat beneath the canopy of an overgrown shrub. As content as he was to roll about on the ground, she deserved better than his soiled fantasies. He stopped only when the backs of her knees brushed against the stone seat.

Releasing her only long enough to shed his coat, he draped it over the bench. Then his hands were back on her, memorizing every curve. He pressed his lips to hers in a kiss meant to promise all that was possible when Isabelle leaned closer and demanded more than just promises. He almost smiled against her as he deepened their kiss, his hands roaming over her body.

Her fingers tangled in the fabric of his cravat. She pulled at the knot with impatient movements for a second. Finally, she broke their kiss to tug the fabric loose from his throat. He went still as he allowed her to remove his clothing while he held her close. It was an oddly intimate moment, having her assistance with such a mundane task as removing his cravat, but the air around them sizzled with the intensity of the action. He watched her as she unknotted the fabric, then her fingers trailed down his waistcoat, pulling at the buttons.

A second later she paused, their gazes meeting in the moonlight, but her eyes had gone dreamy as she looked at him. "This is it."

"What?"

"I've always wanted to live within the pages of Tristan and Isolde's story, and now I am. This really is the shining, beautiful moment I always envisioned."

"I'm familiar with the tale," he hedged, though he refused to admit to any similarity between their time together and such a tragic story. Tonight was not the night for honesty about their future or even honesty with himself. Tonight was about Isabelle.

She sighed as she slid her hands over his chest. "The sweet floral scent on the night air, I'm here alone with you... I've always wanted to have a romance like Isolde's."

That was what she wanted? He hated to poke holes, especially since she was running her hands over his body at the moment, but her thinking was somewhat flawed. "You're aware that she marries Tristan's king, has scandalous talk surrounding her most of her life because of her relations with Tristan, and then dies of a broken heart in the end, aren't you?"

"That isn't the important part of the story," she whispered as she rose to her toes and brushed her lips across his. "Those are simply unfortunate details. For a time she had Tristan, and they slept in the trees."

"And for a time you're here with me in an over-grown garden," he finished as he studied her. There was something more that she wasn't saying, and he could guess it had something to do with the love she'd proclaimed to have for him before. It was odd that the sentiment that made him flee not too many days ago now made him pull her closer. And even more frightening for his sanity, he realized he wanted to hear those blasted words from her lips again. They were better off not speaking of it.

Words, in his experience, were dangerous things. They were to be avoided at all costs.

With that in mind, he kissed her—hard, the type of kiss that choked out all thought. Her fingers tangled in his hair. No confessions of love and tragic endings to romance this evening. The night was theirs, and he knew precisely how he wished to spend it.

He began gathering her dress in his hands, dragging the thin material up her body. But a heartbeat later, Isabelle grabbed it from him and ripped it over her head. The honest and open action would be surprising with any other lady, but not with Isabelle. She was the curious one who threw open doors to see what hid behind them, the one who gave her heart out with ease, and the one who stood before him now, bathed in moonlight with a look of anticipation on her lovely face.

He let out a harsh breath and pulled his shirt over his head in one swift motion, tossing it to the ground at their feet. He allowed his fingers to skim down her sides, slowly. There was no hurry, no ticking clock or place he needed to be. None that he cared about at any rate. He needed only her, and there was no burden of time between them tonight.

The moon cast a pale glow across her skin. He raised one hand to cup her cheek, unable to take his eyes from such a beautiful sight. "Moonlight suits you."

"Have you ever wanted to dive into the silver light of the moon and swim about for a while?" she asked as she trailed her fingertips over the ridges and valleys of the muscles on his abdomen.

"Only if you're with me." Fallon couldn't stay still any longer. He needed to touch her. Pulling her close, he lifted her from the ground and placed her on his coat he'd thrown over the stone bench. He crouched down in front of her to look in her eyes as he smoothed his hands down her sides.

Surprise turned to excitement as he watched her. She was exquisite. Cool light washed down on her body, pouring over her delicate shoulders and her arms. She held them spread to the sides, grasping the bench on either side of her rounded hips.

The moss covering the gravel around the bench cushioned his knees as he shifted to kneel before her. He ran his hands down the outside of her thighs, wanting to touch her everywhere—as much to feel her body as to prove to himself that she was real. "You look like a mythical creature come to life. I'm fairly certain this exact piece of statuary lives in a garden somewhere."

"You're perfect," she whispered, her gaze on his. "You do know that, don't you, Fallon?"

He shook his head. "You are." Leaning forward, he captured her lips beneath his.

She slipped her hands up his arms, trailing her nails over his shoulders in tantalizing strokes as she matched the movement of his tongue. Forever—he could remain here forever with her. Even kneeling on moss-covered stones was worth it if he could just kiss her like this for the rest of his life.

When she finally broke their kiss, she had a dazed look in her eyes and drew in ragged breaths. He dragged his lips across the line of her jaw. She tilted her head back as he moved slowly down her neck to the swell of her breasts. Beautiful, round… He moved his lips over her soft skin, unable to satisfy his hunger for her. Her smooth curves glided beneath his mouth and his cheek as he drank her in and swam about in her moonlit body.

Everything about her was soft, inviting, and more than willing to discover the next secret this night possessed. Flicking the hardened peak of her nipple with his tongue, he glanced up to watch her reaction, only to see the desperation that must reside in his own eyes reflected back at him. She pressed forward in a quiet request for more of what he'd done to her in his bed last night, and he smiled against her. He wanted this and so much more with her. He wanted everything, and most of all he wanted it to never end. He moved his palms over her soft skin, learning every detail of her body with his hands and his mouth.

Only pausing the wandering touch of his fingers when he reached the point where her legs curled over the garden bench, he rubbed small circles against the insides of her knees with his thumbs until she relaxed into him. He traced his hands up her thighs as he gave her breast one last kiss. Shifting her arms to rest her weight upon and leaning back on the bench, she watched him, curiosity burning bright in her eyes. It was a position of complete trust and openness. And he wouldn't betray that trust—not tonight, not ever.

Dipping his head, he followed the path his hands had made up her thighs, trailing his lips over her sensitive skin. Her breathing grew harsh in the still of the evening.

"What are you..." she began, but her words slipped away as he brushed the backs of his knuckles over the apex of her thighs. He glanced up at her. If she wanted him to stop, he would mourn the lost pleasure of touching her like this, but he would do as she wished. But when he saw the wide-eyed look of amazement on her face, he almost chuckled. Isabelle seemed to have no concerns about "being sensible," and this moment was no different. He continued to tease her with touches of his fingers until she exhaled a harsh breath and opened farther to him.

Continuing the caresses, he moved closer, allowing her to learn his touch as much as he was learning from her body. Unrushed, no matter his own slamming heartbeat or her harsh breathing, he drew his thumb in closer to the bud above her core. Drawing slow circles around the sensitive skin there, he pulled a choked *oh* from her lips.

She tilted her hips toward him and grabbed his forearm in the next second, and this time he did chuckle. Only she would be this eager when other sheltered ladies would faint or some such at the very idea. He slowly slid his tongue first up one side of the silken skin of her lips, then down the other. And he watched her, wanting to understand every nuance of her body and what brought her pleasure. After traveling the same path with his tongue for another moment, he drew her outer lips into his mouth, sucking on her until her breath caught and she arched into him for more. He grinned at her show of enjoyment.

Dragging his teeth gently along the folds on the other side, he flicked his tongue over the sensitive bud. She almost arched off the bench, but he held her steady. Pulling the most delicate part of her into his mouth, he sucked on her, alternating with teasing flicks of his tongue. She might have come apart right there if he'd continued to do just that, but she deserved more. She should have it all. Not to mention he wanted to feel her, to have her mad for him. He waited a moment, a heartbeat, then as she relaxed he drove into her, tugging her closer to the edge of her own desire. She was wet, beautiful, wild, and pushing into his hand for more. And he was in awe of her.

Licking and sucking at the very heart of her while he pushed his fingers deep inside, he looked up to see her brows draw together. Her head fell back, and she let loose a scream that could be heard across London. She was amazing. He pulled back as she began to shake. He would give her anything in the world, and tonight he'd given her pleasure. A swell of pride bloomed in his chest as he ran his hands over her body once more.

Pushing himself up from the mossy ground, he shifted to the bench beside her and dragged her bare legs up to drape across his own. Holding her close to his body, he listened to her racing heartbeat, relished every shiver of her body as she came back down from the peak where he'd taken her. She leaned her head against his shoulder and squirmed even closer into his embrace, and he wrapped her tighter in his arms.

His beautiful Isabelle.

There were no words that could do justice to what he felt for her in this moment. The entire garden glinted in the fragile, cool light of this magical night. She was his, and he was hers, and for now nothing could break the spell that had been cast between them.

Sometime later, leaves rustled around them in the breeze, but all he heard now was his own heartbeat.

He wasn't certain how long he'd sat here with Isabelle in his arms—not long enough for his liking.

For the first time in years, he wasn't rushing to his next destination. There was no agenda for them tonight, no meeting to hurry away to or operation to oversee. He pulled her closer to his body, not wanting to let her go. If he were to be honest—and he clearly had trouble with such a notion—he must admit he didn't want to *ever* watch her walk away. It was unrealistic to think that he could keep Isabelle in his life forever though. Even if he could balance his work with marriage, there was so much about his life that she didn't know.

Would she stay curled in his arms as she was now if she knew the truth?

He couldn't bring himself to tell her about the Spare Heirs Society. Not with ongoing operations taking place just downstairs from where they sat. He'd done too much wrong already, led men into too much danger. And he would be risking too much to tell her the truth—he would be risking the loss of another evening like this one. Dipping his chin, he pressed his lips to the top of her head, and she sighed and wiggled closer to him.

He had to hold on to her, not just tonight but forever. There must be a path forward from this place in which he didn't lose her in the end. It was perhaps the most important operational plan he'd ever attempted to make, yet he had no idea how to proceed. All he knew was he didn't want to let her go.

This isn't logical behavior, you know that. You'll have to allow her to return home soon. But he couldn't hand her over to her father. She'd be gone, beyond his reach forever. He needed the light that she brought into his life, the laughter, the freedom she pushed him to take from his tasks even if for only a few minutes. He needed to protect her and cherish her. Who would listen to her fantasies if not him?

And then the truth was in front of him. How had he not considered it before?

Nothing about this situation or his actions in it was logical as he had come to be accustomed in his life because *love* wasn't logical.

Fallon ran a now-shaking hand down her bare arm. He loved Isabelle. He loved every fanciful thought in her head, the way she curled up beside him in the evenings, the sparkle in her eyes when she looked at him, and the way she offered the generosity of her heart to anyone who might be interested.

He was more than interested; he loved her beyond reason. And the implications of that fact were more frightening than any seedy London alley he'd ever walked down at night.

❧

Fallon stared out across what once had been a drawing room. The gentle clank of balls from the billiard table accented the leather-scented air. It was a quiet afternoon at headquarters, and he sat back in his usual chair in the corner.

He had founded the Spare Heirs so long before that he couldn't remember what it was like not to govern over a large band of men. He couldn't recall having an excess of free time in his early days in town, but how had he filled his hours without his endless rounds of meetings? One thing, though, hadn't changed a bit in all that time: Kelton Brice, Lord Hardaway, would still talk his ear off whether he was listening to the man's story or not.

"You won't believe what he said to that. He told me that he'd never set foot in Tattersalls—when he bought that horse out from under me not a fortnight ago. And when I compliment his new mount, what does he do? Not act sheepish about it, I know that much. No." He drew out the word and stretched his arms to the sides. "Instead he suggests we race. There I was an hour later…"

Perhaps the length and frequency of Hardaway's stories were the reasons Fallon lacked time for himself. If he had less responsibility to the Spares, would he have enough hours left to devote to Isabelle? She may think Isolde's life pleasantly dramatic, but a life surrounded by talk and scandal wasn't a reality that would suit her. She deserved to be happy. Happiness was all she wanted—happiness with an honorable gentleman in a normally functioning home. He couldn't offer her anything but the first. After all, he wasn't the least bit honorable. He'd flouted more rules of society than he could count, and he was skilled with numbers. His entire life's work had been built upon creating his own law, his own fiefdom within the land in which they lived. And how he lived…the men who milled about this room from day-to-day relied on him. His home was far from average.

Survival. Conventional notions such as honesty and virtuous actions couldn't always be adhered to if one was to survive, let alone manage the lives of others when they would otherwise have nothing.

If Isabelle knew the truth of who he was, what he'd neglected to tell her about his past with Grapling, what he did every day in order to protect and maintain the Spares, would she even consider him a friend anymore? She teased him about being a pirate, but she didn't really want a future with someone who secretly lived outside the bounds of law and society as he did. Last night she'd been pliable and warm in his arms, and he wanted to hold her close again. He wanted to allow her the freedom to wander wherever pleased her, not just secluded gardens where her view of his life was limited. Perhaps it was time to change a few things at headquarters. It was *his* home, after all. And he loved Isabelle.

"And that's when Lord Forth and I swung from the stars and slid down a merry arse beam of moonlight to dance together in Hyde Park because you are not listening to anything I say."

"I'm glad to hear that your evening was amusing," Fallon said in an attempt to reassure his friend.

"Damn, St. James! That was disgraceful. I've long admired your ability to hear me without truly listening. You're the only man I know who can think of three things at once and give them all his full attention. But this—" He broke off with a wave of his hand that nearly knocked the drink decanter off the table. "This is a shameful show of your talents."

"Apologies for disappointing you." Fallon rubbed his eyes. He hadn't had much sleep last night. Not that he was complaining about the particular events that had kept him from his bed.

"I've never seen you in such a state. Perhaps if you took up drinking. I know you're opposed, but you can't do much worse than what I see here. A nice glass of whiskey makes me a bit more cheerful about my circumstances, I know that."

"I'm plenty cheerful."

"Oh, yes. You're correct, of course. When I think of you, I think, 'Now there's a cheerful fellow.'"

"I've been practicing my smile. Laughing more often as well." He'd actually smiled more in the past few weeks than he had in years. Isabelle had that effect on people. She'd lured him into the light, and now that he was there, he wasn't certain what to do with the darkness in his life.

"Your grin is positively blinding. And I'm sure your distraction has nothing to do with the lady you have locked in your suite of rooms—for her protection, of course."

Fallon stared his friend down. He owed Hardaway no answers. But for all the words this man had poured into Fallon's ears over the years, Hardaway was now quietly listening.

"With Crosby Steam Works predicting a healthy profit as well as a few other endeavors here and there, perhaps it's time for the Spare Heirs Society to change. We could invest in more legal ventures. End the schemes. No more dark alleys or exchanged sacks of coin. Fewer men lingering about the place. We could live on the proper side of the law, not dirty our hands with threats or payoffs. We could be proper gentlemen, noble and honest even…"

"The Steam Works Claughbane set up for us does show potential. I don't know, stepping away from the shady side of society would be a change. But what of the others? The Spares is bigger than the few of us who began this misguided venture all those years ago. Not to mention that we'd no longer have allies to keep us aware of potential threats."

"Proper gentlemen don't require such things."

"Then you have no wish to hear about the arrival of three different men in our fair land with interests in importing a specific set of stolen goods?"

"You talked of your jealousy of a horse's flanks for twenty minutes when you knew we had word about the Fairlyn art theft?" Fallon asked, leaning forward to pin a glare on his friend.

"It was an amusing story, and you didn't even listen to half of it."

"Is this word from the docks, or does Grapling have someone who talked?"

"The barmaids in London are a wealth of information. Grapling hasn't been back to the tavern where I got the information yet, but if he returns, I'll hear of it."

"Do we know anything about the potential buyers? And how perceptive is your barmaid? Grapling already applied dye to his hair once. He could escape even those who remember him."

"St. James, we'll find him. I wasn't the one who heard of the arrival of the buyers, or I would have tackled Grapling to the ground right there. You know, the type of devious activity you don't want me to do anymore."

"I'm only trying to—"

"Please Lady Isabelle?" Hardaway cut in.

Fallon fell silent, watching his friend. To be brutally honest, he was torn. He wanted to be good enough for Isabelle. The best way he knew to solve her problems was the way he worked for everyone around him—in an underhanded, scheming manner. But as soon as he did, she would be gone.

Hardaway pushed his empty glass of whiskey away and leaned his forearms on the edge of the table. "Let's keep her safe and alive for now by using every underhanded, illegal trick that we have."

"You're only saying that because you want to bash in Grapling's skull," Fallon countered.

"That's true. But, St. James? The Spares do a great deal of good as well. My grandmother always told me—"

"I've already suffered through a story of a horse. Now I'm to hear Grandmother's wisdom as well?" Fallon sat back in his seat, preparing for a long tale.

"I'll summarize then. Balance—it's all about balance. Good, bad, it's quite relative."

"Your grandmother told you that being bad was acceptable?" He raised a brow.

"Hers was a story involving rotten fruit and jams for winter. It's a nice tale, though I always thought she lacked my sense of excitement. Now if she'd added a wager on a nice piece of horse flesh…"

If his problems were as simple as setting aside jam for winter, he wouldn't have the lady he loved locked upstairs while he planned crimes against good sense. But balance wasn't a bad concept.

Fallon stood from his chair. "I've sat here long enough."

"You don't want to hear more? I'm quite knowledgeable about life after a glass of whiskey," Hardaway said as Fallon rounded the table.

"Like you said, it's about balance." And right now, he was leaning in Isabelle's direction.

Sixteen

Isabelle Fairlyn's Diary
March 1817

Today is a perfect day! The first hint of spring is in the air. The flowers in the garden will bud within the week, greeting the most cheerful of seasons with their first blooms. I ventured to Bond Street with Mother and Victoria for the last necessary item before tonight's ball—dancing slippers to match my pale-blue gown. Although I've attended a number of events thus far, tonight's ball is anticipated to be one of the largest of the season. I'm having trouble containing my excitement. Soon music will fill the air, and I will twirl around the ballroom beneath the glow of a thousand candles. I do hope the beads on my dress sparkle there the way they do in my bedchamber. Their shine reminds me of starlight. I will savor every second this night has to offer and every swish of my gown as it billows out around my ankles.

—Isabelle

"OH, SWEET, SWEET ISABELLE. YOU HAVE NO IDEA what I have in store for you this season." Reginald chuckled and tossed the diary back into his bag where he'd found it this afternoon.

If only he could see her weeping face now. Being locked away in St. James's home was enough to make anyone sob, and Isabelle had been there for some time now.

He clucked his tongue. "Protect the little pawn, St. James. Don't let her father down in such a horrible fashion."

He moved to the table in the corner of his new room where he kept a bottle of whiskey and poured a glass. He smiled as he brought it to his lips and took a swallow.

"I'm going to win, you know," he muttered to the empty room.

With the addition of St. James's own maid Emily to his ranks, Reginald would now know every move that was made inside the man's precious headquarters. If Isabelle flinched, Reginald would know of it within the hour. The man couldn't hide her away forever, imprisoned in his home. At some point, she would want to wear those ball gowns and dancing slippers she was so fond of discussing in her diary. And whenever she showed her sickeningly sweet face, Reginald would be waiting. He drained the last of his whiskey and set the glass down with a loud clunk. "I promise."

Isabelle slipped the brush through the ends of her hair where it fell over her shoulder and smiled at herself in the small mirror on the table. She was in love, and true love really was divine! She'd never known such happiness as she now experienced, and it was all because of Fallon. She sighed and stroked the bristles through her hair again.

Last night, as well as every other night as of late, they'd talked until she was certain the sun would soon rise. The topic was never of any importance, but she knew the rhythm of Fallon's thoughts now, when he would chuckle, what made him smile. Then they'd drifted off to sleep together, wrapped in sweet thoughts and each other's arms. Their relationship may have grown out of a necessity for safety, but like vines from far-cast seeds on the wind, they'd grown together, intertwining further with every passing day. He remained her friend, but now that friendship was layered with anticipation for his next words, his next touch of her skin, their next night together... She craved every moment spent with him like flowers longed for the sun. *This* was love. She knew it. This time it was real, and it was finally hers.

Fallon had risen early this morning, as was his custom, and left her to rest. But what lady could rest when she'd finally found love? Not Isabelle.

That had been several hours ago, though. And now she looked to the door at every creak of the house, wanting to see Fallon again. Just then there was a sound in the hall, and she spun to see him walking toward her.

"Get dressed and come with me," he said in greeting, an intent look turning his face quite grave.

She wasn't certain what he had planned for her, but as she would likely follow him to the gallows, she rose from her chair, tossed her brush aside, and crossed the room to quickly pull on her petticoats and stuff her feet in her slippers. A moment later she joined him.

"Are we going to your garden?" she asked hopefully as she wrapped her fingers into his steady grasp.

"No." Something that looked almost like worry drew his brows in for a second. It couldn't be, though. Fallon rarely showed such emotions in his gaze. He took a breath and laced his fingers more firmly with hers. "It's time I show you my home."

"Oh!" His home! He was going to give her a tour of his home in its entirety? Her heart pounded with excitement mixed with trepidation. "Won't someone see me? I thought it wasn't safe."

"Trust me," he said as he held the door for her.

"I do," she said, but her pace slowed as she reached the threshold of the door. She'd been here so long, and now she was to leave the confines of his bedchamber. It was a rather momentous occasion and worthy of a pause for appreciation.

Sighing, he turned back to her. "It's a quiet day. No one is about." Clearly he misunderstood her hesitation, but she didn't stop to explain. She wanted to see his home more than anything.

She smiled and moved into the candlelit hall that stretched off in one direction. There was no one in sight between his bedchamber door and the far corner, and a spring bounced in her step as she allowed Fallon to lead her forward. Was this one step closer to being asked to stay here forever? She hoped so. "Is it the staff's day away?" she asked as they moved down the hall together. "I can't recall when I scheduled it... I suppose it was today."

Fallon made a noncommittal sound in his throat and kept walking.

"Mrs. Featherfitch, the poor dear. She brought me food this morning on her day to leave the house and see to her own needs. I'll have to thank her for her sacrifice."

Fallon veered to the side of the hall, pulling her with him. Opening a door hidden in the molding, he revealed a service stairwell that led to the lower floors, but he paused before entering. He looked back at her, his eyes containing some fond sentiment she couldn't quite define. "You're beautiful."

She hadn't dressed to her usual standards since she'd arrived here. As long as she was Fallon's prisoner, it hadn't seemed necessary to pin her hair—or wear shoes, for that matter. Today she'd only gone one slight step beyond that with her petticoats. "I'm a wrinkled mess," she countered.

"Not where it matters most." He reached out to caress her cheek, and she tilted her head into his palm as his lips met hers. It was a brief kiss, but it held the promise of passion ahead.

Three words sprang to her lips, and she worked to choke them back down to the stew of phrases that boiled within her—all of them better left unsaid. *I love you. I don't want to leave. Please ask me to be your wife.* But she said nothing as she squeezed his hand and followed him into the darkness.

He'd made it clear when he abandoned her for two days that he didn't want to hear her professions of love, even if it was the largest truth she'd ever known. She'd realized a few nights ago as he held her in the moonlight that she loved him—fully and completely. All the feelings that had come before didn't compare to the hold Fallon St. James had on her heart. He'd been right about Hardaway and right, for that matter, about what she'd claimed she felt for Fallon before. After a month almost solely in his company, she knew him now, and she understood her own heart. For the first time, she was in love. But she couldn't tell him, not when her words could chase him away again and their time together could end at any moment.

"Where are you taking me first?" she asked, her voice echoing in the staircase.

"What would you like to see first?"

She wanted to see the parts that Fallon inhabited most, to learn more about the man she loved. "Where is it that you go when you leave me during the day?"

"The library," he replied. "My desk is there, my work—"

"That is what I would like to see," she announced.

He grumbled something that she didn't quite hear and led her to a narrow door and then into a wide hall where a rug ran the length of the expansive area. Artwork filled the walls, and candles burned brighter than on the upper floors of his home, lighting the length of the space with a warm, beeswax-scented glow. His home was not what she'd expected of a house left to a secret caregiver. The size of the building was more fitting to be a ducal residence. In fact, her friend Roselyn's home was considerably smaller than Fallon's. A simple bachelor residence this was not. But there was nothing simple about Fallon.

She looked up at him, wondering what other surprises he held, and she saw him glance around as though to check that they still hadn't been seen. Then he led her through a large wooden door that proved to open into one end of his library. The comforting, welcoming scent of wood paneling, books, and leather hung in the air around her. A large desk stood centered on the tall windows that lined one wall. Everything in Fallon's home was of a grand scale, more so than she'd imagined—which was quite the feat. This room was no different. Above, the high, painted-yellow ceilings were accented with beams that stretched from wall to wall, and her feet sank into a thick rug. This was the sort of room she could be happily locked away in for weeks on end.

It wasn't terribly masculine, even with the leather furniture that sat around the fireplace and in front of the desk, but compared with his bedchamber, this room was certainly intended for a man's use. She smiled at the thought of Fallon spending his days here. It was as if a small mystery about the man had been solved in her mind. She turned to watch him as he closed what appeared to be the main door at the opposite end of the room, keeping her hidden from the view of any passersby. Fallon was always thinking, always protecting her from harm.

Her love for him swelled in her chest, and Isabelle turned away from him to further examine his library before he could read the emotion in her eyes. Trailing her hand over the back of the nearest chair, she said, "This is where you come when you're away from me?"

"It is…for the most part."

"I know I said I wouldn't pry…but you know of my curiosity."

"I do," he replied as he took slow steps back toward her.

"Fallon, what is it that you *do* with your time that consumes you so?"

His brows drew together for a second before he spoke as if what he did took great thought to explain. "I have interests in certain endeavors, investments to look after, and lately an art theft to solve. There's also a lady residing in my bedchamber who is taking up an ever-larger portion of my days—and my nights." He grinned as he finally neared where she stood. "Not that I mind."

She looked down at her hands where she picked at a decorative nail head on the leather chair in front of her. "I suppose this lady you keep in your bedchamber will be gone soon and your life can return to normal." Forcing herself to look up, she met his gaze, finally discussing what had become as off-limits a topic of conversation between them as love. "I will, won't I? We never speak of it, but we both know that day will come."

"It will," he confirmed. His low voice sounded haunted in the large room.

Truth be told, she dreaded the day she would be forced to leave here and return to her family's home. She had no wish to leave. For her part, she loved him. Isabelle cleared her throat and looked away in search of a change of subject.

"Is that one of Lady Herron's relatives?" she asked, gesturing to the nearest painting hanging on the wall between bookshelves. The work depicted an older gentleman.

"I believe so, though the provenance of the pieces isn't documented anywhere, not that I've found." He moved closer at her back as he spoke, finally placing his hand on her shoulder and looking at the portrait with her. "I'm particularly fond of this fellow."

"I had a great-uncle who wore the same sort of look on his face whenever my sister and I would visit," she mused. "He was a good listener. Unfortunately that skill wasn't the least bit diminished in the middle of the night, when Victoria and I tried to steal sweets from his kitchen."

Fallon chuckled, the sound rumbling through her body. "This man is skilled in the same fashion. I discuss things with him often."

"Do you?" She turned to smile up at him over the similarity between them. Until now Isabelle thought only she conversed with paintings as if they were friends.

He grasped her hand once more and gave it a tug. "Come. I want to show you more of my home."

Twining her fingers through his, she walked with him toward the main door he'd shut earlier. "Your home is quite large, especially for a London residence." She shouldn't ask the question that lingered in her mind, but then she did. "Do you ever think of... sharing it with someone?"

He paused just inside the main library door and looked at her. "Are you interested?"

Yes! Was he serious? She licked her lips, searching for words that wouldn't make him run from her. "I don't want to leave you. Even once it's safe to do so."

He squeezed her hand and met her gaze with the most intent look she'd ever seen there. "My situation is a bit different from usual bachelor residences. There are things you should know, Isabelle, things about my life. Secrets—"

The door opened, and a humming Mrs. Featherfitch almost walked into her.

"Lady Isabelle!" The housekeeper clutched her heart and took a step back, looking at them. "You gave me a start. I wasn't expecting—"

"Isn't it your day to be off?" Isabelle asked, wishing the woman hadn't interrupted the most important conversation of Fallon's and her lives.

Mrs. Featherfitch shot her a questioning glance, then looked at Fallon and back again. "I was only checking that the fire had been tended since daybreak. There's a new maid, and she's forgetful with such things. I'll come back later."

"Stay," Fallon commanded. "We were just leaving."

Mrs. Featherfitch nodded, and they moved around her and out into what appeared to be an alcove off the main hall. Isabelle's heart still raced at both the possibilities opening in their discussion and then almost being knocked to the ground by the housekeeper. She studied the floor before her feet for a moment while she tried to regain her composure. Had he mentioned secrets she should know? And Mrs. Featherfitch hadn't appeared to know that this was her day off from her work. The entire encounter had been odd.

"You work your staff too hard, you know," she mused. "You work too hard as well."

"I've always thought I didn't have a choice in that regard."

"And now?" she asked, finally looking up to meet his gaze.

"Nothing has been the same since you came into my life."

"You still work overlong hours."

He shrugged and gave her a wry smile. "I'm here now, strolling the halls of my home with you midmorning. I trusted someone to carry out some business concerns on my behalf. I never do that. Ask anyone."

"You have a man of business?" Finally, she was learning a bit about the part of his life that was such a secret. She watched him, waiting for more clues that would complete her image of him.

He glanced to the main hall ahead for a second before replying. "In a way, yes."

"If I could only convince you to employ a valet, you might appear to be a respectable gentleman," she teased.

"Appearances can be deceiving," he replied, but that was when they stepped into the main hall.

This was the main hall of Fallon's home? There were cherubs painted on the ceiling, paintings framed in gold, a large chandelier heavy with candles, and a wide staircase. It was like something out of a fairy tale, and he used it as a bachelor residence?

She dropped his arm at the sight before her and rushed forward, staring up at the ceiling and twirling around to see the plump, little cherubs from all angles. "Oh, Fallon, this is lovely!"

"Those are Mortimer and Henry," he supplied as he joined her. "They watch over the activity in the house, but they never tell tales, so you have nothing to fear."

She laughed up at the merry depictions above. "They're the perfect housemates for you, then, my secretive one."

"I don't want to have secrets from you anymore," he said, pulling her attention from the ceiling.

She swallowed and turned to look at him. "Nor I you." She wanted to tell him that she loved him. She was about to burst with the containment of such news, but would he push her away again if she told him? She always rushed in, never considered consequences—until now. She couldn't risk losing him even for a day.

He glanced around, suddenly uncomfortable with their location. "This isn't the place for the discussion of secrets though, is it?"

"Secrets aren't things that flee into the night if not told. They'll be here for us tomorrow." And perhaps by then she would have found enough steel in her gut to tell him that she loved him.

"Tomorrow," he confirmed, looking relieved.

"Today I would like to continue our tour. What is this room?" She moved toward the large double doors nearby.

"The drawing room. Or it was when the house belonged to Pearl."

"You don't use it as a drawing room?" she asked. Her hand was on the doorknob, but a second later his fingers covered hers.

"Perhaps that's for tomorrow as well."

She frowned up at him in confusion. Secrets—apparently he was steeped in them, but tomorrow she would learn them all. And then she would finally tell him she loved him. She released the doorknob and took a step away from the drawing room door—for now.

～

After they'd returned from walking around his home, Fallon had left her alone for the rest of the afternoon to attend a meeting of some sort. He'd promised to return soon. Yet it wasn't soon enough.

Isabelle had reviewed the menu for the upcoming week, read a chapter in a book, examined the painting of a vase of roses that hung over the fireplace, sorted her own attempts at paintings, and now lay draped across his bed with her hair trailing nearly to the floor, waiting for him. Had it been an hour or days since he'd left her side? She wasn't certain, but it seemed like days.

"Practicing your fair-maiden-trapped-in-a-tower bit again?" Fallon's voice sounded from the door as he watched her. "I think soon you'll be ready to take the stage."

She turned toward him with a smile. "I've considered a life in the theater, but I think I prefer my own life at the moment."

"You enjoy being my prisoner?" He turned the key in the lock and cut his eyes back at her, amusement shining in their depths.

"It has its benefits."

"You're fortunate, you know," he mused as he pocketed the key and took a step in her direction. "I could have put you in chains in my dungeon if I chose to do so."

"You have a dungeon beneath your home?" she asked as she sat up from her dramatic position with wide eyes. Why hadn't he included *that* on the tour?

"Some believe so."

"Really?" she asked, scooting to the edge of the bed with her gaze on him.

"On second thought, you sound a bit too excited by the prospect of being chained to a dungeon wall."

"It would make for quite the ending to a story, if I were to ever tell anyone of my time here."

He took another step toward her. "Do you want our story to come to an end?"

No. I don't want it to ever end, her heart screamed, but she could hardly explain that to him without speaking of love. And they'd decided secrets were for tomorrow, not tonight. She licked her lips and looked down at her bare toes where they peeked out from the bottom of her day dress. "I'll never be able to tell anyone about this, so it hardly matters."

She glanced back up at Fallon to see something in his expression snap, as if a long-awaited decision had been made. She opened her mouth to ask if something was wrong, but he spoke first.

"On your feet, prisoner."

"What?" Isabelle asked, confused at the sudden change in him. "Are we going back to the garden? Downstairs?"

"No. You're a lady trapped in the tallest tower of a castle. You're not going anywhere."

Isabelle knew her smile must have covered half her face, and she giggled as she clambered to her feet. But a second later, she'd arranged her face to be that of a tortured lady. She squared her shoulders to Fallon, staring him down. "I only came here to save my family from harm. We had a bargain, sir. A bargain."

He raised a brow in question at the story forming in her mind. Wrapping his hands around her arms, he said, "The terms of our agreement have changed, my lady. You shouldn't have trusted me. I'm quite the wicked gentleman."

Isabelle gasped and looked up at him. "What will you do with me? I only ask that you spare my life and release my family from captivity."

"And if I'm so generous?" he asked, his voice dropping to a low rumble as he watched her.

"I'll stay here forever. I'll be yours forever." The raw honesty of her words hung between them for a moment. No matter the parts they played at the moment, at least that much was true.

Judging by the flash of emotion in his eyes, he knew she meant what she said. Yet it didn't force him away this time. Instead he leaned closer to ask, "Will you? That is tempting, but you may regret that offer." He lifted his hand to her jaw as if inspecting her. Then he slid his fingers down her throat and traced the line of her breastbone in a move that spoke of possession and hinted at what was to come. "Forever is quite a long time."

"I'll regret nothing," she countered, taking a tiny step toward him until she had to look up to meet his gaze. "If it saves the lives of my family and the poor village folk under their care, it's worth my sacrifice."

"The poor village folk?" He raised a brow at her in question. "I *am* wicked, aren't I?"

"Everyone says so."

"They don't know the extent of it. But you're about to." He took a step away from her. "Off with your dress."

Oh! This story was getting interesting! "If that's your command," she said.

"It is, or I'll put the chains back on you and rip the dress from your body myself," he warned.

"Will you?" She repeated his own words from a few minutes prior back to him with a grin.

"Do you dare to question me, prisoner?"

She eyed him for a second, but as she was actually rather fond of this dress, she pulled it over her head and dropped it at his feet.

Fallon didn't move instantly; instead, his gaze swept over her body. She could feel it like a featherlight touch, warming her bare skin. She stood before him completely naked while he still wore even his coat. Her heart pounded, and her breaths became shallow. Thus far he'd barely touched her, but the promise of what might happen next was thrilling.

Finally, he reached for her, lifting her from the ground. Her body was pressed against his in an instant. The rough wool of his coat abraded her breasts with every breath she took. He held her close, his hands cupping her rear and splaying across her lower back. This man she knew to be gentle and kind now, in this moment, only radiated power. But this wasn't part of the act. Fallon did possess a quiet strength; he simply didn't reveal that side of his character to her often. She found she loved this side as much as the other.

"What would happen if I dared question you?" she

asked as she slipped her fingers through the knot of his cravat, pulling the fabric tight at his throat even as she worked to remove the garment.

The look in his eyes was dangerous in the fading light of day that came through the windows. "Do you really wish to find out?"

"Yes."

He forgot to be her captor for a moment, laughing as he walked with her to his bed. She could remember a time when his laughter had been rare. That was no longer the case. But a moment later, the laughter faded as he looked at her. Without warning, he tossed her to land in the center of his bed.

When she gasped, he raised a brow at her and began stripping off his clothing. She'd seen his chest before, but that made it no less exciting now. She would likely always be awed by Fallon and what he kept hidden beneath those dark-gray ensembles. He kicked off his boots. Then with his hand paused at the top button of the fall of his breeches, he looked at her. "There's no going back from this point."

"I don't want to go back, Fallon," she confirmed, understanding fully his meaning. "And anyway," she added, "I made a bargain with a wicked gentleman, and now I must pay the price."

"You're perfect," he whispered almost to himself before shifting his attention to the buttons of his breeches.

"You'd best set the poor townsfolk free, unharmed, for what I'm pay...ing..." She was staring. She'd been taught that it wasn't nice to stare, but how could she not? He was all lean muscle with dark hair accenting his chest and tapering down to trim hips. "You're quite handsome you know…and…that." She gawked at the length of him, protruding in front of his powerful thighs. "I know the overall idea here, and you're *large*. You're going to—"

"Shh, I don't believe you're supposed to find your captor handsome," he said, stepping closer to her as he rounded the bed.

"I find it quite helpful, actually."

"What a difficult prisoner you are." He grabbed her ankle, dragging her closer as he crawled onto the bed.

She slid her hands up his arms to his shoulders, then down the planes of his chest, and around to glide down his back. Looking up into his eyes, she was caught in an instant by the emotion she saw shining in his gaze. She couldn't look away. And in that instant she knew—as much as he joked that she was his prisoner, he was just as much hers. Then his lips were on hers and she was melting beneath him.

His arms were braced around her in support of his weight, keeping space between them. But she wanted more. She wanted it all. She loved him. He trailed his lips over the line of her jaw, and she pressed her heels into the bed and squirmed closer to him. Arching off the bed, she pressed her body against his, loving the abrasion of his rough skin against hers.

Sensing her impatience, he shifted his weight and slid his hand down her belly, pressing his palm down against her body. He slipped two fingers farther down in some form of delicious torture. She writhed beneath his touch, wanting everything yet struggling to remain still to receive it. Then he dipped his fingers into her as he had last night, and her head fell back on the bed. "Fallon..." she breathed his name.

"Look at me," he murmured, and she opened her eyes.

It was growing rather dark in the room, but she could still see the care and concern for her in his eyes. His gaze was precious and tender. She couldn't look away. Her heart pounded in her ears.

He slid his hand around to her hip. She knew what was next, and she wanted it now. She wanted to embrace everything that made this man who he was. She wanted this. Gripping his back on either side of his spine, she tipped her hips up toward him.

He gave her a cautious smile just as he plunged into her. Her body stretched to receive him, and she stared up into his eyes. All at once, she had both a feeling of complete wholeness and the need for more. A second later the look of concern on his face passed and he pulled back to drive into her again. Only this time was different, and a new tension began to build within her. Each time he pushed into her, he brought her closer to the tipping point.

Shifting to his knees, he pulled her with him, still keeping the steady rhythm against her body. But now he moved his hands up her abdomen, pausing to gently pinch the sensitive peaks of her breasts. She bit her lip to keep from screaming. Somehow, even without words, he knew exactly what she needed, and she loved him all the more for it.

Then sliding his hands down her belly, still moving against her, he held her hip with one hand and touched her core with the other. She couldn't endure much more, but she wanted to more than she could say. She reached out and grasped the bedclothes for purchase, needing to hold on to something or fall into oblivion forever. Then he began to stroke her with his fingers, coaxing her closer and closer until she cried out. Every muscle in her body clenched around him, as if trying to hold on to him just a bit longer before she was reduced to a shaking heap of body parts beneath him.

"Fallon, you—" she began. But he was already moving again, pulling her back up the steady incline with him.

"I'm not done with you," he murmured.

She could sense an even higher point nearing ever closer on the horizon. Fallon was pure intensity. She'd seen the look in his eyes before, dark and needful, but this was far greater. She wanted to help him as he always did her, but she wasn't certain how. All she knew was she wanted more of him, every secret and every hidden thought, forever.

Placing her hands over his where they were splayed out over her hips, she curled her fingers around his. She met his gaze without wavering.

He increased his pace, driving into her with abandon. She braced herself against him, wanting to go with him wherever he went. A moment later he pulled her close as their bodies pulsed together in unison, murmuring, "Isabelle, my sweet, beautiful Isabelle."

He ran his hands over her hair and kissed her forehead before collapsing beside her. She smiled and curled up beside him as she did every night now, resting her cheek on his chest. She could remain here forever.

"Happiness when in the constant company of a man *is* possible," she mused some time later.

"Didn't you always believe that to be true?" Fallon asked. "You live in stories about unending love. You want to be like Isolde, no matter how flawed I find the notion."

"Yes, but I've only ever seen such love in stories or in the look in a lady's eyes in paintings. What I've witnessed with those around me has been quite different. I didn't know if what I sought was truly possible... until now."

He rubbed his hand over her back in soothing strokes down her spine. "You're Isabelle. You seek out joy and beauty in everything around you. You're drawn to them. There will be no quarrels or anger you can't overcome in your future simply because of who you are and what you choose to surround yourself with. Rest assured, you won't have the same fate as your parents."

"Neither will you."

"I'm aware. I'm nothing like my family. I never have been. A fact that brought my father much anguish before I left home."

"Because you're Fallon."

"Yes. I don't consume large amounts of alcohol and yell at everyone within earshot on a daily basis."

"That is true, but I was thinking of how you control everything in your life. You won't become your father if you loosen your grip on the reins a bit. Just as I won't become my mother."

"Survival has been my focus for so long—"

"Well, you weren't surviving very well without

my assistance, were you?" she teased with a grin. "Walking about in wrinkled shirts and eating awful food in a dusty home. You needed my help."

"I'd be lost without you, Isabelle," he said as he hugged her tight. "I don't believe I've ever talked about my family with anyone but you."

"See? You even control your words."

"I'll show you how in control I am." In a swift motion, he flipped her to her back and smiled down at her. "I'm glad I kidnapped you."

"I quite like being your prisoner. I want to stay here with you, Fallon." It was as close to *I love you* as she dared, and even still, she watched his reaction warily.

"Always," he murmured, and he kissed her again.

In that kiss, the promise of happiness lingered on his lips. Would they have it all: marriage, children, and love forever more? A life lived out together beneath the gaze of painted cherubs in their home? She smiled at the image and wound her arms around him with no wish to ever let go.

Seventeen

Dear Mr. Grapling,

It's as you thought. Lady Isabelle was in Mr. St. James's company just today. I saw her in the main hall with him this morning, looking about the house. They were quite cozy together. You can meet me Tuesday next around the corner at sunrise for my payment.

—Miss Emily Rushing

❧⚬☙

"MRS. FEATHERFITCH, BELIEVE ME, IT'S BEEN PROVEN to be perfectly safe. Why would he mind this? I only want to retrieve a book from his library to occupy my afternoon." Isabelle crossed her fingers behind her back at the small lie. In truth, she wanted to see Fallon again, to explore his house more, to twirl in the shining light that was her love for him.

Surely Fallon wouldn't mind her brief departure from the room. They'd shared his bed in the most intimate fashion only last night. There was something between them now that had gone beyond words. But if there had been words involved, they would have held some sort of promise of happiness together. There was a future for them. And this was his home, not some foreign field where a war raged and enemies brandished weapons at every turn. He would want to see her, no matter his opinion about surprises. She was certain.

Fallon would be in his library, seeing to some work matter or other. He told her that she was safe with him; therefore, visiting the very room where he sat at his desk wouldn't be a problem.

Fallon's housekeeper, however, wasn't convinced. "My lady, I have strict orders—"

"You saw me downstairs with Mr. St. James only yesterday," Isabelle cut in.

"That is true," the woman hedged, the tray she held still blocking the open bedchamber door.

"I'll come straight back," Isabelle promised, taking a step toward the door. "I've been trapped here for a month."

Mrs. Featherfitch adjusted the empty dishes on the tray so as not to drop them on her way back to the kitchen, muttering, "I've never agreed with this arrangement."

"Then look the other way while I slip out the door."

Mrs. Featherfitch studied Isabelle for a long second before giving her a sigh of defeat. "Very well, but be quick about it. I wouldn't want Mr. St. James to become angry with me over this."

"He won't," Isabelle promised as she ran to stuff her

feet into the slippers that she'd worn only once during her entire stay there.

She'd dressed properly and sorted her hair the second she'd had the idea to go downstairs. Then she'd waited for her opportunity. Last night Fallon had loved her, even if it had been only in the physical sense. She was his and he was hers even if he'd yet to make an official commitment to her. She may well be the lady of the house soon, so she shouldn't be seen barefoot and with her hair a mess. Although she was determined to go unnoticed, it was always a fine idea to be prepared. If she did meet one of Fallon's staff along the way, she didn't want to give the wrong impression.

Isabelle was out the door before Mrs. Featherfitch could change her mind. Moving down the hall, she retraced the path she'd taken yesterday with Fallon. After her night with him, she couldn't simply sit and wait for his return. Her heart was pounding with the memory of his body against hers, her mind whirling with thoughts of him. Even her limbs danced to a merry melody as she moved down the narrow stairs toward him.

When he saw her, would he sweep her up in his arms? They would sit together and talk until the evening hours. Or perhaps he would lay her out on his desk for a thorough study of her body. Then she could do the same to him... The possibilities for the afternoon were endless. But as she neared the library door, many male voices rang out in laughter.

He was entertaining? That was disappointing for how she'd imagined spending the day. Just then a young maid rounded the corner at the far end of the hall. Isabelle only had a second to react or she'd be seen. Diving across the rug, she tucked herself in behind the open door to the library. Holding her breath, she waited until the girl passed. There was an open stretch of floor between where she stood and the stairs that led back to the safety of Fallon's private quarters. She would have to cross the space without being seen by any of the gentlemen in the room. All this time hiding, and on her first attempt to visit Fallon, she would be seen. Spy work was quite difficult, no matter how simple Roselyn had claimed it to be. Isabelle sighed and leaned her head back against the wall.

From here she could see Fallon through the slit where the door was hinged. He sat at his desk, looking in command of the room. Her pirate. She bit her lip and leaned closer to get a better view. He was so handsome. Her good fortune was boundless.

"Jackson, when can you have that report to me?" he asked someone in the room.

Jackson must be his man of business. But this was a rather large gathering for a meeting. How odd.

"With necessary figures? Two days."

"I'll make a note of it." Fallon leaned forward and picked up his quill, scribbling something on a paper in front of him. "About the negotiations of the new leasing terms at the Greenly Boardinghouse, did Madam Molloy accept the new rates?"

Greenly Boardinghouse? That was in the worst part of London. She'd passed it once in the carriage, and Victoria had made a jest about the women who boarded there. Isabelle blinked. She knew exactly the sort of house that madam ran, and it wasn't a nunnery. What the devil sort of meeting was Fallon involved in? And worse, he seemed to be in charge of it. Isabelle couldn't move. She should have returned to the stairs. Instead she listened to every word that was said.

"I need a bit longer to settle things with Madam Molloy to completion," the gentleman named Jackson answered.

"I bet you do," someone inside the room replied, and there was a round of laughter.

"We have only one week left on her current contract to finalize the new terms before her girls are out on the streets," Fallon said, and the laughter faded away.

"She isn't pleased with the increase, of course, but the offering of an extra patrol through the area and a new chandelier for her main parlor seemed to appease her. I'll get her full agreement."

"I'm certain you will," Fallon said with a grin.

"St. James, was that another jest?" A loud, jovial voice rang out, a voice Isabelle knew quite well. "Three in one day—I wonder at the cause for such an occurrence."

She couldn't breathe. She knew they were friends, but what *was* this?

"Shut it, Hardaway," Fallon tossed out before turning back to the other man. "Good work, Jackson. I'm glad to see this bit of business find resolution."

"Thank you, sir. I think your idea for the chandelier brought her around. She offered me…compensation for my efforts last night."

"Did she?" Fallon raised a brow at the man.

"And I thought I was special," someone muttered

from the other end of the room, and there was another round of laughter.

Fallon gave the man in front of him a sympathetic smile and said, "Show of hands, who has been offered Madam Molloy's thanks for the Spare Heirs Society's assistance in some matter?"

Isabelle saw every hand in the room rise into the air in unison, including Fallon's. The Spare Heirs Society. Her eyes widened, more concerned by Fallon's involvement with the owner of a brothel than some society she'd never heard of before.

"You'll become accustomed to such things, Jackson," Fallon offered.

"Aye, she even gifted St. James with three of her best women at once last year," someone beyond her line of sight called out. "Of course, we'll never learn the details of it from him."

"Such secrets, St. James," one man complained, only to be joined by others.

"Come now, man. Have a heart."

Three women? What of last night with her? Something tightened in her gut, but she only leaned closer to hear more.

"That's enough," Fallon commanded, shifting his attention to another man who sat in front of his desk. "What was the weekly take from Bennett Street? More than previously reported, I hope. What Hardaway lost at the hazard tables alone matches that small sum."

"It was the same, sir."

"Have they forgotten that we keep them on the proper side of the law by lining the pockets of those who are influential in such matters?" Fallon leaned forward, studying one of the men in front of him. "Have you let them forget about our support?"

"I'll make certain they remember, St. James. You can count on me."

"Very well. You have three days to remind them where their loyalties need be before I step in."

"I'll talk to them," Hardaway offered.

Who were these men? Isabelle had known of Fallon's friendship with Hardaway, but this was something else entirely. Perhaps *associates* was a more apt term for the two men.

"No one wants Hardaway's involvement except perhaps Hardaway," Fallon said, shooting a quick glance at the man. "Remind them of their need to pay for our services, or I'll allow Hardaway to do what he enjoys most, and the blood will be on your hands."

"Understood, sir."

Blood? Hardaway enjoyed harming people? What was happening? She'd been horribly wrong about him. Thank heavens nothing had come to pass between them. And it was a good thing Victoria fled her wedding. He might have hurt her sister. She shook her head and continued to look through the crack in the door.

Fallon made a note of something with the quill on his desk, and the room fell silent as the men gathered there waited for him to finish. He did command a ship of men—only this wasn't a ship. This was an organization of some mean sort. Everything she thought she knew was crumbling and reshaping into a different reality than anything she'd believed before.

Fallon looked down, consulting something on his desk. "I'm told the milliners will reopen their doors on Bond in a week's time. The damage done to the jewelry shop is already cleaned up. It reopened yesterday, even though I'm told the smell of the smoke still lingers. Because of Ayton's interest, we'll need to fix that. We can't have one of our own paying the price."

"I'll see to it, sir," a man beyond Isabelle's sight offered.

Ayton? Roselyn's Ayton? Was she dreaming this entire encounter? How was *he* involved with this group? She had to warn Roselyn, poor, dear Roselyn. She would be devastated, but she needed to know. Her husband... How would Isabelle break such news to her friend?

"Good. And no one is aware of our involvement with the fire, correct?" Fallon asked, and she had to shake the buzzing sound from her ears. "No one has heard whispers of it?"

The fire...our involvement... She couldn't hear any more, but she also couldn't walk away.

"Not a word here."

"Nothing here, either."

"All went to plan, then," Fallon confirmed. "Let's not burn a portion of Bond Street in the future if we can avoid it, eh, Hardaway?"

He'd started the fire. Hardaway had set Bond Street ablaze and then had benefited from it with a title and her sister? Did her father know of this?

"You're quite amusing. Truly you are," Hardaway quipped.

"I'm aware," Fallon retorted with a smile.

A smile...a blasted smile about the single event that had brought her world crashing down around her. He found it amusing? Who was this man, and what had he done with the Fallon St. James who cared about her? She covered her mouth with her hand to keep from screaming. This was the worst moment of her life.

"Now, what do we know about the Fairlyn art?" he asked, and the moment grew worse.

Isabelle went still. Even her heart seemed to cease beating as she listened to the sound of her happiness shattering.

Fallon picked up something from his desk and glared at it as he spoke. "Have we found the buyers?"

"The meeting should be soon," Hardaway supplied.

"Excellent. I'll want to be present for the exchange," Fallon said. What was that in his hand? He was grasping it as if he'd like to squeeze all life from it.

"I thought you would," Hardaway responded.

Just then something gold slipped from Fallon's hand and trailed to the surface of his desk. Isabelle didn't want to know what it was, but she knew in an instant. He was holding her locket.

"And the letter?" When there was no response, Fallon said, "I don't want excuses, gentlemen. I want results. Our foe is somewhere in this city, and we must find him. He wants to bring one of us down. He wants to end us. Will we allow him to do that?"

The answer "No!" rang out through the library.

Fallon stood and looked across the room, making eye contact with each man present as he spoke. "Every one of you was chosen for your abilities to…to…" Fallon stared straight at her. "Oh God. Excuse me, gentlemen." He threw her locket to his desk and was already rounding it to move toward her.

She stepped from behind the door, staggering into the hallway, away from the danger of being seen. She needed a moment to think. She didn't know what to say to him.

"Isabelle," Fallon said as he grabbed her arm and stopped her, there, beneath the gaze of the cherubs on the hall ceiling.

"I came to surprise you," she whispered as she stared into his concerned face. "That." She pointed to the library as she began to find her voice once more. "What was that?"

"A meeting with my men. I don't know how much you heard, but you should know—"

"Enough! I heard enough." Her mind was reeling with all she'd heard. Her illusions about who he was had been destroyed in mere minutes. "I painted you as a hero in my mind. You valiantly saved me, cared for me..." She squeezed her eyes shut against him. "But you're something else entirely. Paints only hide the awful truth."

"Isabelle, what I do here, what I've done, serves a purpose. I'm not perfect, and I've never claimed so. But there are many gentlemen who look to me for support—more than those in that room. There are businesses that are able to operate because of my influence."

"Brothels and gaming hells?" she asked, looking up at him. "Those sorts of businesses? Or are you referring to the ones you burn to the ground?"

"The fire was an accident. That never should have happened."

"But you knew about it," she countered, taking a

step beyond his reach. "You were involved in it. Yet you said nothing to me. You comforted me after it happened. I thought…I thought you were my friend." Tears pricked the backs of her eyes, and she wrapped her arms around herself.

"I am your friend, more than that, Isabelle. Everything we've shared, the time we've spent together…this has been the best time of my life." The look in his eyes was one of complete honesty. If only she could believe him. "I want it to go on without end, just as I said last night."

"And I would live here with you while you cavort with multiple ladies at a brothel and take the profits of gaming hells?" She took another step away from him. "No. I promised myself long ago that I would find love with an honorable, kindhearted gentleman. I wanted him to be many things, but most of all I wanted him to be good. You knew that. You lied to me. You… I was wrong about you, so terribly wrong. I was wrong about everything."

He took a step toward her and reached out his hand before it fell back to his side again. "I know this has all come as quite the shock. I understand why you can't accept the life I lead. I should have told you long ago, but I didn't know how. I knew how difficult this would be for you."

"So you allowed me to believe lies? This isn't some story in a book or pretty setting in a painting, this is my life. I gave you my heart, my body, everything." She exhaled a ragged breath. "I don't even know you. Who are you, Fallon?"

"I'm the second son of a perpetually drunk lord,

the former caregiver of an elderly lady, and the current head of a secret organization that I founded for the betterment of other gentlemen like me."

"Ha! You make yourself sound quite honorable. If I hadn't just heard a discussion of your involvement in various sorts of crime within the walls of your own library, I might believe you." She stared at him, and she looked into the eyes of a stranger. And after all they'd shared, to not know him now broke her heart.

"I'll earn your trust back, Isabelle. Ask me anything." He closed the gap between them, the look in his eyes one of desperation. "I'll tell you the truth."

"Have you beaten a man to the ground?" she asked, her throat tightening around the words.

"Yes, many times."

"Have you killed a man?"

"I've seen it happen, even ordered it twice."

She winced but continued. "Have you broken into a place where you didn't belong?"

"Quite often."

"Have you ever stolen anything that didn't belong to you?"

"Yes."

She began to shake and drew her arms tighter over her chest to hold herself still. "Did you steal my family's art and then convince me it was another man?"

"No!" he said, drawing back in surprise. "I would never do that."

"You just admitted to stealing, breaking into a place where you have no claim, and hurting people."

"I know what that artwork means to you, and I've

had my men searching the city to return the pieces you lost."

"Why should I believe you? You're a bad man, a villain."

Fallon didn't reply.

"I cared for you. I wanted…" She wanted to marry him. She loved him. But this was too much to bear. He wasn't the man she thought him to be. She'd made herself a promise long ago that she wouldn't have a loveless marriage like her parents had. She would find a good man who cared for her. And foolish as she was, she'd thought…

The door beside them opened, and the drawing room he'd kept her from seeing yesterday came into view as two gentlemen walked past them to the front door. Inside there were more men playing billiards and swilling drink. This was a gentlemen's club. He used his home as a gentlemen's club, and he profited from crime. And he'd kept her from this discovery yesterday, just before he'd, before they'd… "Secrets," she muttered. The floor seemed to tilt beneath her feet as this last great wave of truth crashed over her and everything she thought she knew slid to shatter on the floor at her feet. He'd held back who he was until after he'd gotten what he wanted from her, and she'd fallen for it.

"I never meant to hurt you, Isabelle," he said, accurately reading the devastation in her eyes.

"Then why am I hurt?" she asked him, but he gave no defense of his actions.

Turning, she took slow paces toward the front door. The tears she'd pushed back for the past few minutes threatened to fall now.

Surely he would stop her. He would somehow explain that all of this had been practice for some grand play. None of this was real.

But it was real. And he didn't say a word to stop her as she walked out of his life.

～⚬～

Fallon watched her leave, but he didn't move. He watched as his butler stepped in to close the door Isabelle had left swinging on its hinges.

He should return to the library and continue his meeting. He should chase after Isabelle and force her to return. He should have her things gathered and sent to Knottsby. Yet he stood rooted to the floor, staring at the closed front door to his home.

He'd done what was best, hadn't he? The best path was the simple one that led ever forward. But standing still and allowing Isabelle to walk away wasn't simple at all.

She wouldn't come back, he knew that much. But from this moment forward, every step he took was a step away from Isabelle. She'd looked at him and seen a wretched human and had made her decision accordingly. And he'd lost her. It should come as no surprise. He'd lost every woman whom he'd ever loved due to his own damned mistakes. Why would Isabelle be any different?

Claughbane stepped into the main hall from the library and leaned against the wall, watching Fallon as he stared at the closed door. The young man was one of the newer members of the Spare Heirs Society, a con artist and now part owner of Crosby Steam

Works, which was—surprising everyone involved—a legitimate business.

A legitimate business. Fallon should have mentioned that bit of information to Isabelle while she was here, along with countless other things—the fact that he loved her. That he would abandon everything he'd worked for if it meant keeping her in his life. But it would have done no good. None of that mattered.

"Was that Lady Victoria I saw fleeing headquarters?" Claughbane asked.

"Isabelle," Fallon corrected, not turning to look at the man.

"A lady at headquarters? Hmm. She's my wife's cousin, you know. I don't suppose she was simply coming by for tea to check on the recovery of her family's paintings?"

"No." It had been much more than tea. And now it was over. It was as it should be. He could never have been a good match for her. This past month had been a fantasy, but their story was over. He must allow her to be, for her own happiness.

"St. James, I'm unsure if this occasion calls for pistols at dawn, a measure of whiskey, or a fast horse to catch the lady in question, but know that I have all three options at the ready."

"Go ahead and shoot me. End it. It's what I deserve," he muttered.

"Whiskey it is, then," Claughbane replied.

But before the man could move, Fallon stopped him. "The meeting is over." *Over*. The word reverberated in his head until it ached. He couldn't let Isabelle leave. She was still in danger; no matter what she thought of him, he had to protect her. "I need you to go after the lady. Use your *fast horse* and find her. She couldn't have gotten far. And Claughbane? When you find her, take her to her home. Ensure her safety."

"Of course," Claughbane muttered as he sped toward the door.

Fallon watched him leave and turned to walk up the stairs to the upper floors of his home, away from the temptation to chase after her himself. He had no claim to her. He had no place at her side, and now she didn't even want him there. When Claughbane caught up to her in the next block, he would escort her back to her father. It's where she should be. His time with Isabelle was over.

He was a villain, and she was a beautiful lady.

Entering the first unused room he reached, he walked inside and shut the door, not wanting to be disturbed. He'd lost her. He sank to the floor in defeat and leaned back against the wall.

"Every woman I've ever loved," he whispered. He'd lost his mother when he was a boy, Pearl when he had only just become a man, and today he'd lost Isabelle.

He shouldn't have lost sight of reality for even a moment, but with Isabelle that was a difficult feat to accomplish. Perhaps he was destined to be alone. Love was for gentlemen who danced and smiled, as Isabelle had always insisted. He'd mucked this all up. But keeping her in his life had been a dream anyway. This was always going to happen at the end. At least now she could find someone who would dance with her... bring her flowers...

He took a ragged breath and choked back the emotion that threatened to drag him under.

She would return to her home. His men would see that Grapling was captured, the last confession letter recovered, and the art sent back to the museum. She would be free of this entire situation. And he…would spend the rest of his days thinking of the summer month he'd spent with Isabelle and how he'd almost found love.

He sniffed and pushed to his feet. He couldn't linger here any longer. He had a society to run.

Eighteen

Knottsby,

Please be advised that your daughter has left head-quarters. I sent Mr. Claughbane after her to see to her safety on the street. I've yet to hear a report back from him. There is still a threat, one I cannot mention here. Increase your security and cancel all social engagements until further notice.

—St. James

THE FIRST STEP HAD BEEN THE HARDEST. ALL OTHERS were simply allowing her feet to move forward and allowing her to move on—though to what end she wasn't certain. One step, then another, every one taking her farther and farther from Fallon and the life she'd had with him.

She'd spent weeks solely in his company, had opened her heart to him. "I loved…" she whispered to herself and drew her arms across her chest. She was cold despite the season, and the wind bit through the thin muslin of her day dress and petticoat. There was no going back for a pelisse now. There was no going back at all. She'd given herself to him. Tears stung the backs of her eyes, but she kept moving. They were going to be married, have children, live in happiness… in her mind, anyway. Fallon had had something different in mind, it would seem. Someone like that could never offer her the future she wanted. He'd known the truth the entire time and had misled her. She'd given him everything she had, and he hadn't even seen fit to give her the honesty she deserved.

She blinked away the tears that threatened to spill down her cheeks. She should have known, should have seen the person Fallon truly was. She'd been so consumed with her own dream version of the man that she hadn't seen reality in front of her. Fallon St. James was a bad person who concocted villainous plots and lived with a band of rogues.

"Lady Isabelle," someone called behind her, but she kept moving. Ducking around a corner to avoid being seen, she watched a man ride past her. Mr. Claughbane. Her eyes widened. Mr. Claughbane? That was Evie's new husband. Was he wrapped up in this too? They were all evil. Every gentleman she knew. Poor Evie. Did her cousin have any idea? He guided his horse around the next corner and out of sight, still calling her name. She wouldn't go with him. He would only take her back to Fallon—the one place she couldn't go.

Bad men were everywhere, married to her friend

Roselyn, her cousin Evie. Was no one good at heart? She'd been wrong about Hardaway as well, but above all else, Fallon's true nature stung the most. *Fallon*, her heart wailed from deep inside her chest, but not a sound escaped her lips.

She'd rushed in, had trusted him. She'd been so certain about him, who he was, how he felt about her. Her family had been right about her, everyone had been right. She was foolish. "Just a silly girl with silly dreams," she muttered through a tight throat as she continued down the street.

She only wanted love. Was it so much to ask for in life? She shook as a sob was wrenched from her body. A dark carriage drove by, but she hadn't a care who saw her like this. There was nothing left of her with which to care. Fallon had taken it all and then hadn't even tried to stop her when she walked out his door. She meant nothing to him. She was ruined. Tears slipped down her cheeks, chilled by the wind that pulled at her as she moved down the street.

Love wasn't meant to be, not for her. She'd so hoped this time... He'd touched her with such tenderness. He'd held her as if he were holding his own life in his hands. He'd smiled and laughed with her. How had he still hidden so much of himself away?

The clouds were thick overhead as they swirled and shifted in the wind. Gray—the day was gray, the road was gray, and all the homes she passed were gray. Isabelle didn't know where she was. The buildings were unfamiliar. The street was foreign, but she kept walking. It was all she could do.

Keep moving. As much as she wanted to move

on and find another as she had before, she knew she couldn't replace what she'd had with Fallon—for her part, anyway. Perhaps just like this street with its worn gray stone that stretched out in front of her with no visible end, she was destined to walk through life cold and alone.

Another carriage passed, or perhaps it was the same one again. Someone else was as lost and tired as she was this afternoon. She'd lost count of the blocks she'd walked. With no money for a hack or even an idea if she was going the right direction, she slowed her pace. There was no hurry when one came from nothing and was walking toward nothing. She spotted a small park across the street and stumbled in that direction.

Sinking onto a bench, she sat and stared. Only a little while ago, she would have thought the deep green of the grass to be beautiful against the tree trunks. Today it only reminded her of the garden on Fallon's rooftop, lush, green, and filled with false hopes.

She sniffed and wiped the tears from her cheeks. The wind was cool against her face. Perhaps she would simply stay here until she perished on this park bench, eventually turning to stone. Children would look upon her and wonder at the sorrow in her eyes. And she would be a piece of art forever. Unchanging. Unfeeling.

"Lady Isabelle?" someone asked from behind her.

Isabelle jumped. Had Mr. Claughbane seen her enter the park? If so, she would tell him exactly what she thought of his secret club and how she had been deceived by it. She exhaled a breath and turned. Then her eyes narrowed on the man standing only a few paces away. "Mr. Grapling?"

"I haven't seen you in some time," he offered with a wide smile. "I'm not… I'm not disturbing you, am I?"

"No." She blinked up at him in surprise over the coincidence of seeing him here, now. It was a bit startling to be thrown back into life so quickly. She'd imagined she'd have time before having to speak with anyone in town. "Your company is unexpected but quite welcome," she said through teeth clenched into what she hoped was a convincing smile. It would do no good to be rude to the man. It wasn't his fault she was in this mess.

"I hope you had safe travels back into town."

"Into town…yes, of course," she lied. At least her reputation wasn't destroyed over her stay with Fallon, only what made her whole.

He moved around to the front of the bench. He wasn't wearing the bright colors she associated with him. Everyone had changed while she was away, it seemed. She certainly had. "I was disappointed when you left so quickly. We'd only just become acquainted."

"My departure was unexpected," she muttered.

"I'm pleased you've returned. Are you here alone?" he asked, casting a wary glance around the park.

"Ha," she released a harsh exhale. "I find I'm quite alone today."

"Then you must allow me to accompany you. You shouldn't be out alone like this. Would you care to see the rest of the park?"

"I've had my fill of walking for one day, thank you." She sighed and glanced down at her hands, already weary of the man's company. "I arrived here a bit lost, but I'll manage."

"I have a carriage nearby. I was…in the area on some business when I thought to stop for a moment. There's no need to walk any farther than that street right there. I could see you home."

"That wouldn't be proper. I can't."

"My only concern is your welfare, Lady Isabelle." He stepped closer, the look in his eyes a bit intense.

What could be a display of worry over her well-being set off alarm bells in her head. Her newfound lack of trust in gentlemen was as disconcerting as that look in Mr. Grapling's eyes. "Even still," she muttered.

"I insist." In the next moment, she was on her feet and being pulled by the elbow toward his awaiting carriage.

If anyone happened to be watching, they would look like a couple out for a stroll, unless one noticed that Isabelle's feet were leaving trenches in the dirt as she tried to stop her momentum and that Mr. Grapling's grip on her arm was unyielding.

"I can find my home on my own, sir. Really. It would be a scandal. I can't."

"You must come with me."

Isabelle blinked up at the man who had once sent her jewelry and flowers. Had she ever known this man at all? She had spent the majority of the season locked away with Fallon, but this was rather a different Mr. Grapling than she'd experienced before. She pulled against him, but his grip on her arm was too tight. She was still moving toward the man's carriage whether she liked the idea or not. "I should get back to my family now. Though I do appreciate your offer of assistance, I must refuse."

"Nonsense. I'll even ride up top with my driver."

"How…kind of you. But I must decline."

"I won't hear of it, Lady Isabelle. You'll get into my carriage, or I'll place you there."

She gasped and shoved against his hold on her, but he only increased his speed. How had this man been at the top of her ideal match list at one time? She'd been horribly wrong about Fallon, he did horrible things with his time, but he'd never made her feel unsafe. If he were only here, he would help her escape this man. But he wasn't here, and he wasn't coming.

The carriage that waited ahead looked to be the same carriage she'd seen earlier. Had he followed her? Or was her imagination getting the best of her again? Simply because he was forceful with his will for her didn't mean he was stalking her movements. *Be calm. You'll find a way to escape this situation without inviting ruin*, she told herself. And she would—only how? Screaming would hardly help her avoid a scandal. No one was going to rescue her. This wasn't a book, and there was no happy ending.

"Mr. Grapling, I understand that you are attempting to be considerate, but you must let me go. I simply cannot get into your carriage. It would cause a scandal."

"There was a time when I was concerned with saying the proper thing in order to please you, my lady. That time has passed. And it pleases me to no end that I no longer have to fawn over you. Actually, I can now treat you however I choose. It's quite freeing. I'm certain you're familiar with the concept of kidnapping." He opened the door and pulled her closer. "Get in the carriage."

She saw the flash of warning in his eyes at the same time she caught sight of the pistol in his other hand. Reasoning with him was her only option, and it wasn't a good one. "Why are you doing this?"

"Because it's my move." He shoved her into the interior of the conveyance, the shadows swallowing her whole.

She scrambled toward the door, but he blocked her path. "What do you mean, *your move*?"

There was no answer, only the slamming of the door and the sudden jolt of the carriage wheels set in motion. After a minute, her eyes adjusted to the dark carriage interior. She had to get out, but they were moving. She couldn't leap from a moving carriage. Perhaps there would be traffic ahead. There was always a delay somewhere. There had to be. She would wait. "Wait for the right time," she whispered in order to calm her frayed nerves. Well-worn fabric covered the seats, and she slid down to lean her head on the back of the seat. "Wait."

The carriage was traveling quite fast now. The force of corners at high speed pushed her left, then right. Lifting her feet to the opposite bench, she propped them on the edge of the cushion for stability.

The carriage jostled over a larger-than-normal bump in the road, and the seat beneath her feet lifted a fraction before slamming shut once more. Pulling her feet back to the floor, she eyed the bench. There was some sort of storage space beneath that seat. Could there be a weapon in there? It seemed her best option at the moment. She shifted forward and lifted the cushion-covered wood. Peering inside, she saw only a leather bag propped in the far corner. No pistols. Not even a knife. She would have been grateful for a length of wood—anything that would help even the odds of this situation. But it was a blasted bag. It most likely held papers of some business dealing or other. Dull documents, nothing more…

She stared at the bag as they rolled past two buildings without slowing before she shot forward and opened the latch that held the bag closed and lifted the flap of leather that covered the opening. Even if the bag held only papers, they were information. Perhaps there was some document that would explain all of this to her. She'd always seen her curiosity as a weakness, but if she'd pried a bit more where Fallon was concerned, she could have saved herself a great deal of heartache. She wouldn't be making the same mistake again with any gentleman.

Reaching inside the leather bag, her fingers wrapped around several papers and a book of some sort. She pulled the pile of belongings out and looked down—at several official-looking documents and, on top of the stack, her own diary.

She stared at the cover. Clearly her mind could handle only so much before snapping. This couldn't be. Yet…

She flipped the journal open in her lap. Her writing. Her words. Her feelings and thoughts spilled out for anyone to see.

Her heart hammered in her chest. How did Mr. Grapling have the diary she'd misplaced at the beginning of the season? But perhaps the better question was why?

She spun to look out the window still clutching the diary in her hand, knowing what she must do. They were nearing a busy intersection. They would have to slow. Even a little would help. She scooted toward the door, easing the latch open as the carriage continued to roll down the street. There was no more waiting. It was time to jump.

The congested London streets. There was a street vendor moving his wares and blocking the road. The carriage slowed. She had only a second to make the leap. There was a flurry of flailing arms and wind in her skirts as she leapt from the vehicle and collided with a—thankfully—sturdy woman. Carrots tumbled to the ground as Isabelle bumped the woman's cart with her hip. She struggled to gain her balance, taking a step and still clinging to the woman's arm, desperately unsteady.

"Apologies," Isabelle muttered holding the diary over her face to shield herself from view. She didn't dare linger any longer. Glancing up from behind the diary, she spotted the merchant where Victoria had insisted they once slip away to purchase rouge. She almost laughed, she was so thankful to her sister for bringing her here. Taking a right, she ran the path she'd taken that day last year, remembering how they'd had to hide their purchase from their mother. And then Sue had worn the makeup to that masquerade ball at the Rutledges' home.

The roads twisted in front of her, but she knew the way from here. She glanced back over her shoulder after every turn, eventually dropping the diary to her side. Would Mr. Grapling know she'd escaped his carriage? Was he following her again? Isabelle's grip on her diary tightened.

She didn't slow until she reached the rear garden of her home. Flinging open the gate, she ran down the stone path, weaving through the roses she knew by heart. But the closer she came to her home, the more uncertain she became of what to tell her family. Her steps came to a stop, and she hugged the diary to her chest as she looked up at her house.

"Isabelle?" her father called out as he rushed toward her.

How long had she been standing here with the wind cutting through her dress as she wondered what she should do now? She didn't know, but her father made the next step clear when he threw his arms around her.

"It's almost night. I've had every footman out searching the streets for you most of the day. It isn't safe to set off across town alone even in the best of times. You could have been killed."

"I nearly was," she mumbled into the wool of his coat.

"What happened?" he asked as he released her, now staring at her, waiting for answers.

"I was kidnapped by someone I thought I knew." Her tone was flat even to her ears. She was numb from the cold of the day, the immense fear, then relief of having escaped danger, but most of all, she was numb from crying over Fallon through all of it.

"St. James? I'm aware of where you've been hiding, but kidnapping is a bit of a harsh word, isn't it?"

"No, it isn't that. That…" She swallowed and

looked away. She couldn't discuss *that*. Not now, and perhaps not ever. "I jumped from Mr. Grapling's carriage not an hour ago. He saw me in a park and forced me to go with him."

"Did you say Mr. Grapling? He's here? In town?" All the blood drained from her father's face in an instant.

"He stole my diary. Months ago, I suspect," she muttered as if it somehow explained…anything at all, though she knew it didn't. "I suppose that was how he knew me so well."

"Knew you?" her father bellowed, but she didn't flinch.

"Yes, he attempted to court me earlier in the season." That seemed like another lifetime now. So much had changed. She had changed. Fallon had been her friend then. And Mr. Grapling her secret admirer. She stared at her father without really seeing him as she continued. "But that was all false. Father, he had a pistol today. He shoved me…" Her voice trailed off, along with her thoughts.

"It's over now. Get inside. You'll be safe here. You're home." He turned and led her to the nearest door, the one that led to the kitchen. "Everything can return to normal now," he continued. "Your life will be exactly as you left it. You'll see. It will be like none of this ever happened."

Like none of this ever happened? Was it possible to simply step back into her old life?

The familiar surroundings of her home pressed in on her, reminding her of how far she'd traveled from her old life and how much she'd changed as a result. As Isabelle looked up at her father and stepped through the kitchen door and into her home, she knew she was still just as lost as she had been on that street across town.

❧

Fallon shuffled through the stacks of documents on his desk, looking in vain for the reports from the gaming hells. He'd reviewed the numbers a week ago, but one could never be too careful with gamblers. His eyes seemed to be filled with sand, and he rubbed his hand over them. What time was it? The days had blended together without beginning or end since Isabelle had left.

He located the documents he was looking for and glanced up to the man on the opposite side of his desk. "Wentwood, I'll need the ledgers for the boarding-houses by this evening. I asked Lawson to check them against our accounts. We haven't audited those yet this year. I want it done by tomorrow."

"Sir, that will take days," he muttered.

"Then I'll do it," Fallon snapped, staring at the man ten years his senior.

The man shifted uneasily on his feet for a second before replying, "I'll do what I can."

"Porter," Fallon called out to one of the men across the room. He stopped the low conversation he was having and looked over at Fallon from in front of the fire-place. "Do you have the interest statements I asked for?"

"Not yet, sir," the man replied, tossing back the contents of the glass in his hand. "Fields is still completing his part."

"Tell him to hurry." Fallon spread two files in front of him, his eyes darting between the two.

"Has anyone heard the timeline for payout from Crosby Steam Works? I suppose not," he surmised from the relative silence in the group. He made a note to contact Claughbane directly with his questions.

Fallon glanced up a second later, seeing that there was a new arrival to his library. "Hardaway..."

"Is it my turn on the spit?" Hardaway asked in mock excitement as he moved forward. "I'll try to spin better over the fire than the rest of this lot. Nice and evenly cooked. Wouldn't want my arse to be raw, would we?"

"Did you get in touch with Phillips?" Fallon asked, ignoring his friend's antics.

"I did. The terms are much better now."

"Better is the enemy of good, Hardaway," Fallon said as he pulled out another file of reports from the harbor.

"That's it, everyone out," Hardaway bellowed. "I need to speak with St. James alone."

"Why do they need to leave?" Fallon asked, pausing his work to look up at the man. "They'll be able to hear you out in the street anyway."

"Even still. Out," Hardaway commanded.

Fallon sat back in his chair watching his *friend* usher everyone from the room. He was losing time over this show, precious minutes in his day that he couldn't retrieve. He had to remain focused on the Spare Heirs Society. It was the only thing that mattered anymore.

"She left you," Hardaway began without preamble. "I understand. But you're being an arse to everyone who is still here. Did you know Lawson didn't sleep last night working on your blasted report?"

"Audit," Fallon corrected. "And I didn't sleep either."

"*That* has nothing to do with a damned audit that doesn't need to be done for another four months, and you know it."

"Lawson has been complaining, has he?" Fallon would have to have a chat with the man later. "After all I've done for this organization, all I've given—"

"We've *all* bled for this, St. James. Lawson, Wentwood, Porter, Ayton, Claughbane, Dean, me… don't act like this is all you. We were there too," Hardaway growled.

Fallon released a ragged breath and ran his hand through his hair. He knew that, really he did. This group of gentlemen had all come together to support one another. How they'd done so was the sticking point. Isabelle thought he was a horrible gentleman with a black heart, and perhaps that's exactly what he was. He was mad to think she'd understand. And now she was gone.

"She blames me, thinks me the worst kind of blackguard. Actually I'm a *villain*—that was the word she used. I…am a villain. It was foolish for me to think even for a second that someone so…" Pure and lovely, good…beautiful—words paled in comparison to who Isabelle really was. "She was right. We're hardly ever on the right side of the law. This was my idea, my creation. The Spare Heirs Society was supposed to be a place that looked after those who had no place in society."

"And it does. St. James, you've done a great deal of good for this town. Sometimes it's necessary to go about that good by less-than-traditional methods, but you look after an army of men. You've saved more than a few, guided them into more productive lives."

"Productive? I oversee the business of gaming hells and brothels. Only months ago I brought a swindler into town. You call that a productive life?"

"I call it a life that provides for their families." Hardaway sat in the chair opposite Fallon's desk and propped the heels of his boots on the corner. "During my time in the military—"

"The whole year, or are we just counting the three months abroad?"

"Shut it so I can compliment you, ya bastard. During my time in the military, I saw that there were two kinds of leaders: good ones and bad ones."

"Why did I think that was going to be more poetic?"

"You're a strong leader, St. James. The men here look to you. They follow your orders without question. They would die for you. And do you know why? I'll tell you why."

"I thought you might."

"You care about them. They know at the end of it all that you're doing all you can to look out for every one of them. You're one of the good ones, St. James."

Fallon nodded, more to bring an end to this conversation than as a sign of agreement. Although this was, in truth, going better than he'd anticipated. Hardaway had never been one to mince words or pull a punch.

"So when I see you acting like a horse's arse and overworking your men and yourself simply because you lost your lady love—"

"There it is." Fallon should have known the worst was still to come. There was a reason he always sent Hardaway to handle the difficult situations for the

Spares, and this was it. Fallon just wasn't usually on this side of the lecture.

"As your friend, I have a responsibility to stop you from destroying everything you've built."

"By asking them to work?" Fallon asked. "What harm am I doing here?"

"St. James, you look like shite, and you're being a complete arse to everyone around you. When was the last time you stepped away from this desk to even eat a proper meal?"

"Food is for the weak. This is what I do. The Spares are my life, and my friends deserve my full attention."

"You've moved on, then. Lady Isabelle was just a quick diversion. This…"—he waved his hand about Fallon's desk before continuing—"is normal."

"It has to be," Fallon said as he straightened a stack of papers on the edge of his desk.

"I caught sight of her when I returned her trunk to her home."

Fallon froze and looked up at Hardaway. "And?"

"Oh, now you want to hear about it? You don't have three reports to review at the same time or something of that nature? Since this is normal and all." Hardaway shrugged. "She was sitting in the drawing room with the door open when I arrived. She barely spared me a glance before returning to the book she was reading. Knottsby said she seemed relieved to be home. St. James, you should know, he also said she was taken by Grapling on her way there and jumped from a moving carriage to escape."

"Is she hurt?" he asked, pushing to his feet, ready to send for the doctor for her once again.

"She's well and at home with her family. She's where she should be. I'm sorry Claughbane lost her trail. Could have been disastrous, but she survived. Knottsby said she's been quiet about things."

Quiet and relieved to be home—of course she was relieved to be back with her family. It was where she belonged, after all. All was as it should be. Still, a part of him was hurt that she was so pleased to be away from him. And being quiet about things didn't sound like Isabelle. "You're certain it wasn't her sister who you saw?"

"Oh, I would know the difference," Hardaway ground out. "That lady needs to keep her distance from me."

Fallon shouldn't want to know more, but he knew he would never stop searching ballrooms for even a glimpse of Isabelle or clinging to mentions of her in conversation around town. It was wrong, but so was he in every way possible. "How did she look?"

"Like a lady reading a book in a drawing room." Hardaway shrugged. "Well, I suppose."

"Good. That's…good." Fallon stared down at the piles of papers in front of him. This was where he belonged and where he would stay. The Spares needed him.

"For the best. Isn't that what people say in these situations? In similar circumstances, I told Claughbane the story of my uncle showing his bits and pieces around town, and that seemed to help at the time. I could repeat it. It's a fine tale."

"The night of the Rightworths' ball?" Fallon raised a brow at the mention of the night Claughbane tried to destroy himself. "This isn't even close to the same circumstances. He lost his mind and was trying to get himself thrown into prison."

"And you're trying to waste away to nothing. I don't see much difference from where I'm sitting other than the comfort of your surroundings. You've put yourself in the same chains ol' Claughbane did."

"Shove off." Fallon bristled at the accusation.

"Very well." Hardaway stood from his chair and took his time adjusting his coat on his shoulders as he watched Fallon. After taking a step away, he paused and turned back to his desk. "While I'm thinking of it, did you still want information on that stolen artwork? It's being sold tonight."

Fallon sat forward in his chair, suddenly on alert. Isabelle's paintings. "You went on about my work habits when the art is changing hands tonight? What's wrong with you?"

Hardaway grinned. "I knew you wouldn't listen to the rest of it if I led with the informative bit. I've known you long enough to know that."

"You're such a bastard," he said, rising from his desk. He had to meet with his men, form a plan of attack...

"St. James, can I ask you one last question?"

"At this point, I don't see why not," Fallon muttered as he ran a hand through his hair. There was much to do to be ready for tonight.

"Is this about stopping Grapling from taking his revenge on us for tossing him in prison? Or is it about retrieving Lady Isabelle's paintings and acting the hero?"

There was no hope where Isabelle was concerned.

Acting the hero would do no good. Isabelle was gone and had no desire to return. If he could return the paintings and wrap up this scandal for her, perhaps he could see her smile one last time as he walked away. "What time is the meeting?"

"I thought so. The sale is at nine o'clock tonight in the Rockport building by the docks."

Once Hardaway had left the library, Fallon leaned a hand on his desk. His friend's question had been ridiculous. Reginald Grapling was finally within his reach. Of course that was all that mattered. The man would pay for all of his crimes—especially for daring to place a finger on Isabelle.

❧

Isabelle had often wondered what it must be like for the lady in the story to return to her home after being rescued from the villain by the brave knight—and now she knew. It was blasted uncomfortable.

Perhaps in her case the difference was that the villain was still on her mind when she ate or went to bed or thought of something amusing that would have made him smile. Tears stung at her eyes when she did anything at all. Fallon was everywhere she looked, even here in her home. This is what came of ladies who fell for the villain and not the hero. There was no brave knight at hand, no noble steed, and no hero's love to cling to. There were only her parents screaming at each other, Victoria keeping her distance, and the maids eyeing her like she might break at any moment. And she wasn't even allowed as far as the garden. The walls of her home made a more formidable dungeon cell than Fallon's bedchamber ever had.

"Father, I think it would be best if we left London. I would be safer in the country. We would all be happier if we packed immediately," she recited to herself once more on her way down the stairs.

She'd perfected a rather rousing argument to sway the man into taking the family back to the country before the end of the season. Now all that was left was to confront her father and make her case in favor of leaving town—as soon as trunks could be packed.

She couldn't recall ever confronting her father about anything at all, having preferred to slip beneath his notice and wait for life's storms to pass while in the garden. Two days ago, however, she'd escaped captivity, walked across London, and jumped from a moving carriage. She'd suffered enough at the hands of gentlemen, and she would have this conversation with her father now.

There was nothing left for her here anyway. Once outside town, she would be able to breathe. She wouldn't feel as if her heart had been trod upon by a coach and eight. She wouldn't be reminded of blasted Fallon St. James at every turn. Or at least that was her plan. Move on. And the first step on that journey was here.

Rounding the corner into the library, she stopped. It was empty. Turning back to the hall, she spotted a passing footman. "Do you know my father's whereabouts this afternoon?"

"He left an hour past, just after the post arrived. He mentioned a meeting."

"Thank you," she murmured. Isabelle paused at the door to the library, tapping her fingers on the doorframe. Idle hours hadn't eaten away at her this much when she'd been at Fallon's home. She'd read books, painted, dreamed, and sorted out his chaotic life. She almost smiled at that. Her own home was different from her experience there. What had once filled her time now seemed empty. She'd been content before Fallon kidnapped her, hadn't she? At least she'd thought so at the time. Once she was away from London, things would improve. They had to.

The library wasn't a large room—not like Fallon's, with its grand artwork and tall windows—but it was filled with books. She inhaled the scent of hundreds of leather-bound volumes and stepped inside the room. It was her father's domain, his retreat from her mother, but he wasn't home just now.

The fire hadn't been stoked since this morning and now burned low in the grate. Flickers of light danced over the two chairs and the table that sat on the thick rug. The post still lay scattered on the table from where her father had scanned through the letters before he left the house. One was open on top of the pile. Isabelle glanced back to the door and picked up the page.

Sharp angular writing of only a few lines covered the center of the paper. A red wax seal was broken on one edge, but she could still see the letters pressed there—*SHS*.

"Father isn't in," Victoria said from the door behind her.

"I know that. I was only—"

"Looking through his things. I suppose some things never change."

"Victoria…" Isabelle began, turning to look at her sister but unsure of what to say. "I'm sorry. I was angry with you before I went away, but I shouldn't have turned my back on you."

"Oh, but our aunt, whom we've met on only the one occasion, needed you. You had to leave immediately. It hardly mattered that I was to marry someone I detest. Our aunt required you. It's all quite understandable."

"Victoria, that isn't how it happened," Isabelle said quietly. How much could she tell her sister? Her parents had obviously told her the same tale that had been spread around town. Suddenly, her sister's distance since she returned home was clear—Victoria was hurt by her absence.

"I'm sure the story is quite dramatic—with you they always are."

Isabelle searched her sister's face, willing her to see that the decision to abandon Victoria on her wedding day hadn't been Isabelle's. "You don't understand."

"You're correct. I don't." Victoria turned and walked away.

"Victoria," Isabelle called after her, but there was no response. She would have to explain everything to make things right between them, and she would, but not right now, not when Victoria's anger toward her was still so raw. Her sister would never listen to her admittedly dramatic story when she was in such a state.

With a sigh, Isabelle looked at the page from the post and scanned down to the signature. She blinked, thinking she'd imagined it, but it was still there, shining in black ink.

St. James. Her heart pounded, and her eyes darted over the words scrawled there.

Knottsby,

The event we have waited for is happening this evening. Your art collection will be sold at nine o'clock tonight at the Rockport building near the harbor. Come alone.

—St. James

"What?" she whispered, flipping the paper over to search for more. Blank. Nothing.

The event we have waited for. Fallon's words made it sound as if her father had been in on the theft as well. That couldn't be. Her own father?

She'd been hit over the head and left for dead. She'd spent weeks in a man's bedchamber.

Fallon—her heart still screamed his name even with what she knew of his true nature. She'd been wise enough to know he wasn't a good man and to walk away even though it killed her to do so. Surely her father could see the same. Her father couldn't be involved with a man like Fallon. She was missing something. *Why did he send a note to Father, then?* A voice that sounded a great deal like Victoria's echoed in her mind.

Isabelle wasn't certain what was going on, but she was sure her father wouldn't be going to meet Fallon alone. Her breathing quickened at the thought of what she was about to do. But she had no choice. She needed answers. Her hands shook as she looked down at the paper in her hands one last time.

Abandoning the note where she'd found it, she went to the hall, spotting the same footman as before. "I require a carriage."

"Yes, m'lady. Where will you be going this afternoon?"

"Thornwood House," Isabelle said as she pulled a shawl from a nearby table and tossed it around her shoulders.

"The Mad Duke's home?"

"Yes," Isabelle stated, her confidence in her quickly hatched plan increasing by the second.

The duke's younger sister, Isabelle's dear friend Roselyn, was surely still away with her new husband, Lord Ayton. But it wasn't her friend she needed just now—it was the use of her black muslin day dress. The one Roselyn had used to spy on her husband. There would have been no need to take an article of mourning attire with her on a wedding trip. And what were friends for if not to loan out their clothing in times of need? And this was surely that.

For the first time in her life, Isabelle wanted to know the truth—not just some dreamed-up version of events that she pieced together in her mind. Tonight she would follow her father and finally discover the ugly reality of the gentlemen in her life. They'd kept her in the dark in matters that concerned her. They'd kidnapped her. They'd lied to her. "No more," she whispered to herself.

Nine o'clock tonight at the Rockport building.

She would be there, and she would certainly be attending alone.

Nineteen

Dear Isabelle,

I'm sorry. If there were stronger words than those that captured the pain I've caused you, I would say those as well. I never deserved having you in my life. It was a fact I knew well, but I was weak in the one area where I should have been strong. You were hurt as a result of my carelessness, and I'll carry that knowledge with me forever. Someday, long from now, I will see you waltzing at a ball in the arms of an honorable gentleman, and I hope to see you smile. It won't be a smile for me, of course, but I long for it nonetheless. I will always love you—

⁂

FALLON LIFTED THE PAPER FROM HIS DESK AND WADDED it into a ball in his fist, tossing it across the room into the fire. His words sizzled, popped, and then turned to ash just like all the others he'd written since she had walked out the door. His love for Isabelle, just like so many other secrets in his life, would never be spoken aloud. It was over.

⌘

The wind blew through the rough-hewn doors of the old stone building, stirring whirls of dirt on the floor. Soon it would be time.

Fallon glanced out the nearest window. The street outside was still quiet. Knottsby's carriage had arrived only minutes before, and Fallon's men had sent the driver on around the corner. Fallon wanted only Hardaway and Knottsby inside the abandoned building with him—Knottsby to identify the art as the originals and Hardaway because he enjoyed violence.

Wooden columns stood scattered across the open space, but it was otherwise as empty as it had been for years. On clear nights, the clerestory windows lit the building enough for an exchange of funds or an interrogation. Fallon knew the space all too well. Tonight, however, the clouds kept the corners of the room shadowed, which worked in the Spares' favor. The three of them could easily wait out of sight until the paintings were brought inside.

"I came alone as instructed, but I see you didn't," Knottsby said as he joined Fallon beside the window.

"Never," Fallon replied as he scanned the street once more. One of the Spares lingered in a doorway at the bend in the road, but there was still no sign of Grapling.

Hardaway moved in behind them and greeted Knottsby. "We have men stationed around the building. Nothing will move in or out of here without our notice."

"Always on top of things," Knottsby murmured.

Not always, or tonight would be quite different. He would have seen through Grapling years ago. He would have met Isabelle under different circumstances, and perhaps she wouldn't despise him. It seemed the only thing he *could* manage in his life was a successful operation.

"The intelligence behind this exchange seems to be accurate," Fallon said, eyeing the empty street outside and the harbor beyond that. The place held all the usual marks of being a sale location—proximity to a ship scheduled to leave port by morning, a quiet building, and a lack of homes in the area. For these same reasons, Fallon had used it on occasion. Unfortunately, he'd trained Grapling well.

"Was there bad information before?" Knottsby asked in surprise. "Hardaway, you're going too easy on your informants."

"He's been distraught ever since the wedding," Fallon answered with an innocent shrug of his shoulders for Hardaway's benefit. Fallon was still on edge from their talk earlier, and the chitchat while they waited for Grapling wasn't helping matters. *"Heartbroken*, wasn't that the term you used?"

"Ha!" Hardaway exclaimed.

"Keep your voice down." Fallon jabbed Hardaway in the ribs with his elbow.

His friend drew back and narrowed his eyes on Fallon in the dim moonlight. "Is this sharing of confidences time, St. James? Because I know a thing or two that I could say. You wouldn't want me to say what I could say, but say it I would."

Fallon almost grinned—almost. "Hardaway, would you say it? I am not certain I understand if you would say something."

"Bloody know-it-all," his friend ground out.

"About the wedding," Knottsby cut in. "Hardaway, you have my utmost apologies for—"

"Not now," Fallon bit out as a carriage drew to a stop outside the building. This was it.

He took a step back into the shadows and nodded for the others to do the same. They watched from the edge of the window as Grapling stepped down along with two young men. They each possessed the rough look of boys who had grown up on the streets. Their wary eyes darted around, and pistols were visible at their backs. Grapling, on the other hand, walked as if he owned the air around him.

They paused outside the carriage, a swaying lantern lighting the scene. Grapling was giving directions to the driver, appeared to be instructing one of the men to stay behind. The artwork could be in the carriage. Unless there was another conveyance still to come.

"He has blond hair?" Knottsby asked. "When did that happen?"

"When he discovered Isabelle's fondness for fair-headed gentlemen and attempted to court her." Fallon shifted back from the window to avoid being seen.

"Grapling shouldn't be allowed in the same room as Isabelle." Knottsby's gaze lingered for a second on Fallon's dark-brown hair and frowned in an all-too-obvious thought.

Fallon had never been right for Isabelle. She would go on to marry some lordly man who had the hair color and principles that she preferred. He swallowed down any further thought about what could have been, focusing on their present situation. "I tried to warn her away, attempted to alert you—as best I could, anyway, without endangering her life, but I failed on both counts. He lured her to the museum that day for revenge against you…and me. I'm sorry I couldn't tell you he was the culprit. He'd threatened to kill her if I spoke."

"On her sister's wedding day… I've neglected my family for too long. I don't even know what happens in my own home. Did you know that Grapling sent my Isabelle that blasted necklace and she wore it to a ball?"

Yes, as the jewelry now resided in Fallon's own desk drawer. He was still angered that for a time he'd thought this was about recreating a crime from years ago and not about art theft. Only someone who knew Fallon would know how to manipulate him in such a manner.

"My daughters are running amok," Knottsby said at his side. "My family's art collection has been stolen. It's all because of my own inattentiveness. I got caught up in having this blasted title and all that went with it. This is my fault."

"No. The blame is mine," Fallon stated.

"Not everything is your responsibility, St. James."

That wasn't the least bit true, but he didn't argue. A door opened a fraction on the other side of the room, and he heard light footsteps. Glancing back, he noted that Grapling was still outside, only just coming up to the nearest door. Fallon squinted into the dark of the opposite corner but saw nothing. He'd instructed his men to remain outside the building. Whoever had gone against his orders would have to be dealt with.

Just then the door banged open and Grapling entered, drawing Fallon's attention away from the noise and the dark corner.

"A fine night for wealth and revenge."

"We can drink to that tonight," the young man replied.

"We shall. As soon as we're rid of the paintings, my boy."

"Never would have thought some paint would fetch that kind of price."

"That's why you have me about. I know about the finer things and how to get them. You just have to follow my lead."

"Yes, sir," the young man said as he leaned back to look out the door. "When will he be here?"

"Not long. You should always arrive early to meetings such as this one. It gives you the advantage of knowing your surroundings. I can teach you much about this business."

Hardaway glanced to Fallon, and Fallon curled his fingers into fists. Arriving early was *his* advice to new recruits. He'd told it to Grapling in similar circumstances, only he hadn't acted like a high-handed arse when he'd said it. Little did the man know that he hadn't arrived early enough.

Something moved outside the building, and Fallon turned. The buyer. Fallon watched as another carriage arrived. He could feel the anticipation radiating off of Knottsby and Hardaway. A second later the door opened, and two men stepped inside. Grapling greeted the first man, finely dressed in tailored clothing and with a refined look about him. He must have been the art dealer. The buyer nodded to his man, and a leather bag was produced. Fallon waited.

"Where are the paintings?" Knottsby hissed in his ear.

Fallon held up a hand to silently tell the man to be patient. These things couldn't be rushed. They had to move at just the right time, or the entire operation would fall apart. Lives would be put in danger.

A moment later there were loud scratching and banging sounds outside the door. Knottsby shifted forward, but Fallon caught his arm. It was nearly time but not quite.

"Easy with that," Grapling called out as the man he'd left by the carriage heaved one end of a large crate into view.

"Sorry, sir. It's blasted heavy."

The crate started to shift, something slid inside, and it toppled farther. The young man was going to drop the crate, but there was nothing Fallon could do at this distance but wince for the paintings inside. Hopefully they were well packaged to survive their journey.

Except there was a flash of movement at his side, and Knottsby was already out of range of Fallon's grab. He ran forward into the central lit area of the building even as he reached for his pistol.

"Always was impatient," Hardaway mumbled at his side, and then he and Fallon were off as well, running into a fight two minutes too early.

Fallon checked the location of his pistol at his back and noticed Hardaway already had one in each hand.

Backup in case one misfired or was needed elsewhere, no doubt. Fallon sped forward, all the while doing the math of their situation. Most of his men were stationed around the building to prevent escape. Inside these walls, it was five men against three. Hardaway had two weapons, which would leave them evenly matched as long as the art dealer wasn't armed. It was a gamble, and one he didn't like the odds on.

Knottsby was moving toward the boy with the crate while Hardaway was at his side, focused on the two young men on the other side of the crate. Fallon wanted to pummel only one man tonight, and he was headed straight for him. Grapling looked up as the three moved out of the shadows, but had no time to react. Fallon reached the crate and dug one toe of his boot against the edge, launching himself over the top to come down on top of the man.

He'd been longing to punch the man again after their fight at the museum had been cut short, especially after what the man had done to Isabelle. His fingers dug into Grapling's shirt, and Fallon pushed him hard down onto the floor. Landing with an echoing thud, Fallon wasted no time landing a punch in the man's stomach, then kneeing him in the side. Grapling tore at Fallon's clothing, but he was no match for Fallon's size; he never had been.

Fallon had lost sight of the rest of the fight, but only one opponent truly mattered—the one who had dared hit Isabelle. Fallon's fist collided with Grapling's jaw with a satisfying thwack, but a second later he was pulled off the man and slung onto the floor.

Knottsby's opponent must have gotten away from

him. Grunts and blows sounded all around Fallon as he scrambled to his feet searching for his attacker. Grapling was on his knees now, slowly climbing to his feet. Fallon chanced a quick glance to the side. Hardaway was fighting two of the men by using his pistols as clubs, while the buyer stayed back and clutched his bag of money to his chest. Perhaps he should have wagered on the outcome of this fight after all.

Hearing a struggle behind him, Fallon turned just in time to see Knottsby fighting for control of a pistol. Pulling out his own pistol, he reached for the man's shoulder. Knottsby was a solid fighter, but he had thirty years on his opponent. Fallon had to help, or someone would get shot.

As he moved, he saw motion in the shadows. And a flash of an image where the light fell—soft blond curls framed round eyes. But he blinked, and the vision was gone.

Isabelle? It couldn't be.

How had she slipped past his men? Why was she here?

Fallon turned back to Grapling just in time to see the man raising a pistol and aiming it at Fallon's chest. He held a knife loosely at his side. Throwing knives had always been his specialty.

Fallon raised his pistol as well. A shot fired into the air behind him, and everything went quiet, aside from the ringing in his ears. Fallon glanced to the side. Pistols were raised around the room. Blast it all, Knottsby's opponent must have had a second weapon. No one was getting out of this alive. But it wasn't his life he was thinking of just now. It was Isabelle's.

❧

Isabelle backed away from the fight with hurried footsteps, her borrowed black dress blending her into the
dark stone walls behind her. Bumping into something
solid, she jumped, but it was only one of the wooden
columns. She slipped behind it and peeked out from
the edge. The wood was rough under her bare fingers,
but she held on anyway. Watching.

Had Fallon seen her? She was almost certain he had.

Looking at him now was like watching the ghost
of a lost loved one. Hair she'd once run her fingers
through, lips she'd once kissed... She wanted to rush
to him, but there was no longer anything there to hold
on to. He was standing still now, pistol raised just like
the others. She had no business being here tonight,
but it seemed Fallon *did* have business to attend to—
murderous business.

She'd been so wrong about him. But in the end,
she'd been right—he was a villain just like the rest of
them. Oddly, that confidence in her actions offered
her no comfort. She looked over the scene. Pistols
were raised in every direction, holding everyone in
check. Every man in her life was in this room: Fallon,
Lord Hardaway, Mr. Grapling, even her father. All
dogs fighting over a bone. She'd been wrong about
more than just Fallon. He wasn't the only villainous
gentleman here tonight. Perhaps there were no noble
knights in reality—there were only untrustworthy
men, all guilty, all out for their own gain.

She straightened her spine a bit. She was Lady
Isabelle Fairlyn, and she didn't require saving by any

of these so-called gentlemen. Once she had answers to all of her questions, she could put this mess behind her and walk away—only this time for good. Leaning against the column, she listened.

"Fallon St. James," Mr. Grapling crooned. "You found me, just as I'd hoped you would."

"Could have fooled me," Fallon retorted.

"I couldn't make it too easy for you though, could I? Where would the fun be in that?"

"My idea of fun is quite different from yours," Hardaway cut in.

"You're bluffing," Fallon accused. "You're only sorry that you finally slipped up and got caught."

"Neither of you likes my little party?" Grapling sneered. "It wouldn't be an evening with St. James without his pet, Brice."

"It's Hardaway now, you miserable sod," the man ground out.

"Oh, that's right. I *would* congratulate you on the new title, but I would wager you weren't pleased about receiving it at all. Did it put your membership in jeopardy with the secret club for the titleless? I suppose not, since you're here. The rules never apply to St. James's true friends. All the other Spare Heirs are there only to do your bidding, aren't they, St. James? No questions allowed. Everything done in the name of serving the great master." He waved at Fallon with the barrel of his pistol.

"We're a brotherhood. Something you never understood, Grapling." Fallon shifted on his feet but otherwise didn't flinch.

"Three years. Three years I did as I was told!

Three years I collected coins, wrote up accountings of events, assured the good women of the Westminster Boardinghouse that I would see to their needs on behalf of the great St. James."

"You were paid for your services," Hardaway cut in. "You were well taken care of. You were given rooms, food, and a weekly stipend."

"While he became wealthy," Grapling retorted, fixing his pistol aim between Fallon's eyes.

"It was never enough for you," Fallon mused. "Nothing was ever enough. I should have seen your greed and your ambition then. Is that why you're doing this? You think you can destroy Knottsby, steal from him, and take me down in the process? I have an army of men who beg to differ. Men who are loyal to this organization—something you never understood. They won't go quietly, and neither will I."

"Such a poignant speech, oh great leader. Tell me, when you rally your troops with words of togetherness and survival, do you mention the whores and the down-on-their-luck gentlemen you gather your coins from? We're no different, you and me."

"I've never killed for sport or siphoned funds simply to fill my own pockets. You're a murderer and a thief. I'm far from ideal, but everything I do is to help those around me. I may *gather coins*—as you put it—but I keep the people working in the establishments no one cares for safe from harm, from both the unjust law and men like you. I've never taken anything we didn't earn. I've never struck a lady over the head and left her for dead, placing the blame for a crime on her shoulders. I've never murdered—"

"Are you still on about that? It was four years ago, and she was a whore."

"She was an innocent woman, and you killed her."

"Those women are there for men's entertainment. And I found my time with her quite entertaining."

"And Lady Isabelle? Did you find that amusing? You could have killed her!" Fallon's words echoed off the walls of the abandoned building.

Isabelle swallowed. The truth struck her as directly as any one of their bullets might—Fallon might still be a criminal or even a villain, but she couldn't deny one thing: he still cared for her. "Her life or death was inconsequential. Sometimes pawns must be sacrificed to win the game. It's simple strategy."

She'd danced with this man. She'd worn the blasted locket he'd sent to her. How had she fallen into such a trap? The thought of it made her ill.

"The scandal will still fall on Knottsby's shoulders. I knew if you rushed to her rescue, then she would serve as a distraction while I took my time and enjoyed the city as I stole from your good friend here and blamed it on his daughter. And if you didn't come to her rescue… Well, we both knew you would attempt to save the girl's life. You have no idea how much I've treasured watching the great St. James powerless to stop my plans."

Isabelle sucked in an unsteady breath. He really was awful.

"I should have filled you with lead four years ago. Sending you to prison was too lenient."

"And become a murderer—just like me?"

Suddenly everything became clear. Well, perhaps

not *clear*, precisely, but far less muddied. Grapling was the villain here. It was just as she'd realized in his carriage—only somehow worse now that she knew the reasons behind his actions. He was the one who'd murdered some poor girl. He was the one who'd arrived with her family's artwork in crates, who'd stolen her diary and used the contents in whatever sick game he was playing. Fallon might not be the perfect gentleman she had previously thought him to be, but neither was he villainous. Yet she'd painted his heart black in her mind all the same.

She'd wondered for some time now who Fallon St. James was, and she had to admit that, even now, she still wasn't certain. But she took a step toward him anyway, leaving the cover of the column behind.

She watched as Fallon shifted his weight, his focus on Mr. Grapling. Then movement beyond them grabbed her attention.

Her father lunged forward. "I've heard enough. You stole from me, and I've come to take back what's mine."

No! In the cover of the shadowed perimeter of the room, Isabelle moved forward. She had to do something. She had to help them. Her private thoughts in her diary had caused this, had led this madman to threaten everything she held dear.

Father wasn't watching the men, only Mr. Grapling. In his inattention to the raised pistols all around him, one of the men cocked his weapon, aiming it at her father. Isabelle leapt forward just as Fallon turned to knock the pistol from the man's hands. Time seemed to slow.

She saw it all in the span of a heartbeat.

The gleam of victory in Mr. Grapling's eyes. Fallon's head still turned toward the pistol as it fell to the ground. The knife in the moonlight that lit the center of the room. Fallon.

Mr. Grapling raised his arm and threw the knife. Fallon didn't see it as it flew through the air. Fallon. Fallon! Her mouth couldn't form words of warning fast enough. She dove for the knife. Hot, slicing pain. Silencing pain. A bellow of rage. Grapling's shocked face. Footsteps. Gunfire.

Fallon. Secure arms holding her. Warm brown eyes watching her. Her name on his lips…

⁓

The building had erupted into chaotic madness all around him, but Fallon was still. His knees pressed into the wood plank floor as he held Isabelle in his arms. He brushed the hair back from her face and caressed her cheek.

"Isabelle, you're going to be all right. I've got you, love. Stay with me, Isabelle. Stay with me. Dear God, you have to stay with me. Please, Isabelle. Please don't go."

Her eyes were already closing. He was losing her.

"Isabelle? Isabelle!"

He could hear his men's footsteps as they swarmed through the doors. Hardaway had somehow ended up on top of Grapling, pinning the man to the floor with his forearm. Knottsby was in front of Fallon, crouched in front of his daughter. But Fallon didn't care about any of them. None of it mattered.

"I need a doctor!" he screamed.

"He can't arrive here fast enough, St. James," Knottsby said in a low voice that was hollow with fear.

Fallon blinked through the tears that filled his eyes and looked at the knife that still punctured her side, deep red now covering the black of the dress she wore. "Give me a knife and a length of cloth…your cravat." He sniffed, knowing what he must do.

"You're going to remove the knife yourself," her father accused him, already removing his cravat. "She'll bleed out. You can't!"

"I have to try," he said, still looking down at Isabelle, still warm in his arms.

"St. James, let me do this." Knottsby moved closer, holding the knife in his hands. "She's not completely gone. If we attempt this… If she wakes when I pull the knife out, you must hold her still. You have to trust me. You can't do this alone. You need my help."

Fallon swallowed and looked up at Isabelle's father. "Make sure the dress is cut back from the wound to prevent infection. If even a thread of fabric—"

"I'm her father. I care for her too. Trust me."

Fallon nodded, unable to speak through the knot of emotion in his throat. This had to work. He couldn't lose her completely. She had to live on and find happiness. He only brought her pain. But if she lived, was he strong enough to let her go again, as he had before?

Tightening his grip on her shoulders and bracing her head in the crook of his arm, Fallon looked back down into Isabelle's ashen face. Right or wrong, he would always love her. And right or wrong, he would never let her go.

Her father ripped the dress back from the hilt of the knife and braced a hand against her rib cage. But then he looked up, stopping. "We can't do this. We need a doctor. We could kill her."

Fallon couldn't speak, but he gave Knottsby a grave nod.

"Where should I take Grapling?" Hardaway asked from what seemed a great distance away.

Fallon was watching shaking hands tie the cravat tight around Isabelle's waist, putting vital pressure on the dressing, holding it—and the knife—in place and stopping the blood that made his hands sticky and warm.

Isabelle didn't move. There were no screams of pain or instantly alert open eyes as he tightened the dressing even more. There was only silence.

Knottsby had done a nice job with the field dressing even if it didn't save Isabelle's life. Fallon couldn't have done any better.

"St. James," Hardaway said again in an attempt to draw his attention.

The Spares, he had to finish this mission. "Send for…" he began, but his mind was consumed by the woman in his arms.

Hardaway kept talking. "I'll see to the men and send for the authorities. It's time this man returned to prison where he belongs. I'll make sure he receives the worst treatment possible, you can be sure. And I'll have the artwork returned to Knottsby's home. The doctor will be here in a few minutes." Hardaway gave him a nod and moved away, for once not speaking a single word that wasn't necessary.

But there were a few words that Fallon owed his friend. "Hardaway," he called out. "Thank you. For taking charge."

"You've done the same for me a thousand times over, my friend. I'm glad I can help you in return. All of us are."

Fallon glanced around at the men under his command. Stern, sorrow-filled faces met his watery gaze. They watched as the most heart-wrenching, private moment of his life was laid out before them for all to see. But the truth these men were witness to didn't weaken his position as their leader, as he had always assumed it would. It made him stronger. It made *them* stronger. He had these men at his back, just as he was there to support them.

He trusted these men, and he trusted Isabelle. If she lived, he would tell her so every day. *Please live so that I might love you forever*, he silently begged.

The room was silent as Grapling, his men, and the art buyer were bound, gagged, and gathered together against the far wall until assistance could arrive. Outside there was the sound of a carriage coming to a stop.

"The doctor is here. She can still be saved," Knottsby muttered at his side, the desperation clear in his voice.

But Fallon didn't have the strength left to hope. He hugged Isabelle to his chest and squeezed his eyes shut as he took a last inhale of her hair, pressing his lips to the top of her head. It was too late—too late for the doctor to save her and too late for Fallon to tell her how he felt for her.

"I'm so sorry. No more secrets," he whispered to Isabelle. "I'm a wicked gentleman who has done a great deal wrong in this life, and I will love you for the rest of my days. You saved me, my lady. I wish I could have done the same for you." He sniffed and kissed her forehead, refusing to let her go. "Rest well, my love, and dream of fairy tales with…" He choked on the emotion of good-bye for a second as a tear traced down his cheek before whispering, "Happy endings for all."

Twenty

St. James,

The last confession letter was finally found in the incoming post for the Times. *It seems he was waiting until he fled for good to have the note hit the papers. There will be no story now, of course. I left the note safely on your desk. Grapling was taken back to prison, one with higher security than before. There's no chance of his escape. He'll regret his actions for the rest of his life. When you return to headquarters, we can discuss any other details you require. Until then, my thoughts are with you, Knottsby, and Lady Isabelle.*

—*Hardaway*

THE SCENT OF FLOWERS SURROUNDED HER, PRESSING IN on her senses. A garden was one of her favorite places to spend an afternoon. Isabelle shifted her head on the pillows. Pillows? What garden had soft pillows? She blinked her eyes open, her blurry vision seeing an array of colored blooms. She couldn't be back in Fallon's bed. A comfortable bed in a garden? Perhaps this was the end after all. "Am I dead?" she murmured, waiting to be answered by some ethereal voice.

"No. Thankfully not," came a male voice from some distance away. She tried to shift in his direction, pain shooting through her side as she did so. "You did have me worried there for a bit, though."

"Fallon?" she asked, but even as his name left her lips, she knew he wasn't there.

Her father drew closer, adjusting the cloth on her forehead. "Why did you follow me? It wasn't safe."

"I can see that quite clearly now," she murmured, her voice scratchy and rough. Her mother was in the room as well and joined her father at her bedside. How long had she been here? The last she remembered was the searing pain of the knife…and Fallon. He'd held her in his arms.

"Thank heavens you're awake," her mother said. "The doctor wasn't certain when you would rouse…" She squeezed Isabelle's hand. "If ever."

Her father continued to twitch the cloth on her head this way and that until he was satisfied. However, it wasn't her head that ached; it was her side. Still she didn't move, only watched.

"Don't dwell on that now, darling. Isabelle will make a full recovery."

Darling? Isabelle looked up at her parents, watching them cling to each other, their fingers twined together. Perhaps she was dead after all. Her parents were on more-than-friendly terms, and she was surrounded by blossoms.

"Your father and I didn't lose all hope, but it was in short supply."

Isabelle shifted to take a closer look at the flowers and noted that they weren't planted in dirt. They were real, arranged in what must have been every available vase in the house, filling her bedchamber. The scene reminded her of a certain other flower-covered room. Her eyes pricked with tears, knowing she would never go back there. Turning back to her father, she said, "I'm sorry I got caught up in this mess, not just following you, but the museum, Victoria's wedding—"

"You are not to blame, Isabelle." His eyes were troubled as he spoke, which defined the lines there and made him look every bit his age. "That plot began long before you went to that museum. It began when you were still in the schoolroom, even if he did become fixated on you in the end. Reginald Grapling is to blame for this, for all of it." He ground out the man's name, and her mother placed a hand on her father's shoulder to comfort him.

Isabelle ignored her parents' odd behavior and continued, "I shouldn't have ever looked in that man's direction. I've done so much that was wrong this season. How you must have worried over me. I should have found a way to write to you after the wedding, to let you know I was safe…and well cared for." She sniffed, blinking away the threat of tears. It would do no good to cry over what once was. It was over, no matter what she'd overheard at the harbor. The way he'd looked at her was concern—that was all. Too much had happened. There was no turning back now.

"We knew you were in the safest place you could be," her father reassured her.

"You did? I knew you sent a trunk with my things, but you knew…about everything?"

"I've—" Her father broke off, tugging at the knot of his cravat as if it had been tied too tightly. "I've been in communication with St. James for some time now."

"You mean about the stolen paintings."

"Not only that."

"You talked to St. James about me, of course. My condition. To ask after my health."

He sighed and sat down on the edge of her bed, looking her in the eye. "I received a note from one of his men within the hour of your arrival at headquarters. He kept me updated since then."

"Headquarters… Then you know. You know the sort of place where I was held?"

"I do. Quite well actually."

"There's no sense keeping this from her," her mother said over his shoulder. "She knows most of it already."

"I'm confused." She looked from her father to her mother and back again. There was more to this yet. She was caught on the notion that her father had been aware that St. James ran a secret gentlemen's club from his home, and he had still allowed his daughter to stay there. She'd only just woken from what was apparently near death. Couldn't they just explain things to her outright?

Her father shifted uncomfortably, drawing her full

attention. "Isabelle, I didn't always have my title, the estate, an income that would provide for your mother, your sister, and you. You were too young to recall the lean years when we had to rely on the benevolence of relatives. By the time you were old enough to notice such things, my situation had improved."

"We always managed, though," she cut in.

"Yes, we did. And that was because of St. James and his organization. I met him when he was just a young man—driven, cunning as they come, and with a wild idea in mind to start a secret gentlemen's club. I followed him, as did many others. I was one of the founding members of the Spare Heirs Society. That was until three years ago, when I became Lord Knottsby. I had a title and inheritance, so I stepped down out of respect for our rules, but if not for that, I would maintain my membership today."

"What?" She croaked out the question and stared at him. Her own father? Then the pieces of the story began to slip together in her mind.

Three years ago…his refusal to take her with him on any of his trips to London. Hardaway's presence at their home on occasion. Last night. Father was involved with Grapling and the stolen paintings, just as Fallon had been, and for the same reason—because of this secret society. No. She was spinning fantasies again. This couldn't be true. "I've never heard of your involvement with such a band of—"

"Gentlemen?" he cut in. "Men born of quality upon whom society has turned its back? Without inheritance, lands, the ability to work in trade… Not everyone is suited for a life in the military or the church. I'm proud of my former involvement with such a group. I owe St. James my life. He offers men like me—many men like me—a chance to belong, to have the funds we require to provide for our families, to right wrongs that are beyond the gaze of the authorities."

"You're claiming that the organization is an honorable one? That St. James leads this group like he's some sort of Robin Hood character? Father, he may have been on the right side of that one art theft, but when I was there at headquarters, I heard things… awful things."

"Only an honorable man would…" His words trailed off as he glanced to his wife. "I don't think it's my place to explain it to you. I will say this, Isabelle. There is no other man I would trust with my daughter's life. Even you admit you were well cared for while in his home."

"I was." She clutched the blankets that covered her in her fists, pulling them tighter. "None of that matters anymore, though."

"Doesn't it?" He shot a glance to her mother that Isabelle didn't understand.

Isabelle stared at her father. "Why would it?"

Her father looked at her for a moment, clearly considering his words carefully before speaking. "Isabelle, you have always had the gift to see the good in everything around you. That ability has helped you to keep your cheer even in the worst situations, but it's also blinded you to the true evils that exist. The world isn't all good."

"I've discovered that on my own, as it happens,"

she grumbled, well aware of the knife wound in her side, the scar above her hairline, and the broken heart she now had.

"Yes, I suppose that's true. I never imagined that you would get injured in all of this. And your wounds and firsthand experience with Grapling make it that much more difficult for you to see things for what they are."

"I'm well acquainted with reality as of late, if that's your meaning."

"My meaning is the world isn't all bad, either. St. James isn't all bad. And neither am I, for being one of the Spare Heirs. He lives an unusual life, to be sure. You know that better than most. But I also believe you know the kind of man he is at heart better than most as well."

Heat filled her cheeks, and she looked down at her hands. "It hardly matters what kind of man I believe him to be." Talking about him with her father was only making this more difficult. Didn't he understand? She may have had the wrong idea about Fallon St. James's character, but things had ended poorly between them. It was too late for a change of heart now. She had walked away, and he hadn't stopped her. What more proof did she need that he didn't want what she had to give? "It's time I carried on with my life. I'd like to leave London as soon as I'm able."

"Isabelle, I understand your desire to move ever forward…" her father began, his voice rising, but he seemed to catch himself before he reached a true yell.

"Isn't that the wisdom you've always imparted to me?"

Her father took a breath and studied her for a

second before continuing. "Who do you think had our entire home filled to the rafters with flowers for you to enjoy when you woke? You've seen his home. You know the truth."

She looked around, taking in the layers of blooms that covered every surface of her bedchamber. Her gaze landed on the vase of pink roses closest to her bed. Her favorite. She'd told him so the night he'd taken her to the rooftop garden. But it couldn't be. She'd called him a villain, and he hadn't argued. He'd let her leave as if he didn't care for her at all. Yet her father was right; she knew the truth.

"Fallon." His name slipped from her lips with such ease. If only everything between them was so easy.

"If you'd like to see him, he refuses to leave the chair outside your door," her mother chimed in. "The maids are starting to complain of his scowls, constant questions about your well-being, and demands for more tea."

This must have been a fever dream. He'd come to watch over her even after all she'd said and done? "He's here?" she asked in wonder. "But he… I left and then…"

She loved his scowls and his smiles that were just for her. She loved him. No matter what he was involved in, she knew him, the true Fallon who sat at her side when she had a head wound and made up stories with her when she couldn't sleep at night.

Her mother stepped forward, removed the cloth from her forehead, and set it aside. "*And then*," her mother repeated, "he tracked down the man who hurt you at the museum and took back the paintings that mean so much to you." She glanced to Isabelle's father and nodded, as if checking off a mental list. "He sent for the doctor he keeps on staff to see to you—none other would do. He brought you more flowers than I thought possible. His concern for you was inspiring." She tossed a smile over her shoulder to Isabelle's father, who winked at her in return.

Her father stood from the edge of her bed and took her mother's hand. "She needs rest. We've said too much already."

"You're leaving?" she called after them, but they were already out the door by the time her reeling mind formed the words.

She craned her neck to see into the hall. Was he really there, guarding her door? But her question was answered a second later when Fallon stepped inside her bedchamber.

❧

Fourteen hours and twenty-six minutes he'd waited to hear her voice, give or take the few seconds since he'd checked the time. He'd had forty-two vases of flowers delivered, had waited twenty minutes too long for his doctor to arrive, had driven away two maids, and had berated himself the entire time for allowing that bastard to hurt Isabelle again.

When Knottsby led his wife from the room and she held his hand and dabbed at tears in her eyes, his heart stopped, just as it had last night.

No. She had to survive. She simply had to. His limbs grew heavy and time slowed even further as he watched Knottsby look around at his wife. Then Fallon heard Isabelle's voice. In an instant, he bolted to his feet and rushed into her bedchamber. Hang what was proper; those rules didn't apply to them.

"You're awake. The doctor…" He couldn't bring himself to repeat what he'd been warned could happen. "I see you got my flowers," he said as he moved farther into the room.

"Pink roses," she whispered with a hint of a smile.

"Every bloom that was available in London." He watched her for a moment, pale from blood loss and appearing small and frail surrounded in pillows as she was. Flowers were the least he could do. He wanted to fix this, to heal her, but he couldn't. His lack of control over her fate had driven him to near madness. Even seeing her awake now didn't take away the need he possessed to fix this somehow. "Isabelle, why did you dive for that knife? I could have stopped him."

"Then you would be the one injured," she countered.

"That's as it should be." He sat on the edge of her bed, careful not to jostle her too much but unable to stay away all the same. "I should be the one with a wound in the side. This was my battle to fight, not yours. I thought I'd lost you." He glanced down at the cuffs of his shirt, still stained from where he'd held her in his arms, begging for her to live.

"I thought you'd lost me too," she murmured. She gave him the same starry-eyed look she had that night in his bedchamber, but she was just this side of death. Starry eyes were to be expected in such circumstances. They didn't mean what they once had.

"You do know that the lady is supposed to be the one who is rescued in the story?" he asked, brushing a lock of her hair from her face.

"Not in this story." She almost laughed but shifted in pain instead, making his heart ache for her.

"If I were a noble, honest gentleman who wore bright colors, danced at balls, and smiled on occasion, you wouldn't have gotten wrapped up in this. You would be whole and sitting in the garden, enjoying the warm weather."

"That isn't much of a story, Fallon. Where are the danger and excitement? I think I prefer the version with the wicked pirate."

His pulse quickened as a flicker of hope lit deep in his bones. Did she mean him, or was this another of her stories? He needed to know. "Wicked pirates... gentlemen of that sort are troublesome creatures, Isabelle. Always wrapped up in devious plots."

"Far more dramatic a tale, don't you agree?"

"Isabelle..." This wasn't the time for this conversation. She should be well, but he needed to settle things with her. "There are details to the story that you don't know, and I want you to know everything. No secrets."

"My father told me already. You could have mentioned your alliance with him at some point."

"Apologies. I'll never keep anything from you again. However, it is a *secret* society."

"I suppose."

He swallowed, knowing there was a cliff he was about to leap from and hoping he would find clear waters below. "Is that all he told you? That he was once a member of my organization? He was. That's where he first met Grapling. I put them together, overseeing one of the projects we had at the time. It wasn't until later that I discovered the kind of man

Grapling was, but by then it was too late. Your father was his opposite, trustworthy, honorable—as much as gentlemen of our ilk can be.

"Did your father mention anything else by chance?"

"There's more?"

"You may like this part—I hope so anyway. I know you have a fondness for such tales when they involve characters in a book or something you saw once in an opera."

She remained quiet, her eyes on his as she listened to every word he said. This was it. There was nothing to be done but to toss his hand of cards on the table and see if there would be a winner.

He took a breath and dove in. "When I took you back to my home from the museum that day—"

"Kidnapped," she corrected.

"Very well, *kidnapped*," he said, unable to contain his smile. "I wrote to your father."

"He said that. You asked for my things to be sent over. You mentioned it over dinner that night as well. Remember?"

"I didn't tell you everything," he confessed.

"Oh."

"I also promised him that if anything went awry, if word of your whereabouts got out and your reputation was harmed, that I…would marry you."

"What?"

She tried to sit up, but he placed a hand on her shoulder. "Don't move. Your wound could reopen. My timing with this conversation is—"

"Did you truly want to marry me? That was more than a month ago, Fallon. You kept me locked away."

"To protect your future, not to preserve my bachelorhood," he insisted. "I know your thoughts on marriage, Isabelle. I didn't want you to be forced into marriage because of a rumor. I'm well aware of how hurtful that can be. Ever since the debacle with Hardaway and Lady Victoria, believe me. I was responsible for that as well, since I'm confessing truths. I was attempting to erase the scandal of the fire, but on some level I think I was glad to have Hardaway away from you permanently. Even then…" He noticed he still had a hand on her arm but didn't remove it. He didn't want to lose that connection with her, especially not if it was to be his last. "Even then, I only wanted you to be happy. And I knew firsthand that Hardaway wasn't the one who could do that. I didn't think I could either. You wanted to be with some gentleman who dances and wears red or some hideous color like that. Not me. I'm—"

"Not a villain. I shouldn't have ever said that, Fallon. It's not true. I know that now."

"Nor am I a gentleman with leisure time who spends afternoons riding about the park and complaining of ennui. You know what I do. You know the truth of my home and what occurs within those walls, and I can't change that. My life… Isabelle, no lady would want that life. And I wasn't going to have it forced on you."

"Forced on me? Fallon, what of all the time we spent together? Did you think that wouldn't sway my thinking? We spent nearly a month sharing a bed," she whispered with a quick glance to the crack in the door. "You kissed me thoroughly, repeatedly, and we—"

"I recall," he assured her as he slid his hand down her arm to her wrist. He would never forget his time with her. If she refused to forgive him, those memories would be all he would have of her. They would become his most prized possessions. But he wouldn't concede defeat without at least trying. Even if all was lost, he had to try. This was Isabelle, his Isabelle.

"That wasn't simply sport for you, was it?" she asked in a small voice.

"No!" God no. How could he explain this to her? "What happened between us was never meant to happen, but…it did. You are the only thing in my life I didn't plan. You were unexpected, and I made a mess of things. I was trying *not* to hurt you, Isabelle."

The room fell silent for a second, and Isabelle only examined him. He kept his hand over hers on the bed, but she made no move to reassure him with a touch. Perhaps it really was too late. He'd made too many mistakes and truly lost her. He barely dared to breathe. *Let her forgive me, let me hold her again.* All his future happiness in the world rested in the palm of her hand. And he waited.

"Why did you stop me?" she finally asked.

"What?"

"When I tried to tell you that I loved you. You stopped me, and you left me alone for two days. Two terribly long days! And you'd already spoken to my father! Isn't there *supposed* to be love in marriage? Isn't love good?"

His own foolish fear of everything he'd built falling apart was the very thing causing this to fall apart? He released a harsh breath. "Of course there should be love. I love you too, Isabelle, but that's precisely why I tried to keep my distance. I didn't want to hurt you. I didn't want you to feel as though you had to marry me and live at the headquarters for a secret gentlemen's club for the rest of your days. I love you enough to want a better life than that for you."

"You love me," she stated as if she had just received the last clue in a great mystery.

"More than anything," he murmured. He searched her eyes, her beautiful round eyes that saw love everywhere. Was there a chance she still felt for him as she once had?

"That's why you let me walk away. You're afraid you can't provide me with a life of stability. But I can manage a home. You've seen that. And you're the head of a large organization." She grabbed his fingertips with her own, and his heart caught.

"I lead an organization of misfit gentlemen through a life some see as one of crime. I'm horribly flawed— villainous, some say—and I want you back regardless of any logic." He sounded desperate, but he didn't care. "I know my life is…"

"Exciting and dramatic—two of my favorite descriptions. But you already knew that."

Of course she would see it all in such a light. She was Isabelle. He sighed and lifted her hand to his lips, placing a kiss on her palm. "I've missed you. You changed everything in my home, and now I can't eat without thinking of you. The food tastes—"

"Entirely unlike sawdust?" she asked with a wry smile, and he reached up and touched her cheek.

"I can't sleep at night. I'm driving my men mad."

"I've changed as well, Fallon. I don't belong here with my family anymore."

"You belong with me," he said as he stroked his fingers through her hair, unable to stop himself from touching her. He'd been involved in enough negotiations to know when a deal was closed in all but signatures. Sometime later, when all was quiet, he would consider how close he'd come to losing her, even after her life had been saved, but right now he needed to settle things once and for all. "Would you consider returning to my home? And not as a kidnapping victim this time?"

"Will you let me leave your bedchamber?"

"Perhaps. We can discuss the terms of your freedom," he said with a grin.

"I can't think of anywhere I would rather be." She slipped her hand inside his coat and splayed her fingers over his chest. "I love you, Fallon. You're all the things I thought you were—friend, pirate, lover, hero, gentleman. I'm sorry I doubted what I already knew of your heart."

He leaned forward and kissed her, grateful for her life and her love. He didn't deserve her, but he would cherish her forever. "For someone who falls in love twice a week, you're not very practiced at the nuance involved," he teased as he looked down into her eyes.

"I never loved before I loved you, not really. I'm glad it was you." She added the last bit in a low murmur just before she tugged on his shirt to bring him close enough for her lips to meet his.

She was so sweet, such his opposite in every way,

and she loved him. The words that once drove him away now pulled him in. "You forgot one item in your list—husband. Will you marry me, Isabelle?"

"Yes, but only if I can be the grand matron of the Spare Heirs Society. Doesn't that sound fabulous?"

He laughed, something he often did now because of Isabelle. "I love you."

"I'm glad you agree." She beamed up at him. "I might need a walking stick with a jewel on the top for a proper entrance into the drawing room."

"We can discuss the title and costuming later, once you're healed. For now, what about becoming Mrs. St. James?"

"It's perfect!"

July 1817

I had the most wonderful day of my life today. I have an awful pain in my side. There was the part where I almost died. That was unfortunate. And Victoria is still barely speaking to me. It makes me sad that she still believes I abandoned her. In time, I know we'll reconcile, though. She's my sister. We fight and we forgive; it's what we do. But near death, pain, and lingering anger don't matter in light of what happened next. I'm engaged to be married! It was the most romantic proposal ever. The room was filled with flowers he brought me—my favorite flowers. Fallon, the man of my dreams, was sitting at my side. And he asked me to be his wife. I said yes, of course, after a bit of discussion.

It was odd, that conversation—though rather heated on occasion—wasn't one of anger but of desperate need to understand. There was confrontation, but it didn't lead to screams or slammed doors. Instead it led to an agreement to marry, to joy, and to a future better than any found in the pages of a book. I'm in love.

When he kissed my hand, I nearly melted down into my bedclothes. He loves me. Fallon St. James loves me! I will spend the rest of my days at his side, and happiness will bloom forever around us.

—Lady Isabelle Fairlyn,
soon to be Mrs. St. James

Grand Matron of the
Spare Heirs Society

Epilogue

December 1817
Headquarters—London, England

FALLON WAS RECLINING AT HIS DESK IN THE LIBRARY, studying a stack of documents in his hands as he did every morning.

He was surrounded by papers in a quiet room, yet the lines around his eyes had eased over the past few months. He certainly never missed an opportunity to take an afternoon to walk with Isabelle in the park, visit her in the now-tidy rooftop garden, or come to their bed at night. And he was about to eat before noon, whether he liked it or not.

Isabelle smiled at him as she crossed the room, the platter she'd taken from the housekeeper braced against one hip. "I have something for you."

"Cakes?" he asked with a curious smile as he spotted her and set his papers aside. "It's barely eight in the morning."

"I know, but they smelled delicious. I couldn't resist. Try one." She lifted one of the small lemon cakes and threw it across the room to her husband.

Reaching up and grabbing the cake from the air above his head, he laughed. Laughter was often heard in the halls of headquarters now. "You don't have to throw sweets at my head to get me to eat, you know."

"You know I'm fond of sending platters of cakes to the floor. Not to mention if one hits the rug, you'll be forced to flee the scene of the crime before Mrs. Featherfitch scolds you for making a mess." She threw another. "That was your own advice, after all."

"Isabelle," he said in a halfhearted attempt at admonishment as he grinned at her. "I'm reviewing the investments that you had a hand in, but since you're here…" He stood, dodging one cake, then catching another and taking a bite. "That *is* delicious. Come with me." He rounded the desk and wrapped her icing-covered hand in his, taking the platter from her and leaving it on a side table.

"Where are we going?" she asked, turning to follow along at Fallon's side. "To the garden? Back to bed?"

He smirked at her, his look filled with promises for later this evening. Then lifting her fingers to his lips, he sucked the lingering icing from her fingertip. She slowed to a stop beside the staircase that led to the upper floors of their home, looking up at him. She would follow him anywhere, but it would be a pleasant change to know what he had planned.

"You aren't going to tell me where we're going, are you? One day I will get you to tell me all of your secrets."

"You know all my secrets. You and only you, my beautiful wife." He kissed the backs of her knuckles. His eyes were locked on hers in a piercing gaze, as if he were willing her to believe him. And she did. They'd lain awake nights for months, telling each other stories, not of legend or myth, but of experiences from their own pasts. She knew Fallon St. James first as her friend, then as her lover, now as her husband. But there was still an air of mystery surrounding his actions that she rather thought he enjoyed.

"I don't know where we're going right now," she complained, but he only tugged her to move past the open door of the drawing room where gentlemen's voices could always be heard.

"There's a difference between secrets and surprises," he said as he led her to the dining room door.

"Oh! It's a surprise?" She almost bounced in her excitement but clung to Fallon's arm instead as he opened the door.

Stepping inside, she looked up at the painting that hung on the most prominent wall of the room—her painting, her *stolen* painting and the one that had ultimately brought them together. She released Fallon's arm and moved forward to admire it.

"I contacted the librarian at the museum. He oversaw the repairs to the frame, and I had it brought here. Most of the house is still full of Spares, but this room isn't ever used by the men. Your friends will be here to visit in a few days' time…and I thought the two of us could dine together here, perhaps someday with a family. I want this place to be your home. I know I have no castle to offer you, but this—"

"It's perfect," Isabelle said as she looked up at the painting of the castle on the large wall of the dining room.

Fallon placed a hand on her shoulder as he moved

closer behind her. "Quite realistic, isn't it? You could almost move in."

"It is lovely, but I much prefer my true life here with you."

"Your life here with a houseful of misfit gentlemen?"

"There's one gentleman in particular that I'm grateful to share a home with," she said, turning to face him.

"I know this house, though on the large side for a London residence, isn't ideal—"

"*Our home* is better than ideal. I have a happy life with you, Fallon. You've given me everything I've ever wanted. I don't have to be afraid of quarrels anymore. There's nothing to escape from here. I'm free to live, encouraged to do as I please. The gentlemen who reside here have become my friends. The only words ever spoken in anger are between your men, and you quickly settle them because you lead with love."

"Keep your voice down," Fallon teased. "If Hardaway hears you say that, I'll never hear the end of it."

"You care for those men. You look after them, keep them safe, just as you do for me. I find I rather enjoy the bustle of a busy home."

"It's never dull, to be sure," Fallon agreed.

"I always wondered when I first met you what kept you so busy. Now I know—you needed me. You, my pirate captain, required my help, and I am pleased to keep your ship afloat while you wage war against injustice on the open seas." She smiled up at him as he wound his arms around her waist.

"I'm a pirate again, am I?"

"Oh, quite. Cannon fire is blasting through dangerous waters as the battle goes on day after day. Men are requiring your direction, and you, my husband, were trying to manage a staff and keep the ship in working order at such a time." She poked a playful finger at his chest.

He gave her a wry smile. "It *is* nice to have a tidy ship, and now food simply arrives without my arranging it."

"See? I'm a valuable lady to have on board."

"I'm glad I kidnapped you," he murmured as he rested his forehead against hers, pulling her even closer within his embrace.

"No more working day and night."

"My nights are all yours," he promised, and she had no doubt that he meant it. He angled down and placed a searing kiss on her lips, one that had her leaning in for more and blinking for a moment when it ended.

"Like I said, it's perfect," she said with a grin. "My life is filled with happiness and love—"

"In a headquarters for a secret society full of roguish gentlemen," he added with a chuckle.

"Don't forget the flowers and paintings of cherubs. I love Pearl for those little fellows in the main hall. Every dream castle should have cherubs and flowers."

"She would have liked you, Isabelle."

Isabelle nodded, grateful that he thought the lady who had been like a grandmother to him and had shaped him into the man he was would have approved of their match. "And I will care for this house, her former home, just as you have."

"I think it needs more artwork and perhaps some more works of fiction. Care to help me with that?"

"Are you suggesting a leisurely pursuit?" she teased.

"Only if I get to be leisurely with you, my love." Fallon trailed his hands over her body, and his gaze turned heated. She could stare into those dark eyes forever, and as fortune would have it, she would get to.

"Pardon the interruption," the butler said from the door, pulling them both from the private moment. When Isabelle peered around Fallon's shoulder, she saw the man had his eyes purposefully averted. "You have a caller."

"Spares' business," Fallon muttered as he kissed her cheek and stepped away. "You stay and admire your painting. I'll return in a moment."

"Actually, it's a lady, sir, here to see Mrs. St. James. Although your presence may be needed as well, sir."

"A lady knows the location of headquarters? Is she the wife of a member?" Fallon turned to shoot her a questioning look.

"I'm on my way," she said with a nod for their butler. "Thank you for the message."

Isabelle offered her husband a smile and left the room. But as she stepped through the door to the main hall, she suddenly understood their butler's concern. She stopped, staring at the woman who waited in the center of the room.

"Victoria!"

Her sister had been peering inside the drawing room with curiosity, but when she spotted Isabelle, she turned to face her. "Your new home suits you."

Isabelle hadn't seen her sister since Isabelle had married and moved to her new home. She'd sent Victoria letters, but they'd all been returned unopened. She'd called on her but had been turned away. Would this hurt that had already lasted too long between them ever heal? For Isabelle's part, she would never cease her attempts. That had been the one fly in the ointment of her perfect happiness—the nagging worry over her sister. And now…

The woman before her was but a ghost of the lady Isabelle had once known so well. Her skin was pale, as if she hadn't seen the light in weeks. She'd lost weight too. Not so much that anyone else would notice while hidden beneath a dress, but Isabelle saw it immediately. But worst of all there was a cut on her swollen and bruised lip that hadn't been properly cleaned. Had she been in some sort of brawl? Isabelle moved closer. "Victoria, what's happened to you?"

Victoria raised her chin, clearly digging for the dignity she required to continue with this conversation. Her gaze met Isabelle's for a long moment before she parted her lips to speak. "A large drink would be most welcome."

"Of course," Isabelle muttered, reaching for her sister, but before she could excuse Victoria from the main hall, footsteps sounded on the stairs behind her.

"Lady Victoria Fairlyn," Hardaway grated. "Would you like to turn and flee out the door? For the sake of fond memories and all."

"Hardaway, really," Isabelle admonished. She'd come to understand the man's wit, but this was no time for such ribbing. "Can't you see she is in some sort of trouble?"

Hardaway's steps slowed as he looked at Victoria, apparently noticing her bruised state for the first time.

"Isabelle, why don't you show your sister into your private parlor," Fallon murmured in her ear. She hadn't heard him approach, but she was glad to have him present at such a tense time. She was friends with Hardaway now, her old infatuation with the man gone, but he was being less than gentlemanly with her sister, and she wouldn't have it.

But before they could move out of the hall, Victoria looked past Isabelle, her focus on where Hardaway stood at the bottom of the stairs. "I didn't know where else to go. I thought to impose on my sister."

"It's no imposition—" Isabelle began, but Fallon silenced her with a touch of his hand.

Victoria looked up at Hardaway, battered from some fight and appearing desperate for the first time in Isabelle's memory.

She licked at the blood on her lip and winced in pain. "Kel...Lord Hardaway, I need your help."

Please enjoy this sneak peek of
Lord of Lies by *USA Today* bestselling
author Amy Sandas

London, June 1817

PORTIA CHADWICK WAS TERRIFIED. AND FURIOUS.

And *terrified*.

Perched on the edge of her seat in the racing carriage, her legs braced for action, Portia clenched fistfuls of her skirts in a vain attempt to contain her panic.

Not twenty minutes ago, her sister Lily had been abducted right off the street in front of their great-aunt's house in Mayfair. They had just arrived home after an evening out when the assailant had come out of nowhere, knocking their driver to the ground with one blow and hauling Lily off her feet. Portia had scrambled from the carriage just in time to see her sister being tossed into a waiting vehicle that took off as soon as the kidnapper climbed in after her.

Portia's immediate instinct had been to chase after the carriage with her skirts lifted to her knees. If her great-aunt hadn't shouted after her with the uncharacteristically rational observation that she had no chance of outrunning a racing carriage, Portia would still be sprinting down the street.

Angelique had insisted there was another way.

And now here they were, driving at breakneck speed to the East End to search the streets for a boy wearing a red cap.

It was ludicrous! Angelique had clearly lost her mind this time.

Portia's gaze darted toward the elderly lady. Despite the perilous nature of their current plight, the Dowager Countess of Chelmsworth appeared shockingly unperturbed. "We should have contacted the authorities," Portia argued once more, fear making her combative.

"The authorities will do nothing but write up a report. Word of this will spread like a disease through the gossip mills," Angelique replied. A heavy French accent still colored her words, though she'd lived in England for decades. "We need to save your sister, and quickly, but the authorities will be more harm than help."

Portia wasn't sure she agreed, but she had accepted Angelique's lead on impulse and now had no choice but to follow it through.

She hated feeling so ineffectual, so bloody useless.

If only she had gotten out of the carriage first, then *she* would have been abducted instead of Lily. She would give anything to be in her sister's place right now. At twenty, Lily was more than a year older than Portia, but she was far too gentle and trusting to fare well in the hands of a ruthless kidnapper.

And Portia had no doubt her sister's abductor was quite ruthless. The kidnapping had to be the work of

Mason Hale, who had been sending threatening letters to their oldest sister, Emma. The same man who had accosted Lily just two nights ago, demanding repayment of a loan their father had incurred before his untimely death.

But Hale had given them until the end of tomorrow to come up with his money. Why would he kidnap one of them now? It made no sense.

Unless it was not Hale after all…

Portia's throat closed up in fierce rejection of the thought. It had to be Hale.

"How in hell is a boy in a red cap going to help us?" Portia pressed again, desperately needing assurance that they were not on a fool's errand as they raced toward a corner of London's East End where no gently bred lady should ever consider visiting.

"The boy knows how to get in touch with a man who can help us," Angelique answered. "Trust me, darling. It is our very best chance to save your sister."

Portia's stomach twisted.

"What kind of man?" she asked. "Who is he? How do you know he will help us?"

"He is known to do many things…for the proper incentive," Angelique replied evasively.

"Incentive?" Portia's anxiety spiked. "But we have little money."

"We have enough to bluff, *ma petite*. Now stop arguing." The elderly lady leaned forward to peer out the window. "We are almost there. Keep your eyes alert for the boy. Remember to look for a red cap."

Portia shivered—from fear, anxiety, and the effort it took to suppress the urgent need to take action. Her heart was wedged firmly in her throat, and her jaw ached from clenching her teeth against the desire to shout her sister's name as loudly as she could into the night on the insane hope that Lily might somehow hear her and know they were doing all they could to get her back.

She was desperate to be moving, running, talking. *Something* to produce progress. While they rolled through the narrow, twisting lanes, Lily was being taken farther away from them.

Instead of bolting out of the carriage and scouring the streets uselessly, Portia focused all of her energy on scanning the streets through the window. Streetlamps were sparse, casting deep shadows through which anonymous figures moved about. It was near midnight, and the East End was rife with activity.

Questionable activity.

The carriage slowed as they wound their way along the dark lanes. Portia saw various characters moving about in the night—men, women, and far more children than she would have expected, but not a single red cap.

And then, as they turned another corner—there!

A boy strolled casually with a chimney sweep's broom. One hand was stuffed deep in the pocket of his oversize woolen trousers, a red cap sitting jauntily on his head.

"Is that him?" Portia asked, a flash of hope making her chest tight.

Her great-aunt leaned across Portia to peer out the window. "Let us hope so." She knocked on the roof, signaling for the carriage to stop. A moment later, Charles appeared in the doorway. A heavy bruise had already formed above his temple where he had been struck by Lily's attacker.

"Go fetch that boy there," Angelique said.

"Yes, m'lady."

While the loyal servant did as requested, the ladies waited in tense silence. Several moments later, the carriage door opened again.

"Wot do you fancy pieces want?"

The boy in the red cap peered in through the open door while Charles stood stiffly behind his shoulder. The lad's young face was smeared with soot, making it hard to discern his age. But judging by his size, Portia guessed him to be about eleven or twelve. A bit old for a chimney sweep.

He stood warily scanning the interior of the carriage, expertly assessing what danger they might represent. He dismissed Angelique quickly enough, but took a few extra seconds studying Portia. When he gave her a jaunty little grin and tipped the brim of his hat, Portia realized with a touch of shock that the child was flirting with her.

Angelique leaned forward from the shadows, bringing her face near to the boy's. Her age lines looked deeper in the uncertain light, but her dark eyes were piercing and direct. If Portia hadn't known better, she would have been intimidated by the sudden intensity within her great-aunt's stare.

"We are looking for Nightshade." Angelique spoke in a dramatic whisper, though there was no one beyond Portia and the boy near enough to hear her.

The child snorted and eyed Angelique as though she was daft. Portia worried again about having followed her great-aunt's suggestion so readily. The dowager countess was generally just a harmless eccentric, but so far she had led them on a search for a boy in a red cap, and now she was asking for a poisonous herb.

"I ain't no apothecary," the boy said.

Angelique flashed a coin in the palm of her gloved hand. "You know whom I seek, boy. We haven't the time for games and subterfuge."

A shadow of respect crossed the boy's face, and he reached to take the coin, testing it between his teeth before shrugging his shoulders. "Can't take you to 'im. Not how it works. I deliver a message, an' his man'll contact you."

"No, please," Portia said, drawing the boy's eyes back to her. "We don't have time for messages." She finally had some hope her great-aunt had not led them astray, and she was not going to let the opportunity slide away. "You must take us to this man directly. Immediately."

The boy narrowed his sharp gaze and flashed another grin. "Fer another coin an' a kiss, I may change me mind."

Angelique made a sound that could have been a scoff or a chuckle or something in between. But she reached back into her purse. "Here is your coin." She waved a hand toward Portia. "Give him a kiss so we can move this along."

The coin quickly disappeared into the child's pocket before he swept his hat off his head and turned his face to Portia. Feeling more than a little silly, Portia leaned forward to briefly brush her lips across the child's cheek.

He gave a quick whoop then smashed his hat back on his head.

Turning to Charles, who still stood beside him, he said, "Head down the street a ways, then swing right after the butcher's place. Keep going till you pass the park. There'll be a row of houses that all look the same. Go to the one nearest the broken streetlamp. That's where you'll find Nightshade's man." He looked back to Portia and Angelique. "And I'd be grateful if you don't tell him it was me who sent ya. He'd have me hide fer not following the rules." The boy tossed a jaunty wink at Portia. "I like me hide."

The boy was ridiculously charming, and Portia smiled despite her anxiety. "Thank you. We do appreciate your help."

The boy tipped the brim of his cap then backed away. Charles quickly closed the carriage door, and a minute later they were off again.

Portia stared across the carriage at her great-aunt with a dose of newfound respect. "Who is Nightshade?"

The lady's expression was vague as she replied, "No one knows, *ma petite cherie*."

"What do you mean?"

"He never meets his clients face-to-face." The old lady gestured toward the window. "There is a strict process to getting in touch with the man. We are fortunate your kiss is so highly regarded," she added with a sly glance.

Portia resisted the urge to roll her eyes. *Among young boys maybe.* "Can this Nightshade be trusted?"

"He would not have gained the reputation he has if he were untrustworthy or incompetent. They say his insistence on remaining anonymous allows him to move through any environment undetected; that he is capable of infiltrating even the most elite social groups."

Portia leaned forward, captivated by the idea such a man existed. "How do you know of him?"

"Word gets around when there is someone willing to do what others cannot. Or will not." Angelique paused and looked down at the ring on her left hand. "A few years ago, I hired him to help me with a certain personal matter. If anyone can find Lily, it is Nightshade."

Portia fell silent, hoping her great-aunt was right.

After several minutes, the carriage reached the area the boy had mentioned. It was a more residential neighborhood, and both sides of the street were lined with brick row houses two stories high with narrow fronts and identical entrances. Portia peered through the window, straining to locate the broken streetlamp that would mark the correct house.

There. The moment she saw it, the carriage pulled to the side of the street. Charles must have seen it as well.

Portia took her great-aunt's arm in silence as they made their way up the walk to the dark front door. She swept her gaze in all directions, trying to pierce the night surrounding them, alert for any threat. The shadows were deep in front of the house, and no number marked the address. Two small windows bracketed the door, but no light shone from them. Portia tipped her head to look at the windows on the upper level. All was dark.

Blast. What if no one was home?

Angelique lifted the tarnished brass knocker and issued a loud, echoing announcement of their presence.

Silence followed. And then a soft noise.

The door opened unexpectedly on well-oiled hinges, revealing a petite man in his later years with a smallish head and iron-gray hair worn back in an old-fashioned queue. Despite the man's diminutive height, he somehow managed to look down at them along the length of a hawklike nose.

"Wot?"

His one word, uttered with none of the graces assigned to even a poorly trained butler, threw Portia off. She stiffened in affront, then prepared to respond to the discourteous greeting with a bit of insolence herself.

Angelique saved her the trouble as she pushed through the door, past the little man who was helpless to stop her, and into the hall, saying as she went, "We have a matter of vital importance that requires Nightshade's immediate attention." She swung around to cast the little man a narrow-eyed look. "Where shall we wait?"

"Don't know who yer talking 'bout."

"Yes, you do. Now fetch your master, or I will seek him out myself."

Portia was infinitely impressed. Who knew the woman who barely remembered to put on her shoes before leaving the house could display such an air of unquestionable command?

The little man pinched his face into a sour expression as he glanced toward the door then back to Angelique as though debating the benefits of tossing them both back onto the street. He cast a critical gaze over their appearances, seeming to take mental note of the quality of their clothing. Then he snorted and turned to amble into the shadows at the back of the hall.

Angelique released a pent-up breath, her previous arrogance falling away like a discarded cloak. She turned to Portia. "Come. Let us find somewhere comfortable to wait."

The front hall was dark and narrow. Stairs rose up along the left side, and three doors opened to the right. The hall itself contained nothing but a small table set near the door. Portia wandered toward the first door to peek into the room beyond.

It was a small parlor.

"This way," she said as she strode into the room.

The room was also quite dark. Only the faint glow of distant city lights filtered through the window, but it was enough to see the outline of the furniture and a small candelabrum set on a table near the sofa. Angelique took a seat in an armchair while Portia went directly to the cold fireplace, looking for something to light the candles.

It felt good to finally have something to do even if it was as mundane a task as lighting candles. It kept her thoughts from flying in all sorts of wild directions. Once the candles were lit, she found herself unable to sit still. Though she tried several times to take a seat, she inevitably jumped to her feet again in a matter of moments as fretful energy continued to rush unheeded through her body.

Rather than perpetrating a pointless battle against the urge to move, she took to pacing the tiny room.

Two

IT FELT LIKE THEY WAITED FOR HOURS IN THE DIMLY lit parlor for Nightshade's man. Angelique sat quietly, her eyelids dropping in the semidarkness. Portia almost envied the old woman her drowsiness as her disquiet steadily grew. The longer they sat unattended, the harder it was going to be to track Lily down.

Portia wondered if perhaps the rude little butler had simply gone to bed rather than informing his master of his guests. After making her hundredth turn at the fireplace, she took off toward the door at the opposite end of the room with purposeful strides, determined to go in search of someone herself.

Just as she neared the door, however, a figure appeared in the dark frame. The man made such a sudden and silent appearance Portia was nearly startled from her skin. As it was, she was under the force of such fierce momentum, she barely managed to stop herself from colliding with the man by bracing her hand hard on the doorframe.

She looked at the newcomer sharply. Her worry

and impatience coalesced into anger now that he had finally appeared.

He was a rather nondescript man in his later years, perhaps in his fifties, with light hair that was going to gray, a pale, almost sickly complexion, a beard that had grown a bit bushy, and small, wire-rimmed spectacles. He was dressed in a brown suit with matching waistcoat and stood with sloped shoulders, his hands stuffed into the front pockets of his coat.

Seemingly unconcerned with their near collision, he looked down at her from almost a foot above her with an expression that could only be classified as annoyed.

The longer she stood there staring up at him, the more annoyed he became, evidenced by the lowering of his untamed brows and the pursing of his thin mouth. And yet he was the one who had kept them waiting while her sister was dragged off to who knows where.

She pushed off from the doorframe and planted her hands on her hips.

"It is about time. Do you have any idea how long we have been waiting?"

The thick eyebrows shot up, reaching far above the top rim of his spectacles. "You have been waiting less than fifteen minutes," he replied in an entirely unhurried tone. "Do you have any idea what time of night it is?"

"I would say it is nearing one o'clock in the morning, which should signify that our issue is of such importance it cannot wait until a more reasonable hour, which should in turn have pressed you to a more hasty response."

The man made a sound in the back of his throat—a

sort of abbreviated snort—then stared, saying nothing more. His lips pressed into such a tight line they lost all hint of color, and his eyes narrowed to a squint behind his spectacles.

"Portia, come sit. Allow the poor man into the room so we may conduct our business."

Portia realized then that her challenging stance essentially blocked the doorway, keeping the new-comer stranded on the threshold. Executing a little snort of her own, Portia turned with a whip of her skirts and strode to where her great-aunt was pushing herself a bit straighter in the armchair. Rather than sitting—which she knew wouldn't last long anyway—Portia took position beside the chair and waited for Nightshade's man to step forward and take control of the situation.

Taking control was not how Portia would describe the man's next actions.

After a slow glance at Angelique, he strolled into the room, keeping his hands in his pockets. He walked past the lit candelabra, his brows shooting upward again, as if the fact that they had lit the room was more of an affront than their untimely visit.

Portia studied him, irritated and curious.

This was the go-between for the highly skilled and ruthless Nightshade? He looked more like someone's daft uncle or a confused schoolteacher.

"Mr. Honeycutt," Angelique said, "we met once before, a few years ago—"

"Of course, Lady Chelmsworth," Honeycutt inter-rupted without turning to face them as he wandered to the window overlooking the front street. "I recall

Romance Writers of America. For your encouragement, support, sacrifice, laughter, and hard work, I thank you. Without you, these books wouldn't be possible.

Hugs to everyone!

—E. Michels

About the Author

Elizabeth Michels is the award-winning author of the Tricks of the Ton series and Spare Heirs series. She grew up on a small Christmas tree farm in South Carolina. After tiptoeing her way through school with her focus on ballet steps and her nose in a book, she met a boy and followed him a thousand miles away from home to Kansas City, Missouri, where she earned her bachelor's degree in interior design. Years later she returned to the South and settled down in a small lakeside town in North Carolina. When she is not writing, she is caring for her husband and little boy. Elizabeth loves to hear from her readers. Please visit www.elizabethmichels.com for more information.